Welcome to the Damned

Astraea Long

Welcome to the Damned

Paperback edition ISBN: 979-8-9888946-0-5

E-Book ISBN: 979-8-9888946-1-2

Amazon Kindle ASIN: B0CP7JTRC6

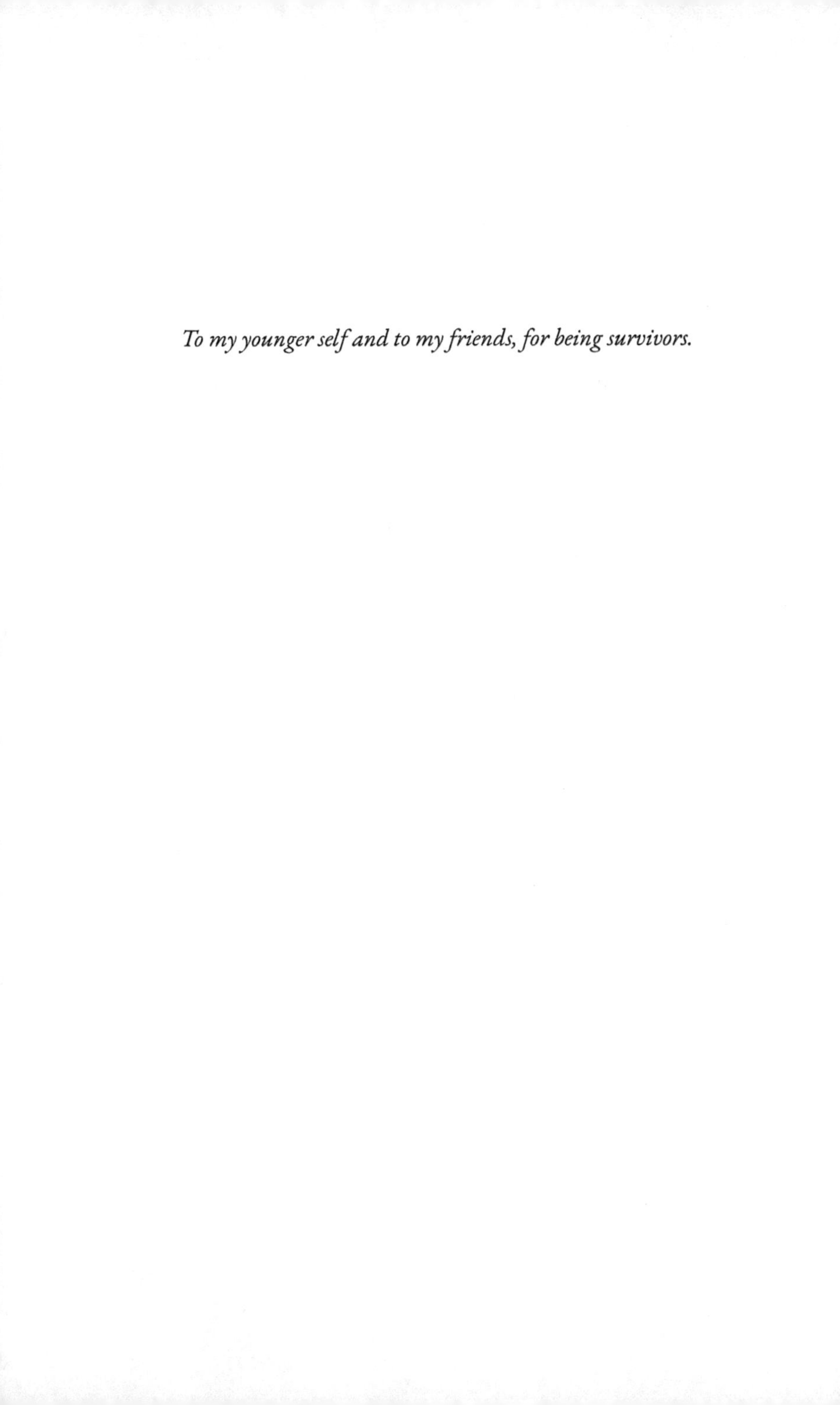

To my younger self and to my friends, for being survivors.

"Your life began the day it nearly ended."

(*Captain Marvel*)

Contents

Note to Readers — VII

1. Heartless Games — 1
2. Between the Reckless — 18
3. Welcome to Dyvris — 36
4. The Agency — 56
5. Ace of Crowns — 75
6. Disk Boot Failure — 92
7. Machine Malfunction — 110
8. Metloxcy — 129
9. You Can Run — 145
10. The Scavenger — 161
11. Strange Goodbyes — 175
12. Starless Night — 188
13. No More — 202
14. Hello, Vengeance — 217
15. Tomb's Day — 232
16. Young Lunacy — 247

17. Everyone Has Secrets   261

18. Nothing Lasts Forever   274

Epilogue   289

Acknowledgements   298

Appendix   300

About the Author   304

Note to Readers

This book includes alcoholism, mentions of abuse, blood and gore, mental illness, murder, mind-control, self-harm, suicidal ideation, mentions of suicide and suicide attempt, and violence.

Thank you!
Astraea Long

1

Heartless Games

P**ills spilled out of the bottle and clattered into the toilet.**

I watched myself flush them down, heard myself telling my friends that I was leaving, and felt myself walking out of the dimly lit restaurant. Sunrays bore into my skin and pricked my eyes when I halted in the middle of the parking lot, feeling the weight of the second bottle of pills in my pocket.

The sky was a sickly orange, and the flowers were pink and yellow, but I only saw them as distant and dull projections concocted by another world. After all, I didn't know what my reality was any longer. I had almost overdosed by choice on two bottles of painkillers in a public restroom mere minutes ago.

It was like I was in a trance, manipulated by an evil overlord to end my own life and lose control over my own body. And like every other mental game the Devil plays, I had no sense of time. Maybe that poisonous haze only lasted the minutes that my thoughts zeroed in on escaping life's tortures. Maybe it was rooted from the day I was born in this corrupted world that was built to demolish fragile souls like mine.

But the most crippling realization was that the Devil was me. All this time, the harrowing voice in my head was my alter ego, the self-destruct button in my programming, an adversary of my own creation. I didn't even realize I was walking towards the edge of the cliff until rocks were tumbling down its side from underneath my feet.

Then there was the swerve. The swerve of my consciousness out of this paradoxical dream. The swerve of my speeding car away from crashing through Death's door. The swerve of my hand holding a gun right before the bullet flew. The swerve of my pen, turning the period into a semicolon in my story.

What I didn't know, after all these crashing waves of epiphany about my existence, was what to write after that semicolon. All these years, I allowed myself to deform into a machine, a ghost, an uninteresting tale. So now that I've woken up, how do I become sentient?

Esme sucks in a sharp breath, jolted out of her flashback when Caitlyn tightens her grip on their linked hands. She blinks the memory away and lets out a soft sigh. The dark sidewalk before her eyes ripples with shades of pink, purple, and blue as rain beats down on the puddles reflecting the urban lights of Torch City.

They just got out of the shuttle in the late evening after work, but now Caitlyn is dragging her along at a faster pace. Their boots make larger splashes with every step they take. Although an umbrella formed from pure energy floats above their heads, her shoulders start to catch rain as their walk home turns frantic. Esme flicks a quick look out of the corner of her eye to the road and almost trips over her own feet.

A black van trails a short distance behind them.

Her heart begins to pound, and she nearly forgets how to breathe.

Given their field of work, no ordinary person would dare to mess with them. Esme and Caitlyn are scientists working directly for the government, and they live in the safest, most protected neighborhood of the country. Breaking through the sixteen levels of security technology would take incredible skill, way beyond the programming education of any university or military training.

Esme's hands are damp from rain and sweat.

Because this can only mean one thing.

It must be the Damned, criminals who will do anything they want, infesting the shadows of every street in Pureland, inciting chaos for their amusement and wealth, forsaken by any divine powers that one is willing to believe in.

Every child has heard of the stories. The most haunting ones whisper of the slow corruption of ordinary teenagers, where the lures of lawlessness prey upon their innocence until their hearts turn black, so heavy that it drags them down to the bottom of society. It twists and morphs their souls into something unrecognizable, something wicked beyond comprehension, something rancid and hideous and sickening. They are cautionary tales, because nothing is more frightening than the very possibility that even the sweetest child could grow up to become one of *them*.

They are not just the petty thieves that steal a wallet on the street, or the poor students who occasionally shoplift.

No, the Damned thoroughly shatter the lives of anyone who catches their attention.

They are the wraiths lurking on the roofs of abandoned buildings, hanging off of broken wires, always watching.

Esme has no idea when or how she or Caitlyn got on their radar, but none of that matters when the Damned have already come knocking at their door.

"Caitlyn," Esme says tightly.

"We're fine," Caitlyn hisses back.

Esme purses her lips, though she can feel the tears pricking her eyes. She suddenly feels cold, despite the thick jacket. They both know it's too late.

The van keeps the same amount of distance as it follows them, as if taunting them.

A warm drop of tear slips down Esme's cheek.

"Caitlyn," she says again, hopelessness thick in her lover's name.

Caitlyn finally stops and looks back. Her face screams of anger, of denial, of fear.

Esme's lips tremble. "I—"

But Caitlyn doesn't let her say it. Instead, she pulls Esme into a brutal kiss, pressing her into the glowing wall of blue and white neon. After all, there is no such thing as a happy ending when the Damned are involved. This mess of fingers grasping tangled hair and stealing breaths is their last goodbye.

They break apart, a long look passing between them that speaks of everything they can't say. Esme's chest aches as she remembers the afternoon when Caitlyn passed her the lost file of chemical experiments she needed to organize in the messy lab, with a soft smile that warmed her like the coffee she was holding.

Esme reaches out to tuck a wet strand of hair behind Caitlyn's ear. Caitlyn tries to smile now, brushing Esme's cheek gently with a thumb, but her face starts to crumble. Esme shushes her and presses their lips together one more time.

The van pulls to a stop next to them.

Holding up a hand, Esme gazes steadily into Caitlyn's eyes. Caitlyn sets her jaw and grips Esme's hand, determination shining behind her tears. No matter how terrified they are, they will not give those criminals the satisfaction of seeing them break.

Together, Caitlyn and Esme face the van as a door slides open, showing nothing but darkness inside. Two women and two men prowl out, like fairytale monsters coming to life right before their eyes. Esme shrinks back into Caitlyn's arms when she sees a glass eye shining an unnatural blue on one of the women's faces beneath the black hood. The four criminals split up to trap Caitlyn and Esme on the sidewalk, two on each side of the girls.

A heavy boot drops down from the van, bulky and black with ominous red designs glowing in the night.

Esme's chest tightens, her fingers going numb.

A man with tawny beige skin emerges from the darkness, a crimson shield hovering over his black curls, where the raindrops bounce and resemble streams of blood.

Caitlyn squeezes Esme so hard that she's sure that neither of them can breathe.

He wears a blood-red dress shirt beneath a black jacket, his steps slow and casual. His eyes flit over the two of them, glinting with danger and mania. When his lips stretch into a crooked grin, Esme is suddenly sure that he must be one of the worst monsters to exist, even among the Damned.

A knife appears in between his gloved fingers. The man toys with it as he considers the girls in front of him, his smirk sharpening.

"Aw, don't look so scared," he coos. "We haven't done anything yet."

At that, another pair of black boots land on the wet pavement, a much heavier sound that almost matches the pounding of Esme's heart.

Measured strides bring another man into view beside him beneath the illusory umbrella of blood.

This one is taller and bulkier, wearing a violet button-down, skin a golden shade of brown. A gleam of metal catches Esme's attention even as her legs begin to shake. She squints, just a little, through the rain to see a thick, golden hoop hanging from his right ear.

When Esme shifts her gaze to the man's face, she flinches at the cold eyes staring right back at her.

"Get in the car," he demands, his gravelly voice controlled yet sharp enough to cut through the rain.

"No," Caitlyn spits out. "Crawl back to whichever hell you came from and rot there."

The man in red laughs. "Maybe later, sweetheart," he winks at Esme and tosses his knife, a relaxed gesture yet a clear warning. "Don't worry, we don't even want you. Just her, and we'll be on our merry way."

Esme's breath hitches, but when Caitlyn lunges at him, she has to haul her back with weak arms. Caitlyn narrows her eyes at them. "You can try."

"Oh!" The man in red taps his head with his knife. "You think we didn't catch your pathetic attempt at sending a distress call to your supervisors?"

Esme looks down to see Caitlyn's silver cuff blinking red. Her heart drops. Foolishly, she hoped that someone, anyone could help them. Mind racing, she exchanges another glance with Caitlyn, feeling the dread crawling through her veins.

"We've blocked all signals in the area and looped all the cameras," the man continues. "No one has any idea what's happening to you. My darlings, who do you think we are?"

She closes her eyes. Her head spins even more wildly, so much that she could not tell up from down. Resentment burns her chest as these monsters steal away her future and crush it to dust, and she can do nothing to stop them. She has no choice. She never did. Esme feels faint even as she steels herself to open her mouth. Her lips feel dry even though her feet feel cold and wet.

"Caitlyn," Esme whispers. "They just want me."

"*No*," Caitlyn growls.

"This is the best case scenario, you know this."

"I am *not* in the mood for your martyr complex right now."

Esme laughs softly, pained. "It's not like I'm choosing to surrender myself to barbaric criminals."

Caitlyn tries to argue more, but the man in red interrupts them again.

"Ah, lovers' quarrel," he drawls. "We don't have all night, you know. Dinners to attend, crimes to commit."

Caitlyn clenches her jaw, seething with hatred. Everything around them falls eerily silent, except for the shrill howls of cars flying down the main street. Indecision and looming violence feed into the suffocation of the contaminated air.

A metallic click of the safety on a bullet gun cuts through the invisible chokehold.

"I'm running out of patience," the man in violet says, his barrel aimed at Esme's head.

Releasing a long breath, she brings up their linked hands and presses her lips against Caitlyn's fingers.

"I'm sorry," she says softly, snatching her hand away before her resolve could waver and walking backwards into the van. The rain immediately soaks through her hair and her clothes. Esme blinks rapidly when a couple droplets sting her eyes.

"No," Caitlyn hisses, emerald eyes flashing with betrayal, with grief, with bitter acceptance. She attempts to follow, but a gunshot lands before her feet. She stumbles, then howls, "*No.*"

"I'm sorry," Esme repeats, when someone snatches her arm.

"Esme—"

"I love you, okay? Remember that."

Then she's hauled onto the van and the door slides shut. Esme's face contorts as she slumps against it, fingers curling into fists. The wheels beneath her feet speed off without wasting a millisecond.

The girl sighs, straightening.

She turns and passes a tired gaze over the six wary expressions, apprehension so thick in the air that it could almost choke her.

"Well," she says, attempting to break the tension, swaying with the motion of the moving car. She doesn't lose her balance, despite having appeared as though her legs might give out mere moments ago.

The girl tilts her head, narrowing her eyes.

The girl is no longer Esme Min.

"Long time no see," she finishes.

The girl is, in fact, one of the Damned. Those sinister monsters that children hear about in their bedtime stories? She's one of the most rotten of them all, one that wears any skin that she chooses, one that leeches off of her victims' greatest desires.

The man in red grins fully now, the knife disappearing from his hand. "Welcome back, Zero. We've missed our little Ace of Crowns."

Zero holds up a finger. "Before someone explains why I'm getting pulled out right now, there's something we need to deal with."

She lifts up the ends of her hair to reveal a black device shaped like a scorpion embedded in the back of her neck. Ignoring the soft gasps and subtle flinches behind her, Zero taps the right glove of the man in red, which she knows covers only part of his metal arm.

"Tal, get rid of this for me."

The man's face drops, narrowing his eyes with annoyance.

"Ah, dear Zero. Why is nothing ever simple with you?" Tal laments, turning her around by the shoulders to inspect the scorpion. After a moment, he says, "This is going to hurt."

Zero rolls her eyes at the useless warning. It's not as though she has any other choice. "Hurry up."

Her vision almost completely blacks out when her neck feels as though someone ripped her skin and muscles right off her vertebrae. She grits her teeth and breathes heavily until she's able to see the vague outline of a shadow towering over her.

As colors start to fill in again, she realizes that the vehicle — a Shapeshifter — has transformed into what seems to be a party bus. The dim lighting swirls around various colors on white cushions, which does not help with Zero's dizziness. Tal has apparently set her down in a seat to keep her steady and to stitch up the wound. The other members are already preoccupied with clearing their way back to base, operating like a well-oiled machine per usual, though the presence of the Avyrian pair in the back is a new advancement of which Zero does not approve.

Raven Ly, a woman with sharp features and dark eyes, hair cut short and swept back, is wearing a green bomber jacket over a white tank top, though everything else is black. The combat boots, the baggy pants with too many pockets, the fingerless gloves made from leather, the thick choker around her neck, the small hoops through her earlobes and orbital conch piercings: all black.

Raven Ly has changed since Zero last saw her.

Raven Ly should not be here.

And Jacek Zou, the bony man working on a laptop across from Raven, should definitely be staying at least ten worlds away from this place. His outfit is similar to Raven's, though he's wearing a black short-sleeved shirt and silver chains on his belt. At least his fashion sense hasn't changed.

The next person Zero sees gives her even a greater headache. Sensing her attention, Kagiso Ihejirika shifts his gaze, always full of mischief, and smirks. He only ever wears the same black coat over his bare torso, even though he has probably stolen thousands from rich houses all over Pureland. His dark skin accentuates the gleam of his layered pendants under the lighting of the Shapeshifter. With fingers clad in thick silver rings, Kagiso lifts his glass of whiskey as acknowledgement of her return.

Zero doesn't dignify that with a response. She moves onto studying a much friendlier face, though not any less dangerous— Daleyza Etienam, her mentor and sister figure. Her dark blue hair drapes over one side of her face, half-covering her real, brown eye, while the other side is undercut with a design that resembles a computer chip. Her glass eye shines a bright blue in the iris to match the glowing studs dotting the outline of her ear. Her black leather jacket is decorated with a strip inside the collar and spikes of the same neon.

An odd group to put together for a simple extraction, Zero notes, especially with Tal in the mix. Underboss of the Aconite gang, he's known for his ruthless violence. When unsheathed, the sharp claws of his metal arm are often dripping with blood, a poetic image for his full name: Talon Gierkas.

Needless to say, it's not quite morally promising for Zero that Tal is also the closest thing she has to a brother.

"I see you brought all my friends." Zero tilts her head at the man in violet, who's standing over her at the moment. "*Boss.*"

Arms crossed, he narrows his eyes at her. "You heard."

Zero's sure that every single wretched creature of the Damned has heard about the man's rise in power, so she doesn't bother wasting her breath with a verbal response.

The man clenches his jaw at her lack of answer. "We had to be prepared."

"By which you mean you appointed five people who can handle me in every way in case I genuinely refused to come." Zero scoffs. "Three Reapers, too. Daleyza, Tal, you. Did you expect a lot of bloodshed? Well, this must be important. Though I must say, I don't think it was necessary to come personally for little me *and* bring your second-in-command. One would suffice."

"Aw, are you not happy to see me?" Tal pouts. "Or is it Rovis? I do hope it's him, because I already bought you a 'welcome back' gift."

"Don't ask questions you already know the answer to," Zero shoots back at him.

At that, Tal schools his expression and glances at Rovis, who does not look at either of them. "You're right," Rovis says to Zero without acknowledging her. "It's important."

Rovis opens the door to the private room behind the driver's and passenger's seats, which Zero knows is soundproof.

Tal moves to follow, but Rovis stops him with a look and says, "I can deal with her."

"It's not you I'm worried about."

Zero raises an eyebrow. "I can deal with *him*."

Tal considers that. "Okay, I'm worried about both of you."

Rovis shakes his head. "Stay out here."

Tal frowns but doesn't argue any further. Zero gives his arm a light squeeze before shutting the door behind her. It's a small room that barely fits a table with surrounding seat walls. She plops down across from Rovis, the farthest away from him possible.

Any hint of amusement evaporates from Zero's face. "What?" she snaps.

"Someone sold us out," Rovis states. "Six of our operations got squashed by the Purish patrolling bots last week."

Zero blinks at him, surprised.

He meets her eyes when he says, "You're the only one who works with the government."

"Ah." Zero leans back and crosses her arms as she understands. "So you think I did it."

Rovis must know that she infiltrated the deep state *for* the Aconites. The last boss, Quade Bianchi, agreed to send her in so she could find more important investors for his poison weaponry business. Except Rovis shut down the weapons production as soon as he took over. Zero can't trick him as easily as she manipulated Bianchi.

Rovis, unfortunately, isn't as corrupted.

"Do you plan to defend yourself at all?" he asks calmly.

Zero shrugs. "Trying to convince you of anything is a waste of energy."

Rovis gives her a long look. Two years ago, she'd try to read him, try to see if he had any emotions left behind that stoic mask. Five years ago, she didn't need to try, because she always knew exactly what he was thinking. Or so she thought. Now Zero just doesn't care at all.

"Give me your arm," Rovis finally says.

That's when Zero stiffens. Traditionally, the head of the Aconites punishes any members who betray the organization by burying a long knife into the forearm where the ornate tattoo, an outline of the wolfsbane flower, is inked to mark their loyalty. Blood and torn tissue would mar the beautiful image, just as the culprit's bond to the family is severed. Even when advanced technological devices of tissue regeneration can heal the cut without a scar, the tattoo would never look the same again.

Zero doesn't really feel like bleeding at the moment.

"You don't want to believe it, do you?" she asks to stall time, voice blank while she calculates a way to talk her way out of this.

Rovis clenches his jaw. "Did you do it or not?"

"Of course I'll say that I didn't do it." Zero tilts her head. "But how exactly do you want me to prove that I didn't do something, *Boss*?"

"Did you do it," he repeats slowly, "or not?"

"No, Rovis." Zero rolls her eyes. "I didn't even know it happened. I don't see how a chemist can connect to crime-watching federal robots. You've known about my fake job since the beginning. I've been sending *you* information the whole time. You know I didn't have the time to do something like that."

"Do I?" Rovis asks darkly. He drops the scorpion onto the table, still stained with Zero's blood. "What the hell is this? What kind of job did you take to warrant this? And shall we talk about how you knew I'm in charge and didn't come back? I gave you the benefit of the doubt, but what am I supposed to think now? You pretended to be oblivious, because you know I don't care about Bianchi's old business. It's been a *year*, and what could you have possibly been doing? You could've turned."

"Which question do you want me to answer?" Zero says icily.

"Stop it," Rovis hisses in Toullish, the language that he taught her a lifetime ago. "Tell me what you've been up to."

"The same thing I've been doing since before you killed Quade," she answers in Toullish as well. "I just didn't feel like coming back because you are very annoying."

Rovis narrows his eyes. "You know how I feel about liars."

"And you know how I feel about men older than me failing to get to the point," Zero retorts, switching back to Purish.

"Zero, I'm still trying to protect you. That never changed. But encouraging me to think the worst of you is seriously undermining my efforts."

"What do you want me to say?"

"Simple as always. The truth."

Zero wants to slap him. The nerve this man has to demand the truth out of everyone when he's a nationally wanted thief.

But she sighs and says, long-suffering, "I did not betray you. I did not turn. I did not provide anyone any information that did not belong to Esme Min, a woman I fabricated to up Bianchi's game in the weapons black market. Happy?"

"Not when you're still hiding things from me," Rovis snaps in Toullish.

"I cannot care less."

"Find out whoever's responsible, then," Rovis says.

Zero stares at him stonily.

Rovis looks away and adds, *"Biv'ye nu wanotai."*

Zero's fingers twitch in surprise. He must be truly desperate to bring back those words between them. She frowns. Rovis likely believes that Zero isn't the traitor but still can't rule out the possibility due to her personality and circumstances. However, ordering her to help him solve this takes another level of trust. He knows better than anyone that she could easily frame someone if she were the one who betrayed him. This must be more than the six operations that got broken up last week.

"Fine." She stands up and grabs the door handle. Even though Zero wants to ask Rovis why Raven and Jacek got involved with this, she cannot stand the sight of him any longer. "I've reached my quota of interacting with you for the day. Allow me to socialize with people my own age."

Zero doesn't wait for a response and shoves the door open, briefly making eye contact with Tal. Knowing him, Tal likely gathered how irritated she is, but Zero can't bring herself to care. She has other issues to deal with.

"Raven," she calls.

The girl looks up, but in that moment Zero hears Tal ask Rovis, "Are we ready for Wyatt Revyxon now?"

Zero whips her head around, forgetting about her so-called quota. Seeing her violent reaction, Rovis swears under his breath.

"I'm sorry," she glares at him. "Wyatt Revyxon?"

"Tal." Rovis rubs his temples. "Don't you know to check who's in the room?" He turns to Zero before Tal can defend himself. "You're not coming."

Zero's hands curl into a fist. "Rovis."

"No." His voice is firm. "It's an easy one. I don't need a distraction, which means I don't need you."

The vehicle comes to a stop behind a nightclub. With a flick of fingers from Rovis, Tal leaves first with Kagiso, Jacek, and Raven, all without a word, to get on another Shapeshifter hiding in the shadows. Rovis follows and moves to the door, but he looks back at Zero, with that overbearing frown that she knows too well and feels a bottomless urge to punch.

"Stay in the car. Or I'll actually shoot you this time."

As soon as the door slams shut, Zero digs into the duffel bag next to Daleyza for a party dress. The organization always packs spare outfits in case someone needs a change in venue for a job.

Daleyza sighs. "Zero, you really shouldn't."

Zero rolls her eyes. "I'll go after Rovis finishes his thing. He probably will shoot me, but he won't kill me."

"You sure about that?"

"Nope," Zero answers. She has a terrible habit of pushing Rovis's limits. "But I don't care. I have to do this. I've lived longer than I thought I would anyway."

She locks herself in the private room and quickly switches out of her clothes into a short, silver dress, then pulls on black high-heeled boots.

Daleyza doesn't stop Zero, too used to her doing whatever she wants regardless of the consequences. Zero walks into the club and immediately spots Revyxon, surrounded by a crowd of girls at the bar on the ground floor. She scopes out the area first, stalking up the neon stairs in the corner, unflinching as the flashing disco lights assault her eyes with too many shades of color. When she rests her elbow on the railing of the mezzanine, she notices that Rovis is speaking to Revyxon, a rare but undoubtedly false smile on his face. Rovis and Revyxon shake hands, and Rovis claps the boy on the shoulder.

Zero can't help but roll her eyes again. She mutters, "Fake."

When she focuses her attention back to the bar downstairs, Rovis is already gone. Zero didn't see him make the switch and doesn't know if he got what the organization needed from Revyxon, but she never figured out how he does what he does over the past two years anyway.

Every organization of the Damned, for whatever reason, groups its people the same way: Reapers who kill for their boss, Sleightists who steal, Mechs who build, Digitals who breach anything that runs on electricity,

Heartless who manipulate their targets, Menders who patch up wounds, and Clockworks who keep everything running smoothly.

Rovis worked as both a Reaper and Sleightist until he became the boss of the Aconites.

Zero shakes her head, not wanting to think any more about what Rovis has accomplished since he joined the Damned. She treads down the stairs, heels clicking against the shining steps, as her stare remains glued on Wyatt Revyxon, who's now in the middle of the dance floor with his arms around two girls twisting their bodies like snakes.

Adjusting to the beats of the music, Zero joins a couple girls a couple feet away from Revyxon and runs her hands through her hair as she tilts her head back. The girls are cute, too drunk to care that they've never met Zero before, and they cheer loudly as her movements grow bigger. Any other day, she'd let herself just enjoy it.

When she feels a stare burning into the back of her neck, Zero snaps her head to the side, and her hair flips over one shoulder. Her chin dips as she catches Revyxon watching her through a sidelong glance. The corner of her lips lifts.

Keeping the rhythm in her swaying, she struts towards him until her hand is on his abdomen. Without breaking eye contact, Zero drags her hand up to his chest and over his shoulder.

"Wanna dance?" Zero asks the young and witless man before his attention could turn to anyone else, a suggestive smirk growing on her face to reflect whoever this nameless persona she improvised is.

Revyxon's eyes drag down and up Zero's body before he nods with a hungry grin. It almost makes her nauseous, but revenge and spite can do crazy things to one's mind, so she latches her arms around his neck and degrades herself to Revyxon's foolishness with her dancing.

Just a few more drinks, a couple more songs, a bit more stupidity, and Zero has him alone against a dark wall, far, far away from the club.

A thrill runs through her chest as she pretends to lean farther into Revyxon and lifts up her right foot behind her. Of course he's too aroused to notice that one of her hands has disappeared. Her fingers wrap around a hilt. Zero smiles then, a savage monster waking up in her blood.

This was what I've been waiting for. For two years.

Grinning fully now, Zero shoves the knife she hid in her boot through the fabric of his pants, right next to his zipper.

2

Between the Reckless

"Oh, you've got to be kidding me."

Tal's sigh coming through Rovis's earpiece is as dramatic as it would be in person.

"What?" Rovis asks absently, leaning against a dim wall of a closed store, watching the silhouette of cars dance across the paved ground. The sun sets later around Torch City, compared to the Dyvrian Mountains; the sky is still orange from the wildfires ignited by the drying climate, rather than the ominous color of dried blood during the night.

"Well, you see, our favorite little feral bunny has Revyxon right now." There's a pause, as if Tal is waiting for Rovis to wail in anguish for the unsurprising fact that Zero ignored his orders again. "Oh, let me guess. You already know."

Rovis hums, counting down his mental clock. After all these years, he can almost predict every move Zero makes. The more he discloses his position on a situation, the more likely she's going to do the opposite of what he says.

"Oh, no!" Tal gasps, and Rovis thinks that the man on the other side of this line should've gotten a career in the film industry. It would certainly be more interesting than watching camera feeds when the Aconites go out for illegal information-shopping. "She stabbed him in the worst place possible. Ouchie. Would not want to be him right now. Or ever. Any orders, Boss?"

"No, give her a few minutes." Rovis starts walking down the crowded and noisy street. Bright streaks of cars flying by, just barely above the ground, embellish the ostentatious buildings of the capital and pulse with the beat of techno-pop music rumbling the concrete beneath his feet.

"For what, exactly?"

Three narrow alleys pass by. Five. Seven.

"Boss? I'm bored," Tal whines. "Give me something to do."

Rovis feels his lips twitch. "Do you still have the whole area covered?"

"Local cameras are still looped, and our drones are surveilling. Zero is still within perimeters. No sign of any Purish patrols nearby."

"Good. Stay put, and I'll let you keep Levi to yourself for tonight."

Tal sputters, and a faint laughter that must be from Levi, the Clockwork driving one of the Shapeshifters tonight, cuts on top of his voice.

"Oh, don't tease him, Boss," another voice pipes up.

"Summer," Rovis greets the woman. "Is it done?"

"Yes, Boss."

At the sight of a former flower shop under construction, a dreary void of darkness hidden by the neon city, Rovis makes a sharp turn and slips into the shadows.

"Amazing," Tal breathes, as though whispering a secret into Rovis's ear. Ignoring the fact that seven other people are on the communications line, of course. "I didn't even tell you where she is."

A smirk tugs at Rovis's lips. "The criminal world calls her the Ace of Crowns, but they truly do not know how much of a wild card she is."

In the popular game of Keepers and Thieves, the Ace of Crowns is the greatest card, inferior only to the annihilation card named after the god of death, Drokklo. Zero did not earn that name without outsmarting some dangerous figures of the Damned. She's one of the greatest assets to the Aconites, their lead Heartless.

Such a mysterious name, such an enigmatic person. Rovis has yet to find out how Zero managed to build her reputation within a few months. He knows even less about how her old life got lost to this depraved world, though he supposes it was only a matter of time. In Pureland, a simple school girl becomes a parasite to the lowlifes, effective in stealing information and giving nothing in return. Even the most cautious felons may wake up one morning to find a violet card with a single, ornate, green crown in their pocket, and they'll know exactly who they spent the night with.

But she's not nearly as monstrous as Rovis.

"Fortunately," he says to Tal. "I make the rules here."

Creeping around the broken building, Rovis finds Zero looming over Revyxon, a sharp heel digging into his throat, while the knife is still lodged in his body.

She doesn't turn around or acknowledge his arrival. Either she's so overcome with rage that her mind is barely on this plane of existence anymore, or she doesn't care that Rovis is seeing this. There are very few people in the world that Rovis can't sneak up on, and Zero is on the top of that list. On any other day, her wicked ears could pick up even the sound of someone's change in breathing the second they wake up from a different room.

Her bloody knuckles, however, are glaring signs that today is no ordinary day.

Revyxon's face is a crimson mess. The blank expression on Zero's lacks any of the fake personalities she takes on. Suddenly, Rovis realizes that the comms have been silent, and he understands. Zero has never been a physically violent person except out of self-defense. She prefers breaking down her targets' psyche by emotional manipulation or verbal bloodshed.

Rovis almost regrets bringing Raven and Jacek to see two of her worst sides: a Heartless at work and a vicious girl seeking retribution.

"Remember when a Purish boy shot up Lime Gateway High School two and a half years ago?" he says into the comms, knowing they would want an explanation.

Pushing off the wall without waiting for any response, Rovis reaches Zero's side and firmly presses two fingers on her wrist. He waits. Though her chest still heaves with fury, she eventually drags her eyes away from Revyxon's limp form to glare at Rovis.

"Enough," he says in Avyrian, Zero's mother tongue. His eyes don't break away from hers, no matter how much the hellfire in them threatens to jump out and burn him.

Slowly, she tilts her head while maintaining her glare.

Why?

It's a challenge, a demand. A threat, even.

Rovis only looks back at her, unwavering. He understands her hatred, her vengeance, and all her pain from that school shooting. Even if he wasn't there that day. He knows that she knows he always has a reason. He also trusts that she can make the right decision to listen to him when it matters. They've been through too much for the last crumbs of trust between them to go down the drain because of one Purish boy.

Seconds pass by, then minutes.

Rovis can feel Zero's trembling arm and wild pulse beneath his gloved fingers, but he doesn't move. He doesn't grab her, push her, or step away from her. He only waits for her to decide.

Zero juts out her chin, her glare so sharp that would probably kill him if he weren't a monster himself, too. The girl is young, and much smaller than him, but he doesn't doubt that she could do some damage to him if she chooses to ignore him this time. Rovis wouldn't blame her. Revenge is like oxygen to the Damned, forgiveness a myth.

But in the end, Zero steps back slowly, releasing Revyxon. Her lethal gaze doesn't waver or settle down despite her surrender. The fingers Rovis had on Zero's wrist slips off, and he lets his arm drop by his side.

Something stings in his heart, but he ignores it. Maintaining eye contact, Rovis nods at Zero, then says to the others, "Now."

Melting away from the shadows, Daleyza puts a hand on Zero's shoulder to guide her away. Tal strides over from where he parked the car, shoves a gag down Revyxon's throat and plucks out the knife, chuckling at the muffled screams, then drags the boy out. Summer pours chemicals over the blood on the concrete to clean up after Zero. Rovis watches his people complete their tasks with crossed arms, leaning against the wall with a calculating gaze.

After Summer erases all traces of violence in the area, he flicks his fingers, signaling her to leave him. She disappears without a question, and suddenly Rovis is alone, staring at the spot where Revyxon previously lied in his own pool of blood but now looks as though nothing has ever happened.

"So you're still in there," Rovis muses in the empty alley. His fingers twitch in his black leather gloves. "You're not the hollow shell of infinite faces that you insist you are."

Rovis lifts his head, gazing at the red to orange gradient painting the sky. The pain in his chest returns now that Zero's gone. Memories threaten to flash through his mind, but he keeps them at bay by sheer will.

He sucks in a breath.

One, two, three, four, five.

And exhales.

Six, seven, eight, nine, ten, eleven, twelve.

He forces his feet to move and returns to the Shapeshifter, silently noting that Tal was smart enough to direct Raven and Jacek back to this car. The rookies wouldn't want to witness what comes next. If Rovis is known for his savagery as a ghost who pounces in the shadows, and Zero for her trickery as poison that slithers into her prey's heart, then Tal is feared for his cruelty as a monster that tears everything apart from the inside out.

The streets whisper about him, his sharp grin, his deadly claws. Little do they know that the deadliest thing about Talon Gierkas is his brain. His work in the labs, on both hardware and software, carries half the weight of the Aconites' survival.

When he was merely fifteen, the Damned gave him a name.

Lithium.

For the metal burns bright red when drowned in flames.

Wyatt Revyxon doesn't stand a chance, not even in his next hundred lives. After Rovis got what he needed from the boy, he no longer needed him. Tal can have fun finishing what Zero started; Rovis only wanted to spare her already tormented mind from the weight of taking a life. Not that she'd ever know or want to know his true reasons for stopping her.

"Boss."

Daleyza's voice pulls Rovis out of his thoughts. He glances at his head Reaper, who jerks her head toward the back of the party bus. Zero is leaning against a pole with her hands behind her back, now in a leather jacket, speaking to Jacek and Raven. The pose looks casual enough, but her right hand looks... wrong.

"She won't listen to me," Daleyza says, seeing his expression change when he understands. "Not in this state, at least."

Without thinking, Rovis stalks over and snatches her arm to inspect the broken bones.

Zero jumps away, but Rovis's grip is too strong for her to free her arm.

"Don't touch me," she hisses.

He lets go without a word, remembering himself. Rovis reaches inside his suit jacket, tosses an instant ice pack and a roll of bandages onto Jacek's lap, and glances at Zero.

"I shouldn't have done that," he says in Toullish. "But you should let your friends help."

Zero doesn't respond, only allows Jacek to take her hand.

"Make sure Ofir sees her when we get back," Rovis adds in Purish, nodding at Raven before turning away. "Tal. Status?"

"Aw, don't ruin my party, Boss."

Rovis scoffs. "Dinners to attend, crimes to commit," he mocks Tal's words from earlier. "We've committed the crime, so can we go to dinner now?"

Tal laughs. "As you wish, Rov. Only because you asked so nicely. We'll meet you back at the mountains."

Shaking his head, Rovis tunes back into the soft conversations in the Shapeshifter. He frowns when he realizes Jacek is speaking to Zero in a language that sounds like Ezclovese.

Strange, he thinks. Why, exactly, do these kids speak the language of the former colonizing empire? Ezclovia is now merely a tourist country, but speaking the language is hardly necessary when universal translators exist and Purish is the lingua franca across all six countries.

More interestingly, Zero is staring at Jacek like he's a stranger. Which, Rovis supposes, is his fault. He brought in Raven and Jacek while Zero was away, even though it was quite clear that she wanted her friends to be far, far away from the Damned. But now isn't the time to unpack that.

Rovis watches Daleyza move to the other side of Zero and study the younger girl's face. His head Reaper clucks her tongue and says, "I thought I taught you how to punch properly."

"My school records show that I'm not exactly a great student," Zero says, apathetic.

"Well, good thing your greatest weapon is manipulation," Daleyza says lightly. Zero's face darkens. Or the lighting of the Shapeshifter wavered as they passed under a magnetic bridge. "Stick to being a Heartless, and let us Reapers do our job, alright?"

Zero nods. She glances over at Raven and Jacek again before dropping her eyes to the floor, as if deciding that she's too exhausted to process their presence after practically punching a boy to death. Daleyza ruffles Zero's hair with rare affection then moves to lie down across the seats on the other side of the bus for her mandatory post-mission nap. After a quick exchange of glances at Zero's silence, Raven and Jacek both hesitantly return to focusing on watching over surveillance devices scattered all over their way back to the desert. Silence falls between them, and Rovis listens to the heavy metal music drifting through the comms from Tal's end.

He thinks everyone might have dozed off when an hour passes by, but he passes another glance over his people and catches Zero staring at his hands.

"Ask," Rovis says, blunt and indifferent.

Zero blinks, as if she didn't realize where her eyes went. Rovis sees the moment his request registers in her brain. She says, "What are you hiding?"

Rovis almost scoffs. Of course she went straight for the throat. Living in a lawless society, they always have to watch out for signs of danger, anything that may deviate from the normal routine. Zero wouldn't buy his practiced lie about the gloves being new fashion choices. Rovis thinks back to when he grabbed her, wondering if he accidentally gripped too hard and gave away what's beneath the leather.

He doesn't think so, but maybe he was too distracted. Either way, Rovis doesn't plan on telling Zero the truth. It's not her burden to carry. He doesn't see why she'd care anyway.

"Scandalizing tattoos," Rovis says dryly instead.

The only response he got was from his earpiece, when Tal huffs out a laugh, restrained, likely because everyone else except the driver on his side is asleep, too. Zero only seems to accept Rovis's obvious lie as a sign to let the subject slide, and she stares off into space.

Rovis stays vigilant as the hours pass, though he doesn't need to wake up the others when they pass Dyvris, the flashing city of the Eastern Desert with neon buildings, on their way to the edge of the mountains. While Torch City architecture demonstrates the capital's shallow culture of competition by building taller and taller, Dyvris has far more interesting external designs. Each building takes up more space for its individual shapes and even unique lighting patterns, whereas Torch City is cramped with identical rectangles like a toddler's first attempt at building blocks.

And, well, the blasting alternative pop rock electronic music is enough to wake up anyone.

Levi parks at the back of an Avyrian restaurant, far from the three-story building that glows a bright red against the night sky, with streaks of gold that dance across the surface. Rovis watches the second Shapeshifter pull up on the other side of the parking lot, right next to the back entrance, when he gets out of the bus. The restaurant appears to be filled with tourists, as there are vehicles of all shapes and sizes gathered in the lot.

"Speeding all the way?" Rovis raises a brow when Tal climbs out.

"You know it." Tal grins. "Why follow traffic rules when we break every other one anyway?"

"Some logic," Rovis comments as Zero greets the two other Aconite members from Tal's car that she hasn't seen yet. Gray, another Clockwork who mostly drives for the organization, claps her on the shoulder, and Summer, a Reaper under Daleyza's command, messes up her hair until it looks like a bird nest.

The restaurant's owner welcomes them warmly and gives them the largest room on the third floor, with ten round tables draped in white cloth that each seat eight, even though there are only ten of them. Rovis stays behind at a table next to one of the exits, while the rest of the group settles in the center of the room. Tal lingers by the center table as he speaks to Levi for a moment before kissing the top of Levi's blond hair. He catches Rovis's eye and winks.

Heat pricks the back of Rovis's neck and his cheeks, but he shoves down the feeling and decides to ignore Tal walking over to him by listening in on the conversations.

"What would you say about us killing Caitlyn Fuller?" Daleyza is asking Zero, who idly swirls a straw in her glass of water with her uninjured hand.

"Who?" Zero asked, evidently exhausted.

Summer chuckles, with mild amusement colored by disbelief. "The Purish woman you seduced for twenty months. You know, the one you were just with a few hours ago when we snatched you."

Rovis glances over to see Zero blink, face blank. Maybe she really doesn't remember. Rovis doesn't know, understand, or care. She says, "Oh, right. Do it. Or don't. Whatever you're in the mood for. She works for the bioweapons division but never really made anything useful."

Daleyza smiles, shark-like. "Good, 'cause Summer already killed her. Poison in her drink while she was grieving over you."

Zero nods, sipping on her straw, apathetic.

Summer whistles. "You Heartless are made of something else. None of us could be sure if you were still with us or not. I almost thought we got the wrong person from the way you looked, to be honest. Terrified and weak, clinging onto your 'girlfriend.' I mean, you *were* in there for quite a while."

"Her?" Raven snorted. "Working for the Purish government for real?"

While Raven seems well-adjusted, Jacek looks grim at that interaction, and Rovis can't blame him. He's too kind-hearted to be around such a casual conversation about murder and manipulation, especially when it involves his best friends. Raven sticks with the Mechs and Digitals, but Zero? She's a Heartless for a reason.

What a pity, Rovis thinks, shaking his head as he drags his focus away from them. The girl Rovis once vowed to protect wouldn't have such little empathy. Part of him can see that Zero suffered way too many tragedies to remain kind and generous and soft. But another part of him believes that this is just another one of her masks. The Ace is practically fluid, constantly changing to fit her needs, and sometimes Rovis isn't sure if he knows what's real and what's not.

At least he found a thread today that might lead him back to the past she's buried. Their past.

Tal sits down next to Rovis, flipping out the bloody knife and wiping it with a napkin from the table. When he catches Rovis looking over at him, puzzled, he just snorts and shakes his head. "This is mine. Drokklo's favorite daughter over there used it on Revyxon. I have no idea when she stole it from me. Maybe she can add Sleightist to her resume."

"I don't know." Rovis leans back, instantly relaxing in Tal's presence. "Maybe you just have too many knives to keep track of."

"There's no such thing." Tal smirks, showing Rovis his dimple. Mischief shimmers in his eyes, and they remind Rovis of the foxes that used to run around the desert before they went extinct. Black eyeliner boldens the edges where lashes fan out, suitably matching Tal's personality. Rovis couldn't stop the twitch of his own lips even if he wanted to.

An android, shaped like a pomegranate with unsettling yellow robotic 'eyes,' comes by and sets down a steamy plate of food that makes his stomach growl, and Rovis realizes he's been staring at his second-in-command for too long. He snaps his gaze to the food, ignoring the heat creeping up the back of his neck. As he picks through the dish on the turntable with a pair of chopsticks, movement in his peripheral vision pulls his attention to the center table again.

Another android gives Zero a piece of paper. Zero only scans the words on it once and stands up, looking at Rovis. He resumes picking out food as she walks over, while several more human-sized pomegranate robots bring out the rest of their dinner.

The conversations quiet when Zero settles down at Rovis's table, but when she props her chin casually on a hand, elbow resting on the table, and looks back at the larger group, everyone dutifully starts talking again.

Zero turns her attention back to Rovis.

"Would you stop watching me like I'm a bomb that's going to explode the second you look away? I'll do it," she says. It only takes him a beat to realize she's referring to the private conversation they had on the Shapeshifter. When he doesn't say anything, she continues, "I already have some ideas on where to start. But tell me what useless approaches you took first."

"Hey," Tal points at her with his chopsticks before Rovis could shoot back with a scathing remark. "No work talk. I'm enjoying my dinner, and you should, too."

Rolling her eyes, Zero slides out of her seat and strolls downstairs. Rovis frowns after her but starts to eat as his head tries to work through a detail that's bothering him. It isn't until he hears the center table's conversation drifting over again that he realizes.

"Hold on a second," Rovis says. His brain is just now catching up, awakened by the jarring dissonance of two languages. "We're speaking in Lasan."

"Yes," Tal says slowly, an exaggerated smile stretching his face. "We are."

Rovis ignores his impertinence. "Since when does she speak Lasan?"

"Since always." Tal narrows his eyes. "You speak it."

"Because of you. You taught me."

Tal's mocking grin morphs into a proud smirk. "I did, didn't I?"

"Yes, yes, you're the best teacher ever." Rovis rubs his temples. "That's five out of the six main languages. What's next, Riyssolan?"

Tal pauses to process what Rovis is implying.

"Purish, Avyrian, Toullish. Lasan... She speaks Ezclovese?" he asks, the smirk slipping off his face. "Why?"

"With Raven and Jacek. I don't know why."

Tal frowns. Clearly, they both missed something when they brought in the Avyrian pair. It's especially a notable error on Rovis's part, since Ezclovia still has some economic control of Lasantirk, Tal's home country.

"I need you to tail Zero for a few days," Rovis says.

Tal's jaw drops, his face lit up with intrigue. "My, my, Boss. You truly believe it was Drokklo's little proxy who sold us out?"

Does he? Rovis doesn't know, because speaking five languages is unnecessary in a world where translation devices exist except for dubious affairs that even the Heartless avoid, which Zero should not be involved in and does not need to be if she's under the Aconites' protection.

Truthfully, he doesn't know what he would do if Zero did betray him. He wonders if he can bring himself to do what's usually done, or if he would just stow her away on a ride and ship her off to a different country with enough money to start a new life.

Yet he's also the head of the Aconites now. These people, no matter how monstrous or callous or cruel, they're his family. He cannot forgive whoever is selling them out and causing his people to die or get injured by the Purish patrols, which should be and usually are too stupid to catch them. What's more is that something is stirring within the organization, an undertone of unrest, and Rovis is not about to wait around to watch the Aconites turn on each other and destroy themselves.

His eyes drift over to the center table and cherishes the dangerous glint in Daleyza's eyes as she recounts the incident where she had to fight off several members of the Purity Syndicate, a criminal organization of Ezclovese descendants who believe they're the true heirs of this country and made it their life mission to terrorize all immigrant groups. Rovis watches as Summer throws back a shot of bourbon and adds to the story with animated gestures, a huge beam practically radiating on her face. Kagiso listens, an amused smirk etched on his face while he swirls his own crystal glass, leaning back in his chair. Gray slaps Levi's shoulder and coaxes him into talking about the car chase that came after the fight, while Raven and Jacek very obviously try not to laugh at them.

They are the Damned, but that doesn't mean they don't protect each other.

But Rovis doesn't say any of that, only tilts his head at Tal and lifts a brow. "You heard yourself just now, right?"

Amusement gleams in Tal's eyes, as if knowing where his mind wandered off to and seeing through his avoidance. Rovis hates that his breath catches at the look. Tal drawls, "Alright, Rov. Let's say she needs to be watched. Fine, fine. It doesn't need to be me, though. Just use the drones."

Rovis looks away and shakes his head, both at Tal's lazy suggestion and at himself for acting bizarre. "She'll just break all of them."

"What? No. My designs are too good."

"Tal—"

A resounding boom vibrates the walls and tables. Every single person in the room springs up. Rovis whips out a large blaster and holds up a hand when Daleyza and Summer start rushing out. They immediately freeze in place, waiting for his instructions.

"You two," Rovis orders, "stay with the rest. Protect them. Kill any intruders as needed. Tal, come with me."

He leaves no room for arguments because he's already sprinting downstairs and out to the back to inspect the damage, waving off the frantic apologies from the restaurant's owner. Some other customers are already outside processing the ruins of their cars, shocked and horrified. The radius of the explosion wasn't large enough to touch the Shapeshifter Gray parked next to the restaurant, since it's not even in the lot, but even at the door

Rovis can see that the vehicle he was in earlier is now scattered in smoking pieces.

"What the hell," Tal swears beside him.

Rovis grunts in agreement and moves forward, stepping over the debris where the remains of several cars are still in flames. While he's come close to getting blown up before, those incidents have always been on the job. But this is his territory. The city, the desert, the mountains. All of it is his. Every single person residing in this area is his, from Aconite members to business associates to neighborhoods under his protection.

So who the hell had the audacity to cross Rovis tonight?

As he approaches what used to be his Shapeshifter, feeling a dangerous fire starting to burn in his veins, his eyes make out a shadowed figure crouched down in the middle of the wreck.

Rovis holds up his blaster without a second thought, electricity already charging up.

"Wait, Rov," Tal yells and throws out a hand in front of Rovis. It's merely a gesture for him to pause and far from enough to actually stop him, but Rovis listens and holds back from shooting.

Tal holds out the palm of his metal hand, where light gathers in the center and form into an orb, and turns it over to send the light toward the lump of shadows.

The streetlights got destroyed by the explosion, but Rovis can see clearly now, from Tal's makeshift flashlight, the crouched figure is Zero. She's frozen in a side lunge, one hand planted on the ground in front of her, her other arm held up as if shielding her body.

Rovis's heart stops.

"Zero," he calls out, mind racing.

She doesn't move.

Before Rovis could shout again, Tal takes off and pulls Zero forcefully off the ground. Rovis doesn't see what happens after, since Tal took the light with him, but he runs to them as fast as he can while pulling out his own light orb. Tal's shaking Zero by the shoulders when Rovis reaches them. Her vacant eyes seem to come back to focus when Rovis takes her from Tal, gripping her elbows.

"Oh, hey," she rasps.

Rovis breathes a heavy sigh of relief, bowing his head so she doesn't see the look on his face.

"'*Hey*?'" Tal snarls. "You almost got blown up, and you say '*hey*?'"

"It kept ticking," Zero says, haunted. "I could hear it, but I couldn't find it."

Rovis schools his expression and looks up again. His voice is tight with dismay when he asks through his teeth, "What were you doing out here?"

She blinks at him. Then Zero's fingers fumble inside her jacket, and she holds out the note she got earlier. Rovis snatches it so that he and Tal could read it. He crumples up the paper when it only says, cryptically, 'Meet by Shapeshifter in back.'

"Raven," Tal says into his comms. "Go through the tapes and trace the android that gave Zero that note. I doubt whoever did this is still in the area, but if you can find out who messed with the droid, let us know."

"Understood," Rovis hears Raven's response over the line.

As Tal walks off to the side and explains the situation to the rest of the group through the comms, Rovis pulls a medical scanner over his knuckles and runs it up and down Zero's body. Ashes cover her hair and arms, and some parts of her dress are charred. The right sleeve of her jacket has been burnt and ripped, where some shards of metal are embedded in her arm. When Rovis sees the results from the scanner, he sighs.

"Are you trying to beat some record of how many bones you can break or fracture in one day?" Rovis grinds his teeth as he sends a dozen medical spider bots from beneath his sleeve to deal with her surface injuries. "I don't think I've ever witnessed this level of stupidity from you."

"I thought it was Aconite or Dyvris business," Zero says, voice empty, her gaze still far away from the present. She doesn't even twitch when a couple spiders pull the shards out of her arm. Rovis tugs at her left sleeve, and she takes off her ruined jacket without thinking. He throws his own jacket around her shoulders.

"The only people who are supposed to know that you're back," he informs her quietly, "are the ones you saw today. No one else in the organization knows yet. And who the hell do you think you're taking orders from, other than me?"

"I am a Heartless," she contradicts, though without any sharpness. "I have some contacts in the city that might want to meet with me."

"In *my* city," Rovis corrects her.

"You don't know the people of your city like I do, Rovis."

"That may be true," Rovis concedes. "But even then, none of them should know that you're back."

Zero only nods.

"She hasn't been in the field for over a year," Tal interjects, rejoining them. "Give her a break. Our Ace will be at the top of her game again soon enough."

"She should've come back to either one of us," Rovis insists.

"That, I agree with. Zero, that blast could have killed you. Do you even remember how to disarm a bomb? Wait."

Tal narrows his eyes at the spiders all over her closing up her wounds. He grabs her right hand and pushes one side of Rovis's jacket out of the way. Melted plastic stuck to her wrist where a couple spiders are attempting to remove the toxic material and heal her skin, with some fried wires sticking out of the hump. Tal lets out an exasperated growl and shoots Rovis a look.

"This energy shield device is outdated by two years."

"That's pretty good, then," Zero comments absently.

"Stars and bloody cities, *no*." Tal points a metal finger at her. "I'm giving you a full upgrade to everything you own as soon as we get back."

Rovis looks around once more around the area, studying the angles and positions of the cameras. Despite being in the back, there's likely footage of every angle of the Shapeshifter before it got blown up, which meant the bomb was planted before Zero's extraction. And there were likely multiple sources synced together, given the level of explosion. If Zero left the scene like she should've, she would've been far enough to have survived even without the shield.

Unless whoever planted it knew she was going to look for the bomb, and they knew her ears would be sharp enough to hear the ticking when it started.

Because then, even if she survived, she would've been caught on camera searching through the car. It's a terrible plot, but someone still tried it.

An unsettling theory turns in his stomach.

"Zero," Rovis sighs.

The girl looks over at him, still not completely there. Tal narrows his eyes at Rovis's expression. Rovis shoots a meaningful look at him and shifts his gaze back to Zero, who still blinks at him blankly. He shakes his head, knowing he has to say it, even though she's clearly still in shock.

"I suggest you get on the case of what we talked about, because someone's either trying to kill you or frame you."

3

Welcome to Dyvris

Tal is going to kill Zero the next time he sees her.

Metal clanging, the broken parts of three drones plop lifelessly onto Tal's workstation in his private lab. The first drone successfully followed Zero for all of fifteen minutes before she turned a corner too fast, and it mysteriously went offline. The second one made it through five minutes. The third found itself staring into her unimpressed gaze after three minutes.

He makes a mental note to figure out a way to fix the fragility of the drones as he plants his hands on the workstation and bows his head, grieving the short existence of his creations. In Tal's defense, stealth often does not go well with strength when it comes to technology. He turns his head and grits his teeth at the sight of a purple card. Metal fingers snatch the card off the table and flick it into the trash can.

Zero had the audacity to dump all the parts in a paper bag from a local bakery-café, throw in one of her obnoxious Ace cards, and unceremoniously leave the bag outside the door to his lab. Tal's valuable inventions should at least be ornately packaged, even if they're brutally murdered by the human equivalent of a wasp.

Levi's soft chuckle draws his attention.

"What?" Tal snaps.

"I haven't seen you this riled up since that one time Quade sent Rovis on a heist without you." Levi leans on the table, facing Tal. "This isn't really about the broken drones. What is it?"

A resounding crunch is the only warning before the worktable shifts and topples over, causing a series of cacophonous chords of metallic parts crashing onto the marble floor and against each other.

Tal stares down at his metal fingers gripping the only corner of the table left standing on a leg. Jagged edges extend out from the dent created by his silver thumb. Then the remaining material in his fist shatter and sprinkle on the pile of safety hazards on the floor.

The last leg of the table topples over, bounces once, and rolls a few paces away.

Tal puts his fists on his hips and looks at the ceiling, feigning innocence.

"Damn, I wonder how that happened," Levi deadpans.

"It was the table's fault."

A beat of silence. "You built it."

"Hey, I built the arm, too." Tal crosses his arms and finally drops the act to look at Levi. "Now we know that in a fight between the table and the arm, the arm would win."

Levi only raises a brow.

"It's crucial knowledge," Tal adds. "In case you need to win a bet."

"Tal."

"Who are you, my mother?"

"Have I ever thrown you out onto the streets?" Levi shoots back.

Tal squawks and points an accusatory finger at him, racking his brain for a better comeback. But then he snorts and puts a hand on his knee, laughing so hard that he starts wheezing. "No, I can't beat you this time. That was too good."

"Uh-huh." Levi doesn't even smirk, only continues to stare at him, unimpressed.

Forcing himself to calm down, Tal straightens and rakes his fingers through his hair. At Levi's serious expression, he schools his own, wiping away all remaining attempts to use humor as a cover. There are exactly three people in the world who can get the truth out of Tal anytime they want to: Rovis, Zero, and Levi.

"There…" Tal sighs. "The reason why we rushed Zero's extraction is because one of our Digitals found a list. You know all the anti-Avyrian hate crimes going on right now? They're especially bad in the capital. The government is purging all of their Avyrian workers because they think the employees are spying for their home country, meaning Zero's alias was coded red. It doesn't help that another war might be coming, since the Purish government thinks it can take on the Riyssolans, as if they even have the resources to go against a better equipped military force. Now the Purish are targeting the Avyrians because of the technological superiority of the islands they come from, but they're going to come for the rest of us next. The Toullish, the Lasan, the Riyssolans, maybe even the Ezclovese in the country. Who knows? Zero's now missing from her employment, so they may send people to hunt her down if they realize she wasn't who she said she was."

"And there was the bomb. So you and Boss want to keep her under constant surveillance, and you're annoyed she's taking down all your drones because that was going to be your backup in case you can't be there?" Levi guesses. "But she's back in our territory now, and there isn't a single Reaper in this mansion that wouldn't protect her. It doesn't need to be all on you two."

"Now, hold on a minute." Tal reaches for a wrench. "Just the Reapers? Who in the rest of the organization do I need to put through a re-orientation?"

"Stars, will you calm down?" Levi chides, wrapping his fingers around Tal's fist. "I meant she's in the safest place possible. You know how much I like that girl; I wouldn't lie to you about this."

Tal lets Levi take the wrench.

"On another note," Levi says, picking up Zero's metal scorpion with a frown. Tal doesn't miss the flash of concern in his eyes before he looks up, business only. "I've copied the program from this thing. Did you want me to modify anything to repurpose it?"

"No." Tal shoots him an easy grin. "You've been here long enough. Go take a break. I'll let you know if I need anything."

Levi nods, setting down the scorpion, and Tal watches him leave. Something's clearly on his mind, but Tal stops himself from asking. After taking another look at the drones, he sighs and tosses them to the junk pile. They would need to be completely rebuilt if Tal still wants to use them as drones.

"Is now a bad time to say 'I told you so'?"

Tal spins around, a knife flying out and embedding in a car he's been trying to upgrade. Rovis smirks in his holographic form. Right. He's checking in with Aconite fronts downtown. The most involved members live in a mansion in the mountains, but many more reside throughout the desert. Rovis is only here virtually, and N.A.D.E., the traitorous artificial intelligence program that *Tal* created with twelve years of hard work, must have answered the call while he was busy seething.

"Don't look at me like that," Rovis says, insufferably smug. "Zero can probably hear that thing from three blocks away. Besides, she always knows more than she should, including where all the weak spots of your groundbreaking tech are."

"She hasn't even been here!" Tal throws his hands up. "Where did she find the time to memorize that stuff? Wait. Did you just call my drones loud? Excuse you, the whole point of them is to spy for us. I made them *soundless.*"

Rovis shrugs. "It's better to follow her in person. She's always around other people."

"Some of which are Purish officials aiming to take us down," Tal deadpans, not bothering to hide how unconvinced he is of the theory that Zero is plotting for the Aconite's downfall. Rovis doesn't even believe it himself, so Tal doesn't understand why he insists on pretending that he's suspicious of her.

"We may have another problem, which is why I'm calling you. Quite a few reports are saying that there has been Syndicate activity around here."

"Like what?" Tal snarks. "Looking for more middle school kids to terrorize?"

"Tal." Rovis attempts to scold him, but the corners of Rovis's lips twitch. Tal considers that a win. "The rebellion is getting stronger. The Purish are getting agitated, which means the Syndicate is growing. We may get caught in the crossfires."

Feeling petty, Tal mocks his words with incoherent, high pitched noises and rolled eyes.

"Talon Gierkas."

"Oh, save me the lecture, Boss," Tal drawls, waving a dismissive hand.

On a dying planet with a greedy puppet for the chief of Pureland, a revolution is inevitable. The privileged descendants of Ezcalese colonizers, who drove the natives of this land to extinction and decided to call themselves the Purish, are rich enough to hide from the increasingly frequent and severe natural disasters, to buy miracle cures for all the new diseases, to take as much land as they want. Meanwhile, they use minority groups as shields, as expendables, as steps beneath their feet.

For instance, if it weren't for the intelligence and knowledge of resources of the Avyrian immigrants, the coastal cities would all be useless when the sea levels rose and drowned the shores. The Purish fled inland when it happened, raising prices of housing as they did so. Out of all immigrant populations, Avyrians are the most highly concentrated near the coasts due to their lineage tracing back to the islands. When they couldn't follow the Purish into neighborhoods that were safe from the floods because of the inordinately expensive costs, they enhanced the cities to unparalleled technology. They established underwater facilities and built taller. They organized public transportation systems with speedboats, submarines, floating pods, highways, and inter-structural bridges.

The Avyrians of Pureland survived, despite having been left to fend for themselves.

Most of them turned their backs on the laws and joined the Damned. They formed the largest network among the world of criminals and called themselves the Water Lords. The Avyrians essentially rule the coasts now, so of course the Purish government is eager to get rid of them.

"Lithium," Rovis says, mildly annoyed now.

"Fine. I'll send some Reapers to look into it," Tal says. "But I highly doubt that they can touch us. The Syndicate has been around for almost a century, and they've accomplished nothing."

"We should still be careful. They won't care that we aren't part of the rebellion."

"Yes, yes. We all look the same." Tal smirks. "I'd like to see them try to kill all of us. We don't even recognize them as part of the Damned because all they do is go around preaching Purish supremacy."

"You know things are changing now. Things are especially tense between the Purish and the Avyrians right now. Don't tell me you've forgotten the reason we rushed over to Torch City to get Zero." Rovis pauses. A glint of mockery sharpens his eyes. "How are your drones doing, by the way?"

Tal glares at him at that last taunt. "I'll go tail her now. Because I decided to do that myself. Not because of anything you said, just to be clear."

He ends the call without waiting for a dry response that Rovis was bound to have, retrieves his knife, pulls on a black leather glove over his metal hand, and locks the lab behind him. The elevator shoots up and opens on the main floor, where the halls are bustling with members of the organization. Tal's knife slips into his hand, and he tosses it as he walks, lunatic smirk already plastered onto his face. Older members nod at him, and fledglings scurry to avoid him.

The Aconite mansion is a shadow above a natural lake hidden by dangerous mountains prone to landslides, kept afloat by antigravity engineering honed by the most brilliant mechanics who worked for the organization. Including Tal, of course.

There are four main buildings, the largest one housing the head boss and underboss, the Reapers, the Menders, and the Clockworks. It's a massive, white, circular construction that glows a faintly ominous violet with a sliding transportation track that wraps around it like a venomous snake. The hollow center grows the deadly plant that gave the organization its name: wolfsbane. Vials of the aconitine poison extracted from wolfsbane form the interior circular wall. Above the wolfsbane garden, a glass dome protects the plants from the toxic gasses that accumulate in the air everyday.

They call the monstrous building the Poison Core.

The three other buildings are home to more specialized groups. The Tech Hall, a sparkling blue, geometric home to the Digitals and Mechs, connects to all floors of the Core with sapphire-colored glass tubes. The Opulent House, an ornate establishment for the Sleightists, who are ridiculously fond of heists and showcasing their riches, as well as being the most maddening pranksters of the universe. The fancy bridges that connect the House to each floor of the Core look as though the original architect couldn't choose what style to use and just decided to add all of them. And the Wraith Tower, an aggressively gothic tower looming over the Core in its black splendor, is the only building to house only one group and to provide only one entrance for outsiders. They even have an iron gate and a black cat.

Tal finds the Heartless fascinating. They are masters of manipulation who work with all the other groups, since their line of business almost always requires a distraction, yet they stay isolated and armor themselves with their grim reputation and intimidating quarters. Even though Zero's the only one who managed to make a name for herself among the Damned, the rest of the Heartless are equally vicious.

Tal's anti-gravity car rumbles to life, and he drives off the edges of the floating premises. He hovers over the lake's surface and ashen trees until he reaches the ambiguous line between mountain and desert. When the tires touch the ground, Tal sets the vehicle on full speed on the track to Zero's location, a faint red dot on the screen in the heart of Dyvris.

The buildings may not shine as brightly during the day, but the architecture remains impressive even without the colorful tricks and animations. Busy people bustle along the streets, dressed in all kinds of fashionable yet protective desert clothing. Since today's winds are relatively strong and picking up a significant amount of sand, everyone has their nose and mouth covered. The locals often wear scarves and tinted goggles, whereas commuters wear full face helmets. Dyvrian fashion has evolved over the last century to include variations on face covers, which is one of the city's greatest attractions for tourists.

Tal flies down the main street until he can catch Zero's familiar figure ahead of him.

She's riding a motorcycle lined with the Aconite's violet glow, dressed in all black with the tail of a long coat flowing behind. A shiny black full face helmet, with the cracks lined in neon purple, protects her face from the harsh air of the desert. She slows to a stop next to a vintage bookstore and leaves her bike there. Tal drives past her through a couple intersections and turns onto a side street, which is equally crowded as the main street.

After parking in a discreet corner near one of the organization's fronts, Tal zips up his leather jacket, all black except for the scarlet glow inside his collar, and pulls on a helmet similar to Zero's but with extra red linings. He starts trailing the girl on foot after she exits the store with a package in hand.

"Zero," a surprised voice catches both their attention. "Is that you?""

Tal steps over to a meat skewer stand so that the shadows give him a bit more coverage. A tall man walks over to Zero, his black helmet shiny under the sun. The familiar lines of violet marks him as an Aconite, and Tal recognizes the clothing as one of the Ezclovese.

"Oh, it really is you," the man says, delighted, when Zero turns and crosses her arms, a cotton bag hanging from her wrist. Tal finally pinpoints the voice as Noah Williams, one of the middle-aged Digitals. Williams continues, "I heard you came back, but I haven't seen you around the mansion."

"I've been staying in the city," Zero says. Her helmet gives away nothing, but Tal knows her well enough to know she already wants to leave this conversation. He shares the sentiment, since Williams was one of the most hostile members when either of them joined the Aconites.

"Ah, the young generation," Williams says. "You all crave the excitement of the city, to fill the emptiness of your soul."

Tal snorts. The vendor of the stand flinches and hurries to offer him a bundle of at least five skewers, each protected by thin paper bags from the desert wind, all while he hears Zero say, "Yes, of course. That's exactly why I'm staying here. The simplicity of my generation is astounding."

Then Tal loses track of the conversation as he shakes his hands at the vendor, who's trying to shove the paper bags at him.

"It's free for you, of course, sir," the vendor says, then bows way too many times. "Thank you for watching over this city."

"Right." Tal often forgets he's Lithium to the locals, too. "Thank you!"

All the local businesses serve Aconite members for free, in exchange for their new homes in Dyvris after getting displaced, as a result of natural disasters or the Purish buying out their towns. Tal holes up in his lab too often to leave the mountains and take advantage of that.

Giving up, he accepts the skewers and tucks them inside his jacket. Tal hurries away before any more awkwardness and finds that Zero, fortunately, has gotten rid of Williams. Her route is incredibly tedious, winding in and out of side streets, probably as complicated as her neural pathways. She passes by people who say hello, and she asks a few questions about the last couple years while giving out various sorts of gifts. Tal has to wonder how she's so popular when she went off to Torch City after barely spending time here, and hasn't reappeared until now. How do people even remember her?

To make things worse, Zero makes her way down to one of the abandoned subway tracks, filthy and rusty and swarming with pests. As if they need a reminder of what they are to society. Tal watches her from the shadows against the musty walls, ignoring the dozens of centipedes that are now exploring the outside of his helmet. The screen in front of his eyes has switched into night vision mode.

Zero treks down to the end of the track, where large pipes converge into a massive well, its diameter three times Tal's height.

"Oh, *no,*" Tal mutters, knowing exactly where it leads to.

He internally groans when Zero hops into the void, followed by heavy clangs when her boots land on metal platforms while descending, with even intervals in between like a metronome. Tal sighs and makes his way to the edge of the well, peering down at the spritely girl leaping her way to a lower level of hell.

Tal hasn't been down there since he was fourteen. He's way too old for this now.

When he's sure that Zero has reached the bottom and left the vertical tunnel, Tal grudgingly follows. He pulls out a thick disc the size of his palm from his jacket and flicks it out with two fingers. It flies out and hovers by his legs, stretching into a much thinner disc with ten times the area. Tal steps onto it, and it lowers itself past all the minor platforms in the walls of the tunnel. When he finally sees light, the disc slows, and he steps off to land on the ground. The disc shrinks and flies back to under his sleeve like magnet.

The underground town is quiet as it usually is at this time of day. It only becomes busy at night, when the desert is too cold for comfort. Tal used to hide here all the time, to find jobs to support his family, and because no ordinary tourist would ever find their way down here.

One downside is that there are too many stars-damned stairs and ladders because of the oversized pipes.

"My knees," Tal complains as he clambers down another flight of rusty stairs. He grunts when he lands on the ground again. "My *spine*. Stars, all my joints."

Finally, when Zero slips into an internet cafe, Tal rounds to the back to observe through a window, rubbing his back. Her visor disappears when she's inside, though her helmet stays on. He watches as she sits down across a very familiar head of blond.

"Levi," Tal says, suddenly cheering up.

Zero pulls out a book from her cotton bag and slides it across the table with a small grin. Levi picks it up and drops his jaw, then attempts to cover up his reaction by slapping a hand over his mouth. Zero props her chin on her hands and watches Levi with excitement.

Tal can't hear what they're saying because he hasn't bothered to turn up the sound reception frequency in his helmet, but even an amateur could read their lips right now.

"You found it?" Levi asks, practically beaming at Zero.

Her smile broadens. "I found it."

"Aw," Tal comments, when Levi holds his hand up for a high-five. "This is adorable, actually."

He watches the rest of conversation while munching on the meat skewers, since the sand can't fly into his food underground. When the conversation ends, Levi reaches out to knock the top of her helmet, and Zero glares at him half-heartedly before saying goodbye and walking out the store. As much as Tal wants to go in and hangout with Levi, he has to keep an eye on Zero for the coming weeks, so he shakes out his legs and proceeds following her.

Tal does not gather any useful information in the next hour, only more aching joints when he has to follow Zero back up to ground level.

"How peculiar," he mutters to himself when Zero has spoken to exactly five homeless people and three street cleaners since they've returned to the surface. "I'm confused yet entertained."

He's almost forgotten how useless the local government is when it comes to public housing. Rovis offered his help to the homeless when he came into power, and some people took it and set up successful businesses or joined the Aconites, while others refused a life associated with the Damned and stayed on the streets. Which is why Tal doesn't see Zero's reasoning to talk to these people.

Either Zero and Rovis are both out of their minds and this whole charade with Zero on the manhunt is fruitless, or there's actually useful information from the wanderers most easily forgotten on the streets.

Tal knows better than to assume the former.

He steps into a coffee shop when Zero rides off on her motorcycle again. Tal pulls off his helmet, thinking.

If someone planted a bomb to either kill or frame Zero, they have to know her relatively well. And if they made a plan like that, maybe Tal isn't approaching this correctly. He needs to know more, see more, get a better view somewhere.

He should probably get on the roofs.

The barista smiles uncertainly at Tal when he wanders over to order his drink.

"Good morning," they say, handing over a warm and full cup.

Slightly puzzled, Tal accepts it and takes a sip. He hums, content to find that it's his favorite. Medium roasted Lasan grounds, triple shot espresso.

"How'd you know?" he asks, unable to recall interacting with this employee before.

"I, uh." The barista's gaze darts around the room, clearly unsure about how to speak to a local gangster. "Our boss made sure we all knew your favorite drinks during training. That is, all the important, frequent customers... Of your status. Lithium, sir."

"Ah." A practiced grin appears on Tal's face at the use of his street name, and he reaches inside his leather jacket for cash.

"Uh, uh, no," the barista stammers, waving at Tal. "It's on the house. Sir."

"I know." His lips tilt into a smirk. Tal tosses an ingot worth a hundred units onto the register, glancing at the name tag. "Your tip, Baron."

Leaving behind the speechless child, Tal strolls out of the shop, only to walk around to the back. He taps his metal forearm, from which a red holographic screen lights up. A few selections, and a grappling hook shoots out of his palm for him to climb the wall.

Once he reaches the roof, Tal checks Zero's location again.

"You're really making me work for it, aren't you?" Tal scoffs.

He stomps his feet once, activating the nanotech that climbs its way out of his boots and around his legs like a vine, circling one last time right above his knees. Along with its energy absorption material, Tal designed these shoes for situations that involve unhealthy stunts.

For example, when he has to jump across seventeen roofs to spy on the Ace of Crowns. Especially since the buildings in Dyvris aren't exactly regularly shaped or closely spaced. It doesn't eliminate the impact on his body, but his joints have been a lost cause anyway.

When Tal settles down on the edge with a good view of Zero sitting next to a dweller, shielded from the wind and sharing food with her visor off again, he activates the parabolic microphone hidden in his middle knuckle, connecting it to his audio transmitters to listen in on the conversation.

"Not really," Zero is saying.

"Very well," the dweller answers. "Time and hatred cement. Turmoil is the sea where wolves have drowned. The queen of poisons shall crawl out of the grave."

"What the hell," Tal mutters. He feels particularly unintelligent when Zero does not appear to be as confused as he is.

"I can't believe I didn't think of that," Zero says slowly.

"Well," the dweller says, patting Zero's knee. "You've had quite a lot on your plate."

Zero nods absently. Then she tilts her head. "Why didn't *he* think of that?" She twists her ring in her lap, eyes glazed at the wall in front of her. "Well, I suppose they hid their true feelings enough to pass as acceptance. I should've paid more attention."

She moves to stand, but the dweller grasps her sleeve.

"A conflagration followed the phoenix," they say.

Zero pauses, narrowing her eyes at the dweller. "Interesting. Thank you. You know what to do if you ever need me."

The motorcycle rolls out of the alley and heads down the street. The dweller continues eating. Tal sighs at his lack of success once again. Literally none of that made sense. But he dutifully gets up and continues tailing Zero, jumping between rooftops to watch her next contact.

Zero turns smoothly into a quiet alley, next to a virtual reality gaming nightclub called Arden's Sunset, and the bike rumbles to a stop. She slides off the seat and leans back on it casually while taking off her helmet. Instead of long black hair, however, a wavy pink and purple bob falls around her face. A thick gold ring of a neon choker glows around her neck, and her makeup appears much darker and bolder than before.

Something in Tal settles down just slightly, seeing that Zero is smart enough to change up her look to make it harder for someone to look for her.

But then Tal makes the mistake of shifting, leather boots grating against concrete without nearby cars to drown out the noise.

Zero sighs and rolls her eyes.

"Is this really the best you can do, Lithium?"

Tal squawks, affronted. He heaves himself over the edge and flexes his right hand, metal blades unsheathing at his fingertips. His boots land on the ground in a controlled descent with his claws digging into the wall of pink and blue dancing circles.

"You wouldn't be able to handle me at my best," Tal announces.

"Was this necessary?" Zero asks blandly.

"No, actually. You are more than welcome to continue consulting your wide variety of friends, and I'll continue to follow you."

"Tal." Zero tosses and catches her helmet. The name somehow sounds like an insult on her tongue. "Do me a favor. Tell His Royal Highness that I'm working, and I work much, much better without a loud, clumsy, distracting, vexatious—"

"Hey, hey, hey," Tal protests. "Watch who you're talking to."

Shaking her head and rolling her eyes once again, Zero pushes inside the gaming nightclub, which is in fact one of the Aconite fronts. The first floor is dark, only lit by holographic games that tourists are interacting with. Raves often fill out around gamers. The second floor is more of a mezzanine, open in the middle, mostly for those in the mood to gamble on the larger, multiplayer games visible on the first floor. The third floor is a bar only allowed for Aconite members, as well as a few private rooms.

On his way up the stairs, lit up with waves of rainbows, Tal notices Ayssa Lan marching towards Zero from behind on the second floor.

"Ooh, yikes." He chuckles, slipping between drunken bodies around the railing.

Someone — someone who clearly doesn't want to finish the day with all their limbs — grabs his wrist, and Tal uses the momentum to slam the other person into the wall. A knife slips into his flesh hand and presses against the assailant's neck. Claws unsheathed, the metal tips slice through fabric and rest on the skin covering a thudding heart.

When he finally sees who he pinned to the wall, Tal slackens.

"Oh, hey, Rov."

But Tal's too distracted by the man staring back at him to move away. Two pieces of stray black silky hair dangle above one arched brow, where a golden barbell with a small raven skull glistens. A thick gold hoop pierces through Rovis's right earlobe. Sharp brown eyes reveal nothing of the man's endless calculations.

He looks every bit the unofficial king that he is.

The Scavenger of the Eastern Desert, he rules the land abandoned by the Purish, even the fiery sun could never burn such a survivor.

Although Tal thinks he might want to see that. He imagines that Rovis would be glorious in the midst of fire, passion like nothing else blazing in his eyes. This man has always been a steady flame against Tal's fickle lightning.

But right here, brushed by fluorescent colors and painted by the shadows, Rovis Bozyd-Wei radiates power, even under Tal's claws.

He is the most regal monster.

He is the angelic demon.

He is the seal of death for Tal's weak heart.

Yes, Tal has been gone for Rovis since the day they met.

"Hello," Rovis says, dragging Tal out of his stupor. He tilts his head, a dangerous, *dangerous* smirk dancing on his lips. "Are you going to put your little talons away, or has it been your plan to snatch my heart all along?"

Tal jerks back.

Then covers it up with a laugh, though the words *You have no idea* almost choke him.

"My beloved boss," Tal says, "you've interrupted my spying mission."

Rovis's smirk fades. "Well?"

Shaking his head, Tal looks back across the mezzanine to see Ayssa waving her arms at Zero. He reactivates the microphone and audio transmitters, this time connecting to Rovis's earpiece as well.

"Maybe finding a partner will fix that dreadful personality of yours," Ayssa is saying. "Everyone knows you stay single for attention. But you don't really want to grow old and die alone, do you?"

"I don't know," Zero says, indifferent. "I've always had a feeling I'd die young. No growing old for me. What a shame."

She turns to leave, but Ayssa grips her arm.

Zero stops, her posture sharpening.

"Do not," came the quiet yet deadly hiss, "touch me."

"Or what?" Ayssa challenges. Tal tuts, shaking his head. Zero smiles, cold and still hidden from the other girl's view.

Suddenly, Ayssa jumps back, cradling her hand. Zero tilts her head at Ayssa, as if the bloody switchblade in her hand has nothing to do with the new injury.

"Sweetie," she says, with no affection in her voice. "Ever heard of this concept called 'boundaries'?"

Ayssa says nothing, but the hatred in her eyes makes Tal consider a new possibility for the organization's mole.

Levi did let slip that not everyone in the Aconite gang likes Zero, did he not?

When Zero turns away, Ayssa spits out, "Lila would despise what you've become, S—"

She chokes when her back slams against the wall.

A blade flashes against her neck.

"Lose that name," Zero whispers into Ayssa's ear, lips carved into a grin that's anything but friendly, "or lose your tongue."

"Nice one," Tal comments quietly but proudly. He loves one-liners. His shoulder bumps against Rovis's. "She's got a bit of Lithium there, right?"

"Lila's dead," Zero is saying, voice flat. "The dead don't hate or love anything. Her best friend's dead, too. You won't find her in me."

Unfortunately, Tal has to end his entertainment when Kagiso approaches them.

The boy nods at Tal, then reaches up to whisper into Rovis's ear. Judging by the scowl on the Scavenger's face, it isn't good news at all, and Tal regrets not being able to turn up with anything more concrete on the matter with Zero.

"I have to go," Rovis says. "We'll talk about this later."

Tal watches him follow Kagiso out. His long coat billows after him, almost like the cape of a champion marching through his battleground.

"Stars, I need to stop," Tal berates himself and tears his gaze away.

When he sees that Zero and Ayssa are gone, he wanders upstairs to the bar, delighted to see Levi nursing a beer while scrolling through his phone. It's been hard for Tal and Levi to catch each other lately, with all the business they each have to take care of in the city and in the mansion.

Tal walks over and leans sideways to face Levi, mimicking his posture from earlier in the lab.

"Hey." Levi smiles when he looks up. "You need anything?"

Tal reaches out to run his fingers through soft, blond hair. "Not today."

Levi nods and offers the rest of the bottle. Tal's fingers twitch, hesitating. Images of crushed glass and blood flashed before his eyes, and he can almost hear the familiar cacophony of his parents' screaming matches.

That was six years ago, he reminds himself.

Tal blinks the memories away, shoves down the panic starting to stir in his chest, and takes the drink. "Do *you* need anything? You drove quite a lot yesterday."

Levi hums, considering. "Well, we had some fun afterwards, didn't we? But how much work do you have today?"

"I'll make time for you."

"Then your room tonight?"

Tal smirks. "Sounds good."

He revels in the comfortable silence, taking small amounts of the alcohol at a time. No expectations weigh him down or wind him up here. This is one of the many gifts that Levi has given him, though Tal isn't sure he deserves it. His metal fingers twitch, and he frowns at the locked chest of ghosts in his head threatening to break out and haunt him again. For a moment, he sees the girl again. She looks a lot like Daleyza, except her skin is lighter and she still has both eyes, and she favors green a lot more than blue. Then the light in her eyes begins to fade.

Tal finishes the bottle in one gulp, and he shakes his head as the burn runs down his throat. He hears some shifting next to him. Then Levi's taking his hand, concerned eyes searching his face. Uncomfortable with the attention, Tal turns his head away and lets his eyes close, wishing he were drunk enough to feel dizzy again.

Kindness always ends with tragedy in Tal's life.

The door creaks.

Tal's eyes shoot open, and his grip on the bottle tightens. His metal hand morphs into a blaster as he whirls around, despite knowing that the Aconites own this place, that if an intruder broke in, they would never make it to the top floor.

Zero walks in, face wiped free of expression. Her tired eyes reflect the light of the energy buzzing through the blaster pointed at her, an aesthetic complement against her new hairdo.

"What did I do now?" she sighs.

"You." Tal points the bottle at her, suddenly excited for the distraction. "We need to talk."

4

The Agency

Zero blinks at Tal's manic beam and Levi's apologetic glance. Even though she spent most of her time as an Aconite undercover in the deep state, she knows well enough that those two's relationship is neither platonic, nor romantic. Rather, it lies somewhere in between, and there's definitely some arrangement going on.

"No." She turns on her heel.

A knife whooshes past her head and lodges in the door. "I outrank you, did you forget?"

Zero only falters slightly before taking a step, mostly surprised by the loud sound the impact made, and somewhat amused by Tal's attempt to use the hierarchy card.

Tal sighs dramatically. "I'll make you coffee."

Usually she wouldn't settle for such a cheap bribe, but after that tedious conversation with Ayssa — which Zero assumes Tal, and probably Rovis, eavesdropped on — she really needs it.

"Alright." She stalks into Rovis and Tal's office, turning on the television. It's a simple but cozy room, with an excessive amount of blankets on the leather couch. Rovis must have replaced all the pictures on the walls, as they all consist of candid shots of current Aconite members in various places on their territory, rather than old, boring portraits of the lineage of Ezclovese bosses Bianchi kept.

Zero's phone buzzes with a call when Tal walks in, but she declines.

"One dark and bitter coffee for one dark and bitter soul," he announces with a flare.

A high pitched beep assaults Zero's ear drums, and she fails to stop the violent flinch in her body. The television screen gets scrambled, a mess of switching channels, before it cuts to red silhouettes of five figures. Dark electro music fades in. The image twists and spirals into a black and red symbol of five snakes hissing around a shield and a torch.

"Stars, not this again," Tal grumbles.

"Leave it on," Zero says, taking the coffee from his hand, eyes glued to the screen.

The symbol of the Faceless bursts apart like a firework, and the video clips start playing. A disfigured man screams in a small cell, banging at the door. Unfinished space ships sleep in a shiny research center. A low income neighborhood flooded to the roofs. Blurry men trading suitcases. A girl with white veins crawling all over her body takes her last breath.

The scenes return the red silhouette, but this time there's a woman holding a finger up to her lips. Zero takes a sip of coffee to hide the hitch in her breath, assuring herself that no one can actually see the woman's face because of the lighting and editing.

Then Zero almost chokes when the words appear across the screen.

THE AGENCY OF JUSTICE IS REAL.

All the video clips from before start to play again, but in full length, with the location, date, and time of each footage on the bottom.

In Torch City, three days ago, in the morning: A Purish man in a three-piece suit injects unknown drugs into a prisoner, before locking him in a cell. A team of scientists take notes on the prisoner's descent into hallucinations and insanity.

In Ferrisque, five days ago, in the evening: Rich couples sign contracts with Pureland's top engineers to build an escape from the dying planet. Other documents show that they bought out lands that used to be lower-class homes. At the same time, on the other side of the city, groups of cloaked figures pour mysterious contents into the water supply.

In Ferrisque, two days ago, during the day: All previous residents fall ill and are transferred out to an unclear destination.

In suburban Hilobis, a week ago: Deals were made between city officials and agents in suits.

In suburban Hilobis, yesterday, midnight: Mayors neglect sending out flood warnings and ignore distress calls sent from the drowning neighborhood. People beg drivers of transportation vehicles to help them evacuate, but Purish surveillance bots interfere and shove them back into the waters when they fail to pay the cost of transportation.

In Eaglair, one month ago: Lab workers successfully create a vaccine and sell it to the highest payer. They trade for billions of monetary units in Torch City.

In Loveias, this morning: A young couple sobs at the bedside of a little girl. She's screaming, tearing at the bedsheets and clawing out her hair. White veins split across her face, her arms, her legs. They look bioluminescent at first, then they glow brighter, and brighter, until the unnatural fire in her veins takes over her entire body.

The screen blacks out.

Zero closes her eyes, taking deep breaths. For a few moments, she can't hear anything, as if she's deep underwater and nowhere close to the surface.

It seems peaceful, really.

And Zero has been very tired, for a very long time now. Peace might just be the one thing she wants, and the one thing she can't have. Even drowning isn't a peaceful death. So she has to keep dragging her own corpse through the motions, do everything she's supposed to, even when she wants to lie down somewhere and never get up again.

When the ringing fades, she slowly peels open her eyes. Black dots swim before her eyes, and for a moment the room might as well be a shot in an archaic black-and-white television show. She blinks several times, then finally lifts her head to see Tal kneeling in front of her, hands planted on the edge of the couch cushions but not touching her legs. And the man staring at her right now is the real him. No masks, no Lithium, no psychopathic acts. Those attentive eyes seem to search for the real her, too. The girl she was before she called herself Zero, before she became a Heartless, before the Ace of Crowns. The girl he once tried to save.

Zero shoves Tal's face away. "I'm fine."

She takes a sip of her coffee to avoid seeing Tal piece his masks and armor back together. Disappointing him would hurt if she still had a heart. But they are the Damned. Tal became Lithium to survive, and he has to keep being Lithium.

"Good for you," he says brightly. "I didn't ask."

Zero snorts and rolls her eyes before glancing over at him again. He's giving her the usual exaggerated smile, which truthfully would look terrifying to any sane person. He looks like a murderous clown with a good fashion sense.

"That was depressing," Tal rambles on. "Your movie choices are getting worse, dear Zero. The creativity is too extreme. As much as I enjoy the reminders of what a terrible world we live in, I wouldn't go as far as saying that the Agency is real. I mean, given our resources, the Aconites would have infiltrated it already—"

Tal cuts himself off and freezes, like a glitch on a screen. His fake grin fades, and Zero starts to feel herself waking up enough to come to a troublesome realization. She tenses as Tal's eyes narrow at her. The ice in his stare chills her clenched fingers on the mug.

"What," Tal growls, "the hell did you do?"

Zero purses her lips and looks away. She downs her entire cup of coffee, welcoming the burn on her tongue and in her throat. At least now she has something to blame for the tremors in her hands. The caffeine, and sleep-deprivation. Slowly, she meets Tal's glare and sets her jaw.

"You can't tell Rovis," she insists.

"That's not up to you," Tal counters coldly. A lethal look pierces through his calm facade like the first flash of lightning in a brewing storm. Zero often forgets he is as much a ruthless destroyer as he is an ingenious creator.

Zero sets the mug down on the coffee table. "What good will it do? I'm out of there already."

"I have been losing *sleep*," Tal hisses, "worried that a regularly corrupted government is going to take you away from us because of a prejudiced hit list. Now you're telling me you were essentially a double agent for a secret organization in the deep state that no one was sure even existed?"

Zero rolls her eyes. "I did not tell you that."

He slams his human hand on the table and breaks it in half. The mug falls onto the floor and shatters. "Don't you pull that on me right now. We have no idea how many people want you dead."

"Probably less than you. You've killed. You've driven many Purish businesses to bankruptcy with your own inventions. And you're the second richest person in the city, not counting the local officials."

"You're the third," Tal counters. "Not really helping your case here."

"I—" Zero blinks. "What?"

Tal chuckles, a dark sound grating with disbelief and irritation. "You think you're so smart, don't you? All those deals you helped Quade make, *that* made you rich. You have blood on your hands, too, Ace. You thought you were playing with fire, but in truth you were mindlessly wandering in a garden of nuclear weapons that can level the whole planet."

Zero scoffs at the insult. "I knew exactly what I was doing."

"So you just wanted to get us all killed."

"I'll *leave*," she snaps.

"That's not what I meant!" Tal huffs in frustration. "I—"

"But *I* mean it," Zero states, standing and shoving her hands in her pockets. "I'm only staying because I have loose ends to tie up, and Rovis needs as many people to watch his back as possible right now. You won't tell him about what you learned today, because he can't deal with this on top of everything else. Look at how you reacted, Tal. Rovis absolutely cannot find out. After I finish my business here, I'm leaving."

"You can't." Tal crosses his arms. "You took the mark. The only way you can leave is either death or the knife."

A laugh escapes Zero's throat before she could force it back.

She's already tempted death once before. She's been ready to kill herself for years, and on the off chance that she finds a reason to stay alive, she wouldn't even wait for Rovis to do the honors when she leaves. She'd knife *herself* in front of the Scavenger.

Something in her brain is wired incorrectly, she knows. But a savage part of her delights in the fact that no one can hurt her more than herself.

Zero regains control over herself when Tal's expression shifts, and she quickly changes the subject. "Besides, you might want to give the knife to some of the Ezclovese. Senka said that the Aconites who worked under Bianchi hated Rovis for taking over and erasing the easy life of weapons trafficking with our unique poison plant. They want to go back."

Tal frowns, evidently displeased by her diversion yet needing to process the information for a more pressing issue. "Senka's the poetry lady? Or the dumpster diver?" At Zero's unimpressed look, he revises his response, "That does make sense. What else did you find out?"

"Senka, the 'poetry lady' and my friend, caught an Ezclovese meeting up with a government operative to sell information."

"And what about Ayssa? Why the bomb?"

Zero frowns. Are they even having the same conversation still? "Ayssa did not plant the bomb, Tal. Did you hit your head hopping roofs?"

"We— I heard your argument downstairs earlier. It's very obvious that she wants to smother you in your sleep."

"Yeah, she wants to," Zero agrees, indifferent. "She thinks I got her high school sweetheart killed, so she's just taking it out on me. But she's all bark and no bite. She's not actually capable of hurting anyone."

"That sounds like plenty of motivation for attempting murder. Zero, listen to me. You can't underestimate her."

"No, stop going off on tangents. The bomb was a distraction, probably an empty threat anyway. I haven't figured out what else happened at the time, but Kagiso definitely knows something."

Tal opens his mouth to argue, but swears quietly instead, as if remembering something. "I have to go. But this conversation is far from over."

Sighing, Zero rolls her eyes again and waves him off. Tal gives her one last glare before hurrying out the door. Then he comes right back in before she even takes her next breath.

"Wait," he says, stopping right in front of her.

Zero blinks at him, apprehensive.

His cold eyes search her expression. Metal fingers twitch by his side. Taking a deep breath, Tal holds out a hand, the one made of flesh.

Zero hesitates. Then, slowly, she matches Tal and covers his palm with her fingers. He pulls her in and hugs her tightly, resting his chin on top of her head.

"I am so angry with you right now," Tal grits out in Lasan.

"I know," she replies, copying the language switch.

"But don't feel so determined to leave, alright? You are one of us, so your problems are ours. It might be worse than we've assumed, but we won't leave you. Even if no one else is as loyal, you'll always have me. I will lose my temper, but I will never abandon you when you mess up. If it comes to it, I will die next to you if the Agency finds us and buries us in gunfire. Rovis, too. I don't know how deep the issues run between you two, but I know him, and he will do the same."

Zero stills, resisting the urge to stab him in a non-vital organ when she hears those words. Something in her chest twitches, and she has to stomp down that feeling before it registers as pain. The sincerity in his voice makes her skin crawl. She knows better than to listen, to let the words sink in, because she's heard similar speeches countless times before. Yet the child in her is thrashing and throwing a tantrum and desperately clinging on to any signs of love.

Like Tal's little monologue, hope is so treacherously tempting, but she can't afford to lose another game to it again. She can't — she *won't* — allow herself to believe in these lies. Tal may not be lying at this moment, but he might take those words back in the future.

Time is the greatest deceiver of the universe.

"I think," she says, patting Tal's back, "I liked it better when you were screaming at me."

He scoffs and pulls back, and the cool fury in his eyes seems to have thawed just a little. Zero crosses her arms and raises a brow.

"I wasn't screaming," Tal claims.

"You broke the table. I'm not explaining that to Rovis."

"Still, not screaming."

Zero rolls her eyes. This man's priorities. "Whatever."

Tal chuckles then, a low sound in his chest. One corner of his lips curls up as the familiar glint of vengeance returns to his eyes. "You're adorable when you pout. Fine, fine, my precious Ace. I can never stay mad at you for long, anyway. Don't worry, I'll deal with Rovis. I'll find the brainless traitor who tried to mess with you and make them pay."

"Sure," Zero says without enthusiasm.

He shoots her a Lithium grin and ruffles her hair, before he finally leaves with a bounce in his step, whistling and toying with one of his knives.

Zero waits until his footsteps fade, blending into the background chaos of noises downstairs in the club. The ringing in her ears return, so she settles back onto the couch, burying her face in her hands. She feels nothing. She cannot, and will not allow herself to succumb to her weaknesses. Not fear of the Agency, not hurt from her past, not guilt about her own corruption. No, the only thing she feels is bone-deep exhaustion.

Perhaps, she wonders, if there would be nothing to be found if a sick Agent tracked her down and decided to carve open her chest. No heart beating against her ribcage. Truly heartless. She chuckles at the irony, a pathetic sound in the empty office.

When she stopped herself from swallowing those pills two years ago, she wanted to start over and truly live, yet she still ended up being even more pathetic than before.

Once she finishes wallowing in her numbness, Zero makes her way out of Arden's Sunset, feeling like a zombie, and rides back to the mountains. She zones out too many times and spends an extra hour at the edge of the desert trying to find her way to the mansion.

She kills the engine and frowns, brows furrowed, when she passes four secret Aconite tunnels that are sealed off.

Could this be Tal's doing?

The tunnels extend beneath the mountains and slope downward under the mansion's lake, supported by energy shields. It all converges in a larger tube, essentially a three-dimensional intersection, in the middle of the lake that would drive vehicles vertically into the mansion's bottom entrance, where there's a magnetic field to direct the cars into the spacious garage beneath the buildings.

But even the tunnel underneath the old nuclear plant that suffered a meltdown has been blocked off. Only about a third of the Aconites know of its existence, and less than a fifth of those would be willing to use it.

Narrowing her eyes, Zero activates the antigravity function in her bike, and flies through the mountains above the surface, though she barely avoids getting buried by six mudslides. When the floating mansion comes into view, she tightens her grip, tilts the bike to a fifty-degree angle, and cranks up the accelerator to full power. Zero shoots over the edge of the establishment and makes a full circle around before coming to a stop next to the Poison Core.

The Wraith Tower still stands like a bad omen when Zero takes off her helmet and observes her surroundings.

She supposes she should have a proper reunion with the Heartless.

The Heartless. They are the most fiercely loving people Zero has ever known, other than Tal and her old friends. They are a family that understands each other more than anyone else ever could, because they all share the same priceless gift that makes them the most dangerous spies: aromanticism and asexuality. They can't get distracted by attraction, yet they can wield it as a weapon against others. They choose the people in their lives, and they all choose each other.

Though, as much as Zero loves the Heartless, they are also way too energetic. She's going to have to deal with the traitor issue before she gets the chance and the social capacity to return to the Tower.

Shaking her head, Zero enters the main building. It looks the same as it did before she left, not that she expects Rovis to make any efforts of renovation or interior design. She passes by several lounges, where the members drink and game, rowdy as always.

"Ace of Crowns," an annoying voice sings.

Zero whirls around and glares at Kagiso, who lifts a crystal glass from a sunroom, his mocking smirk sparkling under the light like an advertisement for toothpaste.

"Zero?" The person sitting on his lap perks up, stacking the cards in their hand. "You're back!"

"Avery," Zero greets them, walking a few steps and dropping the glare reserved for Kagiso.

Avery Stewart is an Ezclovese Clockwork who keeps track of all the records from Aconite jobs and stolen information, and they are quite possibly the cutest human being in this entire world. A small redhead, they have a respectable fashion sense, with countless plaid skirts with matching jackets, most of which Kagiso likely stole for them.

And no, Avery and Kagiso are not a thing. They never have been, and probably never will be. They are best friends who are physically affectionate, with a long history behind them. It shouldn't make sense, because Kagiso is the baddest playboy in the desert, while Avery is the walking embodiment of sunshine. But Zero is a Heartless; she knows better than anyone that relationships are defined by those in it, not outsiders.

"Do you want to play?" Avery asks. Zero looks down at the current round of Keepers and Thieves, where Avery is obliterating the rest of the table. Even their team members.

"It's your favorite game," Kagiso teases.

Zero rolls her eyes. "I'm busy."

"Aw." Avery pouts. "Not even one round?"

Zero raises a hand and blocks Avery's face from her view. "Don't puppy-dog me right now. I actually am busy."

"Busy sending Lithium after me?" Kagiso challenges, dark eyes narrowed.

Zero tilts her head at him. "You still have all your limbs. Clearly he didn't go Lithium on you."

"Of course not. I told him everything he wanted to know without resistance."

"Which was what?"

"Ah, ah." Kagiso raises a finger. "No information without a price, Ace. You know this. Besides, you'll see soon enough."

"Useless," Zero mutters and turns on her heel.

"You wound me," Kagiso calls after her.

She rolls her eyes without looking back at him and marches out. A few more people acknowledge her in the hall, but Zero does a good job avoiding more irritating interactions before she reaches her destination.

"What are you doing here?" Daleyza asks when Zero approaches her outside the training gym. "How did you get back?"

Zero tilts her head. "So something is going on in the inner circle. Funny how I know nothing about this."

"Boss and Tal ordered a full lockdown. No one's supposed to get in or get out." Daleyza narrows her eyes at Zero. "Don't tell me I failed at my one job today."

Waving a dismissive hand, Zero assures her, "All the tunnels were blocked. You're fine."

"You still haven't answered my question."

"I drove through the mountains."

Daleyza only stares. "You know the survival rate of doing that is three percent, right?"

"Well, given that I found this mansion by myself two years ago by walking through the mountains, I think I *am* the three percent. Anyway, do you have time to spar? I'm rusty."

"Zero, what?" Her brown eye is so wide that it has become even more unsettling than the blue mechanical one.

"Has Tal not told you the story of how we met?"

"No," Daleyza enunciates, apparently aggrieved.

"Take it up with him, then. Do you want to spar or not?"

Daleyza huffs, crossing her arms. "Fine, but it hasn't been long since your injury. We should keep it short so you don't hurt your hand again."

Zero scoffs. "Don't go soft on me now, head Reaper."

She promptly pays for that comment by failing to dodge a punch to her side.

"Who are you calling soft?" Daleyza drawls as Zero catches herself with a couple steps away.

Fighting Daleyza is always humbling. Her older sister, Dakota Etienam, served in the military, solely for veteran benefits, but she got tangled in Quade Bianchi's mess of a business and became a Reaper. Zero hasn't heard much of the story, but apparently Dakota was the one who saved Tal from a rowdy group of no-name Purish gangsters who mutilated his arm when he was twelve. She died before Zero joined.

"I know what you did, by the way."

Startled, Zero forgets to divert a punch and lands on her side. She rolls to stand and looks warily at Daleyza. "That's not very specific."

Daleyza flicks her fingers, gesturing for Zero to continue. "I caught Ofir trying to slip something in people's drinks one day."

Zero stays rooted to her spot.

Chuckling at her reaction, Daleyza adds, "But they explained. I eventually let them proceed with your secret treatment."

"You make it sound so suspicious," Zero says dryly, reluctantly going for another round. "I knew what I was doing, but no one would believe me if I announced it."

"It's true, then? Not only is the Agency real, but so is the mind-control division?"

"Unfortunately," Zero mutters, avoiding another brutal swing by a hair.

"That was extremely risky, Zero. I can't believe you were undercover at the Agency. Rovis and Tal would kill me if they found out I knew before them. I wish you had a safer plan, but I understand why you did what you did. Whatever reasons you had to infiltrate a secret government sector that you somehow knew about before everyone else, I'm glad it hasn't killed you yet. You know, you saved several of our fellow members that day."

"It was mostly Ofir. They're pretty genius. Raven, too."

"Give yourself some credit. You put yourself in the wolf's den." Daleyza swipes Zero's feet out from under her again. Zero decides to mope on the floor, unwilling to fight and have this conversation at the same time. Especially when Daleyza asks, "Does Rovis know?"

Zero slams her fist down on the mat, needing to feel the lingering pain of her injury bounce up her arm. "Absolutely not. He doesn't, and he won't."

"Okay, but look at how much you have to deal with right now. Reverse engineering a complex drug aimed to control the most mystifying organ of the human body must have been time-consuming and draining. Boss wouldn't take it lightly. He'd cut you some slack. I mean, when's the last time you slept?"

"Daleyza. Just don't." Zero throws an arm over her eyes, thoroughly worn out from the sparring session. Her limbs feel like noodles, and her brain is too scattered to argue. She's so sick of telling people to keep things from Rovis. Really, why must they be so loyal?

A pause. "Alright. Your choice."

"Thank you."

Daleyza claps right in front of Zero's face. "Get up. It's been an hour."

Zero squints up at Daleyza. "Has it really?"

"Yep. We're done for today. Go eat some food."

When they exit the gym, Zero almost runs over a black ball of fur. It's Starlight, the Heartless's cat, and ze somehow found zir way to the Poison Core.

"Hello," Zero murmurs when she picks up Starlight. "Miss me?"

"You guys actually have a cat?" Daleyza chuckles. "I thought that was a myth, too."

"Starlight usually doesn't leave the Tower."

An odd sense of familiarity hits Zero as she says those words. It almost feels safe, like security and comfort, like this place is somewhere she can always come back to.

They start walking again, and Zero feels something finally settle inside. Every cell in her body is still protesting, having been awake for what's probably been a hundred and fifty hours, since she had to pull all-nighters in the Agency's lab and investigated through the entirety of last night. But she feels a sense of serenity that's different from her usual numbness.

It must be the cat.

"How are things with Summer?" Zero asks.

"Oh, you know." Daleyza smirks.

Zero blinks several times before she says, "Yeah, never mind. You lost the bet, by the way."

Daleyza groans. "Are you sure? There's no way he doesn't know."

"Rovis is oblivious to this kind of stuff. He still thinks you and Summer are just friends. I'm sorry, but Summer wins."

"But he owns the entire organization now! How does he not know?"

Zero only shrugs, half-listening to Daleyza's grumbling about losing the bet and having to enter some underground cage fights as a result of it. Lost in thought, Zero crashes against someone. Which turned out to be the Scavenger himself. Zero blinks at him through the fog in her skull. Daleyza gingerly grabs her from behind and sets Zero upright.

"She drove through the mountains," she explains when Rovis shoots her a questioning glance.

The only hint of surprise is the clench of his jaw. Rovis then passes an unreadable gaze over Zero and says, "Stay out of the billiard room."

Zero frowns, uncomprehending, then follows him anyway because she needs to know why the tunnels were sealed off. Though she walks at a much slower pace, feeling both too heavy and too alte. A moment later, Daleyza disappears after mentioning something about the basement.

When Zero's feet stop moving, she almost forgets why she decided to enter a room she barely frequents. It's huge, with a black and violet pool table in the center, some holographic video games still glowing, and a lot of empty sofas. Everyone's standing, looking... terrified in the eerie silence.

Zero blinks several times and notices for the first time that there are two people at the pool table. Rovis has Noah Williams pinned down, gripping a huge knife that skewered Williams's left forearm to the carpet tiles darkened with blood.

"You were right," someone says from behind Zero. It takes her a few moments to react, to register the voice as Tal's, and to realize he's speaking to her. A familiar scent graces her lungs. She half turns to see shadows covering most of his face, until he steps forward into the light with intense eyes and a deep frown. That expression doesn't incite much optimism, so she turns back around to continue studying the room.

"I remembered that the night before we left to get you," Tal explains quietly, so that only Zero can hear, "Williams was acting suspicious. The Digitals don't go out unless it's to walk around Dyvris because they don't need to interact with other people like Dealers and Reapers. Williams was leaving in the wrong direction, to the coast-end where we store the Shapeshifters, which we only use for jobs. I went to get Rovis to help me search for camera evidence, and we found it, even though Williams tried to loop the surveillance on that side. Luckily I had a fail-safe for that. Williams planted the bomb. N.A.D.E. also filtered out footage from our downtown cameras. Turns out, he's been meeting up with an Agent on a weekly basis."

"He's not the only one," Zero responds.

"No," Tal agrees. "He'll tell us who else is involved. Kagiso cracked and admitted that Williams stole ten cases of our poison. Likely sold it. He couldn't have done that alone."

Zero nods. She guessed as much. "Let's hope he cooperates."

There's a pause. A snug weight settles on her shoulders. Zero looks down to see Tal's suit jacket draped over her.

"He won't have a choice."

She stiffens at the darkness laced in Tal's voice. Masked with Lithium's crazy grin or not, this man is a walking warning sign. She'd say that she's lucky she hasn't gotten on Tal's bad side, but she definitely should not be in his good graces, given the number of times she's lied to him then admitted it to his face.

A scream reaches Zero's ears, and the cat jumps out of her arms, startling the rest of the room, other members originally too focused on Rovis twisting the knife to notice her.

The Scavenger looks up, rage boiling in his eyes, and Zero thinks he might try to burn her alive with that glare alone. His voice is rough when he says in Toullish, "I told you to stay away."

Zero crosses her arms, nails jabbing into her own flesh, and responds in the same language, "Feel free to ignore me and continue."

Under Rovis's elbow, Williams rasps a laugh. "You freak. You are a useless child who thinks he can become king. But you're nothing. You'll always be nothing in a world where you're not welcome."

When another scream sounds, Zero belatedly realizes she should be watching the others for reactions that may give away who Williams was working with. But her head feels too hazy to even think right now. She needs something to clear away the fog. She needs...

Coffee. That's what the smell is.

Keeping her eyes on Rovis, who throws Williams onto the ground with one hand, blood from the knife quickly staining the carpet, Zero reaches back and plucks out a mug from Tal's hands and chugs all of its content. Surprisingly, he doesn't protest. The espresso only makes Zero' heart race faster, but it's close enough of an illusion of wakefulness to jumpstart her brain.

Rovis stares down at Williams with disgust. "Gierkas."

Tal nudges Zero to the side and strides across to haul Williams up by the front of his turtleneck, the blood stains barely visible on Tal's scarlet shirt.

Zero feels a simmer of anger from the left, where all the Ezclovese stand. She's faintly alarmed to see Levi with them, shifting on his feet. But squinting her bleary eyes, Zero realizes that he's glancing nervously at Tal. She shifts her stare over to the other side of the room, and she's glad to see that Avery's standing next to Kagiso, sipping on a smoothie through a straw and watching Rovis interrogate Williams with indifference.

Back to the older Ezclovese, Zero frowns at Darla Griffith, whose fists are clenched so tight that they're shaking as she glares daggers at Rovis. Then she notices Francis Romero by the window, gripping the glass in his hand, eyes on the ground, as if trying to make himself stay calm. Isabella Brown stands in front of Romero, arms crossed and hip cocked, face blank. Except her fingers are digging into her arms. The rest of that corner only seems unconcerned and desensitized with the violence. Paired with the intel Zero has gathered from her trips around town, she reassesses all of them several times, working different angles and motivations.

To think about it, Levi is relatively new compared to the others, joined only a few months after Tal, not to mention their special relationship. He's not the type to play with power among the Damned, and Zero doesn't think he's interested in changing things back to the way they were. Most people are, from what Zero has been hearing, content with the change in leadership as long as they keep making money. So she's almost certain that Griffith, Romero, and Brown are the only other ones trying to deal behind Rovis's back.

Weapons trafficking was easier, but from rigging popular virtual reality games, blackmailing corporation officials, and distributing money from heists when the House is feeling generous, everyone still makes millions of units.

Rovis says something to Tal in Lasan that Zero misses, though it doesn't look like it was something friendly, judging by the pale looks of other people who can understand the language. Tal starts dragging Williams out by the collar, and Zero moves further into the room to clear the doorway.

"You should've drowned in that flood with your parents." Williams sneers at Rovis. "You are nothing. I don't know what Quade saw in you, but you never should've been head Reaper, you Lasan and Avyrian freak. Or whatever the hell you are. You—"

Williams starts choking, clawing at his neck where a thin metal wire cuts into his skin.

Both Tal and Rovis snap their heads to Zero's direction.

She doesn't remember moving, but her left hand is curled next to her body, her thumb hovering over her ring finger, where the silver dragon usually wraps around the base. Zero must have pressed the button on the ring and aimed at Williams. She didn't even notice when it slithered off her finger and flew, stretching into a wire to wrap around her victim's neck.

She didn't mean to do it. But the vicious sinner lurking in Zero swells at the desperation and fear in those traitorous eyes. It's a shameful yet addicting delight.

Slowly, finger by finger, she curls her left hand into a fist, and the wire tightens.

5

Ace of Crowns

Zero's expression doesn't change as she watches **Williams** choke from her wire, but Rovis swears he can see the god of death's shadow dancing in her eyes. No wonder why Tal always associates her with Drokklo.

This child's temper is absolutely awful.

Tal lets Williams drop to his knees and watches with a faint amusement, as if he were watching a magic show for children. The rest of the room gapes at the scene. Rovis internally sighs. While Zero has rarely revealed her vicious side before, he's one of the few people that know it exists. But seeing Wyatt Revyxon seems have torn something open inside of her, and Rovis doesn't particularly want her to make a habit of excessive violence like the rest of them.

"*Tei-hrute*," Rovis orders calmly.

Stop.

The room remains still like the dead, an odd sight of the mansion, like all the gears in a machine have frozen and pulled everything to a stop. It takes a few seconds, or maybe a few hours, for Zero to snap out of it and obey Rovis's words, spoken in his dead mother's language. With a flick of her wrist, the wire disappears and the dragon ring returns to where it belongs. She crosses her arms and resumes looking bored.

Williams coughs and wheezes. At Rovis's silent gesture, Tal heaves the struggling man up by the back of his collar. As they agreed to before, Lithium will be extracting information out of Williams by whatever means necessary before eliminating him. Then they'll deal with the other traitors for the mess they've made for the organization they swore allegiance to. Survival comes at a price, and every single person in this room is willing to pay it. The Scavenger, especially, did not pick up broken victims of the twisted system in Pureland just for a naive yet ambitious Ezclovese to revert back to Bianchi's rotten ways.

"Don't even get me started on *you*," Williams spits out, attempting and failing to lunge at Zero. She doesn't flinch, impervious to his rage, but Rovis feels his own temper rising. "Your loyalty is a lie. A fledgling who makes a name in a few months is undoubtedly a traitor. Even Abigail couldn't manage that sort of climb before Quade executed her. How many dirty Agents did you sleep with to become the Ace?"

The entire room shifts at the reference to the recent reveal made by the Faceless. Still, Zero only blinks sluggishly at the red-faced Williams, like she can't be bothered to acknowledge him as someone worthy of words.

"Lost your tongue?" Williams sneers. "It's only fair, since you haven't got a heart to begin with."

"This is so boring," Tal drawls, possibly even speaking the words for Zero. "You're simply describing every Heartless in the country."

"And soon there will be one less," Williams shoots back hotly. He jabs a finger at Zero. "You've been nothing but a nuisance. You gained Quade's trust, but you never had any interest to serve the Aconites. You only ever cared about yourself. Parasites like you need to be exterminated. You're not easy to kill, but there will be more traps waiting for you. I failed. Others won't. Trust my disdain for you when I say this, Ace: Someday you'll run out of cards in your deck."

"Wait, Boss—"

A crack resounds throughout the room. Williams crumbles onto the floor in front of the far wall where Avery, Kagiso, and the rest of the Opulent House members have shuffled out of the way.

"There it is," Rovis states, showing no emotion on his face. "The confession."

Something shifts within him, like screws coming loose or a boiling pot beginning to whistle. He stalks toward Williams, who scrambles up on his broken arm and staggers in an attempt to grab Zero. What he plans to do, Rovis doesn't and won't need to know, because Zero steps neatly to the side, no more disturbed than a pedestrian making way for a turtle on the sidewalk. Williams barrels into the opposite wall. A loud crack follows. Rovis stands over him in the blink of an eye.

"Don't watch," he mutters under his breath in Avyrian, knowing that Zero can hear him even when no one else can.

He digs his fingers into Williams's scalp and yanks his head back to align their glares.

"If you love your little poison so much," Rovis says, his tone slow, quiet, venomous, and mocking, "why don't you see what it tastes like?"

"Rovis, *wait*," someone urges, but he's not listening.

Williams widens his eyes, too slow to react when Rovis shoves the vial of concentrated aconitine he hid in his sleeve so hard against the back of Williams's throat that the top of the glass tube fractures.

The body tries to reject the poison, but Rovis made sure it was large enough of a dose for instantaneous death.

He releases his grip on the white hair, paying no mind to Williams writhing on the carpet. Kagiso starts up a pointless traditional chant that people gradually join in. When Rovis meets a tense gaze, he realizes too late that Tal was the one asking him to slow down. The Scavenger took over, and Rovis lost rationality. He looks back to the reason for his outburst and finds that Zero, unsurprisingly, did not listen to him.

She stares at the dying body, pensive.

"We needed him alive," Tal says in Lasan, a tinge irritated.

Rovis opens his mouth to answer, but a soft bump to his leg causes him to look down. Starlight weaves between Rovis's feet, zir tail curling around his calf. He crouches down and holds out a gloved hand. Starlight sniffs and paws at his arm. Rovis takes that as an acceptance and picks zir up, carrying the cat to Jacek, who looks pale and nauseous, his thin body slumped against Raven.

"Here," Rovis says in Avyrian, passing over the cat. "You do not have to stay in this city. You did what I asked for. I will not hold it against you if you leave. I'll help you set up a new life."

Jacek sighs, petting Starlight between the ears. He licks his lips and replies, "I thank you for your generosity, but there is no life without family. The Agency murdered my parents, so these two complicated and troubled girls," he nods at Raven, who scoffs at his answer, "are my only family now."

The boy's admission confirms Rovis's suspicions about Zero's true intentions when she joined the organization. All the pieces of the puzzle are slowly falling into place. He's always known, of course. He just never wanted to think about it.

When Zero was a fledgling, she rarely acknowledged Rovis unless Tal was around. She was alarmingly invested in the work of the Heartless, easily adapting methods of manipulation and new personalities. When Abigail, the previous head Heartless died, Zero had just returned from a job in the suburbs of Loveias and got promoted from fledgling straight to the new head. Less than a week of being in power, she went undercover.

Then, the neighborhood Zero stayed in at Torch City had too many levels of security for it to be an ordinary government job. The Purish would never invest so much in a normal 'chemist.' While the Aconite Digitals were able to get through their security like tearing through spider webs, it was still entirely unnecessary.

The scorpion device embedded in the back of Zero's neck held enough cyanide to instantly kill a man ten times her size. Its legs were connected to the arteries in her skull. Its program monitored her location, heart rate, and chemical levels, and it had a function to shock her entire neural system when called upon by a remote command.

Now that Jacek revealed that he also has a personal history with the Agency, Rovis knows without a doubt that Zero's place in the organization has always been a long con. Raven, Jacek, and Zero have been planning this for much longer than he could have imagined. And they must have learned Ezclovese together, so that they could switch between the three languages for secrecy.

Rovis takes a deep breath and closes his eyes.

He has to face the truth now.

Zero worked undercover at the Agency to investigate her father's suicide, along with every other mysterious case that closed without a reasonable explanation.

It was only a wild guess that Rovis pushed to the back of his mind when she first disappeared off to Torch City, claiming to make larger sales for Bianchi. But with more and more secrets revealed, he can only accept that he guessed correctly, as much as he hates it. Rovis blames himself for Zero acting like she's completely on her own, for her insane risks, and for her secrecy. Yet there's nothing to be done about the past, so he can only hope to wrench back some control and nudge her onto a better path again.

His prediction for what happens next, then, is that Raven and Jacek will take Zero and run, possibly out of the country. They must have a plan, though whether or not Zero stuck to what they agreed to is still unclear to Rovis, given that her friends had no idea where she was when their school burnt down. All he knows is that if they decide to run, he'd help them without their knowledge and find a way to keep watch.

"This violence," Rovis says to Jacek now, "it's only the beginning. You can choose to walk away from this."

"Never without her." He doesn't need to follow Jacek's gaze to know who's at the end of it. Rovis nods and stands to search for Tal, only to see the man leaning down to listen to Zero whispering in his ear.

A moment later, Tal leans back, staring back at Zero incredulously. Then a smile breaks free on his face, light shattering the shadow of his earlier annoyance. He jerks his right arm, and his silver palm unfolds and reforms into a gun barrel.

Before Rovis can even comprehend what's happening, three quick blasts fly through the air. Three of the Ezclovese fall to the ground, unconscious. Rovis frowns, wondering what he missed, since he didn't notice anything particularly special about them that would warrant Tal's stun gun.

Tal waves a hand at Summer, who stands in front of a group of Reapers. "Basement."

They immediately move to drag the three out, and several bots shaped like oversized snails wheel in to clean up the blood, erasing the stains as they pass over it. One of the snails rolls over to Williams and sprays a clear liquid onto his body. The drops of chemical immediately eat through his flesh and produce purple gas, which is then vacuumed into the shell of the snail for the Aconites' poison stock. When all that's left is the skeleton, it rolls over it once, leaving behind a large pile of bone dust. The snail then reverses its tracks, vacuuming the last of the remains and leaving the carpet spotless.

Tal opens his arms, grinning, and spins around to pass his stare over every remaining member in the room.

"Anyone else?" he challenges.

Silence.

"Lovely!" Tal claps his hands and begins blasting techno-pop music, coaxing everyone else to return to their previous activities.

Rovis moves to ask Tal for an explanation on the side, but a light touch on his wrist has him pausing and looking down again. Zero meets his gaze and jerks her head toward the door. She leaves first, and Rovis hesitates before following.

If anyone notices that the Scavenger and his Ace interact at all beyond their clashes, they'd think that their odd use of Toullish sprinkled with Avyrian would be their secret language. The uneven distribution is due to the fact that Zero was younger when they first met and had a knack for foreign languages, while Rovis was older and spoke his mother's language the most to preserve memory of her. No one would ever know this, but Rovis is the reason why Zero sounds like a native Toullish speaker. Considering how his father was Avyrian, though, Rovis should've been the one with the advantage to become trilingual first.

Yet Rovis and Zero's true secret language is largely in deliberate and subtle touches, not that they used it much in the last two years. Anything other than calculated points, anything that's too casual or natural without warning can set Zero off, dry heaving. Long ago, they decided that two fingers to the inside of a wrist where blood pulses means what's about to follow calls for close attention.

Zero lingers by the door, clearly wanting the music to cover up their conversation. Rovis has to bend down to listen, since the top of her head doesn't even reach his shoulders at full height.

"Those were the ones I know for sure in allegiance with Williams. I didn't catch anyone else. Question whoever you want. I'm guessing you want words with all of the Ezcalese, but leave Levi to..." Zero glances back. "Mr. Court Jester over there."

Most of that was in Toullish, but the last bit was in Avyrian. The corners of Rovis's mouth twitch at the nickname for Tal.

"You're sure?" he asks.

Zero scowls at him. "What did I just say?"

Rovis nods, holds out a hand with the palm turned up, and waits.

Zero blinks, taken aback, though appearing much more sluggish than usual.

Suddenly Rovis wonders if she isn't apathetic at all, but incredibly sleep-deprived. He wouldn't rule it out, as he knows very little about the working conditions at the Agency. In another world, he might have asked. In this one, it's better that Zero doesn't know that Rovis knows what she was looking for. He fears that it might bring her more pain that she would just bottle up and shape into weapons.

Eventually, Zero shakes her head.

Rovis drops his hand and says, "You did good. Thank you."

She shakes her head again, this time more of a dismissal rather than a careful rejection. "I'm going to move Jacek to the Hall. I'll take an explanation for his presence any day now."

"Later. You should offer Senka a room here." Tal relayed the name of the dweller when he sorted through camera recordings with Rovis.

"Already did. She prefers the streets. Don't change the subject."

"Later," Rovis says again. "I have some unfinished business downstairs."

"The Ezclovese wouldn't be awake right now."

"Not them. Others that just came in around lunchtime."

Rolling her eyes, Zero walks away. Rovis watches her return to the billiard room and kneel in front of Jacek, who looks slightly calmer now. She's saying something Rovis can't hear, but Jacek laughs softly while Raven shoves her lightly. Only when Zero takes her friends' hands and squeezes them does Rovis head down to the basement.

It's dark and expansive with countless rooms divided by steel walls, and it lacks the neon glow of popular contemporary designs. Rovis guesses that the bosses before him used this for disciplining members or holding people kidnapped for ransom. As much as he wants to say he's a better man, Rovis isn't beyond locking up anyone who's wronged him or his organization, not to mention allowing his Reapers to let out their aggression on the culprits in less-than-moral ways. When his parents died, he had no way of survival except becoming a Damned, becoming lawless and monstrous; he might as well embrace his new identity and take what he can get.

"Anything?" he glances at Daleyza, who taps her foot idly outside two adjacent rooms of muffled screeches.

"Just typical Syndicate monologues." She sighs. "They talk. *So* much. Question: Who's your favorite couple within the inner circle, Boss?"

Rovis stares at her, bewildered. "I— I don't know? Kagiso and Avery? Do we even have other couples in the inner circle?"

Daleyza doesn't respond to that, only looks at him with pity, clearly disappointed. Rovis hasn't been this confused in a very long time.

"Why?" he asks, apprehensive.

"Just some bets." Daleyza says. "I lost. Very badly."

Rovis furrows his brows, but he has a feeling he's better off not knowing. Shaking his head, Rovis knocks on one of the doors, and a Reaper opens it for him. The shrieks subside to whimpers. He waits for the Syndicate member to notice him beyond the pain. Eventually, he does.

"Scavenger," he hisses. "You have no idea what's coming to you."

"Death, I assume," Rovis says. "I should hope so, as it's the one infallible truth of living."

"Your empire will fall. The Eastern Desert and Dyvrian Mountains will belong to my boss, and you'll be tossed aside like trash."

"Is that all?"

He snarls, and Rovis concludes that he's only a fledgling sent to complete a trivial task of making noise in his city. He can't be more than sixteen years old. Still, Rovis finds the scorching animosity stale and banal.

"The people you protect never deserved life," the fledgling says. "This planet is running out of resources, and we don't have room for the weak. The human race is on the verge of breaking through to its next stage of evolution, and you're slowing the process. So *he* is coming for you. Our boss respects your strength, but your hero complex of saving the helpless taints your value."

"Wow. I'm so flattered by your approval that I did not ask for and do not need," Rovis says dryly. "The hero part is a new one, and repulsively inaccurate, because I'm pretty sure a savior wouldn't do what I'm about to do."

The fledgling tenses, but Rovis only turns and pats the Reaper on the shoulder. "Have fun."

Rovis crosses the hall to the other room. This kid is older, around eighteen, and his lips curl with disgust when he sees Rovis.

"You," he spits out.

Rovis raises a brow, hands tucked in the pockets of his coat.

"We found things about you, you know." The boy laughs, a deranged sound gurgling in his throat. "Rovis Bozyd-Wei. You were a killer even before you were Damned."

"Hm. Maybe I was. I can't remember. Who are you again?"

"I'm—"

"Actually, I don't care." Rovis tilts his head. "What I actually want to know is, what makes you think you can set foot in my territory and walk out alive?"

The boy's eye twitches. "He's going to destroy you. He's going to exterminate all you parasites. And he's going to burn everything to ash."

"Have you even met him, kid?"

"I don't need to," he growls. "We all want the same thing, and that's all that matters."

"Right, that's why you work for someone you've never seen."

"It's worth it for the cause."

"Of course. What did you achieve on this field trip, again?"

The fledgling grits his teeth. "It's part of his plan—"

Rovis lifts his chin. "Do you even know his name?"

"I don't need to!"

"This is just sad," Rovis mutters and turns away.

"I am not sad! I am happy! I am very happy!"

When Rovis exits the second room, unimpressed, he tells Daleyza, "You're dismissed. If those Syndicate kids are still alive by the end of it, drop them off somewhere of your choice. Don't get caught."

"Yes, Boss." Daleyza flicks her eyes toward the closed doors. "What are you doing about that?"

"Nothing yet," Rovis answers. "Although, I am annoyed that they're messing with my people because they got brainwashed by an elitist cult. I'll bring it up at the meeting with the officials tomorrow evening."

Dyvris and its surrounding suburban towns have representatives that meet once in a while with the Aconite boss. They are the only Purish residents left in the desert, because the wealth from doing business with the Aconites was too good to pass up. Every other Purish, however, fled to somewhere else where there are no immigrant groups. Although Rovis is doing a decent job of stimulating monetary income as the new head of the Aconites, the officials weren't exactly happy that they lost their connections to military executives when he stopped the poisoned weapons production. Regardless of that, Rovis would rather not collapse from the burden of mass murder and genocide, even if it means a few upset political figures. Killing and being responsible for murders doesn't get easier, even as a Reaper. It still weighs heavier and heavier with every life he takes.

Rovis clenches his fists in his pockets as he strides through the mansion. He nods to the members who stop and bow their heads to acknowledge his presence. But his mind is stuck on one thing that the Purish boys told him.

Do they really know the truth about what happened seven years ago?

He shakes his head. He can't let them get to him. Even if they know, it's all in the past. Everyone who should know what happened already knows. Rovis sets his jaw and keeps his face blank as he climbs up the stairs. When he opens the door to his office, however, he scowls.

"Why."

Zero tosses a glowing pink ball and catches it from where she lies on Rovis's couch.

"What am I supposed to do with eight hundred million units?"

"I don't know," Rovis says irritably, shutting the door and taking off his coat. "Donate it to charity for all I care. How did you get in here? N.A.D.E. is only supposed to open for me and Tal. Everyone else needs my permission."

"Oh, she just let me in. She is artificial intelligence, *Boss*." Zero tosses and catches the ball again. "She's learned to meddle in minor personal affairs. You know that, since you've taken advantage of it when Tal is being a workaholic in his lab, because N.A.D.E. patches you through to him even though he isn't answering."

Rovis narrows his eyes at her from his desk. "How did you know all that?"

"I'm a spy, *Boss*."

Despite his nonchalance, he can't ignore her mocking tone anymore. "Do you keep saying it like that to make fun of the fact that you take orders from me now?"

"Maybe. What can you do about it?"

"Kick you out of my office, for one. Why did N.A.D.E. let you in? What 'minor personal affairs' do we have?"

"What am I supposed to do about all this money?"

Rovis rubs his temple, and he feels as though there should be steam coming out of his ears. "Zero. A man just confessed to almost killing you. Then I killed said man right in front of you and your friends. Now, outside this house, the sea level rise is forcing your cousin to deal with territorial issues within the Water Lords. The Purity Syndicate wants to bully the entire nation back to the last century's way of things. Pureland is on the brink of war with Riyssola. And you broke into my office to ask me for financial advice?"

"Dziye called?" Zero asks, sitting up, eyes glinting with curiosity.

Zero's older cousin, around Rovis's age, is a Marquess of the Avyrian mafia called the Water Lords. Dziye Hong stays in contact with Rovis because they're both notable figures among the Damned. And sometimes to send videos of chubby raccoons, for whatever reason.

"Yes, and he wants you to call him back when you get the chance. Now, for example, since you don't have a real reason to be here."

"Jacek and Raven."

"Ah." Rovis crosses his arms. "Those are the 'minor personal affairs.' How about you explain why you used them to find Bianchi? What made you so desperate to drop out of school, ditch your friends, and run around with criminals instead?"

"No," Zero says, bored, though Rovis doesn't miss the light wavering in the pink ball when her grip tightens.

"What happened," he persists, "after I left, Zero?"

Zero scoffs, tilting her head. "I thought you already knew, Boss. Isn't that why you wanted me to stay away from Wyatt Revyxon?"

"I meant—"

A knock on the door and the mechanical announcement of the visitor interrupt him. Rovis clenches his jaw and curls his hand into a fist. He shoots Zero a look and says, "We're not done." Then to N.A.D.E., "Let him in."

Kagiso appears and only spares a glance at Zero before merely accepting her as part of this conversation.

"Unfortunately for your peace of mind," he begins an exceptionally encouraging report, "I found some Skulls snooping around downtown."

Rovis raises a brow.

"They've even been asking bartenders and waiters where you like to go and when. I'm pretty sure they're also fledglings, but reading people isn't my specialty." The Sleightist's gaze slips briefly toward the couch before he drops electromagnetic-powered brass knuckles on the desk. "Pickpocketing is."

A flip of the weapon shows an engraving of a broken skull with roses growing out of the cracks, a golden image of the tattoo inked on the Lasan organization's members. Gangsters are allowed to tour other cities outside their territories, sure, but those deadly weapons hide drilling spikes and are definitely not representative of an innocent visit.

"Is it open season to ruffle the Scavenger's feathers?" Rovis mutters.

Kagiso laughs and opens a hand, gesturing, rings sparkling on every knuckle. "The Syndicate, none of us are surprised. We're not 'pure' enough for 'their country.' But Boss, this is a message sent from Divako."

"I know. I'll handle it. Thank you."

Kagiso bows and leaves, but not before shooting a smirk at Zero. The girl rolls her eyes and leans back, crossing her arms and propping an ankle over her knee. Rovis remains still in his chair. No matter how hard he tries to stop it, his fingers twitch. Giving up, he reaches up and feels the smooth curve of his golden hoop, thinking.

"Narvaez?" Zero asks, spinning the ball on the tip of a finger.

Rovis hesitates. "Yes."

Damian Narvaez is someone from Rovis's past that he thought he left behind. But of course, while it took Rovis three years to unwillingly snatch the power of an entire organization, it took Damian three months to become the head of the Rose Skulls in the city of Divako after actually finishing high school, unlike Rovis.

It's been a year since Rovis killed Bianchi, and now Damian decides to acknowledge him?

"I really don't have time for his games right now," Rovis says, his gaze far away.

The silence that follows makes Rovis think that Zero crept out of the office or fell asleep, but he blinks to see that she's only studying him.

The two of them, so many secrets they keep from each other, and so many secrets they keep for each other. There's no hiding what this message from Damian means for Rovis, not from someone he used to trust without a millisecond of doubt.

And Rovis carries the weight of Zero's past, too, of a manipulative and mentally abusive mother, of a volatile home, of psychological oppression. He remembers the reason for her tenacity, her rashness, her concealed rage.

No, Rovis can never put a leash on Zero. He can chase after the past all he wants, but he can't expect a cosmic force like gravity to tie them together forever. Zero isn't a child anymore, and Rovis needs to let her go. His promise to protect her still stands, even if it means he needs to figure out a new way to keep it.

"Rovis," Zero says.

He shakes his head. "It's too dangerous."

"You know the Ace is the best card to play."

"The Purish government might still be looking for you. I'm not risking that. And you are not a card."

"It's a job, Rovis. I was right under their noses for almost two years. They can't catch me."

"That's no reason to get cocky."

"Which one of us in this mansion isn't on their radar? We're all at equal risk." Zero tosses the ball and spins it on a different finger. "Besides, I'll be in Skull territory. If the Purish do follow me there, they'd have too many fish to catch. I'm smart enough to get out of that situation."

"But—"

"What else are you going to do, Boss? Send another Heartless? I'm the head, and the only one in the group who has been on a job against a Damned before. Send a Reaper? That'll do wonders to your campaign against inter-organizational blood feuds. Put a Digital team on this? The Skulls can just as well hit us back, likely installing malware on every single device in this mansion. Personally go over there? That is not Scavenger behavior, and it's definitely a trap. Trust me, Rovis. I'm your best choice. The only person who knows Narvaez better than I do is you, and he's never met me. You made sure of that. And don't forget, I am the Ace of Crowns."

Rovis stares. A pang of nostalgia slams in his chest.

When did you grow up so fast?

He hates it, but everything she said was right.

And if Zero could infiltrate the Agency, Rovis supposes, then she's the most capable spy he has, one that not only will do what needs to be done, but also make it back safely.

"You really want to take this one?" he asks wearily.

The ball stops spinning. Slender fingers with sharp nails close over it like claws in one sharp movement. Zero lifts a corner of her mouth. "What do you want me to do?"

Rovis heaves a sigh and texts Avery a short request to send their files on the Skulls to Zero. "Damian wants this to build up. He's trying to see how long I can last without snapping. But I'm not interested in playing."

"Send a message that ends this one-upmanship prematurely," Zero deduces.

"You can do your stupid card thing, but don't do anything stupid."

Zero scoffs, standing up. She always seems more lively when she's about to deceive and exploit people. "Don't insult my skills. You never need to worry about me."

As the door shuts behind her, Rovis stares out the window, alone in his office. He presses a loose fist against his mouth, fidgeting with his fingers, his knuckles, his nails. A soft sigh escapes between his lips, blowing hot air into his palm, and his eyes slowly slide shut as his body deflates.

He whispers the truth into the tiny space protected by his hand, barely audible.

"I'll always worry about you."

6
Disk Boot Failure

Being in close proximity to the Purish officials is only fun if Tal gets to throw them around like rag dolls. Alas, his orders are to do the exact opposite: Make sure this meeting with the Dyvrian representatives goes smoothly, without any physical conflicts.

Rovis takes the fun out of everything.

"You're not listening," the man is saying impatiently. "The Purity Syndicate has no business here other than gathering ideas for their next hate crime. There needs to be a legal leash on them, since my organization needs to be free of inconveniences like them to keep our local economy thriving. They've caused too many disturbances on the streets over the past week, and they're becoming more and more aggressive."

"And why would we get involved?" a particularly obnoxious official asks. "As far as we know, these fights are for you to deal with. We're already looking the other way when you break the laws, and that's only due to respect for Quade Bianchi. I think our working relationship is plenty in balance, Scavenger. Especially when you brought in so many of your... minority groups, driving out the Purish population."

Rovis slams down his glass, scotch whiskey splashing over the rim.

He stares down the mayor until the smug expression of the arrogant man pales. It is, after all, the Scavenger that he's speaking to.

Rovis chuckles darkly.

"This isn't about me. Allow me to start from the beginning. Again. The Syndicate holds outdated beliefs that Pureland belongs to the descendants of the Ezcalese, but this country was first home to the Zessroans —the true natives of Pureland before Ezclovia found it— which your people drove to extinction. The Purish who previously lived here abandoned this city because they failed to adapt to the growing multiculturalism in this country, while all of you, sitting at this table, stayed to profit off the economy boosted by the very people I brought in. You gloat about the diversity of your towns and city on television, but you won't value the lives of the Toullish, the Avyrians, and the Lasans."

"Now, hold on—"

"I'm not done. If you don't pull your weight on this, not only do my people get hurt, your businesses will get hurt, too. Since that's all you care about, I suggest you heed my warning."

Just for fun, Tal decides to unsheathe his claws to drive the point home. The sound turns all the heads at the table. Rovis shoots him a look of annoyance at Tal's redundancy, though a hint of amusement flashes in his eyes.

Tal shrugs, an unnaturally wide grin stretching his face.

He can tell that Rovis's muscles have loosened in the tense silence, so Tal accomplished his mission. And it's just a bonus that beads of sweat are now rolling down those loathsome Purish faces.

"Very well," the mayor of Dyvris finally says with a false smile. Though it doesn't take a Heartless to read that his words are meaningless. "We will take into consideration your requests from this meeting."

"This meeting is adjourned, then." Rovis tilts his head towards the exit. "You may walk yourselves out now."

Rovis leans back and watches the representatives shuffle out of what they only thought was neutral territory in one of the suburbs, but is actually another restaurant that the Scavenger recently invested in.

Tal, previously on guard, sits down next to Rovis and props his feet on the table.

"I'm losing them," Rovis states, face blank.

He's right, of course. As much as Tal wants to deny that Rovis's reign has its flaws, but ultimately the resentment against his heritage as both Toullish and Avyrian makes it difficult for him to keep some of the connections Bianchi had. While the Aconites have too much power now for the officials to turn against them, it might become an issue as they keep sitting back and doing nothing, allowing the Syndicate to turn to violence, and a full-on war breaks out between the Syndicate and the Aconites. Then the streets will turn into a river of blood.

Rovis feels responsible for all of that, and Tal hates it. If he'd known what becoming the Scavenger meant for Rovis, Tal never would have helped him take over. He still would have helped kill Bianchi, yes, because of what that bastard did to Rovis. But they could've put someone else on the poisonous throne. They could've run.

Now it's too late.

He wants to do more than putting a hand on Rovis's shoulder, more than a few quips to lighten the mood. He wants to pay for the sin that they both committed. He wants to hold the weight Rovis carries on his shoulders. He wants to hold *Rovis*. The Scavenger is only an armor; the man inside takes too much of the blame and feels too deeply and cares for everyone around him. The man inside is too good for this world, even when it calls him a savage.

Yet Tal would not dare to cross that line, to close that distance between them.

This is the one thing that he cannot risk being ambitious about. This isn't an engineering experiment where he can start over if he tries something and fails. This is the man who walked into Tal's life and changed the way he looked at the world.

So instead, Tal says, "You think they're working with Marudas?"

Jeffrey Marudas, they found, after the recent reveal by the Faceless, is the director of the Agency of Justice. If he allowed a collaboration with local law enforcement officers to target ex-employees like Jacek's parents, then it would be logical that the Agency has gotten familiar with the officials.

"If they are, we wouldn't be here," Rovis says. "This has been going on for a while. We've only just noticed because of our businesses, but think about residential areas. The Syndicate would've started there."

"Then at least we don't have to worry about them calling in the Agency and ordering a massacre through water contamination or something."

"Yet they're still useless. We have to figure out how to deal with the Syndicate before they inevitably take a life." Rovis rakes his fingers through his hair. "Without getting others involved. This technically isn't Aconite business until they spill our blood."

The exhaustion in his voice makes Tal's fingers twitch. He picks up Rovis's half-empty glass and stares into the golden liquid. "If you really think this will lead to something worse than people getting assaulted on the streets, then I know some of the Reapers are willing to play vigilante for however long it takes to get rid of the Syndicate scum. Daleyza and I can organize it, add more patrolling shifts, widen the scope, maybe."

He looks up when Rovis doesn't respond, and nearly flinches back at the intense stare searching his soul.

Tal suddenly doesn't remember what he just said.

"Thank you," Rovis says, quiet but firm.

"Huh? Yes, you're welcome." Tal snaps out of his reverie. He drains the glass in his hand and stands. "You should say that more often, actually. I'm one of a kind. What are you going to do if you lose your savvy inventor and killer?"

Rovis chuckles, eyes cast down, his small smile a bit too genuine and way less sarcastic than Tal is used to in their banters. "I don't know. Maybe I should."

If Tal drank that scotch a few seconds too late, he'd be sputtering all over the place.

"Anyway," Tal coughs. "Is everything settled with the Ezclovese traitors?"

Rovis nods. "I've interrogated all of them, and everything is as Zero expected. I knifed them and had Daleyza drop them off in the sand dunes. Avery will let us know when they die or escape our territory. Everyone else seems to be clean, but we should keep an eye on all the old members who worked under Bianchi and benefited from it."

"Right, understood."

Then Rovis also stands and touches a hand to his violet collar, frowning.

"I just remembered something," he says. "Do you know where Zero is?"

Finally, a safe topic. Somewhat. Tal forces a grin back onto his face and taps through his watch's hologram tracker. "Bookstore. The one with a cafe." He looks up. "Are we still pretending that we're investigating her as a suspect to being a mole, or are you comfortably assured that she's not going to get snatched off the streets by whatever the hell our shady government sends after a possibly rogue scientist?"

"Neither."

Tal tilts his head. "Would you care to share with the class?"

Rovis gazes at him for a moment. When he opens his mouth, his words are in Lasan, barely audible. "I think she worked for the Agency."

Tal's grin freezes. He asks through his teeth, "Are you sure?"

"I'm almost one-hundred percent certain."

"Huh," Tal answers, pitch too high. "Interesting."

Rovis narrows his eyes. "You already knew. When did she tell you?"

"She didn't," Tal holds his hands up. "I put it together when she was watching the last Faceless intermission with me. She really did not want you to know."

"Pity," Rovis scoffs, a gleam of indignation flashing in his eyes. "I've guessed it for a while now, even before I was sure the Agency was real."

Tal sighs dramatically. "Of course, if I could figure it out, then you would have known ages before me. But don't be too mad, darling. She didn't want you to worry."

"Enough," Rovis snaps, though Tal doesn't take offense. "I have an errand to run."

"Yes, Boss," Tal says with exaggerated cheer as he makes for the south door. "Have fun with whatever you're doing. I will be doing the saints' work in heaven."

"You're going to your lab."

"I'm going to my lab."

He throws a hand up as a goodbye as he walks away without looking back. His chunky boots land heavily down the stairs as his favorite knife materializes between his fingers. Tal whistles and tosses the knife to the even rhythm of his steps. His nanotech helmet shuts over his face the moment he steps outside. He drives out the desert without wasting any more time. If someone else were here, they might tease him and say that he's running away from Rovis, but thankfully he's alone.

Even though the sky is still a sickly shade of orange, the breeze feels nice in the mountains when Tal can finally drive with the top down and helmet-free. For a moment, just a moment, he feels real again. No names, no crimes; just another human being.

I was fifteen, and Daleyza no longer seemed resentful of being around me after Dakota's death. Quade was satisfied with my new blasters that neatly injected a small dose of wolfsbane and killed targets at a painfully slow rate. I didn't love what kind of things my brain came to create under my mentor Lowell, a dual Mech and Digital like me. But I wasn't much good for life before I joined the Damned, either.

And that's when I saw him. Rovis Bozyd-Wei, a new but wicked Sleightist. He was a fledgling who went on heist after heist, while training as a Reaper on the side. There were rumors of a dead boyfriend, but every member has had their fair share of unfounded stories. That day, he came back from robbing a secretary of war in Torch City all by himself, and he brought back the Shapeshifter without a scratch. He did not have a team of Digitals backing him in the mansion, nor did he have a getaway ride at the ready. The courtyard was crowded where he had parked, because everyone knew what his return meant.

Rovis earned his status as a full Aconite, and he'd be getting his mark that night.

Because that job was a suicide mission, not meant to be done by a single person. The level of security was impossible to get through alone. It was a test for fledglings in the Opulent House, to determine who would be strong enough to stay in the organization, and who would be too weak to survive. That was how any full-status members were selected under Quade's rule. Rovis was the first to make it back in three years.

I watched through the window wall of my room in the Tech Hall as Rovis pulled out a large crate from the trunk, the muscles in his arms bulging against the rolled-up sleeves of his black button-up. Quade walked out to the courtyard to welcome him back. That was when Rovis uncovered the crate to reveal stacks of gold bars. Shock rippled through the crowd surrounding him and Quade, and I crossed my arms then, interest piqued. Holding out a fist, Rovis showed everyone a silver watch lined with diamonds, the only thing he was supposed to steal. Eyes sparkling, Quade laughed and patted Rovis on the shoulder.

"Overachiever," I muttered, though a corner of my lips tilted up.

As if he heard me, Rovis looked up, indifferent eyes staring right at me. I stepped back, surprised, before I remembered that the windows were tinted. Knowing he couldn't actually see me, I stared back, until I felt heat curling in my stomach. Next to Rovis, Quade held out his hand. That regained Rovis's attention, and he shook Quade's hand, no doubt swearing his loyalty to the Aconites. Forcing myself to walk away, I hurried back to the lab on inexplicably weak legs. I hammered nails, debugged programs, and designed new blueprints until my mind was filled with equations and numbers again.

I didn't actively seek him out. He found me first in Lowell's lab, to collect some tools for the House's next heist.

"Talon, right?" a voice had startled me while I was welding parts for a new engine model, and I nearly demolished my arm with a blowtorch.

After shutting down all equipment and cursing the intruder to a thousand years of misery without technology, I turned and took off my goggles, ready to snap at the person stupid enough to distract me. But any cruel comments I had died on my tongue the moment I saw him again. Heat rushed to my face as I dropped the goggles onto a nearby table then crossed my arms.

"Yes," I answered, a sharp grin sitting on my face, foreign and still growing into what would become Lithium's warning sign. "But I go by Tal. What do you need? I'll grab it for you."

With a small smile on his face, Rovis listed off the usual items, and I could feel his stare pricking the back of my neck when I shuffled through the tables. He was still studying me when I set the gadgets in front of him.

"You didn't ask me how I knew your name," he said.

I shrugged, ignoring the rapid pounding of my heartbeats. "Residential genius. Everyone knows my name."

Rovis had the nerve to laugh, to steal my breath away.

"You've earned that, I won't deny. But no. I've heard of you before coming here." He took the lock picks, smiling softly. "You were always brilliant, way before your talent and work became profitable."

Right then, when he said those words, he had me. He could've asked me for anything, and I would've given it.

Brilliant, *he called me.*

He'd be quite disappointed in me when three years later, I did something way less than brilliant.

I went to my usual coffee shop, eighteen and no longer insecure, mentally noting the other customers: six tourists, two business people, and two high school students. For some reason, I felt like staying, so I settled down by a window to tweak a weapons targeting program.

A tap on my shoulder had me glancing up to see a shy smile. One of the school kids. She had just ordered another coffee that looked like tar, which I observed from my peripheral vision before she approached me. Nothing suspicious. Just a child.

Or so I thought.

"Hi. Sorry," she said bashfully, then hovered her fingers over my Aconite mark. "My boyfriend and I saw you walking in, and he thinks your tattoo is really cool. Who's your artist?"

My tentative smile faltered.

"My apologies," another voice said. The boyfriend, I assumed, pulled on the kid's shoulders. "She's an extrovert."

"This extrovert is the reason you're passing computer science," the girl retorted.

"No worries," I cut in. "Unfortunately, the artist who did this retired. I heard the shop by the mall is decent. The one next to the hardware store is pretty good, too."

The couple nodded their thanks, and I didn't think much about them until two mornings later, I saw the girl again downtown. She saw me, too, and smiled. She didn't linger or try to talk to me, just kept carrying her books down the street. That also didn't seem out of the ordinary.

When I finished my business and drove back to the mansion that evening, however, I saw her where she really shouldn't have been. She was at the edge of the Aconite's lake, gazing up at the mansion. She must have trekked through dangerous paths into the very heart of the Dyvrian Mountains. Her presence was no mistake.

"Alright," I said, parked next to her with the windows down. "What do you really want?"

She didn't answer, only tilted her head at me with her stare fixed on the mansion to indicate that she heard. I didn't really know what to say; I was never good at small talk, and I couldn't threaten a kid. The stoic girl who stood there was nothing like the version of her I met.

"I apologize," she finally said. "I deceived you."

A laugh bursted out of my chest before I could stop it. "I gathered that."

I was going to say more, but that was when she turned, and the hollowness in her eyes was too familiar, a punch to my gut.

"I lied," she said, and her voice felt like a physicalization of nothingness. "The guy I was with isn't my boyfriend; he's just a friend who agreed to help me with this. I already knew where that tattoo came from, because I was looking for someone I used to know. And I apologize the most for putting a tracker on you."

She nodded at my shoulder, and because I wore the same jacket everyday, I found a tiny black chip stuck under the thick seam.

"Clever," I muttered. "But you should go home now. There are drones that will alert us of intruders, so someone with less patience than I do might order them to shoot. Even if I could help with that, this area isn't safe. When it rains, and it often does, there will be mudslides, and the lake rises. Camping out here is not a good idea."

"Death by laser, suffocation, or drowning," she mused. "That's a variety of choices."

"Okay." I got out of the car. "Where do you live? I'll drive you."

"Tell your boss I want a job."

My blood ran cold. "What?"

"I understand that you're older than me with more experience, and I accept any resentments toward me as a result of my deception, but this is my one request."

Although empty, there was a flicker in her eyes that may have been hope or desperation or determination. All I knew was that I couldn't stop her. If I didn't bring her in as a fledgling, she would've just found someone else.

I sighed then, exasperated. "What's your name, kid?"

She hesitated. "I don't know."

"Pick one."

After a few moments, she said, "Zero."

With great reluctance, I took her to see Quade, and he decided to have her train under Abigail as a Heartless. I didn't want to think about what she'd have to do when the time came, when the Heartless gives her the test. I refused to imagine the consequences if she survived to become a full-status member, or if she fails. The world was cold, and I had to become cold with it. Maybe she *reminded me of Saige, or maybe I was still soft for strays, but I gave my first tour of the premises for her. Once we reached the Opulent House, I found the only other person I could trust to take care of Zero.*

"Hey, Rov," I called, forcing a grin. "Come meet the fledgling I found today."

Rovis caught my eye and gave me a small smile, but when he walked over and saw the girl, his gaze darkened, like he wasn't happy to see her in the mansion.

Maybe I should've tried to keep her out after all.

"Do you two know each other?" I asked, starting to feel uneasy again.

"No," Rovis said while still scowling down at Zero. If anyone else was watching, it would've just seemed like an inner circle member of the organization was trying to intimidate a new fledgling. To me though, it seemed like there was a whole chest of secrets between them, threatening to be unlocked. Rovis looked at me and asked, "Who's this?"

"This is Zero. Zero, this is my good friend, Rovis."

Rovis lifted a brow in surprise, glancing at the girl. "Interesting name."

Zero only stared at Rovis as if she were unimpressed by a man who could no doubt throw her all the way off the edge of the land and into the lake with his bare hands. My feigned amusement froze when Zero turned her stare onto me, which then appeared to be more assessing than bored. Her eyes darted back and forth, and I knew in that moment she figured out my inexplicable feelings towards Rovis.

Finally, sighing, she asked, "Where can I get a list of therapists around here?"

The door to Tal's lab swooshes open. Rovis shuffles in and sinks into a nearby couch, tugging at his collar. A small spatter of orange paint sits on his cheek, and Tal turns away to hide his smile.

A glance at the clock tells him that it's been two hours since he started working. He didn't notice that the view outside his glass walls in the Tech Hall turned into blood red ombre, the sky an incessant reminder that their time on this planet is nearing the end.

He barely lifts up the hammer before the door opens again.

"Did you take my eyeliner?" Zero demands.

Tal resolutely does not look at her and swings. *Clang.* "No idea what you're talking about."

A black wad of fabric bounces off his face. Tal gasps.

"You do not treat my jacket like this!" He attempts to straighten it. "Okay, yes. I did. You took my knife first! Just go get another pen from downtown. You know you can just walk in and take whatever you want."

"I don't have time," Zero growls.

"I thought you already left for Divako," Rovis interjects. Tal shakes the black pen out of his sleeve and tosses it to Zero, who fumbles with it and staggers in her heels and blue dress.

"Nope, I just had a therapy session," she says, shoving Tal into the work station. Clearly, she hasn't worked out her anger issues. "Don't worry, *Boss.* I'll make it right on time."

"Therapy," Rovis repeats, the word strange on his lips.

"Yes. You see, since I have to be alive longer than I expected, I might as well feel marginally less miserable."

"Maybe you should take a page out of her book, Boss," Tal comments.

"Oh, shut it," Zero calls over her shoulder as she leaves the room. "Don't be a hypocrite."

Abandoning his work, Tal lounges in the seat across from Rovis. "Why, exactly, is she going to Divako?"

While it's a gorgeous city, there's no reason for Zero to visit. It's known for all forms of visual art, from murals that decorate every building within its perimeters to classical paintings preserved in museums. If anyone from the entire Eastern Desert is interested in going, it would be the Scavenger himself. Or Lasans who want to go to another crime metropolis controlled by their people, which would include Tal if he ever feels like taking a vacation out of Dyvris.

Rovis takes a deep breath and slowly blows it out, a sign of irritation. Instead of answering, he touches his golden hoop again.

"New question, then," Tal says. He hums, tapping his chin. "Truth for truth. What's the story of that earring?"

"My mom's." Rovis drops his hand and meets Tal's gaze. "A drunk Purish beat her to death one night when I was four and dumped her body in a river. She didn't have much, and Dad burned everything. This is all I have left of her, other than her language. I started wearing this hoop and found Toullish-speaking communities to keep holding on."

He says all of that with indifference, as though it was someone else's story. But neither of them care much for sympathy. There's nothing to say, so Tal only nods. They hush, breathing, the only sign that they're alive, that they've survived all the tragedies of childhood. No words would erase their scars, and no miracle would respond to their unspoken wishes for a better world.

"On the topic of jewelry," Rovis breaks the silence for once, fidgeting with his gloves, "how did you make that ring for Zero? It seems incredibly advanced."

Tal frowns. While Rovis often does ask about and listen to his engineering projects when he's down in the lab, Tal doesn't have an answer for this question.

"Actually, I didn't make it. I always thought it was from the Water Lords. You have some cousins in that gang, right? It's very likely for her to have connections, too. Shame, though, because I wish I could take the credit for creating something like that."

Rovis narrows his eyes, clearly equally puzzled with the origins of the dragon ring, but he shakes his head. "It doesn't look familiar."

"She's had it since Quade made her head of the Heartless, no?"

"I think so," Rovis says. "But I've not seen it anywhere else, not even on any of the Lords that I've worked with before."

"If it's not from the Water Lords," Tal thinks out loud, frowning, "it definitely did not come without a price. Let's hope she didn't make any open-ended deals with a disreputable smith."

"When it comes to her," Rovis sighs, "I'm not optimistic."

"She did voluntarily spy on a secret government intelligence organization without telling any of us," Tal agrees.

"Oh, don't remind me."

Tal smirks at that, and the conversation settles into a lull again.

He watches Rovis, appreciating the privilege of seeing this widely feared and notoriously dangerous man unguarded. He doesn't know why he deserves Rovis's trust, but he's grateful for it nonetheless. Being the Scavenger's second gave him respect, power, protection, and most of all, the chance to be close to Rovis.

He gets to see the way black lashes tilt down over glazed, brown eyes when Rovis zones out, his thoughts far away from this depraved world. Tal gets to commit to memory the loose strands of silky hair hanging over one brow. He gets to—

"I told the Ace to send a message to the Rose Skulls," Rovis admits, looking away.

"What."

That... is enough for Tal's brain to process for the day.

With Zero's temper and affinity for destroying a man's ego, pitted against Damian Narvaez's pride and revolting arrogance, the organizations will be lucky to survive this without having their homes burnt to the ground.

"But the Agency?" Tal questions. "This is your move against the Skull fledglings that have been poking around the streets?"

"If she's made it this long as a double agent in the depths of Torch City, then she should be fine in Skull territory."

Tal furrows his brows. While that makes sense, it's not like Rovis to send someone with special and risky circumstances into dangerous territory with such a flimsy logic.

"Rov," he says quietly. "What are you not telling me?"

Rovis works his jaw. Slowly, he drags his gaze back to Tal. Voice grim, he says, "Damian Narvaez and I have history. Zero is, unfortunately, the best choice for this. And frankly, the only choice."

Metal fingers twitch on the arm of Tal's seat. "Because you and Zero also have history. And there's a connection between Zero and Narvaez somehow. Someday, the two of you will have to explain things to me, you know."

"I know." Rovis doesn't avoid his stare. "We will."

"Well," Tal says, standing. "This will certainly be interesting. I think that's my cue to go to bed, pretend this day never happened, and ignore reality. Have a good night, Boss."

He strides into the elevator, and his smirk is back on his face when he turns around.

Rovis watches him and answers with an unreadable gaze, "Night, Tal."

Tal holds up a hand and wiggles his fingers until the doors slide shut. The smirk slips off his face and he furrows his brows, trying to understand what good could possibly come out of Zero going after the Skulls. The elevator stops at the top floor of the Tech Hall and he trudges out, steps heavy with his thoughts. As soon as he makes it to his room, Tal flops onto the bed and sighs.

"You look tired," Levi remarks, setting his book down on the nightstand and shifts Tal's head onto his lap. "You okay?"

Tal groans and pulls a pillow over his face.

"I'll take that as a no," Levi says, amusement evident in his tone.

A muffled sound answers him from beneath the pillow.

"What?"

Tal throws the pillow at Levi's face. "I said, 'You're being mean.'"

"The great Lithium, everyone," Levi snarks, tossing the pillow to the other side. "Get changed. I'm not letting you into bed in work clothes."

"How dare you," Tal grumbles.

"The less time you spend being melodramatic, the more time you get to be in bed."

A growl rumbles through Tal's chest and throat, before he hauls himself off the comforter with the last crumbs of energy left in his body. He glowers at Levi and absolutely does not pout.

Then he plants his hand on the mattress, tossing his legs over the corner. But Levi's faster, springing up to block his arm with his own. Tal doesn't resist, leaning into the momentum against his arm to fall back onto the bed, his metal arm hooking behind Levi's waist as he's going down. With another roll, Tal ends up on top of Levi, arms and legs framing his body.

Levi blinks several times, surprised. Then he laughs, impressed. "Oh, that was so smooth."

"Why, thank you." Tal says with a tilted smile.

Levi rolls his eyes and pulls him down to a deep kiss, fingers running through Tal's hair and moving down his neck and between his shoulder blades.

All of a sudden something presses against Tal's legs and the world spins. Levi's grip on his wrist disappears, and he stumbles back into a crouch to stop the momentum. He stands up in the walk-in closet, affronted.

Arms crossed, Levi raises a brow at him. "Get. Changed."

Then he slams the door to the closet shut.

7

Machine Malfunction

Mira leans on the bar, blue light reflecting off of her skin, and smiles at the android as she orders another drink. While she waits, she nods her head to the beat of the music drumming the walls of the club. Sharp nails tap the counter, offbeat, but slow and steady.

"What are you drinking?" A clear voice cuts through Mira's idle enjoyment.

She turns her head, swirling the last bit of glittery purple liquid in her glass. A tall man has his back against the bar, elbows resting on the edge. He's looking at Mira with a slight tilt to the head, the disco lights highlighting several piercings on the nose, eyebrows, and lips. He smirks when he introduces himself, "The name's Zeke."

Red lips copy his smirk. "Take a guess."

Zeke hums. "Galaxy cocktail."

Mira raises an expectant brow without a word, not quite impressed just yet.

Taking the hint, Zeke chuckles and adds, "Magic mule, vodka lime and ginger beer. With butterfly pea flowers."

With a sharp grin, Mira slides her drink out of her hand with a roll of her fingers, and the glass skids on the counter to stop just in front of him. His eyes linger on the lipstick stain as he reaches for it. Then he lifts up the glass to see tiny blue flecks accumulated around the bottom edges. His brows fly up, barbells glistening under the colorful lights.

"And if the droids really like you," he says, looking over at her with a curious glint in his eyes, "they sprinkle in crushed *laiedrupna*, a very rare Lasan spice imported from the mainland."

"Come here often?" Mira teases, not really asking. "You look surprised. Do they normally only do that for special frequenters from around here?"

Zeke's expression tenses, just slightly. "Something like that."

"Well, on behalf of all tourists who are missing out on the secret ingredient," Mira says, turning to smile at the droid serving her the mule once again, with blue flakes on the bottom, "I thank the droids for making that mistake tonight."

"Perhaps it's no mistake," Zeke recovers quickly. "You are quite lovely. It seems that even the droids have noticed."

"Is that so?" Mira shifts in her seat so that her elbow rests on the back of the bar stool. Without breaking eye contact, she takes a sip of her the iridescent cocktail. The rip of her glass hides her smirk when Zeke swallows, all words forgotten. She takes pity on him and lowers her drink, holding out her free hand, slender fingers sloping down like willow branches. "I'm Mira."

Zeke blinks, remembering himself. "So, Mira, what brings you to Divako?"

"Vacation," Mira answers, accepting her drink from the android. "I'm a university student from Aurodus. Midterms just finished."

"Oh, I know someone in Aurodus. Xe went to university in Torch City, though."

"The capital." Mira smiles. "Seems like you've got some smart friends."

"We're not friends, really. I just know xem from work. Business trips, you know."

She nods. "Of course. What do you do?"

"I work for a tech company here as an data analyst, but I don't do much. Mostly I just keep the company running when my employer isn't there. Keep people in line, you know." Zeke finishes the cocktail that Mira gave him earlier. "Aurodus is a beautiful city, with all the live music on the streets. Are you involved with the entertainment industry then?"

Mira snorts. "No, I don't have a single creative bone in my body. I agree with you, though. Seems like you enjoy your time there on business trips?"

Zeke grimaces. "Not really. Don't get me wrong, it's a great place. But every time I'm there, it's with my employer, and he kind of ruined it for me. We just went last week, and it was a very unpleasant trip. He's been really agitated and distracted lately. But enough about me. What do you study?"

"Chemistry," Mira says, her smile turning sly. "I've been doing some research."

"Oh, yeah? On what?"

She leans forward, as though whispering a dark secret. "Intermolecular forces. Surface tension of liquids."

"I have no idea what that means," Zeke admits.

Mira laughs, straightening. "Me, neither. I never said I know what I'm doing in the lab. What did you study?"

"Computer science, nothing special."

"That's very useful for the current job market, no?"

Zeke huffs. "Sure."

"Oh, right, you hate your job. My bad."

"I don't *hate* it," he defends. "I just wish my employer would actually work as much as he goes on vacation. He dumps all the work on me when he leaves, and when he comes back, he calls me in for a private meeting, but all he does is gush about his time away. Which, almost always, includes a lot of unnecessary details about the things he does with the person he's dating."

"No," Mira says, horrified.

"Yes," Zeke counters with a grimace.

Mira groans, covering her face with her hands. "I feel so sorry for you."

"Please don't. I'd rather do anything else." He extends a hand towards her. "What do you say about dancing with me?"

The girl smiles and places her hand in his. "I'd love to."

Time blends with music and flurry of moments and alcohol and fickle lights. In the transitions between songs, they'd whisper in each other's ears about funny stories that come to mind. When her feet tire out, Zeke offers to walk her back to the hotel, and she spends the whole time ranting about her latest experiments, eyes shining. Except, her words are jumbled from six shots of tequila, so Zeke pokes fun at her sentences with every chance he gets. By the time Mira finds herself outside of her room, she's laughing and tugging at Zeke's jacket.

"Key first," he reminds her with an amused grin, voice low.

"You're right!" Mira fumbles with her purse and goes through it several times before finding the disk to fit in the dint of the door. When she presses it in, the circle blinks purple, and the lock clicks open. She attempts to pull Zeke in, but trips over her own feet.

Zeke steadies her. Mira huffs and pulls him down for a kiss.

"Ah," Zeke says, keeping a firm hand on her shoulder. "As much as I'm enjoying this, you're drunk. Maybe another time, if you still want it."

"But I have to go back to school," Mira pouts.

Zeke pushes her back into the room. "You'll know how to reach me. Drink water."

The door shuts. After roughly ten seconds, when his footsteps fade down the hall and into the elevator, 'Mira' sighs, her goofy smile giving way to Zero's tired frown.

She staggers to the bed, pulls out a needle from her duffel bag on the carpet, slams it in her thigh, and barely makes it to the toilet before vomiting. Zero makes a mental note to bully Tal into upgrading his instant detoxification compound to something less miserable to take. Her head still pounds as she gulps down water, but the recording device embedded in her stud earrings is enough comfort for her compromised memory. As soon as Zero regains her balance, she changes out of her dress and heels, and into loose sweats, an oversized denim jacket, and thick platform boots. Her lips quirk when she takes out Zeke's fake business card from Mira's purse, which says he's a business analyst.

"You thought you were subtle," Zero comments to the empty room. "Wait until you see mine."

He'll find the Ace of Crowns card soon enough, in the inside pocket of his jacket, where he keeps a vintage lighter and a box of cigs.

Tossing Zeke's card on the hotel bed, Zero hauls her duffel onto her shoulder, throws on a black cap, and walks out. She strides past the glow-in-the-dark murals and trusts her feet to carry her to the right subway entrance as her mind wanders.

She keeps telling herself that this is the last thing she'll do for Rovis before leaving him, just like how he left her all those years ago.

But she can't forget the look in his eyes when he saw those brass knuckles that Kagiso picked from the Skulls. For one of the most dangerous men in the country, Rovis has an impressive number of weaknesses. The ghosts of his past, especially, might just be his downfall someday. And Zero shouldn't care. She doesn't.

The rocking of the train ride reminds her to stay alert, though she only faintly remembers getting on the transport. She frowns, trying to figure out if she got on the right train in the first place. She doesn't even recall riding down the escalators to the subway platforms.

"That's probably because you refuse to sleep."

Zero lets her head roll to the right, blinking at Lila. Well, her brain's reconstruction of Lila. Avyrian culture believes in ghosts, but Zero thinks seeing her dead best friend can be anything from hallucinations to maladaptive daydreaming.

There's no one else in the cart except for Zero and Lila, so she mutters, "Shut up."

"Oh, don't be so grumpy. I'm always here to scold you."

"The irony." Zero laughs, turning her gaze back up to the swaying ceiling.

"Do you even enjoy being the Ace?" Lila asks.

"Of course I do. Enyo turned my weaknesses into a weapon. It's protection."

"And what is the point of this 'protection' if you insist on being so self-destructive?" Lila hovers closer now, soundless and lifeless. "All this manipulation only reminds you of your mother. Irony, you said. Is it not ironic that part of why you're so good at being the Ace is because your trauma taught you how to act the way people want you to? Is it not ironic that Enyo, the woman you almost see as a sister, is a devil you made indefinite deals with? Is it not ironic that you consider *her* as protection, even after what happened when you first met?"

Zero closes her eyes and sighs. "Get out of my head, Lila."

"I'm always in your head," the phantom says, but she stays silent afterwards.

When Zero looks over again, Lila's gone. The train comes to a stop. She registers too late that the robotic announcement called out her stop minutes ago, and she squeezes through the shutting doors at the very last second. Her duffel bag barely makes it out before the janky metal can crush it.

A sigh escapes her lips as she enters the flow of people exiting the station. Time eludes her when she skips too many nights of sleep. Eyes cast down, she steps onto the escalator with purpose, noting that she has indeed gotten on one.

Zero's never been a believer of time travel, but maybe she loses hours in the present every time she sees Lila because her mind is trying to trade back the past.

The escalator beneath her boots approaches its silver end, and she counts the number of steps she takes to reach the exit.

The doors slide open, and her heart leaps to her throat.

Zero sways on her feet. The view before her is blurry, the colors too faint. Even though she can't see well, she can feel in her bones that something's off.

"Let go," Rovis's rough voice sharpens Zero's vision.

She blinks. She's not on the street outside the subway station. The neon walls tell her that she's in the hotel room she booked in Dyvris to investigate the past few days.

Water drips onto the floor. Zero looks down at a different outfit on her body and touches a hand to her wet hair. She just took a shower, Zero realizes. She closes her eyes and tries to remember what happened after she exited the station. But she has no idea how she got back to her room, especially since Dyvrian hotels all look like towers of wildly stacked jelly cubes.

Suddenly she wonders if Tal has made any progress on his attempts at developing teleportation technology.

"Zero," Rovis snaps.

She opens her eyes to look at him, slowly noticing that he's sitting on the bed and holding up a fist that's turning white. A thin wire— Oh.

Zero flicks her left wrist, and the dragon ring appears on her finger again.

"You're not supposed to grab it," she says, the unhelpful words feeling foreign on her tongue. Zero rubs her eyes in an attempt to clear the haze in her head.

"Well, I was certainly not going to wait for you to choke me to death."

She sighs. "What do you want?"

"Not what I want." Rovis shakes out his hand and reaches over to her coffee table to lift up a skull, which Zero really hopes is just a prop. It has a red rose in one eye socket and an arrow piercing her Ace card in the other. "What Damian wants. Tal found this in our office."

If Zero had any energy, she'd ask why Rovis's former friend didn't join a theater group instead of channeling all his dramatics into unnecessary threats. But as always, she has no energy, so she says, "How'd they slip past our defenses?"

"We have files on them. They have files on us. The Rose Skulls are one of the deadliest organizations for a reason. You said it yourself that they would hit back harder." Rovis gives Zero a pointed look. "What did you do?"

"Caught Zeke Reyyez's eye."

There's a pause, as if Rovis is waiting for Zero to laugh it off and say it's a joke. Then he tosses the skull onto the coffee table, temper visibly rising. His hair might even be smoking, if Zero's perception of reality were trustworthy at the moment. "I told you not to do anything stupid, and you decided to seduce the underboss of the Rose Skulls."

"We agreed to send them a message."

"Which does *not* mean pissing them off."

Zero rolls her eyes. "Well, be more specific next time."

"Why would you even go for him? To prove a point? You don't need to prove anything."

"No. I was bored. Did you know Narvaez is romantically committed to Jordan Faal?" Zero smiles unkindly when Rovis steps back. "Oh, right. Instead of talking to them like an adult, you ignored them for five years. This song is getting old."

"I didn't ignore you," Rovis says.

"Get out."

"I didn't," Rovis insists. "I'm not the problem here. You're the one who's staying at a hotel instead of sleeping at home."

"Home," Zero echoes. She lets out a hollow chuckle. "What home, Rovis?"

"R—"

"Nope. Leave. You're the reason why I've been so busy lately."

Rovis clenches his jaw. "Just so you know, Avery reported earlier today that Darla Griffith and Francis Romero died in the dunes today. Isabella Brown escaped, and we've lost her trail. You might want to watch your back."

"Okay. Anything else?"

"Damian called a meeting at midnight, and he wants you to be there."

"Midnight? What time is it now?"

Rovis frowns. "Just past noon."

Zero didn't even realize a new day started, let alone the fact that it's early afternoon already. She snaps her fingers for the dimming windows to reveal a bright scenery where the sun shines a lighter shade of orange than the sky, and the moon carves a faint crescent through the colors, both celestial bodies looming over the bustling city in the middle of a desert.

"Huh." Zero keeps her gaze away from Rovis. "Where?"

The answer doesn't come for a few moments. Then, "A cyborg club in Metloxcy, halfway between our cities. Meet me in my office an hour after dinner. Tal is also going."

"No one is surprised."

"What's that supposed to mean?"

"Absolutely nothing, *Boss*." Zero looks him in the eye and says, "Leave."

"I—"

She holds up a hand for him to stop, subtly trying to stop the spinning of her head. Her voice is quiet from exhaustion when she adds, "*Biv'ye nu wanotai.*"

Though he looks like he wants to say something else, he doesn't. He has to obey her last words. The Toullish phrase roughly translates to 'If it entertains you,' but in meaning it translates to 'please' in Purish. Yet that Purish word never meant anything in the first place.

'Please' never stopped the hand forcing Zero's head underwater.

'Please' never stopped the whip from landing on Rovis's back.

'Please' never stopped the bullets from flying into the student body at Lime Gateway High School.

'Please' never woke Zero's father up, blood oozing from his temple, a gun in his hand.

One of the few things Rovis and Zero still share is their preference for the detached Toullish phrase. They are ruthless criminals now; they do not beg. Still, they only use it when it's a serious request from each other.

Rovis shoots her one last look before stalking out.

Zero is just about to flop onto the bed when her watch chimes.

"Damn it," she growls at the reminder to meet up with Raven and Jacek at the frozen yogurt place in five minutes. She doesn't remember when she set up this rendezvous, but she definitely remembers that she has some important matters to discuss with those two headaches.

Zero doesn't bother to change this time, and she takes her time strolling two streets over in baggy black pants and an old sweater with rips cutting across the sleeves. Raven and Jacek are already sitting at a white table on the balcony, enjoying the desserts.

"Just like middle school," Zero comments, settling in the third seat. The circular glass panel in the middle of the table disappears, elevating a bowl of black cherry yogurt. She begins eating, even though she didn't have lunch.

"You can be less enthusiastic about it," Raven retorts.

"Well, I would be overjoyed with this experience if, you know, we aren't criminals. And by the way, since when did 'we' include you two?"

Jacek lets his spoon clatter to the table, annoyed. "When do you think?"

"I did *not* ask you to follow me. In fact, I'm pretty sure I told you both to stay out of it and let me handle things, because I did not want you to be in the position you're in right now."

"That's hardly possible when you send me encrypted data about mind-control drug formulas from the deep state and suggest in a dead programming language, a code in itself, that I should find a cure for it," Raven says.

Zero considers that. "Yeah, that was a miscalculation on my part. But was it really necessary for you to join?"

"The school got burnt down," Jacek says flatly. "During the cultural festival, by some Purish kids. Lime Gateway High School is gone. And you know what? The Scavenger found us. Some Aconite members in the area stopped the fire and reported back to him, and *he* came to offer us protection."

"And you believed him?" Zero says coldly. Her body starts to feel cold, too. "You saw a big man in a fancy, expensive suit, who barged in with a bunch of violent people and beat up the arsonist kids, and you thought he would protect you?"

"You were gone," Jacek argues. "We didn't know where you were, and we had nothing left. He was the only way we could find you again."

"It wasn't supposed to matter. You were supposed to figure out yourselves without me and move on while I searched for answers. That was the plan, yes? I didn't—"

"*Unconditional love*," he cuts her off, slamming his hand on the table. "That's what you said. That's what we all said. It was the four of us, always, and to infinity."

"Lila's not here," Zero snaps, though it comes out weaker than intended.

"I can see that. You never would have become... *this*, if she were still here."

Zero sighs. Her arms are beginning to tingle from exhaustion. "Jacek—"

"When was the last time you slept, huh?" He waits for her to come up with an answer, but Zero's brain is too foggy. "Yeah, that's what we thought. Is it working?"

"I think so," Raven answers, and Zero doesn't understand until she's staring down at the empty bowl, the spoon slipping from her fingers. Her muscles grow weak, and she struggles to stay upright until Jacek slides into her seat and holds her close.

"Why," she croaks.

"I'm sorry," Jacek says quietly, hooking an arm beneath her knees. "We already lost Lila. I can't lose you, too. I'm not letting you shut us out anymore."

Her brows furrow, and her mouth twists into a frown as she tries to fight the sedative. But of course, there's no stopping it. Her sight fades out. And she starts to hear gunshots.

Her heart immediately seizes. Her breathing grows shallow.

No.

Zero can't see anything, sees only darkness, until her fuzzy vision concentrates to show her a hallway full of lockers. The tiles beneath her are arranged in tasteless designs of blue and yellow. Her eyes sting and her hands shake. It's all too familiar. She hasn't been here in ages, but she remembers it so well that she's certain her prison in hell will look like this when she dies.

A scream pierces her ears.

"No," she breathes. Because it's Lila.

She turns on her heel to sprint down the hall, but her feet are glued to the ground.

The school is on fire.

All around her, the flames inch closer, engulfing her, and she still can't move. Because in the fire, she sees faces. Tal and his little sister, Saige. Raven and Jacek. Daleyza and Ofir. Kagiso and the rest of the Aconites. Rovis. Old friends from school.

They are all screaming.

A sob escapes Zero, the sounds ripping her chest apart. She's burning, but the fire is cold against her skin. No, she's burning from the inside. The blood is boiling in her veins, destroying her organs, and tearing her skin apart last.

She hears Lila's ghost laughing from every direction.

"Stop," she whispers, gripping her hair.

But the lava in her chest creeps up into her throat and chokes her. She can barely see anything through her tears and the smoke.

It's too much.

Her knees fall to the ground as she lets it all out with her own scream. Her fists slam on the floor as her own fire, burning white, bursts out from her body and wipes through the orange flames.

Zero's eyes shoot open, her breath caught in her chest.

She can't move.

Someone says her name. The old one. The wrong one. The one that should not be uttered.

"It's Zero," she forces out. The dim purple lights in the creases of the walls tell Zero that she's in the Tech Hall, and the posters give away that it's Jacek's room.

Jacek, whose chest rises and falls under her head with his sigh, tightens his arm around her shoulders and says, "You woke up too soon. Go back to sleep."

For a moment, she doesn't remember the last five years.

It's really just like middle school again, the four of them cuddling in the same bed when it gets too cold in the winter, with no heating in cheap apartments.

Her chest still hurts from the dream, but her heart cracks at the memories. The four of them, navigating through robotics competitions. The four of them, plowing through homework together at internet cafes. The four of them, trapped in that classroom, when Wyatt Revyxon marched in with that rifle.

Raven sits in front of her now, clearly having rummaged through Zero's belongings. She fiddles with Zero's watch. "Two weeks without any sleep, not even a short, mini-nap. What kind of drug are you taking?"

Zero doesn't answer, still trying to control her breathing.

"Did you have a nightmare?" Jacek asks.

"Screw you," she hisses.

"Hey," Raven warns. "We've been trying to have a real conversation with you ever since we got you out of Torch City, but you've been ignoring us. Jacek only suggested we do this when it became clear that you're running yourself into the ground. We forced you to get some rest, while we caught up on your life."

"By going through my things," Zero deadpans.

"As if you were going to give us any straight answers," Raven shoots back.

"Guys," Jacek interrupts them.

Zero shakes her head. "Whatever. I know I've been a shitty friend. I won't hold this against you. Just don't do it again. What time is it?"

"A bit past dinnertime. Don't go to work. We're leaving."

"Oh, I am so late." Zero sighs, dropping her face into her palms. "I don't know where you two are going, but I'm supposed to go somewhere that is definitely not here. No, listen," she stops Raven from interrupting. "I know you two have planned a way out, probably to live our lives in a small town in Ezclovia like we've always talked about, but I still have some things I need to work out first. Either you leave tonight without me, and I'll catch up, or you wait for me to come back, explain everything, and we all leave together."

"You'd rather go to that meeting with the Skulls," Raven deduces, clearly disappointed.

"I wouldn't 'rather' go; I have to go."

"Why?" Jacek demands. "Because the Scavenger told you to?"

Zero purses her lips.

He doesn't relent at her silence. "Because he's the one you were looking for, isn't he? He's the reason why you got us to help you get into the Aconites."

"I'm not talking about him with you," Zero says, voice flat.

"But—"

A buzzing pattern from Jacek's nightstand interrupts him. He sighs and passes over Zero's watch. When she looks at the screen, a headache starts to pound at her skull.

Enyo is calling.

"I have to take this."

She leaps off of bed, but she pauses and looks back when she reaches the door. Neither of them are watching her go, Jacek too busy fidgeting with the soft blanket covering his legs and Raven glaring at the ceiling while leaning against his desk.

Zero's fingers curl into a fist.

No matter what she does, it seems, she's upsetting everyone in her life. Her friends, by trying to keep them out of the world of the Damned. Tal, by keeping his sister's secret. Rovis, by…Well, stars know what.

"I dreamt about the shooting from eighth grade," she says, giving up a truth as a peace offering. "And the fire. Jacek, you were right. You were always right. Always, and to infinity. I will make it up to both of you as soon as I'm finished. You have my word."

Raven quietly joins her at the door and hugs her. "We trust you."

"You shouldn't."

"Of course not."

Zero squeezes Raven back. Before she leaves, she gives Jacek one last look, an unspoken promise. As soon as she shuts the door, she connects the call.

"Hi, baby Ace," came the saccharine voice.

Zero's arms prickle with goosebumps, and her steps away from Jacek's room falter. She can almost hear the ominous sound of slow, clicking heels on a pristine marble floor. But she doesn't dare freeze up.

"Hello, Enyo," she responds in quiet Avyrian. "Apologies for the wait, I was dealing with something."

"Something like the boss of the Rose Skulls?"

"Not yet. On another note, you're aware of the fact that the Scavenger pulled me out of the Agency, which means our deal expired." Zero doesn't need to ask. There's only one reason Enyo ever calls. Every devil cherishes her deals, after all.

"Yes, you've done well. The Daggers have greatly benefited from the information you gave us. Unless you want to make a new deal, I suppose I no longer require your services."

Pausing by her bike right outside the Hall, Zero considers that. With all the moving pieces on this planet, she knows there's something bigger going on. While she doesn't plan on leading a revolution, she needs to keep some tricks up her sleeve in case she does need to take action in the future.

"I will likely request one on a later date," she replies.

"Very well. I look forward to doing business with you again."

The line disconnects, and Zero shakes her head. She's all too aware of the heaviness in her limbs again. Pieces of her dream flash before her eyes, and Zero tries to force them away by pressing her palms into her shut eyelids. All it does is swirl into a mental cauldron of memories and dream fragments, like a bad acid trip. A hysterical laugh threatens to break out her throat, but she forces it down.

She drops her arms, sighing and looking up at the eerie sky. Sometimes she feels simultaneously too young and too old. Sometimes she feels that if she were dead, everything would be easier, and she wouldn't need to interact with people, to scheme and calculate and have ulterior motives. But she's not dead, so she has to deal with her problems, one at a time.

Putting on her helmet, she rides downtown. First, to get coffee. Then sort out her thoughts before she has to go to a stupid meeting between two emotionally constipated mob bosses. Just another ordinary day.

And when a hand clamps over her mouth and drags her backwards into an alley, that's the final straw for her. Especially when her coffee splatters over the pavement. With an irritated growl, she jerks back into the intruder's chest and drops to a crouch on the ground, drawing out her knife. But before she could move to strike, her back slams against the brick wall, and a bruising grip on her wrist forces her to drop the knife. Zeke Reyyez's livid face appears before her glare. The waves of rage rolling off of him are practically assaulting her like an energy blast.

Zero sighs then grits her teeth. She snarls, "Really?"

"Hello, Mira," he greets coldly. "Or shall I say, *Ace of Crowns*, lead Heartless of the Aconites."

"That was my favorite drink," she deadpans.

Reyyez scowls and thrusts a gun beneath her chin, forcing her head to tilt back. The electric buzzing of a blaster gun vibrates against her skin. And, stars and bloody cities, Zero does not have the patience for this. Violence is exhausting and an absolute waste of time.

"*No* one gets to use me and walk away," Reyyez snarls.

Zero chuckles, vicious and colder than ice. "Then pull the trigger."

As predicted, he hesitates. Zero rolls her eyes.

"You're a Reaper, right?" Then she shifts her voice to the higher register, softens it, and slips into her flirtatious mask. "Go ahead. Reap my soul, love."

Reyyez flinches back with Mira's reappearance. She doesn't wait for him to process the whiplash of her personality switch before grabbing his wrist to angle it away from her face when his finger slips and sends a blast into the wall. Coming back to his senses, Reyyez snarls and raises a fist to take a swing. Before the punch lands, Zero snakes under his arm to flip him over right as he dents the wall with his force. His back hits the ground with a crack, followed by his head. Agitated and merciless, Zero stomps on him between the legs. Her hands smooth over her leather jacket as she kicks Zeke's gun back towards him.

"Oh, wait," she says in her regular voice over his groaning on the concrete, "you can't. One, because that would start another blood feud, which is a horrible idea when the government is trying to exterminate us. Two, your boss would be furious with you, since he's trying to make peace with mine. It doesn't seem like it right now, because they can't communicate like mature adults, but they'll get there eventually. Otherwise, Damian Narvaez must truly be bored out of his mind to reach out to us now, for no reason and with no intention to rebuild a relationship with my boss."

Her watch buzzes again, but Zero declines the call from Rovis. If the Skull underboss can ruin her night by wasting her coffee, then the Skull *boss* can have his dramatic entrance ruined by an empty room where the Aconites have yet to arrive.

"And three," she crosses her arms, peering over at his pained expression, and continues, "deep down, you realize it's a petty move. I was just doing my job; it was nothing personal. You realize that the problem was the fact that my boss sent me, knowing that it was extremely offensive to the Skulls. You realize that it was really up to them, and that we, as their inferiors, should not interfere."

Through the agony of his broken bones, Reyyez laughs, a dark and loathing sound. He rolls onto his side, fingers digging into the concrete as he attempts to get up. Zero lets him. Reyyez glares up at Zero after he gets his legs under him again, with much struggle, cold sweat glistening under the city lights.

"You really are something, aren't you? I'll have you know that when I found that card—"

"Look," Zero interrupts, "I'm having a really bad day, and I really don't care what you think of me, so I would like to have some 'me time' before I have to go to the little meeting with your boss. I would rather be sleeping in my very comfortable bed tonight, but I never get what I want."

Reyyez curls his lips at her, spite and scorn written in his glower. But he doesn't say more. Zero can't help the smirk that appears on her face as she regards his half-kneeling position on the cobblestones.

She activates the electromagnets in her gloves. The knife flies back into her hand. Zero turns to leave, but remembers something and pauses to throw a sneer over her shoulder.

"By the way, you owe me a coffee."

8

Metloxcy

Rovis is just about to storm out of his office when Zero trudges in.

"You're late," he snaps, though he notes that her skin has regained some color compared to earlier in the hotel. Zero looks irritated to hell, but at least she doesn't look empty anymore.

"I don't want to talk about it," she mutters.

"Fine," Rovis scoffs and looks at Tal to make sure he's listening to his instructions. "A few things about the meeting. It's cyborg-run, so neutral ground. That means no weapons when we enter. An attendant will keep them until the end. No talking except for me when it starts. No harming anyone. Break any of that, then the Skulls don't have to stay civil, either. And if it gets violent, the cyborgs will kick us out. Trust me, we do not want to be on their bad side. Questions?"

"Uh, yeah." Tal lifts up his metal arm. "Can I get away with this?"

"Just keep your claws to yourself unless absolutely necessary," Rovis emphasizes the last part pointedly. Tal only laughs and mock-salutes him. "Anything else?"

"And if the Skulls break the rules, we don't have to keep it civil?" Zero asks as she stares into space, her mind far away from the present.

"Correct." Rovis narrows his eyes. "Should we be expecting that?"

"Not necessarily. Just a possibility."

Shaking his head and leaving her to her own calculations, Rovis leads the way out the Poison Core, where their ride awaits. As usual, Tal chats away the entire trip, while Zero stays silent like the dead in the very back, and Rovis entertains his second with two-word responses.

When the car slows down in the small city of Metloxcy, a cold feeling grows in Rovis's gut. It doesn't help that the streets are dark here, barely lit with a couple sodium lights.

Rovis sighs, fidgeting with his golden hoop. He would die five times over before he admits the fact that his palms are beginning to sweat at the thought of facing Damian again, especially after Zero so callously informing him of the romantic development between Damian and Jordan.

An expected and long overdue romantic development, but still too much to process.

Of course he's the odd one out now.

Rovis drops his hand into his lap, then crosses his arms. His fidgeting draws Tal's attention, who notices his mood shift and allows him a bit of silence.

Rovis closes his eyes and inhales.

One, two, three, four, five.

Exhales.

Six, seven, eight, nine, ten, eleven, twelve.

When he opens his eyes, he studies the architecture of the city. Whereas the large and heavily populated cities, such as the capital, Dyvris, and Divako, are flamboyant spectacles of neon lights and loud music, Metloxcy operates quietly with a dark industrial aesthetic. Almost entirely inhabited by cyborgs, every building showcases its metallic structure, with gears rotating and chains creaking. If it were during the day, he'd be able to see the detailed laser engraving on the walls and roofs.

They stop in front of a small pub, black tubes wrapping around the edges. Tal shoots Rovis an unimpressed look. Zero shoves both of them forward when they gawk for too long.

"Stop glaring at me," she says, voice flat. "And stop looking so judgmental. You haven't even been inside."

Rolling his eyes, Rovis walks up and inputs the password of the day on the ten-digit combination lock. The doors slowly slide open with two large gears driving rusted chains, and he has to wonder just how long ago this was built.

Electroluminescent strips on the rusty ceiling light the inside, where a bar is serving a few customers in the red glow. A bot, almost as tall as Zero, rolls by to scan Rovis. Its antennae turn green when his identity is confirmed.

"Welcome, Scavenger," its mechanical voice says. "The Skull King is waiting for you. Please surrender your weapons until the end of the consultation."

A drawer pops out from its belly. The three of them drop in knives and guns of every sort. Satisfied, the bot rolls away, and they follow it to an elevator with a metal gate.

"Seriously," Tal complains in Lasan, "how old is this place?"

"This establishment is six hundred years, seventeen days, three hours, eight minutes, and five seconds old," the bot responds.

Tal stares wide-eyed at the bot before breaking into a fit of laughter.

"You know universal translators are embedded in pretty much everything that runs on electricity now, right?" Zero remarks with her usual boredom, shadows crossing her face as the elevator descends.

"Then why do you find it necessary to speak fluently in five languages?" Rovis counters as they enter a massive underground club that looks just like every other one in a big city, a sea of writhing bodies beneath flashing lights, heavy bass thundering against dark walls.

Zero turns to blink at Rovis. Then she scoffs and rolls her eyes. They land on the ground with a clunk. Zero is the first to follow the bot out into the crowd of drunken dancing.

Of course she doesn't answer his question.

Sighing, he squeezes past clubbers before Tal and avoids having alcohol spilt on his shirt. Eerie eyes of cyborgs follow them, silently judging. At least Zero has the decency to wait for them outside the private lounge that Damian must have booked. Rovis marches in first when the doors slide open.

And he feels as though someone punched him in the gut.

"You were never a punctual one, Rov," Damian Narvaez drawls without even looking up from his glass of red wine, legs propped up on the table.

Wordlessly, Rovis takes the seat across from him. He couldn't speak even if he wanted to; his tongue feels heavier than lead. Instead, he shapes his silence into a weapon, pulls on the mask of the Scavenger, and buries all emotions deep below the surface.

Damian lifts his stare and narrows his eyes at Rovis.

The past few years sharpened his edges, built him stronger, and there's no more love in those steel eyes. He's in a three piece with a silver tie that matches his irises, a long gray coat hung over his shoulders. Ten heavy sterling finger-armor rings glint under the lights.

The room suddenly feels cold, too small for Rovis to breathe. His limbs feel numb, but he can't show it. He's always known that the past can never return the way it used to be, but he never allowed himself to truly think about it. It has merely been a theory in his head, and now it's hitting him like a train wreck. There's no such thing as 'when this is all over' or 'when things go back to normal.' Especially not for the Damned. They all sink lower and lower as life just keeps changing and changing, and there's nothing he can do about it.

"How's business in Dyvris?" Damian speaks again.

Rovis hardens his stare. "Fine."

An electric blue bot floats in with drinks. He picks one up but waits, resting his arm on the table so no one sees it shaking.

Undeterred, Damian asks, "How do you like owning the Aconites now?"

Rovis raises a brow, unimpressed by the small talk. "What do you want, Narvaez?"

"Oh, wow." Damian clicks his tongue. "We're back to surnames? Here I am, trying to have a friendly conversation."

"Damian."

"Very well. Rovis, I'd like to know what you have against my organization."

Rovis scoffs. "Am I the one who broke into your house to leave a skull as a threat on your desk? If anything, I think we're even, and that's already bending the truth."

"Even?" Damian sneers. "I sent you a pawn; you sent me a queen. I sent you a mouse; you sent me a lioness. I put down an expendable card, and you came back at me with the Ace of Crowns."

Rovis can't help feeling a bit smug at those words, despite all the things he's trying to suppress, seeing Damian again. Between the secrets of the past and the lies of the present, he knows he had an advantage here, with Zero on his side.

He leans back in his seat, bringing up the drink to his mouth to hide his smirk, and senses Zero over his shoulder. He's about to order her to stay back when she presses two fingers to his wrist, and he's too startled to stop her from snatching the glass out of his grip.

"You have not been addressed, Ace," Damian snaps.

Ignoring him, Zero takes a sip from the cup and walks slowly, silently, around the table.

Then she pauses next to Damian, who glares up at her, as if he doesn't know what to do about her impertinence. Zero stares back at him, reading whatever it is that the Heartless can see just by looking at someone.

Rovis stiffens at the deadly smile creeping up Zero's face.

And he's utterly paralyzed when she dumps the drink over Damian's head.

The Skull king stands abruptly, and Rovis quickly follows, watching Damian fume, while Zero tilts her head at the much taller man, unimpressed. Tal has come to stand beside Rovis, instantly providing much needed emotional support, while Zeke Reyyez and the other Heartless gape at Zero, wide-eyed and stunned speechless.

"It tastes like soap," Zero criticizes.

"What—"

"I mean," Zero continues, "it tastes like a regular sweet drink, but just a little salty. Gamma-hydroxybutyric acid, I presume?"

"You just made up a chemical," Damian growls.

"That's gaslighting. I used to take it for narcolepsy, before I decided sleep was just too much work and started taking the no-nightmare-never-sleep drug in my coffee. Besides," she says, taking out a metal plate from beneath her tongue when both Rovis's and Tal's watches flash on with a notification, "I have the chemical analysis."

Rovis doesn't move, but Tal opens the file they've both received for him, putting it on a holographic display.

"You *are* a chemistry major." Reyyez points at Zero.

Damian's face twists with confusion that Rovis shares. "What?"

Zero ignores him and says, "No, sorry, I'm a high school dropout."

Reyyez glares daggers at her. Damian shoves him back, clearly irritated.

"You came prepared," he says, looking as though he's trying to melt Zero with his glare alone.

"Look who's talking," Zero shoots back. "I say we're done here."

"That's not up to you."

"Damian," Rovis hisses. "Lautaro. Narvaez."

The Skull king merely looks back at him.

Zero rolls her eyes and slams the glass onto the table, miraculously without shattering it.

"You two are acting like children," she says in a bored tone. "You have unresolved high school drama, and you've both forgotten that you're adults now. Let's not talk about the Scavenger, alright? He's not the one who tried to drug the other. *You*." Zero tilts her head at Damian. "You just performed the petty crime equivalent of hazing on my boss. We get it: You missed the college frat boy experience. Breaking news? None of us care. We don't need to be here for this. If you two aren't going to get couple's counseling, then at least have a conversation without the theatrics. You hear that music out there? I'm bored, and we're in a very cool night club, so I think I'm going to go dancing. Anyone want to come with? Stormie? Reyyez? Tal? No one? Okay."

And then she just stalks out.

At Damian's incredulous expression, Rovis rubs his temples and orders in Avyrian, "You better come back to me right now."

Zero definitely hears him, but will she listen? That always seems to be a hit or miss.

Damian opens his mouth, but Rovis holds up a finger with a scowl. "I'm dealing with it."

"Oh, hello, Boss." Zero walks in several minutes later with the serving bot from earlier, disabled. Lowering her voice, she says in rapid Avyrian, "I have about seven minutes before I'm compromised from the stupid drug. Get me out of here." Then Zero switches back to Purish with false cheer. "Long time no see! I filed for a reboot for this little deviant with the owner of this club."

She tosses it onto the table, its broken wires poking out from cracks between dented panels.

"I—" Damian crosses his arms. "How old are you?"

"Mentally?" Zero laughs. "Older than—"

"*Zero*," Tal snaps, speaking for the first time since entering the room.

The girl finally stops her taunts, tilting her head at Rovis and silently deferring to him whether or not to answer the question seriously. He waves a hand impatiently as permission granted, since she seems to be doing everything else on her terms anyway. Her age is her information to give, especially since the Skulls have already seen her face.

Zero smiles again. "Seventeen."

Reyyez chokes on the water he's been chugging.

Something like recognition flashes in Damian's eyes, and *that*... That is not good. Rovis realizes too late that Zero was asking if he thinks Narvaez is to be trusted with the information, rather than for permission to do as she wished. Because she knew Damian would put it together. The misinterpretation was a bizarre mistake that makes Rovis all too aware of how much his head is spinning, how he isn't thinking clearly at all. Anxiety spikes in his chest, as he doesn't know the answer to Zero's unspoken question.

"Alright," Damian says, eyeing him. "Let's entertain the child. Everyone out."

Forcing himself to focus, Rovis grasps Tal's arm and tugs him close.

"Get a hotel room for Zero," he says quietly, mouth dangerously close to Tal's face. "Signal the others to stand down but still standby."

Tal's jaw twitches, clearly not liking the thought of leaving, but they weren't dumb enough to come alone. There are Aconites out on the dance floor waiting for Rovis's signal in case of an emergency. Tal nods and takes Zero's hand, following the other Skulls out of the lounge.

Now it's just Rovis and Damian. Rovis's heart speeds up, apprehensive. He braces himself for the inevitable question.

"Is she—"

"Don't you dare," Rovis cuts him off.

"No wonder why we barely have any information on her," Damian says, eyes cold. "Is this your way of protecting her now?"

"Damian, shut up."

"What's the point?" Damian opens his arms, a challenge. "She's not only a Damned; she's a formidable Heartless with a name. The bloody Ace of Crowns. How did you manage to let that happen?"

"I don't know," Rovis snaps.

"What do you mean, you don't know? She works for you, does she not?"

"That's none of your business."

"Oh." Damian raises a brow, intrigued. "The little one has grown up to outsmart you, hasn't she? She did that all by herself, and you have nothing over her anymore."

Rovis glowers at him. But Damian's too smart; he always has been. He's figured out the truth that none of the Aconites know about in mere minutes.

"What gave her away?"

"The age was just a confirmation," Damian admits. "It was the overprotectiveness that first gave me suspicions. She looked like she wanted to cut off my limbs and choke me with them when she figured me out."

"And what, exactly, did you think you were going to accomplish with spiking my drink?"

"What do you think, Rovis? You may be able to pretend Griffin never existed, but I can't."

Rovis sits back, breath caught in his chest. Hearing that name again is like a hundred daggers piercing through his lungs. "I loved him, Damian. I still blame myself everyday."

"*Good*," Damian hisses. "Because I blame you, too. Jordan never hated you for killing xyr twin, but I did."

"So, what, you wanted to lower my lucidity so that I'd start crying to you about causing Griffin's death?"

"What if I did?" Damian's face darkens. His lips twist into an unhinged grin. "What if I wanted you to admit that you killed him? That you betrayed all of us and destroyed yourself in the process? What if I wanted you to apologize and beg me for forgiveness? You walked away so easily, when you were the one who broke us."

The hatred in his sneer and his words stunned Rovis into silence. While they're no longer friends, he never thought that Damian's resent has festered into something so ugly and rancid.

"Nothing to say?" Damian laughs coldly. He looks away, letting out a long sigh, as though the anger burned all his energy in those few sentences, just like that. "You really are pathetic and spineless now."

"Is that all?" Rovis asks tiredly. "I thought you had something new to tell me."

Damian downs the rest of his wine and slumps against the back of his chair. "The Syndicate."

"What about it?"

"Hate crimes all over my city. Jordan's, too."

"It hasn't come to that in Dyvris."

"It will." Damian looks at Rovis again. "I'm sure you've also figured out that Hilobis isn't just under quarantine from the new virus outbreak."

"A city with only immigrant populations and no Purish," Rovis says. "I think everyone knows what it really is."

Damian nods. "We need to do something before everyone decides that we need to be wiped out. I'm asking for your help, Rov."

"This is when you know the world is actually ending," Rovis mutters.

Damian laughs bitterly. "Not if we combine our resources. My Skulls, your Aconites, Jordan's Crystal Ring."

"Attempting to drug me was not the most promising way to start a pact," Rovis says dryly.

"That was all me," Damian says, with no hint of remorse. "You don't need to trust me, because I sure as hell don't trust you, after everything you've done. You just need to trust Jordan. Xe actually wants to make this work. If only you'd talk to xem again. Xe misses you, Rov. For whatever reason."

"Why would xe?" Rovis tilts his head with a sharp grin. "Xe has you."

"Ah, so that's what your little Ace got out of my second. Clever one, isn't she? Yes, after you disappeared, Jordan and I got closer, and we realized a lot of things that we should have seen way earlier. But you don't have the right to be offended."

"I'm not. I'm just saying that you two can be the power couple and leave me out of this. I want nothing to do with either of you. The past is dead. Our paths diverged a long time ago."

"You made that choice," Damian says, eyes flashing with fury. "Even after Griffin passed away, Jordan promised to help you with anything. And I loved xem more than I hated you, so I would have done the same. *You* chose to take everything on yourself and become a criminal at the age of sixteen."

"As if either of you could have helped," Rovis answers coldly. "My dad died, and I needed money. Zero needed money."

"And she must have been, what, twelve? So you just left her all by herself?"

Rovis stands. "I don't need to explain anything to you."

"She's *seventeen*, Rovis." Damian raises his voice, though something about it makes Rovis pause. "She's only seventeen. What you have her doing, do you not see how messed up it is? How many people has she targeted after becoming a Heartless, and how *old* were those people? What kind of things did she do to earn her title as the Ace of Crowns? I have no idea who the man I'm looking at is, and I don't know who she is to you now. But I know the Rovis I was friends with, before Griffin died, and he never would have let this girl slip through the cracks."

"Why do you care?" Rovis grits through his teeth. "You'd never met her before."

"Because you didn't let her see us," Damian points out. "You loved her so much back then, that you were worried she'd get attached to us and get in trouble with her mother. You think you were helping her? Look at how the two of you turned out."

"Stop."

The relentless words turn sharper, like thin stakes flying burrowing into his body. "She used to shoplift grocery stores to make sure you had enough food for our wrestling tournaments. To make sure all of us did, even though you never let her meet us. She made scarves and gloves for all of us, when the winters got colder and colder. I even remember that she would write Toullish jokes on scraps of paper and slip them into your backpack to cheer you up when you got stressed during exam season. Yes, we all saw those, even though you tried to hide it. And now. Now, she's just a card to be played in your Scavenger games?"

"Enough," Rovis hisses.

Damian must have noticed Rovis's trembling fists, or he was momentarily replaced with a nicer version of himself from an alternate universe, when he repeats, softly, "She's only seventeen."

Rovis forces himself to walk out before he breaks down in front of Damian. He raises a hand to dismiss the rest of the Aconites. Tal already sent him the address of the hotel he picked, so he drives there instead of returning to the mansion after he recollects his weapons. The bot's tray was otherwise empty, so Tal must have already taken care of his and Zero's.

Thankfully, the hotel doesn't look as archaic as the night club.

Tal opens the door when Rovis knocks. He takes one look at Rovis and offers his cup of tea. "I bought some when I secured the area."

"Thanks. How is she?" Rovis takes the cup, glancing at Zero's sleeping form on the bed by the window.

"Out like a light as soon as we made it in here. I wish she slept this well normally."

Rovis nods, thinking back to when Zero was younger. Her mother always yelled at her for being tired during the day, and she once mentioned that she often woke five or six times at night. He thought she dealt with it when she joined the Aconites, since money was no longer a problem, but something must have changed.

"Take the other bed," he says. "I'll keep watch."

"You should sleep," Tal counters. "I'm fine."

"Tal." Rovis places a hand on Tal's shoulder. "Thank you."

Tal blinks, his usual mask faltering. "Of course, Boss."

"I can't sleep now, no matter what I drink. It's been a long night. I need you to drive in the morning."

"Okay." Tal nods. "Understood."

Rovis gives him a small but grateful smile, squeezing his shoulder before letting go. He sits on the edge of Zero's bed and faces the window while Tal settles into bed. Damian's words still ring in his head as Rovis stares into the darkness of the night.

He doesn't know what the other man is up to, since Jordan clearly doesn't know about their poorly planned meeting, otherwise xe would have been there or sent a message. Damian might be planning to steal the Aconites' information and resources, sure, but Rovis believes that he wasn't lying about the Syndicate.

Yet Damian's hatred for what Rovis did to Griffin will never go away. And though Rovis can understand that, he can't trust Damian for that very reason, and it's no longer just his life on the line. He has a whole organization to think about. Even though Rovis has decided to forget ever reconnecting with Damian, his brain refuses to stop replaying fragments of their arguments on shuffle. He always thought he did what was necessary when he left Lime Gateway to join the Aconites, but now he's scared to wonder if that wasn't the only choice he had. After all—

"What are you doing?" Zero's sleepy voice drags him out of the turmoil of his mind.

Rovis runs a hand over his face. A glance at his watch tells him that she was knocked out for about three hours. He looks over his shoulder to check on Tal.

"He's asleep," Zero says in Avyrian, rubbing at her eyes. She shuffles to one side of the mattress. "Sit on the bed. It's fine."

Rovis obeys, careful to not touch her as he shifts to lean his back against the headboard. "If you knew the drink was spiked, why did you drink it?" he asks in Toullish, going back to the language he's most comfortable with.

"I didn't have concrete proof."

"You must have known way before we even got to Metloxcy. You brought a chemical testing plate. How those results ended up on our watches, I have no idea."

"It was a guess. Precaution. Avery texted me today that the Skulls financial account had a new entry of payment at a pharmacy, and I looked into it. So I wrote a program in the back on the way here while you were flirting with Tal—"

"Hold on—"

"—and set an automatic function that would immediately send the results of the test to you two. Honestly, it was so obvious. I saw the drinks when we were walking across the dance floor; yours clearly didn't look right."

"I was *not* flirting with Tal."

She squints at him with puffy eyes. "Really? That's the part you focus on?"

Rovis scoffs. "Why didn't you just dip the testing plate in the drink? Who said you had to have it in your mouth?"

"Oh, that. I just wanted to see the look on his face."

Rovis tilts his head, nonplussed. "What did he ever do to you?"

Zero sighs. "Nothing. I just really hate his personality. What is this, an interrogation? I would rather pretend to go back to sleep."

"Sorry. I just feel naive that I didn't notice anything wrong with the drink."

"Well, you were busy having multiple anxiety attacks about seeing Narvaez."

Rovis doesn't have the heart to glare at her for that jab. Not after Damian's reminders of what she was like before he left her all those years ago. And Zero seems too tired to fight, if the half-lidded and glazed eyes mean anything.

The silence, for once, is a comfortable blanket over them.

Until Rovis has to break it when he says, "I don't want you to work as a Heartless anymore."

Zero sits up and crosses her legs, studying Rovis. "Narvaez had it coming."

"It's not about that." He looks away. "I couldn't do anything about your situation when Bianchi was still in power, but now that I am, I want you somewhere safer. You have enough money, and I know Raven and Jacek have a plan. You should go with them."

"Is that why you took them in? To save me?" Zero's irritation grates against his soul.

"You don't need saving. They did, when the school burnt down. But I also hoped they would give you the family you've always wanted. Even if you don't go, I don't want you out in the field anymore. Switch to either Clockwork or Digital, that's my order."

She says nothing for a while.

Rovis almost dozes off when Zero finally answers.

"I'll think about it."

9

You Can Run

It's been a week since that awful meeting with the Rose Skulls, and Rovis is still holed up in his art studio. He won't even let Tal in. Fortunately, Tal also has his own space to be a workaholic.

"Pass me the solder?" Levi grunts, stepping back from the Shapeshifters that one of the Dealers brought in. It has seen better days, without the patrolling giant robot spiders trying to tear it apart while a team from the Opulent House was in a car chase after a heist.

Tal is just about to give him the iron when a loud crash comes from one of the closets. Without a thought, he shoves Levi back while his metal hand morphs into a blaster gun. "Get to an exit."

Levi knows better than to argue, after all these years. Tal strides over to the closet and flings open the door, the number pad crashing onto the floor with the handle, sparks flying from torn wires.

"Really, guys?" Levi's exasperated voice from behind Tal tells him that he didn't go nearly as far as he should have.

But Tal is too amused by the sight before him to get annoyed at his oldest friend. Daleyza is leaning casually against an old antigravity engine, as if her black shirt isn't half-torn off her shoulder, with Summer leaning against her in a similar state, at least looking somewhat sheepish.

"Oh, by all means," Tal says, his metal hand returning to its original form as he crosses his arms. "Please continue."

Daleyza rolls her eyes but doesn't say anything, pushing Summer off of her and throwing her jacket back on. Not that she has ever said much to Tal before to begin with. Summer mirrors Tal's posture and tilts her head, a teasing grin sharp on her lips.

"I didn't know you thought of us like that, Gierkas."

Appearing next to Tal, Levi exclaims, "How long have you been in there?"

"Oh, not long." Summer inspects her nails. "We hid as soon as you came in."

"We—" Levi finds Summer's blazer and throws it at her. "We've been here for *five hours*."

"Like I said, not long."

"N.A.D.E.," Tal reprimands his AI program for not notifying him of their presence. "What the hell."

"I thought it would be funny, sir."

"And who gave you a sense of humor?"

"You did, sir."

Levi claps his hand over Tal's mouth and shoves him back before he can make a snarky comeback. He narrows his eyes at Daleyza and Summer. "Why were you here in the first place?"

"I was chasing Daleyza," Summer says, nonchalant. "She's being a sore loser about a bet."

"It was a stupid bet," Daleyza retorts with a growl.

"You only started saying that after you lost."

Tal interrupts, curious, "What bet?"

Daleyza scowls and looks away, letting Summer answer. "I bet that Boss would never know that we're together unless someone tells him. She bet that he'd realize it eventually now that he's overseeing the entire organization, at the latest by two years of his reign. The loser has to enter an underground cage fight in Loveias. And of course, as Zero has informed us, Rovis remains oblivious."

Tal raises a brow, surprised. "I thought our head Reaper would enjoy a good cage fight."

"She was trying to get weapons from your lab," Summer says, indignant. "That's so lame! Bare hands or nothing, babe."

"In Loveias? In the territory of the Daggers?" Daleyza retaliates. "I do not have the energy for that."

A high-pitched beep interrupts their petty argument. Tal turns to see Levi frown at his watch and say, "Stars and bloody cities. Avery got shot."

"Avery?" Tal asks, bewildered. Avery never gets involved with anything that could lead to violence. They're probably one of the most popular members among the organization. "Who would shoot Avery?"

"Balsam Rawley."

"Who?"

Levi sighs. "An Ezclovese woman who just joined. She's apparently still causing a raucous at Arden's right now, if you want to reinforce rules while Rovis is taking care of himself."

Tal whirls around and points a finger at Summer and Daleyza. "You see what happens when you slack off?"

"You're the underboss," Summer points out, unimpressed.

"Yes, and?" Tal puts his hands on his hips. "I thought the higher you are on the social ladder in this country, the less work you actually do. I'm supposed to just sit here and look pretty."

"Tal," Levi snaps.

"Right, sorry. Is Avery being taken care of?"

"Yes, they're with Ofir and Kagiso. Rawley didn't get anything important, so Avery will be fine."

"Good." Tal grins and rubs his hands together, digging Lithium out of hibernation. "Come with me."

His frustrations and hatred for the world have been building up ever since Rovis showed up to his lab saying they needed to get Zero out of Torch City. At least for all the drama with Wyatt Revyxon and the purging of traitors in the Aconites, Tal got to take out his anger on them, for hurting Zero, for inconveniencing Rovis. But then he was left out of the loop when it came to the Rose Skulls, because Rovis and Zero were playing at something he didn't understand. Two of the people he cares most about in the world, and they still wouldn't tell him anything about what happened before they joined the Aconites.

Tal saw the emotional damage the Skulls did on Rovis, and he couldn't do a thing about it. Useless. Pathetic. Inconsequential.

Oh, how he craves some violence. His claws are itching to shed blood, especially since he was robbed of that opportunity when Zero decided to handle Damian Narvaez her way.

He takes a bike from the Tech Hall garage and goes through the tunnels to get back downtown, with Levi closely following in a one-seater pod. Arden's Sunset is surrounded by Aconites, who are redirecting tourists to other places. They move out of the way as soon as they see Tal. Unlike the usual darkness in the club to highlight the holographic games, Arden's is fully lit and practically empty.

"What kind of organization is led by rats? All they do is hoard money and steal from the rest of the world!" What's-her-name yells from her spot in the middle of the first floor. "We can be *better*, actually work with the Purish, and have so much more!"

She does not seem to be aware of all the displeased Aconites surrounding her and the unimpressed ones watching her from the mezzanine. She appears to live in her own world, thinking she's the main character, when in the real world everyone's watching her like a bad comedian's show.

Tal clears his throat.

All the Aconites shift back, casting stares downward.

The woman turns to sneer at the intruder, though she hesitates when she sees Tal. Lithium's reputation precedes him, after all.

He smiles cruelly. "Baxter Riley, is it?"

"It's *Balsam Rawley*—"

"Right, right. Blaine Rory. I see you haven't even earned your mark yet." Tal chuckles when she jerks to hold her bare arm protectively. "Such a shame. I would have loved to knife you for what you did to our dear Avery. Of course, I still can. But that takes out the dramatic effect of the traditional punishment for traitors who actually became a full member."

"You're just a boy," she says derisively. "So obsessed with power and hierarchy. Are there any grownups here? Where's your boss?"

Tal breaks into a laughing fit. A knife flies out of nowhere and lands on her shin. The woman gasps, crumbling to the floor.

"Oh! My bad," he says. Really, it's hilarious that she uttered those words. Rovis is only a year older than Tal. Although, Tal does wish the man would have been here.

"You uncivilized bastard!"

Tal snorts and throws another knife at her shoulder. "Woman, you are in the wrong world, expecting the Damned to be civilized. I dare you to insult me again, Bernard Roberts."

"My name—"

"Yeah, yeah, no one asked. Now, where is that pesky gun you used on Avery?"

"One of your *dogs* took it," she spits out, her face pale and covered in a cold sweat. "I would have gutted her, but these meddling weaklings got between us."

"Gierkas," someone calls Tal by the surname. He tilts his head to see that Raven appeared next to him. She holds out a blaster pistol with a bored expression. "Although, I prefer 'hellhound.'"

"You learn fast," he says with approval.

Raven only rolls her eyes and walks away. Tal sees why she's friends with Zero.

Where is that troublemaker, anyway?

"Moving on," Tal says loudly to the rest of the club again. "It seems as though some of you forgot that we have rules. By 'some of you,' I mean Barnaby here, but I'm afraid I have to re-establish what we're here for. Our beloved Scavenger may have decided to not show himself for a few days, but does that mean he isn't watching? Does that mean we all resort to childish lawlessness?"

Dead silence.

No wonder nobody here ever made it to college. They would be terrible students. Negative percent participation grades.

Tal sighs. "Fine. Review session it is. Rule number one."

He holds up the blaster pistol and shoots Blythe or Briscoe or *whoever* in the stomach. She doubles over, choking and gasping.

"An eye for an eye," he says, smiling. "Levi, love, remind me. What did she do again?"

"She's been stealing from other Aconites," Levi answers, monotoned, and clearly exasperated to have been dragged into Tal's performance. "She also violated our code and jeopardized our relations with the locals by starting up uncertified test prep programs tailored towards high school students in Dyvris who want to go to college, overcharging without providing results."

"That's awful!" Tal exclaims. "Rule number two: only steal from rich outsiders. Come on, guys. We're family. You remember the oath that comes with the mark, yes? Good. No stealing from each other. And if you're stealing from the poor kids in our city, then you're just pathetic. Really? They can't even pay for their own housing. What else, darling?"

Levi sighs but answers, "Avery found out when they were checking bank records. Rawley attacked them when she realized she couldn't erase her tracks fast enough."

"Hello? No horse playing, children. Rule number three: internal disputes are settled through our internal system. I'm not saying we don't resort to violence, because we're, well." Tal twirls his hands. "The Damned, of course. But everything has to go through me and the Scavenger first. No one gets to make a move against another Aconite, until we decide what happens next. If you violate that..."

The temperature in the club drops.

He chuckles darkly. None of the Aconites move. Some of them might not even be breathing. Whistling a children's song, Tal saunters over to the woman. He plucks out his knives and wipes the blood on her dress before flicking them back under his sleeve. Then he grabs her by the hair with his claws. She whimpers, but doesn't dare to speak again.

Tal's lips twist with revulsion. "How is it that touching you absolutely disgusts me when this arm doesn't even have sensory receptors? I wonder... Oh, well." He drags the sharp tips across her face, leaving five red streaks through her nose and an eye, then stands. "I'm heading out. Can someone take out the trash?"

He chuckles and kicks open the front doors, drops of blood dripping off his claws and trailing behind him, while Aconites shuffle behind him to clean up his mess.

Even in broad daylight, Dyvris glitters in power and glory. When everything is falling apart, when the government that pledged to serve its people has secretly begun to exterminate the poor and 'unfit,' this city lives on.

All it's missing is its king, its Scavenger, its Rovis.

The man needs space, Tal gets that. But he has no idea how to help Rovis if he refuses to talk about what went down with Narvaez. Tal almost blames Zero. She is the reason why the two mob bosses were left alone in that room, after all. But he would be lying if he didn't expect everything to end in a disaster the moment he found out Rovis sent her to Divako. Narvaez is just too despicable of a person, and Zero is cursed with that awful temper.

When Tal asked her why she had to orchestrate things that way and why Rovis is so affected by the meeting, she merely patted his shoulder and said, "You'll understand when you're older."

So rebellious, that child.

"Well," Levi's voice breaks Tal's train of thought. "You look like you're in a better mood. Did you get it out of your system?"

"Almost." Tal laughs. "There's always a little more monster in me."

"If you insist."

Tal stops walking, and Levi turns around, a question in his eyes.

"Levi, dear." Tal crosses his arms. "You've been quite nervous around me. Is it something I said? Or someone I killed?"

"No," Levi answers quickly, eyes flicking to the side. Not necessarily a sign of lying, but definitely hiding something. Unfortunately, Zero was right again.

"Is this about Williams?" he asks.

"Can we get bubble tea?"

Tal blinks. "That was the least subtle change of topic I have ever experienced. I take it as a yes, then. Levi, I know you're clean."

"Do you?" Levi retorts, his tone subtly taking a dark turn, and Tal does not like it. "You don't know the things I've heard. You don't know the things I've said."

"What could you have possibly heard or said? You don't even know Ezclovese."

Levi grew up in Pureland, so he never learned his home country's language, nor does he share many of the prejudices the Ezclovese have against other immigrant groups. He doesn't have that sense of self-importance and superiority over the historical origins of the Purish. It's not as if the Purish recognize the Ezclovese as their same lineage, anyway.

"I don't," Levi is saying. "But it's hardly necessary to be fluent in any language other than Purish these days."

"Alright." Tal grabs Levi's hand. "We're getting bubble tea, and we're talking about this."

He drags Levi along to the closest shop a few blocks west and orders a strawberry jasmine tea with mango jellies — Levi's favorite — along with a rose water matcha latte. They settle down at a table outside on the third floor, where glass green-tubes with nearly extinct flowers inside surround the railings.

"Speak," Tal says. "Tell me things you've been afraid of saying. If you're scared of someone in the organization, tell me who it is, so I can get rid of them for you. If you're scared of me, tell me what I need to do to fix it. If you're scared of yourself, tell me what you need to feel safe again."

Levi doesn't answer for several moments. He stares at Tal, face pinched with inexplicable emotions. Tal lets him gather his thoughts, both of them sipping on their drinks.

"I guess there's no point," Levi finally says, sighing. "Zero already got all of them."

"Then what's the problem?"

"The Ezclovese, they'd sometimes have debates about the way Rovis runs things. I didn't think much of it, because I rarely paid attention to the details anyway. But in hindsight, I should've reported it. We could've avoided that whole mess with Noah."

"Listen, Levi." Tal leans forward, propping his elbows on the table. "You couldn't have known it was going to escalate to this. Our Ace of Crowns is a feral little thing, right? The Aconites know it. The world of the Damned knows it. Hell, I watched her destroy the boss of the Rose Skulls with words and a glass of cocktail while *drugged* not too long ago. And you said she already dealt with the guilty ones, yes?"

Levi nods.

"Clearly, you're still here. And that girl still adores you. Didn't she just buy you a book the other day? I don't think Zero would do that for someone who might be a threat to the Aconites."

"I was supposed to be like her," Levi mutters.

"You were supposed to be a Heartless," Tal says slowly. "You chose not to be one, because you wanted to avoid situations that would lead to violence. There is nothing wrong with that."

"I'm not strong enough to help you, Tal."

"You do help me," Tal argues. "You help me in the lab. You work on tech that can protect me. You're at the steering wheel when I need a getaway car. You're there every night when I'm stressed out."

"Do you remember that our agreement was non-binding?"

"Sure?" Tal frowns at the topic change. "Do you not want to do it anymore?"

"I don't want you to feel obligated to stay with me," Levi corrects.

"Why—"

"Tal, what are you doing?" Levi tugs at the collar of his own shirt. "Rovis can give you so much more, and you actually love him. And if you're willing to see it, he loves you, too."

"Don't say that," Tal protests weakly.

"No, really, I don't mind what we have right now. You have been the best thing in my life since I got here, and I'm glad I could help you. But I can't change who I am. I'm aromantic and asexual. Rovis isn't."

"Even if you're right, that doesn't make your love any less valuable," Tal says. "It's not less than romantic love; it's just different. Why are you thinking about this now? We've been doing this for years."

"Because ever since Rovis took over, you've been changing. For the better. He's really, really good for you, Tal." Levi reaches out a hand, and Tal grasps it without missing a beat, though his brain is still trying to process the words. "You used to stomp on everything that's beautiful because you didn't believe in life. You thought it was a joke, and you couldn't afford to take anything seriously because there was just so much pain inside of you.

"But when Quade was gone, you were free. You were free, next to the man you love, and you're finally allowed to have hope again. And I've been waiting for you to take a chance, to tell Rovis about how you feel, because you deserve to have good things in your life. But it's been over a year, and Zero's leaving for good this time—"

"Zero's *what*?"

"Oh," Levi sucks in a breath, leaning back. "Oh, no."

"She did not inform me of this decision," Tal says. "I thought I convinced her to stay."

"Let me finish," Levi says. "She still has a couple weeks."

"Fine, fine, go on."

"When Zero leaves, Rovis will need you even more. You can't keep holding back from him, not when things are going to get worse."

"And, what, you think you're the one holding me back?" Tal snaps, irritated. "How dare you consider yourself a *placeholder* in my life?"

"You're only lashing out because you know I'm right." Levi smiles sadly. "You are my friend, Tal. It's not like I'm in love with you romantically and sacrificing my feelings because I have a low self-esteem. You know I never cared much for relationships. This was all just for fun and games, for both of us, and we made that clear to each other from the beginning. The truth is, I'm in love with you platonically, and I'm in love with a lot of people platonically, and I want you to set yourself free. I'm the happiest when all my friends are happy."

Tal shakes his head, words stuck in his throat.

Levi squeezes his hand. "Let's go home. Just think about it."

But I don't want to, Tal wants to protest.

He doesn't want to let go of Levi, because it means things really are changing. He doesn't want to give in to this hunger, for having more with Rovis, because he can't stand the emptiness of being disappointed again. He doesn't want to make the wrong move and lose all the good things he already has right now but never deserved.

But physically, Tal nods numbly and follows Levi downstairs. They walk in silence down the street, heading east towards the mountains. Tal steals glances at Levi, an echo of what he used to do before they hooked up, and catalogs the changes in the other man that he hasn't noticed.

Levi's soft blond hair has grown lighter under the desert sun, and the blue eyes lost the excitement from when they were kids. Now, it's glazed over with a million thoughts, and Tal realizes that he doesn't know everything anymore, because somewhere along the way, Levi stopped telling him everything.

But it's the same the other way around, isn't it? Tal stopped telling Levi everything when Rovis became the head of the Aconites and Lithium had a bigger role among the Damned.

Tal has no right to be offended, but he can't help grieving.

He can't lose Levi, yet he already lost some of him. Apparently, he's going to lose Zero, too. And he's afraid he might lose Rovis if his true feelings ever come out.

But what if Levi's right? Tal doesn't think he can handle the amount of hope that comes with that possibility, because that's too good to be real. It can only live in his pipe dreams.

And what if Levi's wrong? Tal might be okay right now, but he doesn't know if he can always run away from the pain of being close to someone who doesn't love him back.

Tal continues on mindlessly, thoughts circling around and around, his legs doing the work for him as they make their way back to where they parked behind Arden's.

Until Tal hears a very familiar voice speaking briskly in Avyrian.

He makes a sharp turn to find Zero attempting to calm a middle-aged woman in front of an apartment building.

Heavy emphasis on 'attempting.'

The woman cuts off Zero, a high-pitched voice that makes the language sound much less pleasant. Her movements are jagged and angry.

"Hey," Tal yells when the woman grabs onto the front of Zero's shirt.

"It's okay," Zero says quickly, switching to Lasan without blinking an eye.

"Don't lie to my face. You look like you're about to throw up." Tal shoots back. He doesn't think twice about shoving the woman away with his metal arm while wrapping the other one around Zero's shoulders.

Zero opens her mouth, affronted.

"First you don't tell me you're leaving," Tal growls before she can say anything, "now you don't want to let me deal with someone who assaulted you."

"You—" Zero tilts her head, looking past Tal to glare at Levi. "You."

Same word, different languages. Levi, who only technically understands the very last word, must have gathered what the fuss between them is about. He holds up his hands and smiles awkwardly at Zero.

"You know what, I don't have time for this. Levi, you might want to stay back." Zero gestures at the woman. "This poor mother was having a nice walk with her daughter last night when a Purish man with a torch tattoo jumped on them."

"The Syndicate," Tal realizes grimly.

"They killed the daughter," Zero relays. "Slowly. And they made her watch. She wants words with the Scavenger."

"Have you called Rovis?"

"Do you think I'm stupid?" Zero snaps. "He's not answering. You should try calling."

"If he's not answering, what's the point of me calling? Ha, maybe you are stupid."

Zero sighs like she's been alive for three too many centuries. "Because it's *you*. He doesn't want to talk to me right now."

"Ooh! Let me guess, he also just found out you're planning to leave. Do you remember how I said there are only two ways to leave?"

"Tal," Zero says, scowling. "Can we talk about this later?"

"Fine." Tal takes out his phone and dials, holding it next to his ear. "Don't be surprised when he doesn't pick up."

"Tal?" Rovis's voice comes through, and Tal's smug expression freezes. Zero sweeps one arm out like 'I told you so,' and turns back to speak to the Avyrian woman.

"Hey, Boss," Tal says, turning away to focus on his own conversation. "We have a situation downtown."

"Can you handle it?" His tired voice pricks at Tal's heart.

"I'm sorry," he switches to Lasan. "But it needs to be you. The Syndicate situation got worse. Last night they killed a kid, and the mother wants an audience with the Scavenger. You know I would help you with anything, but I'm not you."

"Stars damn it," Rovis curses quietly.

When he says nothing else, Tal says again, "I'm sorry."

"No," Rovis answers quickly. "You have nothing to be sorry about. Damian warned me that the Syndicates would strike. I didn't listen."

"Narvaez?"

"Yes. I'll explain later. This is my fault, so I'll speak to the mother. Can you set up a dinner meeting?"

"Of course. But Rovis," Tal lowers his voice, "are you alright?"

"I'm fine," comes the lie.

"Okay," Tal says, deciding to try something else. "Then why didn't you answer Zero's calls?"

"She didn't call me." Rovis's frown is almost audible. "Why? What's wrong? Is she okay?"

Tal pauses. Then laughs, sharp with rancor. "If by 'okay,' you mean 'tricked the underboss of the organization she works for with a dozen more lies,' then yes. Forget my last question. I will let you know about the dinner details."

"Okay," Rovis says slowly, as if trying to process the drama with Zero. After a moment, he adds, "Thank you, Tal."

"See you later, Boss."

Tal hangs up, fingers drumming his phone as he thinks about his own foolishness. He doesn't know why Zero would lie about something like this, though he also doesn't know why he fell for it. Because Zero never calls anyone unless it's an emergency, Rovis would always answer her calls for that very reason. So why manipulate Tal into calling?

Shaking his head, he turns back to speak to the Avyrian woman, rather than asking Zero. She never gives him a straight answer.

"You'll see the Scavenger at Flan's on sixth street for dinner," Tal says.

"Make sure he isn't late," the woman demands.

Tal gives her a Lithium grin. "He's never late."

She glares at the three of them one last time, definitely wishing she could murder them, before stalking back into the apartment building.

Zero is also somehow gone by the time Tal remembers he needed to yell at her about the whole leaving situation.

"You okay?" Levi asks.

Tal gazes at the street they came from.

"Come to the *Méliaklos* festival with me," he blurts out.

"What?"

"Come with me," Tal says, looking Levi in the eyes. "It'll be fun."

"Okay," Levi says slowly. "It's not for another month, but sure."

Tal breaks into a smile. Hooking his arm under Levi's, he leads them back onto the main road and continues their stroll across the city. It doesn't even matter if it's not the same as it was before. All he needs is a few more moments to feel alive with Levi by his side.

10

The Scavenger

When another ceramic plate shatters against the wall of the private dining room, Zero has to dig her nails into her palm to stop herself from throwing the woman out the window.

"I must request you to calm yourself," Rovis says, impassive.

He hasn't said much of anything since arriving for dinner with the Avyrian mother, and he hasn't even looked at anyone else. Zero is mildly irritated that she's seeing the version of Rovis that everyone else sees: down to business and nothing else. Approach him, and he'll murder you with his eyes. Tread carefully, or he might feed on your corpse.

She can't even read his micro-expressions at the moment.

"You're pathetic," the mother spits out. "I seriously can't believe someone like you is running this city. You are a parasite feeding on the rest of us."

"I've already told you that you have my condolences, and my organization will be taking care of the Purity Syndicate. Unless you tell me what you want me to do, specifically, this is a very unproductive conversation. And I do not react kindly to people wasting my time."

"Listen to this!" the woman yells, with only the inner circle of Aconites as the audience. "How is he so arrogant?"

Without any change in expression, Rovis raises a hand and flicks his fingers.

A pair of Reapers grab the woman by the arms and pull her out. The woman's cursing fades out as the door shuts behind them.

No one else, not even Zero, dares to react, while Rovis picks up his glass and takes his time drinking the last of his cocktail. Maybe Tal would crack a joke, if he were here, but he's at the mansion dealing with something else.

Rovis pushes back his chair, standing.

"Well." He sweeps an arm out, gesturing at the table of food. "No point wasting it. Take what you want. I'm retiring for the night."

Still, no one moves until he leaves the room. Zero breaks the tension by grabbing the bowl of ghost peppers, and the others follow, movements slow with uncertainty. She hurries out to catch up to Rovis, hopping into the car next to him in the backseat before Levi could shut the door. Levi shoots her a questioning glance, and Zero flicks her eyes toward the driver's seat, signaling him to just go with it. He frowns but leaves her be.

Zero doesn't speak to Rovis, only munches on the peppers as the car drives off. The burning of her tongue keeps her mind off of the brooding man beside her, though she does catch him furrowing his brows at her. His mouth twitches like he's put out by her snack choice.

When they reach the mansion, Rovis makes a beeline for his art studio, and Zero follows him like an obnoxious, unwanted shadow. But not before Levi catches her by the elbow.

"What are you doing?" he asks, voice low.

"I need to talk to him."

"He hasn't even talked to Tal for a week. I'd leave him alone, Zero."

Not sharing his concern at all, Zero pats him on the shoulder. "I know what I'm doing."

Levi presses his lips into a thin line. Then, he relents, "Fine, but be careful. Don't push him. You know he's dangerous."

"Aren't we all?" Zero retorts with a ghost of a smirk.

Levi only shakes his head and ruffles her hair.

Surprisingly, Rovis doesn't tell Zero to go away, merely ignoring her, so she continues her stalker behavior.

The lights fade on when they enter his studio, and the doors slide shut behind Zero. Rovis doesn't say anything, doesn't even look at her, as he takes off his suit jacket, embroidered with gold patterns around the edges. He hangs it on a coatrack and pads over to the middle of his forest of easels.

"What are you still doing here?" he finally grunts, setting up another blank canvas.

Zero chomps down on a pepper, holding half of it while chewing. She knows that he's asking why she hasn't left the country yet, but she doesn't think it's necessary to tell him that she drafted a better plan with Raven and Jacek that will take place right after the Moon Festival.

No, she needs to break him out of whatever mental state he's in right now.

"You're acting like my mother when she's about to waterboard me," she says indifferently, tossing the rest of the pepper in her mouth.

Rovis flinches. At last, he looks at her, eyes slightly wide from bewilderment. Zero's lips twitch with satisfaction.

Gotcha.

He opens and closes his mouth a few times, searching for words.

"That's why you haven't said much, isn't it?" Rovis says.

"Neither have you," Zero counters.

"Stop it," he demands. "Stop pretending you're fine and deflecting."

She sighs heavily. "It is not that serious. You're the one who refuses to see people. I know Narvaez got into your head, and I expected you to react like this. I apologize that I forced your reunion to progress faster, but it was unavoidable. Take your time, Boss, but you also have to actually take care of yourself."

"How can you just stand there and say that?" Rovis presses.

"Well, you're already so much taller than me; it would be too awkward to sit or lie down."

"You—" he breaks off, looking away. He takes a deep breath, then exhales slowly. Rovis sits in one of the chairs and leans back, setting an ankle on top of the other knee. "Is that better?" he asks sarcastically.

"Oh, good." Zero crosses her arms. "You're posing as the Scavenger now."

"There is no winning with you," Rovis mutters.

"There's no winning in this universe at all."

He scoffs. "I don't know how you do it. You go on everyday, acting like a relatively normal person, until you suddenly tell me that I remind you of your abuser. And you're still standing in front of me, lecturing, joking— *Why* are you eating peppers like popcorn?"

"Because the restaurant didn't have actual popcorn."

"There it is again."

Zero laughs, incredulous. "What do you want, Rovis? You want me to tell you I don't have feelings? I'm sure you already know this." She tilts her head, assessing him. "Or you're hoping you're wrong. You think Raven and Jacek would remind me of what it's like to love, Wyatt Revyxon to hate, the Rose Skulls to fear."

She pulls a jade pendant off of her neck. It has Rovis's Avyrian name engraved on it. He gave it to her the day she left to deal with the Skulls in Divako. Insurance, he called it, in case Narvaez caught her.

"Speaking of which, I don't need this anymore."

"Keep it," he says, not moving an inch.

"Nostalgia is another thing that I do not feel." Zero grabs his hand, crushing the leather of his glove, and forces the pendant onto his palm. "Save it for someone who loves you."

Rovis curls his fingers over the stone, clenching his jaw.

"Sorry to disappoint," Zero smiles.

"Do what you want, Zero," Rovis says coldly. "Just leave me alone. Don't feel obligated to say goodbye when you decide that your time with the Aconites is over."

"Already planning on that, Boss. Anyway, you need to go to that Avyrian kid's funeral."

He sighs heavily, dragging a hand down his face. "And why would I do that?"

"Everyone in the area has heard about what happened. There are even rumors that you've sold the Aconites to the Syndicate. So if you don't show up, the people will only resent you more. It'd only be a matter of time before the lynching begins, and the people belonging to our own territory would be doing the work for the Syndicate, getting rid of us. But if you do go, you have a chance to show them you're on their side. That way, the Syndicate can't win."

"Your opinion has been noted. You may show yourself to the door."

Zero sighs. "The funeral is today. You don't have time to paint."

"Good thing I'm not going, then. Zero, the door."

"What?" Zero blinks. "What do you mean you're not going?"

"It doesn't concern you. Leave."

"It does. There are quite a few people in the Aconites I want to survive, and I just told you why it's important for you to go to the funeral."

"I have my reasons."

"Look, I don't sympathize with the mother, either. But this is a necessary message."

Rovis stands, fists trembling. "I asked you to get out three times. If this is so important to you, you'll figure something out."

He's right, of course. Zero is only puzzled that she miscalculated something about Rovis. Nodding slowly, she backs away and turns around to find the door.

What is she missing?

There's Damian Narvaez, and there's Jordan Faal.

Except...

Zero pauses with her hand hovering over the door access scanner, turns her head, and notices from the corner of her eye that Rovis is taking off his gloves.

Except Jordan Faal had a twin.

A twin who played sports.

A twin who painted.

A twin who committed suicide.

How could she forget? She passed along so many gifts to him when she was young and stupid, when Rovis refused to let her meet his boyfriend. Something really is wrong with her brain, if memories as important as these ones slip her mind. His death was even one of the files that she had stolen from the Agency while looking for proof that they experimented on her father.

"Did Damian bring up Griffin?" she asks quietly.

A chair crashes against the glass wall across the room from Zero.

She drops her hand by her side.

"You really can't talk to someone without turning their head inside out, can you?" Rovis shouts. "You couldn't just leave it, because every mind is just another round of a twisted game to you, isn't it? You insist that you don't feel emotions, I get it, so you just have to play with everyone else's. You go through people like shoes; you use them until they don't benefit you anymore, and you move onto the next one. No one means anything to you, and nothing from your past can hold you back.

"I'm not like you," he continues. "The people from *my* past, Damian and the twins, they haunt me. I did terrible things when I was a stupid teenager, and I still do awful things now that I know better. And I suffer the consequences. I can't move on, because I'm tied down by all the mistakes

I've made. I am a victim of my past. You want to know what Quade Bianchi did to me when he found out what you were to me?"

Rovis holds up his left hand, no longer gloved and showing her the metal prosthetic that replaced his ring finger.

"This is the man you worshiped, Zero. I could never figure out how he found out. I once made you a promise, and I lost a finger for it. I killed the last head of the Aconites for it. You want to know why I won't go to the funeral? That Avyrian girl who got killed by the Syndicate was the same age as you were when we first met."

Zero is frozen to her spot, her chest heaving with her erratic breathing. Rovis's rant is too much to process. She can barely hear the words gushing out of his broken heart.

Because Zero was the one who tipped off Bianchi about their past, from the security of Agency supercomputers.

She's the reason Rovis lost his finger.

And she keeps breaking him.

"So you may be able to cut off everything and everyone without blinking an eye," Rovis is saying, "but I'm *weak*, and I can't be like you."

His voice scratches, dried out from all the things he never said.

If Zero could still cry, she'd be choking on her tears right now. Even though she has no right to, not when she's the source of his suffering.

"You shouldn't be like me," she says, voice as hollow as her heart.

Rovis only shakes his head and collapses onto the sofa.

"Are you happy now?" Lila says, appearing in the corner, leaning over the back of the seat to look at Rovis. "Look what you did to him."

Go away, Zero thinks. *You're not real.*

"Yes, you keep telling me that." Lila props her chin on one hand. "So, are you just going to stand there, or are you actually going to do something for once?"

It's too late. It's far too late.

"He's right here. You're just being a coward. All you want to do is convince yourself that everyone you know is better off without you so you can feel better about leaving."

With the little strength she has left, Zero forces her feet to move, to inch towards Rovis. Lila's right, of course. She is a coward. But for now, she's willing to sacrifice a percentage of her facade. She flicks her gaze over to the corner, but Lila is already gone.

Zero stands in front of Rovis. He doesn't react, as if she were the ghost.

Slowly, she brings her fingertips up to touch his face.

Neither of them comments on the fact that her hands are shaking.

Gently, she rests her forehead against his, closing her eyes.

I'm sorry.

I'm so, so sorry.

I'm sorry I turned into such a monster.

I'm sorry that I'm not trying to be better than this.

I'm sorry I sold us out to Bianchi, hurting you in the process, while I escaped unscathed.

I'm sorry I underestimated how much our past means to you.

I'm sorry I haven't told you the truth about Griffin's death.

She will send him the file, eventually. Rovis just has to wait a couple more weeks, when she leaves. Zero knows it doesn't rectify all the horrible things she's done, but at least he'll know that it wasn't his fault.

"I'll call Tal to represent you at the funeral," she says when she lets go.

Rovis only nods. He has nothing left to say.

Zero leaves him, and finds herself wandering into the Wraith Tower. She hasn't been here since before she left for the Agency. Thankfully, the ground floor is empty, and the levels have been distributed so that each Heartless has their own floor.

The gothic metal fencing of the elevator glows faintly with violet neon filaments embedded in floral patterns. It shoots up twenty-three floors, and Zero is relieved to see that no one's expecting her to return.

She falls onto bed, dialing Tal's number on her phone.

"Go to the girl's funeral," Zero says as soon as he picks up.

"Could you have come up with a more morbid way of an opener?" Tal drawls.

"Rovis can't, so you need to represent. Keep the people on our side."

Tal must notice that Zero's tone is more dead than usual, as he asks seriously, "What's wrong? What happened?"

"Nothing," she lies. "Rough day. Spend time with Rovis after you're done."

"Zero."

She hangs up, knowing that Tal would do what she asked. The silence claws at her head, but even all of her torment can't keep her consciousness from giving into exhaustion.

Zero doesn't even get a nightmare this time.

A phone call wakes her up a few hours later, but it's not from the Gierkas that she expects.

"Saige," Zero answers it sleepily.

"Oh, sorry, love. Were you napping?"

"It's fine. Why are you calling?"

"We recorded footage of the funeral in Dyvris," Saige says grimly. "The Faceless is going to broadcast it the next time we hack into the television networks."

"You're going to *what*?" Zero sits up. "Is your brother in it?"

"Yes. Tal gave quite a speech." Saige sighs. "We're editing out all the faces, like we've been doing with all the past videos."

"You need to be careful," Zero warns. "Everything is traceable. Stop being in silhouette shots just because it looks cool."

"We haven't gotten caught," Saige points out. "Stop worrying. I called to check on *you*. How are you holding up?"

"I'm fine. Why wouldn't I be?"

"Because you got pulled out of the Agency. Your work got cut off. Do the Aconites know what you were doing in Torch City?"

"Your brother figured it out, and I already told you about the Mender that I had to contact. The head Reaper caught the Mender, but she hasn't told anyone else. I'm safe, for the time being. The bad news is that Raven and Jacek are here."

Saige swears into the phone.

"It was my fault," Zero explains with a sigh. "But we have an out. We're going to take it."

"Good. It's about damn time."

"Yeah, well, unfortunately I can't say the same for you." Zero sighs. Once someone gets involved with the Faceless, there's no turning back. It's even more dangerous than joining any organizations of the Damned. Saige's contact name on Zero's devices is 'Harlow' because they have to do everything to make sure her identity stays a secret.

"Don't worry. I've got people. Listen, I have to go. Take care of yourself and your friends, okay?"

"I will. You, too."

The call disconnects. Blinking through groggy eyes, Zero scans the notifications that she's missed. Tal attempted to call her back when she hung up on him, then texted her several useless messages. Some of her cousins with the Water Lords sent her some updates on the coastal disasters, since those are happening much more frequently recently. Dziye sent her a video of a raccoon stuck on a tree.

Raven also wanted to hangout, apparently.

Wraith Tower gate, Zero texts back, *I'll take you on a tour.*

She showers and changes into sweats before heading to the elevator. Starlight, the bothersome cat, stares up at Zero outside her bedroom. The rest of her floor is more or less an open-style apartment. Never would she have ever thought that she'd have so much space to herself before she joined the Aconites.

"Alright, fine," Zero grumbles, picking up the cat.

She makes her way back to the tower's gate, where two people are speaking to each other in hushed voices.

"Jacek, will you take this cat from me?" Zero interrupts their conversation.

"What about me gives away the fact that I'm a cat person?" he protests, though he reaches his arms out to take Starlight. "Boss did this, too."

"Ze is a trained emotional support cat. You were clearly traumatized."

"Must be so nice to be rich," Raven comments.

"We will be," Zero says, leading them down the path covered made of amethyst crystals, with their famous genetically-modified wolfsbane flowers growing on both sides. "We're going to be in Ezclovia in a few weeks, in a town of immigrants like us, and with all the Purish money I've illegally collected, we're set for the rest of our lives after currency conversion."

"Great."

Zero hesitates, then asks, "Should we bring Ayssa?"

Both Raven and Jacek go still, eyes cold when they stare at her.

"Why should we?" Jacek challenges.

"Seconded," Raven says. "Do you not remember what she did to you? To all of us? Just for being friends with Lila?"

"But—"

"She's toxic," Jacek cuts Zero off. "She was not good for any of us, especially Lila. How can you even suggest something like this?"

Raven puts a hand on Jacek's arm. She asks, "Zero, the friend you miss, she's not Ayssa anymore. That was a really long time ago. I know she was your best friend before us, but you don't owe her anything. Even if you try to help her, she won't appreciate it."

Zero studies the crystals beneath her feet. They're both right, she knows. She just gets these moments of weakness sometimes. Taking a deep breath, she summons all the energy in her body and fakes a smile.

"So anyway," she says with false cheer, "the Wraith Tower."

Raven and Jacek exchange glances but don't comment on her abrupt change in topic and tone. Zero turns to continue leading her tour, knowing her friends will follow.

"How tall is this thing?" Jacek exclaims when they reach the door.

"A hundred and eight floors."

"Must be so nice to be rich," Raven says again, looking up.

Zero puts her hand on the scanner to open the door. "First floor is basically a huge lounge with a mezzanine that has a bar and kitchen around the whole circle. Next five are other common facilities like dining rooms, gym, laundry, recreational areas, and a movie theater."

They enter the tower, and her friends wander off in opposite directions, impressed. Zero thinks all the buildings in the mansion are equally prosperous with its own type of charm. Though she supposes the Wraith Tower is more stunning to non-Heartless members because of its exterior design and their reputation as a misanthropic group.

"The seventh floor is the fledglings' lounge, and the next twenty are each their personal levels. We can access the lounge, but not the personal ones unless we're invited. N.A.D.E. keeps track of permissions and decides what buttons work in the elevator."

"An artificial intelligence system," Jacek says. "Tal is insane for this. I've looked at some raw codes of his, and that man is definitely not human."

"They call him a genius for a reason," Zero agrees. "Alright, so the twenty three floors above the fledglings are buffers. They can be guest apartments, but right now they're just empty. Fifty-first through fifty-fifth are full member spaces, so the fledglings can't go in. They're really the same as the second through sixth floors, but more exclusive."

"How do the fledglings ever feel integrated then?" Raven asks.

"The Heartless are good at including people when we feel like it. We usually only use the exclusive levels when we have to talk about higher-level business. I'll just finish up the summary. Fifty floors above that are personal apartments of full Heartless members, next two are storage, and top floor is another lounge with a glass dome as the ceiling."

"Glass dome?"

"Yeah, you can't see it from the rest of the premises. It's covered by the black spiky design. You can still get out on the roof, just around the top of the dome."

"This feels like a fantasy," Raven says, following Zero into the elevator, where Jacek is trying to access the programs through his watch. "I barely processed the fact that this whole thing is floating over a lake. Aconite engineers really monopolized their antigravity technology breakthroughs."

"Other organizations have their own secret weapons," Zero says.

"Do you still have contacts out there?" Jacek asks, curious.

"In the major ones, yes. I check in with them once in a while."

"Will you still do that once we're in Ezclovia?"

"Maybe. There's no point when we're out of Pureland, but I will probably keep tabs on the ones I was friends with before. In case something happens and they need help, I can just send someone else on my list to help."

Zero takes them to each accessible floor, until they finally reach the top.

All the Heartless, including the fledgling, are gathered in the conversation pit. Sunlight scatters across the soft floor. They jump up when they notice Zero.

"You sure took your time," Rivka, a gorgeous Toullish girl and a trustworthy friend, complains. Zero remembers that she's supposed to transfer her title as the head Heartless to Rivka before she leaves. "We heard you were back as soon as Boss came back from the capital. But you never came to the Tower."

"The Scavenger gave me quite a lot to deal with," she explains dryly. "I haven't been able to catch a break until now."

"That's okay!" Aspen, a fledgling, says brightly. "Will you come to the Moon Festival with us?"

"Well, I was going to—" Zero looks at Raven and Jacek. Raven shrugs, while Jacek beams at the idea like a puppy. "Apparently I will. These two are coming with me, though."

"The more the merrier," someone says. There are too many people talking at the same time for her to keep track of who's speaking. This is why Zero took a nap first upon her return, rather than catching up with the Heartless. She only has so much capacity for human interaction.

But all the smiles on her friends' faces loosen something in her chest.

For most of her life, she got by on survival mode, constantly thinking about the next thing she needs to do.

With Raven and Jacek, though, she might have a future.

A future of peace, on a dying planet.

A future where she can finally rest, with her two best friends.

11

Strange Goodbyes

Black paint splatters against the canvas, already covered in shades of violet and crimson. A sable brush softens the edges of the new stain, as though regretfully soothing a jarring mistake.

Rovis takes a step back, looking over his portrait of Dyvris.

It's a much more ominous rendition of the city, tainted by the dark veil over his mind that has been corroding his perception of reality.

A bleeding moon sits over colorful silhouettes of buildings in the heart of Dyvris. Its hazy depiction materialized from Rovis's dream from a restless night. Perhaps the vision speaks of the uncertainty of the future, since he seems to have lost his sense of purpose ever since Damian frostily reminded Rovis of the blood on his hands.

Perhaps it speaks of a warning, of the inevitable carnage to be released onto his streets. Rovis isn't naive; he knows the violence in their lives right now is nothing compared to what's to come. With the increasingly agitated Syndicates and with the Agency exposed, a civil war will hit them like an asteroid.

"Mister Gierkas is approaching, Boss," N.A.D.E.'s mechanical voice snaps him out of his reverie.

"Let him in," Rovis says, dropping his brush into the nearest cup.

He's washing down his supplies when Tal walks in, but he doesn't bother turning around. He hasn't been in the mood to speak to anyone lately.

"Good morning, beloved," Tal greets cheerfully.

Heat rushes to Rovis's face, and he silently thanks the stars that Tal can't see his face. He coughs and says, "It's mid-afternoon."

"Well, I just had my first cup of coffee, so morning has just started for me." Rovis shakes his head. "Oh, is this new?"

He turns to see Tal grinning at the portrait Rovis just finished. "Yes."

"It's stunning. Although," Tal tilts his head at Rovis, "quite depressing. I think you've been hiding in here for too long. Come downstairs. Some of us are playing Keepers and Thieves in the dining room."

Rovis raises a brow, unimpressed.

"A certain demoness is playing," Tal adds.

This time both his brows shoot up in surprise. If Zero is playing, then this ought to be interesting. As a child, she would gamble against the high school kids and win almost every round. It was half of their unofficial income, but of course it was never enough to provide. When she joined the Aconites, however, she stopped. Zero hangs out with the other members in other ways, but Rovis guesses that she doesn't find playing against the gangsters stimulating.

So if she's playing today, then she really is leaving soon.

And Rovis is still fairly crossed with Zero after their last conversation, even though she apologized in her own way at the end. Something dark stirs in his chest, waking up his lethargic body. Even the Scavenger isn't beyond some petty revenge.

"What level?" he asks.

"Castle." Tal smirks, already knowing that Rovis will be joining the game. "She skipped right through the number levels. Kagiso is close; he's at Shield."

Keepers and Thieves is a ten-person game, played with five decks of cards, that has a Chief during each round, and they form two teams. Depending on the cards that the Chief calls on and what the other players have, the Keepers team is formed by three players to help the Chief get to the next level. The Thieves team is the remaining six, who must gather two hundred points for a chance to play Chief the next round, and two-fifty to possibly advance.

The number levels, from one to ten, can be completed with the winning team, but the last three levels of the game — Shield, Castle, and Ace — must be won as the Chief.

For Zero to win the entire game, she must play a round as Chief to advance from Castle, then wait for the rotation to get back to her to play Chief again at Ace, and win that round. Even if she's on a winning team right now, she doesn't get to move on.

Rovis chuckles, a dark and amused sound low in his throat.

"Well, what are you waiting for?" Tal says, his eyes gleaming with mischief.

When the pair reaches the dining room, the majority of Aconite members are already crowding around the circular table. Avery, arm still bandaged, cheers at the sight of the Scavenger joining the scene with an amused expression on his face, and the others are quick to follow.

Zero, in stark contrast to her usual lack of excitement, is watching Avery with quirked lips. Kagiso elbows her and wiggles his brows. She rolls her eyes and shoves his face away.

The holographic markers by each player tells Rovis that Kagiso is currently Chief, playing Shield, with Zero, Levi, and Rivka on his team. The teams are conveniently split down the middle of the table, since all four of them are sitting in a row.

Raven, on the opposing team, puts down a Drokklo, the largest card of the whole deck. Her team consists of Daleyza, Ofir, Avery, and two members from the Opulent House: Riza and Flan. They still need fifteen points to win the next rotation, and the players that are still on a number level would need sixty-five points to advance.

Zero puts down a ten, sacrificing points. With bewildered expressions, Kagiso and half the room yell at her, the other half whoops, and Raven frowns. Clearly, she has played against Zero enough to know that a trick is coming.

After the cards are buried, Raven plays an Ace of Wineglass, which must be the Chosen suit of this round. The Thieves put down point cards. Kagiso shoots Raven an unimpressed look and puts down a Shield of Fish, just one step larger than her card. Levi and Rivka put down more points for Kagiso.

Zero plays a Drokklo.

Kagiso slams his hand on the table. "What the hell are you doing? I'm the largest."

She shrugs, gestures for him to bury the cards. Scowling, Kagiso taps on the table, and ten sectors of the table tilt inwards for the cards to slide into the middle to get shuffled underneath the top.

Zero tosses all four of her remaining cards into the middle and leans back to sip on her smoothie.

"A *train*?" Tal exclaims, laughing. The room erupts at the pair of tens and a pair of Castles of the Anchor suit scattered on the table. Consecutive pairs, since Shields are considered large trumps during this round. Even though it's the second smallest suit, a train can do quite some damage at the end of a round.

"How do you still have that?" Daleyza complains, dropping the rest of her cards as well. The Thieves lost by five points, so the rotation will continue around the Keepers.

"We didn't clear all the pairs in Anchors, apparently," Raven says.

Kagiso glowers at all the last cards on the table and says irritably, "I would have had the rest. All that I have left are Shields and Drokklos."

"This was faster," Zero returns, nonchalant.

"You won," Raven points out to Kagiso, who growls again and buries the last cards.

"Tal," Levi waves. "Come switch me out. My self-esteem can't handle this anymore."

"You're the next Chief," Avery says, puzzled.

"For level seven." Levi pouts. "I've been on six for three hours."

Tal sits down between Rivka and Flan, but Rovis remains standing as a spectator. Tal gets Kagiso, Zero, and Riza on his team, and they easily win, advancing two levels when the Thieves fail to get one hundred points. It's an average round, but Tal's theatrics makes it entertaining to watch. Even with Rovis's foul mood, he can't help the small smile that grows on his face.

After Griffin passed away, Rovis imploded with self-hatred and grief. Damian resented him, and Jordan struggled to look him in the eye even though xe promised to stay friends. Even Zero, before she changed her name and destroyed herself, couldn't help Rovis carry that weight. And she shouldn't have needed to; she was too young.

When Rovis found the Aconites, he had to build walls around his heart, his mind, and he covered his tragedies with a layer of ambition, barely enough to function.

Then he met Tal. Yes, he became Lithium and arms himself head to toe, inside out, with weapons of every sort, but he has always been *Tal* to Rovis. Somehow, the two of them found each other, saw something in each other, and chose each other.

Tal didn't fix Rovis; he's not sure if he could ever be fixed. But he gave Rovis room to breathe, and that was all he needed to rebuild himself, as terrible of a version that turned out to be.

Drawing himself back to the present, Rovis sees that Tal has made it to Shield after several rounds. The sky outside their glass wall streaks with pink and purple as the setting sun turns the heavens to a brittle shade of copper, and the smell of dinner cooked by the Clockworks drifts into the dining room. Dozens of Aconites leave to eat, and the side conversations subside to idle commentary. Both Kagiso and Zero are at Ace now, and it's Zero's turn to play Chief. Rovis can tell that she has gotten bored and slacked off with counting cards. She has made quite some sloppy plays, just enough to win, but certainly not putting in any effort.

Which is just what Rovis is waiting for.

He steps around Tal and Rivka, and the spectating Aconites start banging on the walls and tables at the sight of their boss deciding to participate in a game. Rovis doesn't smile, but his lips twitch with secret fondness.

Kagiso grins when Rovis stops behind his chair, happily giving up his seat. The mischief sparkling in his eyes tells Rovis that he knows exactly what his plans are. Kagiso's rivalry with Zero has been confusing to Rovis from the start, so he only shakes his head as he sits down.

Next to Rovis, Zero raises a brow, though not entirely surprised to see him switching in. She drops an Ace of Wineglass to claim the Chosen suit. Flan attempts to counter it with a triplet Ace of Maltese to change the Chosen suit. Zero merely enforces her original claim with three more Aces of Wineglass.

Sighs go around the table. Rovis hides an amused smirk by accepting Levi's offer of a glass of liquor.

Zero calls the third Castles of each Crown, Anchor, and Fish, for her teammates. Rovis has a few of those cards that would get him on her team, but he doesn't play them. Tal, Ofir, and Riza end up joining her.

After establishing teams, Zero speeds up her round with lightning quick pair cleanings in all suits. Rovis watches her focus on the Crown and Maltese suits, and does his best to rid himself of Maltese cards. When it looks as though her opponents are running out of pairs, Zero puts down a handful of cards.

The room falls dead silent at the sheer amount of ten cards.

"Stars," Flan curses, as everyone processes the play.

"A five-pair train," Tal says, grinning and already furiously setting down point cards. Five consecutive pairs in Maltese seem pretty hard to top, after all.

Rovis waits until everyone else puts down their ten cards. Since Zero played first, and the rotation goes around the other way, Rovis plays last.

Slowly, he picks out ten cards in one smooth motion and sets it down.

Once again, the room explodes.

"How could you? I thought we were friends!" Tal yells, incredulous and betrayed. One hundred and sixty five points from the Keepers now belong to the Thieves.

Zero, who was leaning her face on her hand, tilts her head over her shoulder to stare at Rovis's cards.

A five-pair train, but in Wineglass.

"Eight pairs in Chosen?" she says, dragging her gaze up. Her question tells him that she didn't expect him to be able to counter her train after clearing out three pairs in the Wineglass suit.

Her eyes, however, tell Rovis that she received his message perfectly clearly. One of her brows inch up, just slightly, and he knows that she's taking up his challenge.

"Not impossible with five decks," Rovis responds.

Nodding once, Zero lets out a soft chuckle and waves the hand on the table, gesturing for him to make his play.

Rovis puts down a quintuple of Shields in Crowns.

Zero narrows her eyes at the table, recalculating, while more Aconites have returned to watch the game. Low murmurs pass around the room.

"Are you guys screwed?" Levi whispers to Tal, but the room is so silent with anticipation that everyone hears him.

Tal shushes him, anxiously waiting for Zero's next move.

She puts down fifty Crown points.

Raven stares at Zero like she grew a second head, but tentatively adds fifteen points. Because who is Zero expecting to be not only out of Crowns, but also to have a quintuple in the Chosen suit?

Daleyza follows Raven, while Ofir decides to play it safe and throws away small Crowns. Avery, Riza, and Flan stuff insignificant cards from other suits.

Tal, however, grins wildly, as he smacks down a quintuple of fives in Wineglass.

Rivka scowls and does her best not to give the Keepers any points.

"You thought we were what, Tal?" Rovis mocks.

Tal sticks his tongue out at him.

The rest of the round intensifies in wrestling for control, so much that no one gets to start a play twice in a row, and it boils down to the large Chosens in the final cards. At one hundred and ninety five for the Thieves, Raven's four of Wineglass starts the last play, leading to Avery's last ten points. Tal plays a meager Castle that's neither points nor large enough to secure points, finally out of tricks to play.

Rovis sets down his Drokklo, claiming victory for the Thieves.

"Zero lost for the first time today!" Kagiso hollers at the spectators in the back, gleaming with satisfaction. "Everyone thank our magnificent Scavenger!"

The aforementioned girl quirks her lips, her last card still balanced between two fingers. With a flick, it flies onto the very center of the table.

Ace of Crowns.

The Aconites get even rowdier at the irony.

When everyone calms down, they play a few more relaxed rounds, with Rovis and Zero on the same team most of the rounds. Even when they're on opposite teams, though, they keep it civil.

That is, until Rovis gets his Chief round at Kagiso's Ace level.

As soon as the players get their cards, Zero puts down a triplet of Drokk-los, a little more aggressive than necessary.

"Anarchy!" Tal drums on the table. "No Chosen suits! Stars, she's out for blood. Didn't even give the overriding system a chance!"

Practically the whole organization is in the room at this point. Rovis can barely hear the sound of his own thoughts.

He tilts his head at Zero and challenges her in Toullish, "You're so ready to trip me over. What if you end up on my team?"

"I'll trash the round, of course," Zero shoots back.

But she doesn't need to, it turns out, since Rovis gets Riza, Flan, and Tal on his team. This round dramatically escalates to a flurry of trains and quintuplets. Every time Rovis manages to snatch back a play, Zero has another trick up her sleeve. Her cards aren't even objectively good; she just seems to know when to gamble with points, when to get rid of trash cards, and when to hit him with an impressive play.

Her Thieves hit exactly two hundred points.

Jacek appears at Zero's side with a giant bottle of soda.

"I swear, if you don't win this game," Jacek grumbles to her in Avyrian, "I'm going to drag you to eat some real food. You're not playing another round."

"*Vye tuhn xaach,*" Zero says.

Don't worry.

Rovis scoffs, and Zero catches him despite the noise. She tilts her head, just enough to glance at him out of the corner of her eye.

"You forget I used to do this for a living," Zero switches to Toullish.

"I would hardly call it a living," Rovis retorts dryly, copying the switch.

"Fair. But you only joined because you knew I wasn't paying attention."

He shrugs. "It's a game."

"Not to you. Not today, it appears." Zero unscrews the top of the soda bottle and chugs half of it. "Very well. I'll play your game."

She picks up her new hand of cards and drops an Ace of Anchor to claim the Chosen suit. Rovis counters with two Aces of Fish. Zero shoots back with three Aces of Crowns. He doesn't have four to override her claim again.

Like the first round he played, Rovis has the choice to join Zero's Keepers, but he decides it's more fun to stick with the Thieves.

And this time, Zero doesn't seem to have any combination tricks. They had the misfortune of the cards being shuffled more evenly across the players, so barely any trains or quintuples make an appearance to speed up the game.

This round lasts over an hour.

In the end, an ordinary pair of Fish from Zero takes out Rovis's sadly single Drokklo, and she wins the entire game by fifteen points.

True to her character, Zero ignores the applause and saunters over to the other dining room while drinking the rest of her soda.

Tal slings an arm over Rovis's shoulders. "That was the most entertaining thing I've seen all year."

Rovis's nose twitches. "How much did you drink?"

"Just a bottle." Tal shakes it in front of Rovis's face. "Don't worry, Boss. I've got it under control."

"Keep it that way," he says, standing and all too aware of the heat radiating off of Tal's body. Tal stumbles, and Rovis catches him by the shoulders, squeezing gently. He frowns, briefly worried at how easily Tal might relapse into his old addiction. His mind flashes back to all the times he had to sneak into Ofir's room to get the Mender to treat an unresponsive Tal, all while trying to avoid Quade Bianchi's violent punishments for non-Ezclovese members who get too drunk.

Without thinking, his gloved fingers brush against Tal's cheek.

"Don't forget how much it took to get here," Rovis says, voice low.

Tal's gaze focuses on Rovis.

Time seems to slow down around them, and Tal looks at him like Rovis is his lifeline, like Rovis's presence is all he needs to keep going. Rovis forces himself not to flinch back. Maybe Tal isn't as drunk as he seems.

"I know," he says softly. *Trust me*, he doesn't say.

Rovis nods once.

The moment shatters when Tal's lips stretch into another exaggerated grin. He turns away and turns the room into a raving party.

By the time Rovis extracts himself from the overly enthusiastic and drunk Aconite members, eats dinner, and finds Zero in the courtyard, it's almost midnight.

"Are you feeling better?" she asks without turning to look at him, though her casual position on the bench says that she's amused, not offended.

Rovis hesitates before settling down on the bench beside her. "Maybe."

"I figured you wouldn't want me to just let you win."

He hums, neither agreeing, nor disagreeing.

They sit in silence.

Slowly but deliberately, Zero holds up a hand. Rovis slants a look at her face, surprised. He waits and studies her to make sure she's not pushing herself to do anything she doesn't want to do. Then he threads his fingers, one of which is made of metal, through hers.

"I didn't mean it," he begins.

"No," Zero interrupts.

"You're not who you want everyone to think you are," Rovis insists. "You are not your mother. I wasn't in my right mind."

"Don't." She sighs. "*Biv'ye nu wanotai.*"

Rovis shakes his head. "Fine."

"Take care of Tal," she says. "Take care of each other."

"We will. We always have."

"Make it your new promise." Zero looks up at him, the moon shining in her eyes. "You've done everything you can with me. Let me go, and hold onto him."

Clenching his jaw, Rovis looks away.

"Rovis. I'm going to be fine. I have my friends."

"You'll be across the ocean," he guesses.

Zero's silence is answer enough. A selfish part of him wants her to stay, even though Rovis was the one who told her to go. He can't help but internally scream at the universe for driving them apart. Zero may blame him for leaving, but even working three jobs back then wouldn't have been enough to support both of them. Then she was the one who left to search for answers in the Agency, because she had to watch her father shoot himself in the head when she was five years old, and what child could ever forget that?

They are the Damned.

They were never meant for a life of family and security.

They could never have anything other than bitterness and paranoia.

"You're all still kids," Rovis whispers into the night.

Zero takes a deep breath, then exhales slowly. "That never meant anything in the world we live in."

She tilts her head back, watching the moon. Rovis follows her gaze, remembering his painting from this afternoon.

No, he thinks, *it's better for them to go.*

It will not be safe here, and Rovis can't afford to put Zero in another situation where she has to lose a part of herself to survive.

"Come to the Moon Festival," Zero says.

"Maybe."

"You never give yourself a break. You're rich now, for stars' sake."

Rovis scoffs. They both know that they got their money in twisted, wicked, undeserving ways. But they are not saints; they're precisely the opposite. Everything they've done that might be interpreted as room for redemption, they did it for profit or their own protection. They're selfish, and they stopped caring ages ago.

They are liars like the moon. They long lost their own identities, lost the taste of their own names, lost the vitality of their souls. All that's left is what they stole; all that others see is the false skin that they've claimed as theirs.

Yet, perhaps, it's the only way to survive the darkness alone.

12

Starless Night

The Moon Festival truly lives up to its expectations.

Mesmerized, Tal wanders down sixth street, where the Avyrian shops have decorated the entire path with red lanterns. Whereas the scarlet hues of the sky hover sinisterly over the country, these jovial lights bring warmth and optimism to their dire lives.

"Would you like to solve a riddle?" Levi asks, beaming with a strip of paper in his hand from his place at one of the street stands.

"What is it?" Tal makes his way over, weaving between locals, tourists, and gangsters. He wraps an arm around Levi's shoulders and leans over to see, but Levi holds the paper away from him.

"Which is faster, hot or cold?"

Tal almost rolls his eyes, but scrunches up his face instead. "Cold is the absence of heat. Why would it have any speed?"

"Nerd," Levi complains, pouting. "Hot is faster, because you can catch a cold."

"In what century?" Tal says, judgmental. "Vaccines exist for a reason."

"Stars, will you stop being so pedantic? These are meant to be silly." Levi lightly shoves him and reaches for another white strip. "Okay, try again.

Who eats leaves, but not meat, and spends all day spinning and weaving for everyone else?"

"Do spiders eat leaves?"

Levi laughs. "Tal, they definitely eat meat. And I think they only make webs for their prey. I'll give you a hint. Today's an Avyrian holiday, so the answer is native to the Avyrian islands."

"Dragons!" Tal answers eagerly, pointing a metal finger at his friend.

"Spiders was closer," Levi says, disappointed.

"Zero as an old lady."

"*No*." Levi slaps Tal's mechanical hand. "That's not even technically correct; she would never give up meat. Oh, I hope she's cooking for the midnight banquet."

"That's true," Tal admits. "And she is. She's out here for a bit with the Heartless, but she's going back earlier to get ready. Boy, do I miss her white cut chicken. Anyway, how about a vegetarian Avyrian elder?"

"It's a silkworm," Levi deadpans.

"Ohhh." Tal laughs. "Fine, fine. Give me another one."

"Your answers are almost as wild as your whole personality," Levi grumbles. He shuffles through the basket. "Okay. What belongs to you, but other people use it more than you?"

"All of my designs for the Aconites. I mean, I give it out willingly, but—"

"Tal," Levi growls.

"Yes, dear. Sorry," he says, not at all sorry. "Work productivity? Money? Reputation?"

"Reputation is close. Kind of. It's your name."

"Oh," Tal laughs again, albeit more forced, and sounding a bit empty to his own ears. His name does belong to him, doesn't it? It doesn't often feel like it.

A name always comes with expectations. His street name accompanies his image of an unfeeling monster and a murderous diva. In a twisted way,

Tal is lucky to have that, because it means protection for himself and for people he cares about.

Less luckily, his birth name came with expectations to be strong and perfect the way his parents wanted him to be, until they renounced him when he came home missing an arm. Only Saige begged Tal to stay. He sighs at the reminder of another person gone from his life. Saige, his baby sister, who was both annoying and adorable.

"Oh, there's Zero," Levi jerks his chin.

Tal shakes off his memories and follows Levi's amused stare.

"Stars and bloody cities," Tal exclaims, "is she *smiling*?"

With her arms hooked with her friends, Zero sways with the music playing for the Avyrian dancers moving gracefully with long silk ribbons, surrounded by the other Heartless. They don't notice Tal and Levi joining their group, too focused on the performance. Aspen, the fledgling, flicks a glance in their direction then does a double take, face lighting up with a huge grin.

"Guys, it's Levi!" he crushes the man with a hug, nearly toppling them both over with the force of his excitement.

Tal tosses up his hands. "*Excuse* me."

"Oh, yes. Hi, Tal!" Aspen waves with barely contained energy. Rivka grabs him by the shoulders and moves him over so that she can hug Tal.

The group shifts around with different permutations of hugging.

Tal really wishes Rovis weren't working today.

When the music ends, and the dancers bow out for the next piece to begin, Levi pulls Zero over by the arm and wraps her in a tight hug, ruffling her hair.

"Have you seen the skits?" she asks when Levi lets go, eyes sparkling.

Levi gasps. "No, where?"

Jacek bounces on his toes. "Oh, I'll take you."

Summoning half of the Heartless and a slightly exasperated Raven, Jacek drags Levi out of the crowd. Zero laughs after them, shaking her head, and reaches out to hold Tal's hand.

Tal lets himself get pulled into the sixtieth hug of the last five minutes, his flesh hand cradling the back of Zero's head, as he presses a quick kiss onto the top of her pink hair.

"You're happy," he comments softly.

"Something like that," she says, her gaze holding more life than Tal has ever seen in the girl. "Rovis is at the art gallery."

"I didn't ask," Tal retorts, though his mind already begins wondering what would be the quickest route to... wherever the art gallery is.

Zero rolls her eyes. "You were thinking about him. I got him to take tonight off and actually come out to have fun. You're welcome. Now go find him."

"Why do you always push me in his direction? What if I just wanted to talk to you?"

Zero scoffs. "Everyone calls you a genius, yet you like to play dumb in front of me. I don't know if I should be offended or flattered, but either way, you're taking ten years off my lifespan. I'm getting too old for this."

"Hey!" Tal squawks. "You're three years younger than me."

"I know. I sometimes do math, too." Zero pokes Tal's chest. "Tell me, are you going to spend all of your twenties pining after Rovis, or is there a ten year plan I'm not taking into account here?"

"I don't *pine*." Tal brushes nonexistent dust off his shirt. "I just help him when he needs me to. Besides, I'm choosing Levi."

"Oh, you have no idea how much Levi's been ranting to me," Zero mutters.

"What?"

"Zero!" One of the dancers from earlier has made her way off stage and is skipping towards them.

"Anyway," Zero says, waving at the girl. "I have some friends to catch up with. Do whatever you want, Tal. I'll see you later."

She disappears before Tal could even open his mouth to protest. He shakes his head, once again reminded of Saige. This version of Zero, especially, is too much like his sister. A deep pang of nostalgia hits him in the lungs, knocking the breath out of him.

"Where are you going?"

My fingers clenched around my backpack strap as I turned around to face Saige. She was eleven, standing outside her door in her pajamas, holding a stuffed bunny. I dug my nails in my palm so hard that they bled, because I was too scared to reach out for her.

"Go back to bed, koneighta*" I whispered, almost choking on the thought of never seeing my sister again.*

"I will if you tell me where you're going."

Even though Saige was only in sixth grade, she knew. I could see it in her eyes. Her face twists at the sight of my missing arm, and she covers her mouth, tears slipping between her fingers. My parents didn't exactly keep their voices down when she got back from cheer practice, so she had to know why I had to leave.

"Saige," I put my hand on her shoulders. "I love you, okay?"

"You never say that. Hrienalo, *what's going on? You're scaring me."*

Hrienalo. Big brother. She hadn't called me that in years.

I sighed, anxiously shifting on my feet. If our parents caught us, this night was going to end with so much more violence. Forcing my fingers to relax, I reached up a hand, the one I still had, and I brushed my fingers against her cheek. "Well, now I did. Remember it."

Saige stared at me. She didn't shove me. She didn't yell at me. She only hugged herself, lips trembling as sadness shook her slim shoulders. "You're not coming back."

"I'm sorry."

She grabbed the hem of my jacket. "I can come with you."

"No," I said firmly. "You're safe here. And everything's going to be better after I leave."

"Tal, I can't live without you. I know we fight, but you're my anchor."

My sister's face contorted, and I looked away. I had hoped that it wouldn't come to this, but I wasn't surprised that the worst-case scenario came true. My parents only ever loved an idea of me, and I failed them when I was too weak to fight back against those Purish gangsters.

My own parents. They chased me out of the house when I came home, missing an arm and still bleeding. They called me a freak, a demon that crawled out of hell, a disgusting imposter living in their house.

How was I supposed to stay?

I pulled Saige into a hug and kissed the top of her head.

"I have to go. I'm sorry," I said again. "Please don't follow me."

And she didn't.

It took everything in me to pretend not to hear her stifled sobs, to open the door without a sound, to walk through it one last time without ever looking back.

"Tal?"

He blinks away the flashback to see Rovis watching him from the middle of art display stands. In his embroidered suit, Rovis stands gracefully among minimalistic ink outlining landscapes. Despite his interest in art, his concerned gaze is focused on Tal. Somehow, while drowning in memories, Tal's feet managed to carry him to where his heart lies.

Tal stretches his face into a grin and adds some spring to his steps, forcing his feet to close the distance between them. "Hello, Boss."

"Tal," Rovis says again, more firmly. He's not fooled by the facade.

"Rov," Tal mocks.

The man doesn't indulge in his childish diversions. Rovis only waits with his steady gaze, letting Tal decide if he wants to talk or to just enjoy the night, but not to pretend he's okay. That's always been the thing with Rovis: Tal doesn't need to be anything around him. He doesn't need to be a perfect son, a capable brother, a daunting killer, a programmer, or a mechanic. He doesn't even need to be 'Tal,' because he has no idea who that is.

"I miss my sister," Tal finds himself saying.

Rovis nods, watching him with attentive eyes, even though Tal has never told him that he even had a sister before.

"Zero seems happy tonight," he continues. "She reminded me of my sister, that's all."

Rovis senses Tal's reluctance to speak more on Saige and focuses on the first part. "It's her last night here. She has a lot to look forward to."

"I still can't believe you're okay with it."

When Tal confronted Zero after going to the funeral as she requested, she sighed like a centenarian and said, "Take it up with Rovis. It's too exhausting when you two aren't on the same page. I have the Scavenger's blessing to leave the organization unharmed. But you are the underboss, so I respect your opinion on this. If you really want, I'll knife myself right in front of you when it's time."

She didn't even flinch when he exploded on her about the stupidity of that last sentence.

"I told her to leave." In the present, Rovis turns, looking down at a painting of two birds resting on a branch with orange blossoms. "You know it isn't safe here."

"But we don't know if it's safer out there," Tal argues. "At least here, we can keep an eye on her. She's going to be way out of our reach."

"Who says I won't have eyes on her?" Rovis whirls back around. He pauses for a moment, studying Tal's face. Then he reaches down to take Tal's hand, the human one, with both of his, their gloves sticking to each other. Tal doesn't dare move another inch.

Everyone is extra physically affectionate today, it appears.

Rovis holds Tal's loose fingers against his chest. "Don't give her a hard time about this, okay? She also has Raven and Jacek to think about. You don't know their history."

And you do? Tal wants to ask. Sometimes he wants to trap Rovis and Zero in a room with him and force them to answer his questions. The two of them, with the past that they won't speak about. But he knows that they're not ready, that it's not just Rovis's secret to tell. Instead, he brings up his other hand, the one he made to kill, to spill blood, and gently covers Rovis's.

"I won't," he promises softly. The corner of his lips twitch upward, a tentative yet genuine smile.

Rovis mirrors his expression, squeezes Tal's hand once, and lets him go.

"She wants us to take care of each other," Rovis says, walking to the next painting. "That's not too hard of a wish to fulfill, don't you think?"

Tal's gloved fist presses against his own lips as he clears his throat, trying to force down the heat pricking at his face. "It's what we do already," he manages.

"It is," Rovis agrees. "Which is why we're going to go watch sword sparring. Come on, the art is boring you."

"What? I'm not bored. I like art."

Rovis snorts, walking out of the maze. "Sure you do. When was the last time you looked at something that serves no purpose other than to be looked at, interpreted, and appreciated?"

"Yesterday," Tal says, following. "I saw your flaming skull painting. Very dramatic, very detailed. Ten out of ten."

"Yeah, but that's because of me. It doesn't count."

"It's *you*. Everything you do interests me. You're not much of a talker. You don't like to say what's on your mind, so you keep it all in, and it comes out through the brush and onto the canvas." They pause at a crossroad, and Rovis turns to look at him. "I don't just barge in that studio to bother you for the sake of interrupting your day, you know. I like to know what's going on inside that head. So it very much does count to look at your work. It counts more than anything else."

Rovis continues staring, not a single word coming out of his mouth.

"Because, well," Tal coughs, "I like you better than other random people I've never met."

Slowly, Rovis smiles. "I tolerate you, too."

A breath catches in Tal's chest. Of course he has noticed that their regular banters have evolved to something different, where every word seems to hold more weight than it used to. But he's been too terrified of thinking about it, to start wondering about the implications of the shifting dynamics between them.

"So where's this sword thing you mentioned?" Tal redirects them onto a shallow topic, being the coward that he's always been, running and running away from what's important. "And what is it?"

Rovis's gaze lingers, as if he knows exactly what Tal is doing, before he chuckles and leads them across the road to the next block. "Swords are one of the earliest weapons in Avyria, during the age of warring islands. It's quite a violent history, but eventually they reached peace and merged into one country. Swords then became a symbol of power, and are incorporated into performances of different types on all seven islands. Each one still has its own distinct culture. Sparring shows come from Xauven, the easternmost island. And sword dancing..."

Rovis nods at the stage they're passing by, where a woman jumps and twirls in the air, her robes billowing with her movements, and lands solidly in a pose, her flexible sword reverberating.

"That's from Oulochess, the northernmost island."

"It's a lot more diverse than Lasantirk," Tal muses. "We've always been one country, one continent. Food has some variations depending on the regional climate, but in terms of performing arts, it's pretty uniform. Why did you suggest the sparring show for me?"

"Because you like violence," Rovis answers as though it's that obvious.

Which, Tal supposes, isn't untrue.

"Look," Rovis says, bumping Tal's shoulder, eyes trained on two girls shifting around each other, dull swords clashing in the red lantern glow.

Tal opens his mouth to respond, a snide remark on his tongue.

A scream cuts through the festivities.

Everyone freezes in a moment of confusion. Rovis whips his head to stare behind them and grips Tal's wrist with too much force, shattering the illusion of a joyful night in Pureland. When Tal's too slow to follow, Rovis tugs at him to turn around.

A good distance behind them, a teenage girl is holding a little boy, tumbling into the ground.

The boy shakes his head frantically, clutching at his hair. The girl asks him what's wrong over and over again, trying to loosen his grip on himself.

Blood is oozing out of the boy's mouth, nose, ears, and eyes.

As soon as that registers, Tal looks sharply at Rovis, whose eyes are wide with shock.

Under the flickering lights, something flashes through Rovis's spooked stare, something like recognition, fear, dread, disbelief, all rolled into one split-second.

"Go back to the mansion," he says, voice tight, without returning Tal's dismayed stare. "Make sure everyone is accounted for. I'll round up whoever's still in the city and figure out what this is."

Tal clenches his fist at the thought of leaving him again. But orders are orders. He forces through his teeth, "Yes, Boss."

Tal takes off, sprinting towards Arden's to get his car and drives back at full speed. He bursts into the Poison Core, mentally jotting down names and faces.

"Hey, Tal—" Kagiso's smirk slips off his face when he sees Tal's expression. He instantly stands, alert. "What do you need?"

"Headcount."

He rushes into the dining room, where Raven flinches back from his aggressive entrance. Only a few Aconites stare back at him, bewildered.

"Where are the others?" Tal grits out.

"Pool," Raven says, voice clipped with fright.

Tal slams the button in the elevator too many times when he crashes against the wall from his uncontrolled speed, and he's never been this frustrated with the efficiency of his own design.

Because despite the confusion and chaos, deep down, he knows what's happening.

It's not enough, it's not enough, it's not enough, I'm too slow—

The doors slide open, and he pushes through tipsy Aconites, scanning their faces. He reaches the edge of the pool and turns just in time to see Levi slamming Zero against a stone column. Suddenly, the room feels cold, like a winter that came too soon and broke into their home to take everything away in a blizzard.

"Levi, what the hells are you doing?" Tal's words race out, his heart beating violently against his rib cage as he tries to get to them.

Zero's face is frozen with surprise.

Then it slowly morphs into terror.

"*Fuck.*"

Tal halts, stunned by the curse. He opens his mouth to ask *what*, what in this cursed universe does Zero know this time, what is happening, when Levi groans, clutching his head, and staggers back.

"Sorry, sorry, sorry," he mumbles, stepping back right into Tal's arms.

"*No.*" Zero pulls at her hair, her face showing more emotion than she ever has since Tal first met her. "No, no, no, no, no—"

Levi's legs give out, and Tal has to catch him by the waist, turning him to face the sky.

Two red beads of blood from at the corners of his eyes.

Tal's whole world turns to ice.

"No, Levi," he whispers.

"I'm sorry," Levi gasps.

"Don't be," Zero snaps over Tal's shoulder, her shadow moving in over them. "I can fix this. I've done it before. I just need— Where's Ofir?"

"They're right over there," Raven's voice replies. "Jacek, what are you doing?"

Tal spares only a moment to look away from Levi, and finds that Jacek is clawing at his chest with one hand.

He coughs, blood spurting out over his lip.

"No," Zero whispers again, and Tal snaps his head back around to focus on Levi. To do what, he doesn't know.

"Stay with me," Tal pleads. "Levi, just hold on until Rovis gets back."

Levi shakes his head weakly, wheezing and squeezing his eyes shut as more blood seeps out. Tal holds Levi's face with one hand, as he sits down on the floor to cradle the other man in his arms. He tries to wipe away the tears of blood with his thumb, but they just keep coming.

"You told me once that you'd do anything for me," Tal says desperately. "I'm ordering you to hold on. Rovis said he's going to figure this out, and I know he will, so just give us some time, yeah?"

Shaking his head again, Levi scrabbles for Tal's arm, and Tal quickly clutches his hand.

"Tell him," Levi rasps, unable to see. "Tell him your truth."

"I will," Tal says urgently. "I promise I will. I'll do whatever you want, if you can just make it through this, okay? Levi. *Levi*. Do it for me. Do it for everything we've been through together. I know it hurts, but it'll be over soon. We'll fix this."

Levi smiles and shakes his head, and more crimson flows out from his ears.

"Levi," Tal warns.

The man in his arms coughs. Blood splatters on Tal's shirt.

Tal's metal fingers brush against Levi's cheek gently. "It's okay. You're going to be okay. You're not leaving me like this, Levi Sparrow."

Levi rolls his head in against Tal's chest, blood dripping from his nose. His ragged breathing makes Tal press his cheek against the top of Levi's head. He feels a weak squeeze on his fingers of flesh.

And Levi's chest stops moving.

"That's not funny," Tal whispers, fingers fumbling for Levi's pulse. "Don't do this. Don't do this to me."

There's no pulse.

Tal lets out a sob, suddenly realizing his face is wet. He vaguely remembers that he's sitting by the pool in the Aconites mansion, but all he can think about, all he can *feel*, is this splinter in his heart.

The crack grows, fracturing his insides, and he feels cold, colder than the heat leaving Levi's body.

His chest is made of ice, and his lungs are dying, and he can't breathe.

He can't breathe, and he doesn't want to.

He can't go on. There's no way he can survive this, not when Drokklo reached inside Tal's body, Tal's soul, and ripped everything out.

How is he supposed to live on after this, without Levi by his side?

How is he supposed to live without that careless laugh?

How is he supposed to live without those playful blue eyes?

How is he supposed to live without Levi's presence?

"I can't do this," Tal hears himself say. "I can't do this, I can't do this, I can't do this…"

A warm hand rests on the back of his neck after a few minutes, a few hours, a few eternities, Tal doesn't *know*.

His head drops, his nose digs into Levi's hair, his eyes squeeze shut, his mouth trembles.

Someone wraps an arm around his shoulders.

Rovis, his mind supplies.

But it doesn't matter.

It doesn't fucking matter.

13

No More

Jacek is dead.

Zero knows that it's true, but she still can't quite process it. Her empty stare breaks when a drop of water lands in her eye. Rivka is still attempting to wash the blood out of her hair.

Jacek's blood.

Ofir told her that there was nothing they could do to save him because the new version of the mind control drug worked a lot faster than the version that Raven had found a cure for a year ago.

"What about the cryo chambers?" Zero remembers asking last night, pacing back and forth next to Jacek's dying form. "We can slow it down and figure it out while they're under."

Ofir only shook their head. "Feel their hands. It'll kill them."

"They're dying right now!"

"I'm sorry, Zero." Ofir brushed a gentle hand over her hair. "They won't make it. It's already too late. It's better to spend this time to say goodbye than to try to move them to the Core and get them in the chambers."

Zero knelt to the ground, clutching Jacek's hand while Raven held the other. They stayed with him until he took his last breath. Raven shared a long look with Zero then, neither of them able to cry from grief.

This is not the first time they lost a friend.

Raven stayed sitting, but Zero lay down next to Jacek's body. She didn't care that his blood was soaking up her clothes and her hair. She wanted to die there, too.

Then Rovis was calling her, telling her to get up. When she didn't, he muttered an apology and slipped his arms under her knees and around her shoulders. Zero immediately started retching, one hand clamped over her mouth while the other grabbed at her stomach. Rovis knew better than to touch her when she's in that state. But he didn't have any other choice; they needed to bury the bodies. Zero didn't blame him, despite the miserable journey to her room.

"Where's Raven?" she hears herself ask distantly. The steam from the bathwater suffocates her. Her throat is sore, even though she hasn't cried or screamed from her grief.

"She's safe, in my room," Rivka answers, carefully running a hand through Zero's hair. "Daleyza is taking care of her."

"I need to see her."

"I'm almost done. Give us fifteen minutes."

Releasing a heavy sigh, Zero closes her eyes. She hopes Jacek finds Lila. A dark part of her hopes that she'd see them again soon.

But maybe there's no realm for the dead. Maybe there isn't a line to cross from life to death. Maybe there's just nothingness, the same nothingness that Zero has been feeling since her father died.

Maybe death is that void that keeps growing inside of you, because you experience more deaths as you live longer, until it consumes you, until you're nothing, until you're dead.

Rivka tells Zero that she's done, and Zero drags herself out of the bathtub, water dripping from her hair and running down her body. She pulls on her clothes like a robot. Kneeling in front of her dresser, she curls her fingers over a small disk with an engraving of a dragon curled around a lotus flower.

When she meets Raven in the main lounge, they need only to make eye contact for one second before walking out of the tower, side by side. They pass the gates and curve into the garden, stopping in front of the fountain, where four empty cauldrons mark quarters of the circle.

Zero holds out the disk, a silent question.

It was their key to leave the country, thanks to Zero's ties with her Water Lord cousins. But now that Jacek is gone, only half of their original family remains, and Zero can guess what Raven's answer might be.

Raven shakes her head.

There's no point in leaving anymore.

Nodding, Zero takes out her lighter, sets the disk on fire, and tosses it into the cauldron.

The two of them watch it burn.

It's their ticket out of the oppressive lies of Pureland, their dare to hope with the strength of their vows to stay together, their last thread to an alternate future away from the doom that's waiting on their current path.

And they watch all of that turn into ash.

"There's something I need to tell you," Raven says quietly after the last embers fade out.

Zero shifts her gaze.

"I'm Zessroan," Raven whispers.

"You're..." Zero blinks. "You're not Avyrian?"

"My father was Avyrian, but my mother is Zessroan. I'm both. But we don't call ourselves Zessroans anymore."

Purish schools taught their students that the Zessroans were natives of Pureland, violent and unfriendly, before the arrival of the Ezclovese drove them to extinction. Zero was never convinced that all of them were gone, and she has heard very rare rumors about the surviving bloodlines. Some of which claim that the remaining Zessroans have formed a secret society within the Damned, hidden among the monsters that rule the shadows.

"Do you happen to call yourselves Descendants of the Originals?" Zero asks, voice barely above a whisper.

"Descendants for short," Raven confirms.

"Why tell me this now? You could have trusted Lila and Jacek with this."

Raven shakes her head. "We were too young. It wasn't that necessary anyway. But now it's just us. And you." She holds up a hand, touching Zero's face when she receives a small nod. "You're a rebel at heart. We're going to need that."

"What do you mean?"

The hand drops. "Lila and Jacek have always wanted to rest. After everything they've each been through, they wanted happy endings. The four of us were prepared to have that together. But then, I think, Lila's death set you off, and you lost grip of everything you've had to carry, so you became a fighter. You joined the Aconites so you'd have more resources, more power, to someday find out the truth behind all these deaths around us. You're always moving, controlling pieces of a game that none of us can see, inciting chaos everywhere. You've had enough of this shitty world, and I respect that.

"The truth is, my mother raised me as a revolutionary. The Descendants have been plotting for generations. I was willing to give that up for Lila and Jacek, but they're gone. And I know you'll never be able to truly rest. The country's current state of unrest means it's almost time. If we can make it through this, I hope we can find peace on the other side. But until then, neither of us will be able to stay put."

Zero's breathing has quickened since Raven revealed her full identity. "What are you saying?"

"I'm saying I have to go," Raven says softly. "I'm sorry."

Zero closes her eyes at those words. People really need to stop saying that.

"Where?" She demands and settles an intense stare on Raven's grim expression. "I'll go with you. Rovis doesn't need to know our plans have changed."

"You can't. I'm going back to my mother and rejoining the forces, so for the safety of our Descendants network, you can't know where I'm going. But I'll keep contact with you, and I need you to stay in touch with all those numbers you have saved on your phone. We'll see each other again soon enough. The criminals and rebels are the same, even though no one wants to admit that. In the end, they're both defying ridiculous laws of the Purish, except the revolutionaries want to change the game, and the Damned like to win the game. They've been walking parallel paths for almost a century now. It's time that they converge." Raven steps closer. "This is a total war."

"Okay," Zero breathes. "I trust you. When are you leaving?"

"After the funeral."

Zero sucks in as much air as her lungs can contain, then releases all of it slowly. She says again, "Okay."

Raven reaches for Zero's shoulders, and Zero meets her with a tight embrace. The uncertainty of when they'll next see each other sits heavily between them, millions of words passing back and forth where they bury their faces in the other's shoulder.

Zero helps Raven pack, though there's not much to pack. None of them owned more than a couple of outfits back in Lime Gateway. They stay up all night after Raven locks her suitcase, talking about unimportant things like movies and music and television shows.

The funeral will begin at dawn, so Zero takes Raven back to her apartment in the Tower when the sky's red lightens to mahogany.

"Chrysanthemums or daffodils?" Zero rotates the mini-greenhouse she's been running in the living room area.

"Both," Raven answers, reaching in for the white and yellow flowers. "Honor their death and wish them a beautiful rebirth, hopefully into a better universe."

Zero nods, preparing three bouquets.

One for Jacek, one for Levi, and one for Ayssa.

The last death surprised Zero, when Rovis muttered about what he found out downtown while carrying her back to her room. It was something the three of them ate during the festival, unsuspecting of the masked person giving away dessert. Zero is both glad that no one else she knows got tricked, and bitter that she still lost people to the government's sick obsession with developing the drugs.

"It's not your fault," Raven says when Zero stares at the third bouquet for too long.

"Maybe it would have been different if I gave her another chance. Before she died. Maybe we could have left on better terms."

"Ayssa changed when she got Lila, you have to know that. She became abusive, and you already had way too much of that at home to deal with it from a former friend. Sometimes there just is no fixing people."

Sighing, Zero gathers her flowers and heads for the elevator.

A sea of Aconites dressed in black and violet is already at the cemetery a few minutes by car south of downtown Dyvris. They stand quietly around the three new Aconite-branded tombstones. The burial grounds are almost overrun with mourners, since the Agency attacked their city, not just the gangsters.

When the sun peeks out over the horizon, Rovis makes his way to the middle and gives a speech that Zero fails to pay attention to. Her eyes remain as dry as the desert they live in. Her heart beats steadily, and her hands don't shake. Surrounded by other grievers, she's suddenly hit with a strong wave of emptiness she didn't think she could feel. Somehow, Zero achieved a new level of numbness.

She doesn't know how many more times she can do this. Drokklo keeps taking and taking, as if punishing her for avoiding the god of death when it was supposed to be her turn. It only makes her wonder, once again, why she hasn't killed herself to escape all this pain in the world.

Rovis must have finished his speech, since Aconites are shifting around and lining up to say their goodbyes to the dead. The boss and the underboss go first, kneeling before each stone, making cuts across their palms and sacrificing blood for the service of each fallen member. Once they finish, Rovis and Tal stand and keep watch next to Ayssa's stone.

Raven sets down her only bouquet before Jacek's stone, whispering promises to make things right and to find their chosen family again in the next life.

Zero follows.

"Sweet Zou Jaa-Xuch," she says his Avyrian name for the first time in ages. "Thank you for everything. Go ahead with the search for peace with Lila, yeah? Raven and I will catch up."

Her lips twitch, attempting to smile. She presses her hand into the dirt for one last farewell before she moves onto Levi's stone. Zero gently adds her flowers to the pile, then sighs as she looks up at the engraving.

"May the fairies guide you to the next world," she says in Ezclovese. She knows Levi didn't speak the language, but she figured he'd appreciate the allusion. He has told her many magical folktales that he learned from translated texts, back when Zero walked around the mansion to shake off nightmares.

For Ayssa, Zero can barely feel the guilt of giving up on her lurking in her chest. Maybe the numbness washed it away, or maybe Ayssa's death made it easier to let go. To the simple tombstone, she only says, "To everything we could have been and could have had."

Flashes of the beginning of their friendship float through her mind. Those innocent laughs and careless hugs seem to have faded centuries ago.

Then everything between them darkened and warped into something else, suffering a sort of corruption driven by a poisonous love and toxic desires. Even though Zero carved Ayssa out of her heart before the cancer spread, she still mourned the loss of what could have been.

"I thought you hated each other," Tal says when Zero joins him, Rovis, and Raven.

"We were friends, once," Zero answers, soft and unfeeling. "Really good friends."

Raven entwines their fingers, subtly yanking Zero toward the gates. As they walk, Zero frowns at the glares that other Dyvrians shoot at the Aconites. When they catch her looking, they quickly turn away, though it's not enough to hide their clenched fists and dark expressions. Zero feels infinitely more exhausted at their reactions.

The Aconites have a rocky road ahead of them, as the blame will fall upon them when the Agency isn't around to take responsibility for what they've done.

A sleek car with tinted windows awaits by the gate. It must be time for Raven to leave.

She's still alive, Zero has to remind herself. *She's only going away for a while.*

One of them has to make it. After watching Lila bleed out from a school shooting, then watching Jacek pass away painfully from the Agency's newest round of experiments, Zero is demanding the entropy, the chaos of the universe to give one of them a peaceful ending. Just one.

"Be careful," Raven says when she opens the driver's-side door.

"You, too." Zero reaches for Raven's shoulder, and they exchange cheek kisses. The last one for a long time.

As soon as Raven drives off, Zero takes out her phone and dials. With the amount of Avyrians gathered at the cemetery today, she rethinks her language choice.

"Hello, baby Ace'," Enyo answers cheerfully.

"I'd like to make another deal," Zero says in quiet Riyssolan to avoid any prying ears. The Mistress of the Daggers was raised by a Riyssolan mafia, after all.

"This sounds serious." Enyo copies her language switch. Her sharp grin is audible over the phone. "What would you like for me to do?"

"An Agent distributed their new wave of drugs in my city. The experiment killed my friends. I want to find out who it was."

"Consider it done, my darling Ace. In exchange, I would like you to look into Didier Whiston. I will send you what we currently have on him."

"Understood. Thank you for your time."

Zero hangs up, her hand dropping to her side and gripping her phone, while her stare stays glued to the view of Dyvris downhill. It looks the same, still bustling and glowing, as if yesterday's disasters never happened.

She might not be able to make the entire Agency pay, but she will make sure that those who were involved with this experiment will have their lives thoroughly ruined.

"You speak all six languages."

Zero turns to see Tal gazing at her, his eyes still glossy. It wasn't a question, so she doesn't have an answer. Behind him, the Aconites have dwindled, the last few members taking their turns at the tombstones.

"Why the hell do you speak Riyssolan?"

Now, that's a question. But she really doesn't have the energy to think back to the lonely days when she decided to learn Lasan and Riyssolan because she loathed not knowing, not understanding everything she sees and hears. If she had no control over her situation, she would find power through knowledge and self-reliance. She refuses to depend on translators, on lines of incomprehensible code that can't possibly capture every meaning of every language, because humans are fickle little things. They lie, they leave, they cheat, and they betray. The Damned may be considered the monsters, but every walking being is tainted. Zero has never bothered to pretend otherwise.

Tal scoffs at her silence, looking away. "Fine. Where did Raven go, and why didn't you go with her? It didn't seem like you two were proceeding as planned when I thought I'd come over to check on you."

Zero shakes her head. This answer, she can't give away.

"You and your secrets," Tal mutters. "It's going to get us all killed some-day."

He stalks away, and Zero absorbs his anger into her void. Perhaps she's supposed to feel guilt, sorrow, or reflected anger from Tal, even. But there's still nothing.

She doesn't know how long she stands there, searching for anything to claim as a sign of humanity within her, until Rovis appears in front of her. A glance at the cemetery tells her that all the Aconites have left.

"Raven?" he asks.

Again, Zero shakes her head, and Rovis accepts that.

"I should have believed you," he says instead, a hint of regret in his voice. "All those years ago, about your father. I know it hurt you when I didn't."

Zero stares at him, startled by the sudden apology.

"It was the drug experiments last night," Rovis explains. "I don't have proof that the same happened to him, but I know it's true. I believe you now."

Words latch onto the inside of Zero's throat. She thinks Tal's slight resentment towards her earlier might have muted her.

"Come on." Rovis tilts his head at the city. "You can ride with me."

She follows. She has nowhere else to go. Of course, Zero has contacts all over the country, and some in other countries, but she'd never be able to stay in those places for more than a month. The Aconite mansion has become the closest thing to a home.

For the next three days, Zero doesn't leave her apartment. She has enough food in the kitchen, and she spends all of her time researching Didier Whiston before she plans to approach him as another fictitious woman. The Heartless keep coming by and requesting entrance, and Zero lets them in but never says anything. Aspen talks her ear off, trying to cheer her up, but Rivka knows that grief works on its own timeline, so she merely shows up to exist beside Zero, without forcing her to speak or do anything other than work.

She appreciates them, of course. She should be sitting down and asking them how they're doing. But she can't afford to slow down, to stop moving, to give the emptiness a chance to take over her body.

Her avoidance routine stops short when she knocks over the pile of books on her nightstand. While picking them up, Zero's heart nearly seizes when she sees the book of Ezclovese fairytales. It was a gift from Levi.

If my corpse of a body can react this way to a book, she forces herself to consider, *how much pain must Tal be in?*

But she's so tired. She doesn't want to think about anyone or anything that's not the task that Enyo has assigned to her. That actually has a purpose, an end goal, an outcome that will solve her real-life issues. Feelings are a useless human trait that she's gotten rid of, so why should it be her problem that other people still have it?

Yet Tal isn't just anyone. He brought her into the organization per her request, even after she tricked him. He shielded her from the hostile members who liked to pick on fledglings. He treated her like a friend, despite his trust issues.

And maybe Levi's death is her fault. If she were transparent about the things she did in Torch City and the things she found out about the Agency, maybe the Aconites could have been better prepared.

But given that she lost Jacek, who was aware of the last round of experiments, maybe it wouldn't have been enough anyway. After all, Zero was too careless to keep track of where the Agency might hit next or the progress of new developing versions of the drug. No, she was too focused on the past, on digging for the truth about people who've already died. She didn't have the foresight to prevent future deaths, and that's on her.

Yes, she finally admits to herself, Levi's death is her fault.

Before she can change her mind, Zero throws on a jacket and strides over to the Poison Core. She slows down once she enters the building.

What, exactly, is she planning to do?

She doesn't even know if she can speak right now. Even if she can, what would she say?

Following the smell of Toullish chicken stew, Zero finds Daleyza in the kitchen. The Reaper looks over and smiles.

"Hey. I haven't seen you in a while. Are you looking for one of the bosses? Because I haven't seen them, either. I don't think they've even come down to have a single meal, trying to figure out who the Agent is."

Zero considers that, nods, and squeezes Daleyza's arm as silent thanks. She takes a large bowl out of the freezer to finish the white cut chicken that she was in the middle of preparing during the Moon Festival.

Her timing is perfect, because Zero finishes carving the chicken around dinnertime. She covers the glass baking dish and piles on a large bowl of rice that Gray cooked, two small bowls, and silverware. Ignoring the odd looks, Zero makes her way to Rovis's office, and the door easily slides open.

Rovis glances up from his computer, clearly expecting her arrival, probably from N.A.D.E., but Tal pretends to busy himself with his holograms.

Zero sets down the dish on the table, and has half the mind to immediately walk back out without any explanation. But she can't be a coward now, not when she owes Tal a confession.

"Thank you," Rovis says, though it sounds more like a question.

Well, I don't know, she wants to say in her weak defense. Food is often the easiest way to bribe someone for forgiveness. Zero breathes in to speak, except no words come out of her open mouth. She tries again, while Rovis watches her patiently and slightly confused.

Still, nothing.

Zero waves a hand and turns away, giving up. Her fingers reach for her necklace, toying with the tiny fox.

Jacek.

Her steps come to a stop, half turning her body back around so that she's facing both Rovis and Tal.

Jacek gave her this necklace when they were twelve, about a week after Rovis left. Zero doesn't wear it when she's out on jobs, afraid to lose it, though she doesn't remember when she last put it on.

She doesn't just owe Tal. She owes Levi, Jacek, and Ayssa, too.

"When I was—" Zero starts, voice scratchy from disuse. She clears her throat and tries again, vacant and soft. "When I was six, my father started to change. He used to sing to me when I couldn't sleep, but one day, he started to break things. His desk, the walls, my door. It wasn't like he became completely violent, like my mother, but there were these moments when he wasn't himself."

Tal still doesn't look at her, but she knows he's listening.

"One night, I couldn't sleep again, and I felt like my skin was boiling, so I went to go find my father. I found him in his office. Rovis already heard this story. I didn't know what my father was doing, or why he was holding a gun so close to his face. I thought, maybe he's checking the barrel. But then he shot himself, and there was blood everywhere, and he was just gone. My mother insisted that he went crazy. That's what she said to justify remarrying so fast. I didn't believe it. As I got older, I heard more things, and I started to build this theory in my head: Maybe it was mind-control. It's not a real thing yet, but the Agency has been trying to make a drug for the last century. They ran out of prisoners to test on, especially with the rising popularity of Drokklo's Playground, so they started secretly testing on low-income neighborhoods. The people that no one would notice when they're gone.

"When I joined the Aconites, I had the resources to infiltrate the Agency. It took me a while to find what I was looking for without setting them off, but I found proof. Not only did I find records of old experiments, I found live entries of current experiments. I found a sample distributed at Arden's Sunset. So I wiretapped communications within the mansion and built a search engine with a burner watch that I stole from Tal's lab before leaving, and I sent Raven the formula of the drug they were testing. She was the strongest in biochemistry, and I knew she could reverse engineer a cure. When I figured out who had the drug in their bodies, I passed on Raven's cure formula to Ofir and told them the names."

Tal has stopped pretending to work at this point. He stares at Zero with an unreadable look. "Who?"

Zero fidgets with her necklace again, gaze falling to the ground in front of Tal.

"You," she answers. "Summer. Kagiso. Riza. Gray."

Neither Rovis or Tal speak.

"I didn't know they had a new version coming up so soon," Zero admits quietly. "It was a huge repository. I didn't know to look for progressing drugs."

Tal sighs heavily.

He closes the distance between them and wraps his arms around her, face pressing into her hair. Zero touches his back with hesitant fingers, then closes her eyes. She knows she doesn't deserve it, but Tal is giving her the forgiveness she sought.

Zero closes her eyes.

Because it isn't enough.

There is no absolution for monsters like her.

And if she's a monster who only knows how to hurt people, she's going to figure out who she needs to hurt next.

14

Hello, Vengeance

"*Once upon a time, there was a beautiful, green country, where colorful birds flew across the blue sky and caracals roamed the land. The folks who lived there were happy. They loved to sing and dance, gathered together every night to feast after a long day of work. It's where you come from, my dear.*"

I smiled at my mother from the comfort of my bed, urging her to continue her story. "What happened next?"

"The Ezclovese Empire wanted what we had. At first, they pretended to befriend us, but they soon ran out of patience and used force. It's what they did to Zessroa, Avyria, and Lasantirk. They wanted to take over the whole world. Once they were done with us, they'd take Riyssola, too."

"But they failed," I said.

"Yes, dear. They took over Zessroa so long ago, the people in power couldn't pay much attention to the bloodlines they stationed there when they were plotting to take four more countries. The descendants of those Ezclovese bloodlines decided that they didn't want to answer to the Empire any longer. They wanted Zessroa for themselves."

"How were they able to fight back?"

"They upgraded weapons and smuggled lots of new designs from Ezclovia. They killed whoever was still loyal to the Empire and declared themselves an independent nation."

"Pureland."

"Not yet. When the Empire didn't recognize them, the Ezclovese descendants combined forces with the Zessroans. You see, the Zessroans were extremely resourceful and skilled in combat. The Purish only came to exist in name when they shook free of the economic oppression Ezclovia imposed upon them for a century, then built up power as its own nation, with the help of the Zessroans. They were so powerful after a couple decades that they formed a navy and freed the Avyrian islands. Then, as the Avyrians regained their technological power, they then joined the Purish and the Zessroans in a vicious war against the Empire. They attacked from the west and freed Toullifuka. It's why so many of our people decided to move here, to Pureland; they see this place as the land of the saviors. But the alliance left Lasantirk to the mercy of Ezclovia as a bargain to end the war."

"Oh, that's why Lasantirk is still a puppet state. But isn't Ezclovia weak now?"

"It is. With Avyria back in the game, they didn't have a technological advantage any longer. And the Purish knew enough about their former mother country to cut off its supplies and force the Ezclovese to agree to conditions in a peace treaty that prevented them from ever becoming an empire again. But Lasantirk doesn't have any allies. The Zessroan natives wanted to help them, but that's when the Purish turned around and drove them to extinction with chemical warfare. That's when they declared the country as Pureland, and the Zessroan nation was no more."

"So what happened to our home?"

"By the time the Purish came to Toullifuka, the Empire had already burned everything to the ground. You see, dear, once they were able to replicate

our plants and crossbred animals to their climate, they couldn't let us keep what they wanted to steal."

I frowned.

"But..." My mother leaned in, brushing hair out of my eyes. "We do live in a world of technology. What none of the Ezclovese or Purish discovered was our underground cities powered by crystals. Toullifuka is still a rich country, only it's a secret."

"But everything on the surface is gone forever?"

"Unfortunately, the world is too warm for that to come back, dear. We can, of course, genetically modify everything, but none of it would be the same as it was before."

"Have you seen the crystal cities?" I asked.

"Yes, and they are beautiful. My favorite was Amethyst Cascades. I want to take you there someday."

"I can't wait for that day, Mother."

She smiled and turned off the lamp. "Go to sleep. I love you, Roz."

❧

"Rovis."

"What?" Rovis blinks away the image of his mother the night before she died. "Did you find anything new on the Agent?"

"No," Tal sighs, sinking onto the couch in their office. "The streets are full of violence. The locals are taking out their anger on us. The Aconites can only think about their survival now, so they're fighting back and injuring civilians, feeding into the bloodshed. It's not like we had an official code, Rov. We just never needed to make moves against the locals, but now that they're turning on us, you can't ask the Aconites to stand there and wait to be lynched. Oh, and did you know Riyssola invaded Ezclovia, which killed most trades with Pureland? Yeah, our businesses are failing, too."

"That's so exciting," Rovis mutters, rubbing his temples. "Forget the rest of the world right now. How are you holding up?"

Tal shakes his head. He sighs, dragging a hand down his face. When he looks up at Rovis, the sorrow in his eyes could drown anyone who peers into them. "I still can't believe he's gone."

Rovis fidgets with his golden hoop, then heaves himself out of his chair and ambles to his kitchenette. He puts milk and chocolate hazelnut spread in a small saucepan, mixing it on low heat until it becomes hot chocolate. After pouring the drink into a mug, he adds marshmallows on the top and hands it over to Tal.

"I know I can't fix anything, but..." Rovis trails off.

"Thank you." Tal shoots him a grateful look, accepting the mug. "You didn't need to make me hot chocolate from scratch."

"It might make everything a little bit easier to bear." Rovis sits down next to Tal. "Does it feel like you're stuck on one thought, the thought that he's gone, and you can't ever move on emotionally, but physically you have to force yourself to keep trudging on day by day?"

Tal shifts his melancholic gaze to study Rovis. "Yes. It does. Sometimes, I don't remember why I keep going. Right now I have revenge, the need to destroy whoever did this to Levi, but once that's over I don't know what will be left."

"That's okay," Rovis says quietly, reaching up to curl a hand around the back of Tal's neck. "One step at a time. Maybe by the time you get there, you'll have found another reason."

"And if I don't?"

"I'll be right there with you. Sometimes, when you can't find a reason, you find out who you can lean on, and you learn that you're not alone, no matter how much it feels like it. I'm not saying you have to feel better right now, or ever, okay? There's no pressure for you to be any certain way. Just do what you need to do, feel what you need to feel, and know that you can always let me know if there's anything I can do to help."

"Wise words." The corner of Tal's lips twitches. "But wisdom is only gained from pain."

Rovis huffs. "You're so dramatic."

"Am I wrong?"

"No, you're almost never wrong." Rovis sighs. "My mom died when I was seven. My dad did everything he could to help me, but he was grieving, too, and he had to keep supporting us. Three years later, I met Zero. She wasn't like how she is now. She was traumatized, but she wasn't self-destructive yet. She was six. And she was the one who helped me find my life again."

Tal stays silent for a moment. Then, he says quietly, "You didn't need to tell me."

"I wanted to." Rovis gently squeezes Tal before retracting his hand. "It is you, after all. I know you've been wanting to know, and I'm sorry it's taking me so long."

"Thank you. For the drink, for saying all those things, for telling me a piece of your story."

"Boss," N.A.D.E. interrupts. "The Ace of Crowns is approaching."

"Allow entry." Rovis crosses an ankle over his leg. "We should really just give her permanent access to this room, shouldn't we?"

It's been a week since Zero came in with her confession about her involvement with the Agency, and she practically volunteered to be their personal meal delivery everyday, though she hasn't spoken at all to either of them. N.A.D.E. for some reason doesn't consider it an important 'minor interpersonal affair' to grant her automatic access. Rovis will never understand artificial intelligence.

"Probably," Tal says, already making the adjustment in the programming from his watch. "Anything we want to keep from her, she'd find out anyways."

The doors slide open, and Zero drops off a tray of Lasan dishes.

"I'm leaving town for a few days with Kagiso," she announces when she turns to face them, crossing her arms.

"Kagiso?" Tal raises a brow.

"You're still working as a Heartless?" Rovis asks, frowning.

Zero blinks at him. "I'm still here. What else would I be doing? And yes, Kagiso. I came here to demand that you two stop skipping meals." She tosses a small bottle of pills at Rovis. "And to actually sleep."

"We're not skipping meals," Tal protests.

"Only because I've been bringing you food— No, instant noodles do not count as meals." Zero sighs heavily. "I'm too old for this."

"Then don't go on whatever job you're taking with Kagiso," Rovis says.

"Too late," she responds flatly. At the look on Rovis's face, she rolls her eyes. "It's too late if you want me to stop being a monster, because this is what I am. And it's too late, because we may have a lead for the Agent. I've also initiated some searches with outside resources. Remind me, what have the two of you found?"

Rovis closes his eyes, trying to regain his patience. He can never manage a long period of peace with Zero. "Not much. We've been tracing through camera footage from around the city, but we lost the Agent within minutes. I don't suppose you have any information to help us, after your time within the Agency?"

Zero looks away.

"It's fine," Rovis says, raking a hand through his hair. He glances at Tal, who's uncharacteristically silent and spaced out. Though, it's reasonable, considering what he's going through right now.

"No, I just—" Zero twists her dragon ring. "I was too focused on their experiment subjects, who I need to keep an eye on, and past records for personal reasons. I didn't look into how they get their data after the initial distribution."

"It's fine," Rovis repeats. "No one asked you to be a one-person surveillance and warning system on mind-control drugs that the Purish government is attempting to produce."

Her fingers twitch, but she doesn't rise to the bait by calling out the edge to his voice. Instead, she pulls out an oddly shaped disk with another heavy sigh.

"Speaking of past records." She presses it into his waiting palm. "I meant to put this on your desk before I left with Raven and Jacek." Rovis hears her voice wobble just slightly with the name. "But, well. I figured I'd wait a bit. One of you needs to be relatively mentally stable at a time."

Rovis frowns. "What is it?"

"It's the truth about Griffin Faal." She takes a step back when his head snaps up. "I think you can guess what that would be, now that you know about the Agency. You don't have to open it; I just thought you should have it."

His eyes shut again as he nods.

One, two, three, four, five.

Six, seven, eight, nine, ten, eleven, twelve.

"It wasn't your fault, Rovis," he hears Zero say in Toullish.

One, two, three, four, five.

Six, seven, eight, nine, ten, eleven, twelve.

"Rovis?" Tal's voice tugs at his mind. Fingers grip his chin and turn his head. "Rovis, name five things you see right now."

Rovis blinks, feeling lightheaded. "Your eyes."

Tal's face freezes, but only for a second. "Okay, keep going."

"Couch. Kitchenette. Desk." His chest heaves with a steadying breath. "Mug."

"Good." Tal studies him for a few moments before releasing his chin.

"I should go," Zero says, already striding out.

"You don't need to," Rovis grits out. "I'm fine."

"And I'm a good person," she mocks. "It's time for me to meet Kagiso. Both of you, stop being stupid and look out for each other while I'm gone. If you're still stuck with the research, look into Emery Marudas and connections he may have with the Purish in Dyvris."

Zero disappears out into the hall.

If his legs weren't feeling like intangible noodles, Rovis would be going after her. Or, at least, he'd order her to stay. He knows Damian got into his head about Zero essentially being a seventeen-year-old seductress, but Damian isn't wrong about this. Rovis doesn't want her to continue working as a Heartless, and not for the reasons she believes him to have.

She's not a monster; she's just a kid who's had bad luck all her life.

Though Rovis doesn't think she'd ever believe him, regardless of how many times he says it.

But stars and bloody cities, the truth about Griffin's death lies in his clutch.

"Rov," Tal nudges softly.

"We had a fight," Rovis begins.

"Just now?" Tal's gaze flicks to the shut door. "That seemed pretty tamed, compared to other fights I've seen."

Rovis shakes his head. "Not Zero. Griffin."

"Oh," Tal whispers, his demeanor shifting to something more attentive.

"Growing up, it was me, Damian, and the twins. When we got to middle school, Griffin and I started to spend a lot of time together, so we ended up dating." Rovis turned Zero's disk in his hand. "Three years passed by, and I loved him more everyday. We weren't without our problems, of course.

We had fights throughout the years, but it became more frequent as we transitioned to high school."

He pauses, taking another deep breath.

Tal silently holds out a gloved hand, an offer.

Rovis takes it, his lips twisting into a poor imitation of a smile. He continues, "I was worried about our relationship, but I didn't ever think it was something we couldn't work through. We were good about communicating. I think we were just growing older, into the age of understanding the world without the naïveté of youth, so that we became more difficult for each other."

He looks up, closing his fingers over the disk. "One day, we had this huge fight right before our wrestling tournament during ninth grade. All four of us were on the team, but Griffin decided to tell our coach that he was sick because he was so angry at me. I still went to the competition, thinking that giving him time to cool down would help, so afterwards we can talk about it. But what really happened..."

Rovis sighs, frustrated.

One, two, three, four, five.

Six, seven, eight, nine, ten, eleven, twelve.

Tal squeezes his hand, waiting. Rovis knows that he can either decide to finish the story or stop, and Tal wouldn't question it. But maybe Rovis really has been holding this in for too long. It feels like the longer he keeps it locked up, the more it poisons him.

"We followed Jordan back to their place. And we found Griffin lying on the floor in the kitchen." Tears prick at his eyes, and he tries to blink them away. "He was holding a knife. There was so much blood."

Slowly, Tal wraps an arm around Rovis, resting his face against a slumped shoulder. When Rovis stays silent, clearly finished, Tal says softly, "You really don't have to open it. Zero's right. You know she always is."

"Tal," Rovis whispers, closing his eyes again. "Does it really make a difference if Griffin killed himself because of our fight or because the Agency experimented on him?"

"You know now that it *was* because of the Agency. I never knew him, but I don't think he would have done it by himself. I think he loved you, too, and that love that you two had was strong. You wanted to work things out, and so did he. Griffin wouldn't have walked away from you like that. Maybe he did feel that low, maybe he didn't. Either way, he would have told you, because you're worth fighting for."

"Yet it was still because of me that he separated from us that day. If I got him to come with us, he wouldn't have fallen into the experiment trap, and he'd be alive."

Tal shakes his head. "I don't know, Rov. I think the same thing about Levi. I think about how Zero saved me from the same fate, but I feel like I cheated Drokklo. Because why do I deserve the luck to survive it, when Levi didn't even stand a chance?"

Sighing, Rovis gently leans his head on top of Tal's. "Maybe there's no such thing as 'deserve.' Because if it worked like that, you and I, we'd both be dead a hundred times over. Maybe it's all just probability and chance, and the universe doesn't care."

"Maybe there's no point in thinking about the what-ifs," Tal wonders quietly, his sorrowful stare reaching worlds away. After what feels like hours of silence, he sighs and asks, "Do you want to talk more, or should we get on with the Marudas research?"

As much as Rovis wants to wallow in their shared grief, he needs to get up. He's the Scavenger. He needs revenge for his people, and answers for all the other victims in Dyvris.

"Let's see who the director of the Agency really is," Rovis answers, shifting to leave the couch, though he very much misses the comfortable position they were in. "Does he have any other names?"

"A few, but once we know one, it's easy to find the rest." Tal opens up his holograms. "Activate search engine, Purish business records in Dyvris, look for Emery Marudas and his aliases, from the branch folder I made a month ago."

"You've investigated him," Rovis says, not quite a question.

"Very little. Only scraped the surface when the Faceless revealed the Agency." The Faceless have shown themselves two more times since then, each time exposing more of Purish cruelty, but not much more on the Agency.

Rovis nods, going through the list of Purish businessmen that Bianchi has dealt with.

"Thomas Revyxon," Tal reads from a list of Marudas's associates, looking up to see Rovis's stare. His holograms flash and flicker all around him, searching and calculating. "Looks like little Wyatt Revyxon's archaic watch from his dad has gotten a lot more useful. N.A.D.E., pull up our decrypted script from the Revyxon watch."

Purple numbers and Purish text hover in the air.

"A few more results from the search engine from our records in Dyvris," Tal says, his brain moving as fast as ever, his program running even faster. "Marudas has met with Sandra Lewis. Jeremy Wright. Deborah Adams."

"I've dealt with Wright before, when Bianchi wanted me to steal things from him while they were having a pretentious meeting." Rovis stands and pulls on a suit jacket. "Get a team of Reapers and Digitals for me, I'm going to Wright's headquarters right now. You can come if you want to interrogate him, or you can stay if you want to work on finding more leads."

Tal rolls up his sleeves, eyes still glued to the holograms. "I'll come with you. The program will keep running on the supercomputer while we're gone, and we'll have everything by the time we get back."

Rovis nods and strides to his room, the one he's had since joining the Aconites. After killing Bianchi, he technically has the penthouse of the

Poison Core, but he always found that idea distasteful. The one he has on the fifth floor is spacious and familiar.

He gathers his knives and guns and wires, slotting them in the usual arrangement of sheaths all over his body.

The Scavenger is, after all, the king of Dyvris.

When Tal meets him on the ground floor, he's got the manic grin of Lithium etched on his face again. Twirling a knife, he drawls, "It's been a while since we've done something like this, hasn't it, Boss?"

"Is everyone ready?" Rovis asks.

"Everyone is at your service, my liege." Tal bows with a flourish, a dangerous gleam returning to his eyes.

Falling into routine, Rovis smirks.

Though he has to ignore the heat pricking at the back of his neck as he leads the way out of the mansion. They take the newest model of a Shapeshifter, and Gray drives them to the city in a limousine. When they stop in front of Wright's headquarters, Tal gets out from the front and opens the door for Rovis.

It's theatrical and completely unnecessary, but as Tal insisted back when they first took over the Aconites, it 'exudes power.' Rovis still thinks he's just making up for all the drama classes he didn't take as a kid.

Like a prowling thunderstorm, the security system of the headquarters shuts down when Rovis walk through the doors, Tal one step behind and slightly to the right of him, five Reapers trailing after them. The poor employees at the front desk stammer with fear, but Rovis pays them no mind.

Because the elevator opens up for him even without card access, thanks to the Digitals back in the mansion hacking into the building while watching Rovis's every move. They take him straight to the top.

He strolls out to ten guns pointing at him and the two Reapers who are now in front of him.

"You have some nerve," Jeremy Wright snarls, "showing up here, *Scavenger.*"

Glass windows surround the man, the views of the city making him seem insignificant in the midst of a vermilion sky and riots in the streets. Rovis doesn't flinch at Tal's abrupt laugh, the one that can make an entire building freeze and everyone in it tremble.

"You do realize whose city you're standing in, Jersey Ryan?" Tal drawls, tossing his knife.

"It's Jeremy—"

"Right, my bad, Jamie Wrinkle."

"*Wright.*"

"I finally got it right? Why, thank you. However, the point is—"

Having had enough of Tal's antics, Rovis holds up a hand. Tal immediately shuts up, with that unhinged grin etched on his face, no doubt.

Rovis tilts his head at Wright and sharpens his gaze. "I merely want to talk."

"Schedule an appointment like everyone else."

"Where's the fun in that? This is a surprise visit, Jeremy."

Wright grits his teeth. "Get out. You're outnumbered. Leave, before I order my team to shoot you."

"Oh." Rovis clicks his tongue. "About that."

Darkness takes over, all the lights cut off and the windows gone opaque. When the lights fade back on, Tal is standing next to Rovis, a wild grin stretched across his face and his chest rising and falling as if he just went on a run.

Rovis's Aconite Reapers now hold two guns each, and the people on Wright's side exchange bewildered glances, hands empty.

Tal sure loves his electromagnets.

"Now." Rovis saunters to the long, curvy couch and sits, leaning all the way back with an ankle on top of a knee and his arms stretched out over the back. "Would you like to talk, Jeremy Wright?"

"I liked you better when you were Quade Bianchi's *toy*."

A knife flies past Wright's head, slicing off a strand of hair, and lands with a crack in the window. Rovis lazily turns his head to look at Tal, raising an eyebrow. Tal shrugs with his hands splayed out, wide eyes falsely innocent.

"What? You said I couldn't take his tongue until after you're done. That was only a hair. Surely you won't punish me for that, Boss?"

"Keep it in your pants, will you?" Rovis says with a bored tone.

The knife returns back to Tal's metal hand with a clink, and he tucks it back where it belongs. He mock-salutes him with two fingers. "As you wish, my king."

Satisfied, Rovis turns his attention back to Jeremy Wright. Face white as a sheet, the man sits down across from Rovis, movements slow with caution.

"There we go," Rovis says, like praising a toddler for swallowing his food without throwing a tantrum. "Now, tell us about Emery Marudas."

Wright glares at him stubbornly.

Rovis raises a brow, unimpressed. "My second has quite the temper, I'm sure you've noticed. If you don't talk, I'm going to be annoyed, and you'll find your throat at the mercy of Lithium's claws."

"I don't know much about Marudas," Wright says tightly, as though pulling out teeth. "He wanted to buy a cure from me, once, but that was the only time I met him."

"Cure for what?"

"The white vein disease. His son got stuck in Hilobis when he was supposed to be there on a week-long trip because of the recent zoonotic virus outbreak, but he was also already carrying the sexually transmitted virus. There's no cure for the white vein disease. My company sells an antiretroviral that hides the symptoms and stops the virus from replicating in the host's body, so the son would live as long as he took the drug. But it doesn't purge the infected person of the virus, and it's still transmittable. Even then, it's the best option in the world, so Marudas bought it from me, and he had already bought the cure for the Hilobis virus. Once he had both, he made an arrangement with a bunch of people to get his son out of the quarantined city."

Rovis scoffs. The filthy rich really can buy their way out of anything, can't they? As one of the most wealthy of the Damned, even he'd have to save up a hundred times more to be able to do what Marudas did.

"His son," Rovis says, "what's his name?"

"You can't find him. They changed his surname."

Rolling his eyes, Rovis raises one hand by a hair and flicks his fingers. "Lithium."

"Wait—"

One of Wright's guards crumples to the ground, her broken neck looking wrong on the pristine carpet.

Wright looks back at Rovis, flushed and fuming, more insulted rather than concerned about the dead woman.

"The son's name," Wright spits out, "is Didier Whiston."

15

Tomb's Day

It turns out that the only crime Didier Whiston has committed is releasing an expensive line of helmets and masks for the impending disaster of poison gas in the atmosphere, and has claimed the patent on it. With the heating climate, a threat of methane eruption and escaping hydrogen sulfide tosses another headache into the boiling pot of political unrest and bloodshed.

Even with countless all-nighters of research, they've found nothing on the Marudas's son. Not even a hint of a connection to the Agency, let alone any leads to who was involved with Levi's murder.

Which is why Tal sits on the roof of the Poison Core, legs dangling off the sides above their wolfsbane garden in the middle of the circular building. The glass dome is deactivated today to give the plants a bit of unfiltered air. For what reason, Tal doesn't know. He doesn't know anything about modern botany, with the world ending and whatnot, but the Aconites are the only producers in the country, so someone in the organization must know what they're doing.

He takes another swig of liquor from Quade's old stash. His eyelids slide shut, and he has to lie down on his back from how much his head spins.

"Another dead end," Tal slurs to the dead sky.

All they found out was Marudas has a spoiled son with a wealthy business that sells overpriced products. It told them nothing about who distributed the drug, why they chose Dyvris, how long it's been planned, or what was in the drug. As much as Tal would love to tear out Emery Marudas's throat and destroy Didier Whiston's business so that he has nothing left except the will of survival like the rest of the population, the Aconites don't have the resources to even get close to the father and son. They have the entire Agency behind them. They have all the weaponized robots owned by the federal government. They are protected by ex-army soldiers and even stronger cybersecurity than the chief of state. Tal knows of that fact personally, given that he successfully hacked into the president's home when he was a fledgling, and now the sight of Marudas's network makes him want to drown himself in vodka.

Burning the entire Agency of Justice to the ground would be the best revenge for Levi, but Tal can't manage that. Even Lithium has his limits. In fact, the Agency is probably just biding its time to exterminate the Damned, and none of the organizations would stand a chance against their resources and coordination. All Tal is trying to do is to find the one, singular Agent who showed up at their city on the night of the Moon Festival, so he can avenge his friend's death before his own sorry demise.

Over the past two weeks, since that useless confrontation with Jeremy Wright, Rovis has barely been at the mansion, running after possible leads all over the city. Tal told Rovis every morning that he'd stay in to keep searching for more, but in reality he's been drinking in the penthouse that Rovis refuses to step foot in while his programs do his job.

He holds the bottle over his mouth again, shaking out the last drops with the bottom pointing up at the moon.

Tal lets his arm drop to the side. He feels like he's asking the heavens for a hug.

As if he isn't a Damned. As if he hasn't already been forsaken.

"Pathetic," he berates himself, pulling his legs off the edge to sit up so he can grab another bottle from the cooler. He pops off the top with his claws and gulps down another mouthful.

When they were fourteen, Tal and Levi loved to drink on the roof together at night. They couldn't see the city because of the mountains, but nature was just as appealing, especially with the stars and constellations dancing across the sky.

Tal kissed Levi first.

Levi warned him that they'd never have anything serious, because he felt no attraction towards anyone. Tal laughed and assured him it was just for fun.

And they had lots of fun. They were teenagers; of course they threw everything else out the window. They went to clubs in the city, drank on the roof, made out beneath the moon, hooked up under the night sky.

Tal still can't remember when they stopped being young and foolish. Fun used to be the default; work with the Aconites was secondary. Even when they were working in the Mechs lab together, they teased each other when Lowell wasn't looking. He can't remember when spending time together started needing to be scheduled, when Levi saw through Tal's feelings towards Rovis, when they both spent almost all their time truly working.

A small, slender hand snatches the bottle out of his lax grip.

He looks up, blinking through his blurry vision until he's squinting at Zero. Her face is blank, and she looks perfectly calm until she throws the bottle to the side. Her eyes don't follow the trajectory to watch it shatter on the ground, its contents spilling out.

"Oh," Tal laughs. "You're angry."

"It's not even close to noon," Zero bites out.

"Whoever made the rules that drinking is only for the nighttime?"

Zero sucks in a breath and lets it out slowly, like how Rovis does sometimes when he's trying to find his patience. They're actually very similar, Tal realizes in his drunken haze.

"Get up," she demands, the soft volume belying her fury.

"I don't want to."

"Get up, or I'm calling Rovis, and you really wouldn't want to bother him today."

Her threat makes no sense in Tal's head. "He's in the city."

"No, he's not." Zero crosses her arms. "Do you even know what day it is?"

"Every day feels the same," he shoots back.

She sits down in front of him, crossing her legs. Her elbows dig into her knees as she leans forward to peer into Tal's eyes with a tilted head.

"Today is your Dance of Wraiths holiday," she says. Then in Lasan, "You do not look like you're planning to go to the *Méliaklos* festival."

Tal sways, chuckling and unfeeling. "I forgot."

"When was the last time you talked to Rovis?"

"Last night." He wipes his mouth. "You said he's not in the city. He's definitely not here, so where do you think he is?"

"Cemetery," she answers as though it's obvious.

"Again? What for?"

Zero shakes her head. "Not here. Not in Dyvris. He's at the cemetery in Lime Gateway."

"And he told you this?"

She snorts. "No, I got back an hour ago, just to find you looking like this. It just so happens that this year, the Toullish Tomb's Day also falls on the same day as the Lasan *Méliaklos*. Rovis is at his mother's grave from sunrise to sunset. I'm visiting him, and you're coming with me."

"Good luck trying to carry me."

"I don't need to," Zero says haughtily. "I'll be downstairs."

She leans over to one side and rolls off the edge of the roof.

Tal looks after her sluggishly, until he remembers that the Poison Core is fourteen stories tall. He stumbles on his hands to look down, only to see the swaying of purple flowers and green weeds where Zero must have fallen through.

"Stars-damned bloody cities and rotten corpses," he curses, staggering back to the penthouse and into the elevator. Tal storms out to the wolfsbane garden, but he can't find her anywhere.

And it's quite embarrassing that he gets lost in the garden.

After finally discovering a way out of that maze, he goes around the ground floor of the Core, and ends up finding Zero stuffing a thermos into a bag.

"Are you out of your mind?" Tal growls. He puts a hand on the fridge to keep his balance, but she hauls the bag over her shoulder and slaps a bottle of water at his chest and leaves.

"Probably," Zero answers breezily.

Tal scrambles after her. "You could've died. Even if you miraculously survived, you could've hurt yourself." He thinks Zero laughs, but he's too dizzy to be sure. "Wait, how are you walking? Your legs should be shattered right now."

She holds a hand, and a new cuff bracelet sits on her wrist. "I stole this from your lab."

Tal squints at the product. His heart lurches when he recalls that it was on his work-in-progress table when he last saw it.

"That's a prototype," Tal snaps. He's been working on a device that would form a flexible bubble of energy shield around the user, automatically adjusting to a wide range of sizes, as opposed to the primitive two-dimensional shields everyone's been using. But right now it can only work for fifteen seconds before it collapses from disequilibrium.

"I tested it for you. It works great. Good job, Tal."

"You shouldn't have—"

"Oh, my apologies," Zero says, sarcastic. "I didn't realize it was only okay for you to fall off the roof, and not me."

"What—"

"You're *drunk*," she seethes, yanking the car door open. When did they arrive at the garage? "I don't want to hear another word from you until you can talk properly."

Zero then shoves the bag at Tal before pushing him into the passenger seat. When she settles in next to him and the doors slam shut, Tal stares at her, uncomprehending.

"What's happening here?"

"No." She holds up a finger at him. "What did I just say?"

Tal narrows his eyes at her.

"Seriously, you know how much I hate driving," Zero grumbles, backing out of the parking spot. "But no, you decided to get drunk. Whatever. There's food in the bag, and you better eat all of it by the time we get to the cemetery. And drink all of the water."

Tal shuffles through the bag. He carefully takes out two bouquets of flowers. The thermos steams with chicken and rice, and another bowl has frozen grapes and slices of bananas. Tal opens his mouth, but Zero turns up the alternative rock music without looking over at him.

He scowls and shakes his head, digging a fork into the chicken. *Message received.*

When Tal's head stops throbbing, and his mind starts to clear up, a heaviness sinks into his chest and his shoulders. He doesn't know what he's doing. He's never known. Running away from his pain, trying to numb himself with alcohol, laughing off every twitch of discomfort, none of that can last forever. In the end, everything still hurts, and he's still alone.

But he remembers Rovis's words.

Sometimes, when you can't find a reason, you find out who you can lean on, and you learn that you're not alone, no matter how much it feels like it.

Tal sneaks a glance at Zero when he exchanges the empty thermos for the bowl of fruits. She's so young, yet she's trying to take care of two grown men in her own way. Rovis has always been looking for her soft side, ever since Tal brought her in, chasing the remnants of their past. But maybe this is it. Maybe, after all the things that she's been through for however long she was separated from Rovis, this is what she became. It's not any less than a conventional image of caring, in Tal's opinion.

The buildings passing by the car window spread out more as Zero takes them out of the city and into the suburbs. Tal swallows a grape too quickly when he sees the burnt rubbles of Lime Gateway High School. Jagged lumps of melted metal must be what used to be lockers, and chars of bricks still cover the entire quarter of a mile that the building used to take up.

Zero doesn't seem to react to the suburban wasteland, zooming past the school without a lingering glance. She parks outside the metal fence of the cemetery and kills the engine. The obnoxious music fades out.

"Thank you," Tal says.

She looks over at him, scans his face and the bag, then rolls her eyes. She unlatches the door and says, "Shut up."

"Zero."

"What," she snaps, exasperated and impatient.

Tal reaches out a hand, slow enough for her to stop him. When she doesn't, only blinking at him with blank confusion, he gingerly touches her hair.

"Thank you," he repeats more deliberately.

Zero nods, movement drawn-out like Tal's a toddler who just told her an incoherent discovery about birds, a single eyebrow lifted. "Okay."

She snatches up a bouquet and hurries out the car. Any onlookers might think there's a swarm of deadly wasps inside. Tal chuckles softly and follows her with the other bouquet.

Rovis is kneeling in front of a short stone, burning incense. A basket and a bottle of red wine sit next to him. Tal watches Zero approach Rovis, who tenses and turns at the sound of footsteps but visibly relaxes when he realizes it's her. Zero carefully holds Rovis's face with her free hand and touches her forehead against his.

Tal pauses, surprised by Zero's display of affection. The relationship between her and Rovis must be improving. It takes a minute for Tal to realize the ends of his lips have curled up into small but genuine smile, nothing like Lithium's menacing sneer.

He schools his expression when Zero straightens, releasing Rovis, and holds out her arrangement of pink orchids and tulips. He accepts the flowers and holds out his other hand, which Zero holds as she kneels down next to Rovis. She watches him pick out the flowers one by one and burn them to ash.

When Tal moves to join them, another familiar figure catches his eye.

Daleyza.

His feet change their trajectory, and he makes his way to what must be Dakota Etienam's stone. A flash of guilt pricks Tal's skin as he realizes he never properly honored Dakota after saving him from those Purish sadists.

Daleyza's sister was the one who threw off Tal's attackers.

She was the one who killed all of them right in front of his eyes.

She was the one who brought him to Ofir to get his arm amputated safely, before the infection spread, then drove him back to Lime Gateway.

"Hey," Tal says softly.

Daleyza looks up. "Tal. Have you been here before?"

"No." He glances at the flowers in his hands. In a moment of decision, he pulls out one orchid and offers her the rest. "I should have done this a long time ago."

"Thanks," she says, taking the flowers. "I didn't really blame you, you know. I know you think I do, and I never bothered to correct you. But I didn't back then, and I certainly don't today."

Words get lost in Tal's throat.

"It was in her nature to help, especially seeing what you had to go through." Daleyza burns a tulip. Her blank expression and empty eyes is jarring, where Tal is used to seeing a poised daredevil. "Quade was the one who ordered her into a trap and basically sent her on a suicide mission."

"She shouldn't have paid the price for saving me. I was lucky that she was there. I owe her my life," Tal says quietly.

"It's all in the past, Tal," she says, burning another flower. "Thank you for coming."

Tal reaches out to squeeze her shoulder, and Daleyza curls a hand over his, squeezing back. Footsteps sound behind him, and he looks back to see Summer trotting over to Daleyza with her own bouquet of flowers. When she sees Tal, she gives him a small smile and a nod.

"Go," Daleyza tells him. "I'm not alone. Go be with him."

Hesitant, Tal glances back at her unguarded expression. At that, she lets out a soft chuckle.

"She'd be proud, you know. You're one of the most vicious monsters to walk this planet, yet you're still hiding a big heart." She turns her gaze to Rovis and Zero. "You've taken good care of them."

"You have, too, with Zero."

Daleyza's ghost of a smile lingers on the girl before she looks back at Tal. Despite the numbness, her eyes reveal the quiet strength that Tal's always secretly admired. She merely says, "We protect family."

"Aconites may not share blood with family," Tal recites his vows, voice low and heavy.

"But we spill blood for family," Daleyza and Summer finish together. Tal lifts his eyes to study Summer's laid-back stance, arms crossed but relaxed, but he knows she'd be ready to slash through an army of Agents within a heartbeat.

The three of them exchange long glances of silent understanding, the most connected Tal has ever felt with any Aconite other than Rovis, before he nods to excuse himself. Leaving them to privacy with Daleyza's sister, Tal trudges back to Rovis and Zero.

Zero sees Tal approaching and stands, while Rovis watches him, head tilted up. Tal kneels down on one leg and sits back on his heel, offering Rovis the last orchid that blooms brilliantly against the black of his leather glove.

Rovis blinks at him, a tentative smile etched on his face, his brows slightly furrowed.

"I didn't realize I grabbed a red one," Zero says.

"Oh." Tal takes another look at the flower. He guesses it does look darker than the other ones. It's hard to tell under the sun. "It's close enough to pink. Does it still work?"

Rovis huffs, amused. "Yes."

His fingers brush against Tal's, the leather materials catching onto each other. They watch the petals turn black and wrinkle in the flames. When it's done, silence rings in his ears, an eerie peace with scattered bird calls and rustling wind among the resting dead. Zero isn't standing over Rovis's shoulder anymore.

"Is it okay if I stay?" Tal asks.

"Of course." Rovis sniffs, frowning. His fingers skim the dried spots on Tal's shirt. "You've been drinking."

Tal sighs. "Where did Zero go?"

"Probably to the high school. Don't bring her into this; she didn't tell me anything. I can smell it on you. Why haven't you talked to me about this?"

"There's nothing to talk about," Tal says. "I don't want to keep feeling like this all the time."

"Tal," Rovis sighs. "I know. But drinking is risky, especially for you. You know it is. Is there any way you can try something else? Something that I can help with?"

"I don't know." Tal's fingers curl into fists on his legs. "I'll think about it, for you. And I don't want you to worry about me right now. Can I give you an answer later?"

"You can, but you should know you're not a burden to me, okay? Whatever you need, you can ask for, and I'll do my best to give it to you."

"Don't say that."

"I'm sick of losing people, Tal," Rovis says, voice tired. "I know you're grieving. You know I know what it's like. Let me help while I still can. I lost that chance with too many people I care about. Don't shut me out, *biv'ye nu wanotai.*"

Tal almost flinches at the Toullish phrase. He's heard Rovis and Zero say it enough times that he knows what it means and why they use it instead of the Purish alternative. What he doesn't know is why it's all of a sudden being used on him.

"Okay," he says quietly. His legs twitch with chagrin. "I want to go for a walk, but I will be back. Are you fine here?"

Rovis nods. "Will you take that walk to the high school? I worry about Zero. She might blame herself for the fire."

"Yeah, I'll do that," Tal answers, standing and brushing dirt off his slacks. "And I'll work on what you asked of me, Rov. I'm used to being alone, so give me some time."

"Anything," Rovis says.

Tal has to turn away before he passes out from the flush of heat in his face, a tragic combination with the desert air in a world on the brink of irreversible damage. His breathing doesn't even out until the high school comes into view.

Rovis is... unreal.

The amount of kindness and compassion he has shown Tal since they first met makes him think that all of this has been a figment of his imagination, a sweet lie of his own subconsciousness, a piteous outcome of his coping mechanisms.

He's afraid that the second he accepts Rovis into his heart, the other man would just disappear into thin air.

When Tal gets closer to Lime Gateway High School, he sees a small but solid figure sitting in the middle of the ruins.

"The Faceless made a reappearance today," Zero says without looking at Tal. "It was a compilation of all the major cities that got screwed over by the experiments."

"Did you run all the way over here to watch the news?" Tal responds dryly.

"Rovis told you about Griffin," she guesses.

"Yes."

"I had something similar. You'd think I've had my fair share of trauma after losing my father to the drug experiments when I was five. In ninth grade, Wyatt Revyxon walked in here and started shooting. My best friend got caught in the crossfires and bled out to death, because no one was coming to help. Raven, Jacek, and I had to watch her soul leave her body." Zero laughs, an empty, hollow sound. "Isn't it funny how both Rovis and I lost someone important around the same age in high school because of Purish hatred?"

Tal's at a loss for words. Before Levi died, he might have had the energy to slip on his Lithium facade and bring humor to everything. But Tal feels emptied out, and this is *Zero*. There's absolutely nothing funny about this.

"Anyway, so I couldn't stay here after I finished out the year," she continues. "I hated being powerless. I found you to submit myself to Quade Bianchi for power, for resources, for revenge. But while I was gone, Raven and Jacek almost lost their lives to a stars-damned fire. Again, Purish hatred. Then I thought I was making it up to them by letting them back in, just to experience an echo of my father, a repeat of Lila, watching Jacek die."

Tal sighs heavily and holds up a hand.

Squeezing her eyes shut, Zero shakes her head.

Tal drops his arm and sits down next to her. "Levi's last words were to tell Rovis the truth. My truth. About how I feel. I promised him I would, but I don't think I can do it."

"You feel like you're betraying him."

"Because I would be. I was with Levi, but I was always thinking about Rovis."

"Levi knew that. You both knew exactly what your agreement was. It's not like you lied to him, Tal."

"He still felt like he wasn't enough," Tal laments.

"No, he recognized that you were changing and could try something different. Listen, you know Levi was supposed to be a Heartless." Tal nods. "He was like me. So trust me when I say this: When we don't feel attraction like other people do, choices are what matter the most. From the time when you two got together until the moment he died, you chose him. You chose to spend time with him, to listen to him when he spoke, to be there for him when he's not at his best. Strong relationships are built on trust and actions and communication. Passion may give you that first spark, but continuous choices keep the flame alive. For people like me, and like Levi, we don't have the advantage of that spark. This society teaches us that we're not love-able since we don't do 'love at first sight.' But you made Levi feel important in this shitty world, because you kept choosing him over and over again. That was an amazing gift to give him, and you should know that he loved you enough to want you to go after the spark you feel with Rovis."

Zero sips from a bottle of water that she must have gotten from the car before coming here. She adds, "And I trust you enough to know that you two will make those choices for each other."

"I'm not ready," Tal whispers.

"None of you alloromantic people ever are." Zero hops down from the charred stones gracefully, and they walk back to the cemetery together. "But I won't push you. It's all your choice, really. How much do you want all the bad things that have happened to you to hold you down for the rest of your life? That's something my therapist asked me. I've been thinking about it, to be honest."

"I didn't realize you actually went to therapy."

Zero hums. "I don't make it easy on her. Anyway, I want to take the car to go somewhere. Are you fine with riding with Rovis? You should take him to *Méliaklos* when the sun sets. Just... don't eat anything."

"Are your not-so-subtle attempts to get me near him also your way of 'not pushing' me?"

"Uh, yes. I'm not forcing your hand to confess or anything like that. You're good for each other, no matter what you are and what you want to label yourselves as. Friends, partners, maybe something else in the future, whatever." She knocks back almost all of the water. "I don't see the point of depriving yourselves of the good things you already have just because you might not be ready to try something different. Life's too short."

Tal peers at her, standing outside of the metal fences again. "Are you sure you're not secretly a hundred?"

Zero shrugs. "I'm taking the car."

"Fine," he says, waving an arm. "Be careful of the riots."

She rolls her eyes, gets in the car, and drives off.

Tal turns away and finds Rovis again. The glass bottle is now empty, its red wine spilt at the foot of the stone. The sun burns above the horizon, ready to take its leave for the day in a couple hours. Tal sits down next to Rovis, and they both remain silent while the golden rays of light wash over the graves.

When the last of the sun disappears, Rovis shifts and stands, shaking out his stiff muscles.

Tal doesn't move.

"Come to the *Méliaklos* festival with me?" he asks, tilting his head back to watch Rovis's expression.

Rovis only smiles, relieved and empathetic and benevolent.

"Yes."

16

Young Lunacy

Lasan music shakes the ground as musicians prance down the streets of central Dyvris and dancers snake their bodies on the rolling stages.

Zero sips on her tea as she watches over the *Méliaklos* festival from her spot on top of Arden's. The neon glow of luminescent buildings has taken over the natural rays of the sun, coloring the pollution in the air. She watches Rovis pull up his car by the club she's sitting on top of, and she almost smiles when Tal gets out of the passenger side.

The pair of men walk closely together as they join the parade, sometimes brushing hands and exchanging quiet and serene glances.

It is, after all, a day of honoring the dead in both their cultures.

Zero pities the people who fear death, who think they can run away from it or buy their way out of it. Death is written in every newborn's story, an undeniable truth that does not discriminate between the privileged and the poor, the kind and the cold-blooded, the blessed and the damned. Only when one makes peace with that fact will they learn to live in the moment and wish their lost ones a painless journey to the next life.

"I'm going somewhere better now," Jacek says, appearing by her side. "With Lila. And Raven can take care of herself. Rovis and Tal are on the way to becoming what they need to be. You don't need to be worried about anything right now."

"I know," Zero says, her eyes flitting over the masses below.

Violence and riots paused this morning to make way for their traditions. Her throat is starting to feel scratchy as if she's coming down with a cold, though she can't recall where she would have caught it, especially when her immune system is bolstered by all the vaccines she had when she joined the Aconites.

"The experiment failed," Lila joins in on her other side. "You know the Agency isn't here anymore. There's nothing to observe, nothing to test, nothing to bring them to Dyvris. They're back on their theory and calculations phase."

"I know," Zero repeats, sighing. Even her own subconsciousness can be so tiresome. "Death is so much easier for the dead. I'm glad you're not here anymore, but I wish you were still with me. It's the innate human selfishness driven by the omnipresent loneliness, I suppose."

She gets distracted when she catches the walls of the Wright headquarters change to a public call for any information on the Faceless. The prize for anyone who provides useful information that will lead to a capture will receive ten million units.

"Saige," Lila says.

Zero fidgets with her dragon ring. One of the leaders of the Faceless have already been captured. A woman named Fyuva Mekonnen. Holographic livestreams popped up in the plazas of every city, publicizing her sentencing to Drokklo's Playground, where she only lasted a few hours of gladiatorial matches before a mechanical elephant stomped her to death.

Zero really hopes Saige is lying low these days.

Her watch vibrates.

Where are you? Kagiso's text flashes. *There's something you need to know about Whiston.*

Frowning, she responds, *Arden's. Where do you want to meet?*

Mansion, my room. 411 in the House.

Be there in seven.

Both Jacek and Lila have disappeared when Zero rises to take the stairs. The team she and Kagiso took to Torch City worked flawlessly, and they got to Didier Whiston without a problem, when Zero disguised herself as a young businesswoman. Of course, they had that usual car chase out of the capital when the girl keeping track of entry logs of the penthouses realized none of the Aconites actually existed in the official system. But that's pretty much the standard experience of going on a heist with the Opulent House.

Kagiso got the documents they came for, and his sticky fingers snatched pockets full of jewelry, somehow already rid of trackers that definitely would have set off alarms if moved out of place.

So, Zero would call their mission a success.

"What?" she demands as soon as she swings open Kagiso's door.

Kagiso doesn't look at her from his relaxed position in his extravagant sofa by the window, legs propped on an oversized coffee table.

He lifts his stemless wine glass and takes a sip.

As usual, he's barely wearing anything. His black silk robes drape over the edges of his seat, untied to display his shiny pendants. Zero supposes she should be grateful that he's wearing shorts, though the entire organization has probably seen him in much less.

Annoyed, Zero turns on her heel to walk out.

"Wait," Kagiso calls.

"Don't waste my time," she bites out.

He scoffs and flicks a small disk at her without looking over. She catches it without flinching. Zero didn't even notice he was holding anything other than the glass. Maybe that's the point of all those unnecessary rings. He's only a year older than Zero, but his jewelry collection is almost ten times as large as hers.

The disk is the kind that the Aconites can fit in their watch and open the files remotely, so Zero slides it into the slit. Holographic folders shoot out from the top of her wrist.

"Check medical history," Kagiso instructs. "Latest entries."

Zero reluctantly follows and searches through the files. The medical history document is irritatingly in chronological order, so she has to scroll all the way to the bottom.

"Oh, that privileged bitch," she mutters when she sees that Didier Whiston was supposed to be in isolation in Hilobis if his rich father didn't buy his way out of the zoonotic disease and quarantine. Zero already knew that he was Marudas's son when she was researching him for Enyo, but she couldn't find any information on his whereabouts from the last two years.

Zero's face slacks with surprise when she sees the other virus that Didier Whiston has.

WVM-67. No known cure. Click for antiretroviral options.

If Whiston has the white vein malady, then...

"You should get tested," Kagiso says quietly when he feels Zero growing tense from gradual understanding, still refusing to look at her.

"Steal a test kit from Ofir's office for me."

That gets his attention. His head snaps over as he stares at her, puzzled. "Why do I need to steal one? You know you can just ask them for an examination."

"Just do it," she snaps. "And don't tell anyone."

"These files are in the archives," Kagiso protests. "Anyone in the organization can find it."

"Only if they're looking." Zero should know; she didn't care to look at Whiston's medical history. That's why it took her two weeks to find out she probably caught a virus from him. "Get a test for me, and don't ask me about the results afterwards."

Kagiso twirls his fingers, and the door slams shut behind Zero. She hears the thudding footsteps getting louder, then fading away as someone passes by Kagiso's room.

Zero raises a brow. "You have movement commands connected to your bedroom door encoded in your rings?"

"It's funny how you jest, Zero." Kagiso stands, wine sloshing in his glass as he saunters over to Zero. "If I recall correctly, the white vein disease goes into effect about two weeks after contracting the virus, starting with a fever before the veins in your fingers start turning white." He tilts his head when he's right in front of her, his intense gaze searching Zero's face. "You're starting to feel sick, aren't you? You already know you're going to test positive."

"Your silence will be generously compensated," she says icily.

A soft but unkind chuckle blows in her face. "The mighty Ace of Crowns. I finally have something you want. Never would have thought it'd be my silence, but something nonetheless."

Kagiso reaches up to curl his fingers on Zero's chin, but freezes when she narrows her eyes at him.

His hand twitches, halfway in the air, before it drops back to his side.

Turning away, he says, "I want your entire earring collection as payment."

"A one-time payment," Zero clarifies, though it may be a pointless attempt to prevent him from asking for more of her property if she's going to die anyway. She thinks of it as insurance to prevent him from demanding information from her in the future.

"Boring, but fine."

"Then it's done."

"Great." Kagiso tosses her a pill bottle. She catches it and reads the label. Cough medicine. "Get out of my room and go to bed. I'll come by your room in fifteen minutes."

Zero leaves and doesn't bother to tell him which floor she lives on. With all the time he spends with Avery, whose sole job is keeping track of the Aconites' archives, Kagiso probably already memorized every single member's room number.

The trek to the Tower takes more effort than usual, her legs feeling heavier with every step, her head hazier. When Zero makes it back to her apartment, she makes more tea for herself, still trying to process the likelihood of her life ending with all her veins turned white from head to toe and burning from the inside out.

As promised, Kagiso walks in fifteen minutes later. He's the head Sleightist of the Aconites for a reason.

Zero takes the plastic bag out of his hand without a word, leading him to her vanity and pointing at the earring tree, before locking herself in the bathroom for the test. When she walks out, she notices that Kagiso also took a box of her bracelets along with the tree, but she can't be bothered to care anymore. The test results won't be finalized until the morning, so she throws back a sleeping pill.

After three and a half nightmares, Zero wakes up with a gasp, sweaty and shivering.

She squeezes her eyes shut and practices breathing.

One, two, three, four, five.

Six, seven, eight, nine, ten, eleven, twelve.

Her lids slowly open again as she lets out a sigh, hauling herself out of bed. All her limbs feel as though lava has replaced her blood. Her head feels as though it belongs to another world. She trudges to the bathroom and picks up the test tube.

Positive.

A laugh echoes from the tiled walls.

Zero clamps a hand over her mouth, hearing how deranged she sounds.

But she's going to die.

I'm finally going to die, Zero thinks, and another laugh bubbles in her chest. She has survived so many things, she almost thought she might be invincible. Of course that was a stupid thought, because no human being on this planet is free of weaknesses.

And of course, she has enough money to pay for fifty years of the cheaper antiretroviral drugs, but what would be the point? What's the point of dragging on her miserable life, when it'll fizzle out within five years, as soon as she stops taking the drugs? What's the point of spending money on herself, when she could give it to someone worthier?

"It had to be a slow death, too," Zero muses out loud and falls into a laughing fit as she stumbles out to fall flat on her back in her bed. "I deserve it, Drokklo. I deserve it."

Her ceiling laughs back at her. Everything swirls into a mess of colors when her stomach aches and her left eye finally lets out one drop of tear, though it's born of madness, rather than sorrow. Only one thought rings in her head like an archaic, broken record.

It's going to be over soon.

She once thought it was going to be over two years ago, when she was ready to commit suicide back in Lime Gateway. For whatever reason, she gave herself a chance to do better, yet she has no idea what she has done in these years to make anything better. Maybe it was worth it to find out the truth behind her father's death. Maybe none of it mattered at all because she only gave herself seven more useless years.

"Fuck it," she laughs. "Fuck everyone and everything."

Her brain feels like cotton candy, her limbs feel like ramen, and her throat feels like lamb skewers. Reality floats away from her like those helium balloons that Purish kids get for birthday parties, silly cartoon characters giggling at her.

With a mind of its own, Zero's body carries her out of the Tower and into the Core, feet drifting to Rovis's office. Around her, Aconites shoot her nonplussed glances. The mirror of one of the doors to the kitchen shows Zero her crazed grin, and she has half the mind to shatter her reflection with the knife that's slipped into her hand.

Five more years. She has no idea what she plans to do with that amount of time, but she knows that she no longer cares about what other people think of her.

"What about Raven's plan?" Jacek demands, materializing in front of her.

Zero twists her lips into an ugly sneer. "Yes, it is unfortunate, isn't it?"

Zero walks right through his apparition, ignoring the bewildered stares all around her. She's perfectly aware that she's speaking to herself, but she has always been on the edge of insanity, so why not simply cross the line and fall?

Rovis looks over when she enters, eyes widening at her expression.

"Good news," Zero says cheerfully. "I will no longer be working as a Heartless. I'm sure you are happy to hear that."

He stares, his mouth forming a cautious response. "What changed your mind?"

Zero's mind flashes back to the way Didier Whiston gripped her hips at the gala in Torch City and to the *POSITIVE* that blinked at her this morning. Whiston is the same age as her, one of her few appropriately aged targets, and it's just her luck that he gave her a virus that has no cure. A chuckle slips out of her lips as she thinks about her pathetic run as the Ace of Crowns.

"Funny story," she says. "But you had to be there."

"Okay," Rovis speaks slowly. "You don't have to tell me, but are you feeling okay?"

Zero breaks into a fit of laughter once again. She feels nothing, yet she feels everything. No words can possibly answer that question.

"Yeah," she wheezes, "sure."

"Don't lie to me," he says, though there's no heat to his voice. "You know better than that."

"Do I?"

Zero certainly didn't know better two years ago, with that bottle of painkillers clutched in her hand. It should have been so easy to drink all of it down.

Rovis clenches his jaw, unsure of how to respond. "Why did you really come in here?"

"How am I supposed to know?"

"What—" He rubs his temples. "What does that even mean?"

She laughs again and plops down on his couch. "I don't know."

"Are you high?"

"Nah."

"Are you drunk?"

"Oh, you know what?" Zero stands again and makes a beeline for the door. "That's actually a good idea."

"No," Rovis snaps in Avyrian. "Don't you dare. Sit down."

She swivels around, tripping over her own feet. Her head spins, and her skin is starting to feel like it could cook chicken noodle soup.

"Do you have chicken noodle soup?"

Rovis blinks. "No?"

His expression makes her laugh again, and she doubles over for so long that she forgets what set her off, which then prolongs her episode. When Zero finally quiets, she straightens and beams at Rovis, who's stunned to silence.

One moment passes.

Two, three.

"I'm calling Ofir," Rovis announces, picking up his phone.

"Don't," Zero responds, voice falsely bright. "They can't help me. My therapist can't help me. You can't help me. No one can help me. It's just me and the universe's probability machine."

Rovis brings his hand down, a million emotions flitting through his eyes as he stares at her. "Okay, what's going on? You're scaring me."

"You're the Scavenger. You're not scared of anything."

"Zero, you know that isn't true." He leans forward. "You can pretend the past never happened, but you have seen every monster in my head. I'm scared of a lot of things. And right now, you look like your mother."

Zero flinches, too surprised to hide her reaction.

She feels as though someone is forcing her head under a running faucet on the highest setting, gripping her hair so that the water flows right up her eyes, her nose, her mouth for endless hours.

That someone used to be real.

That someone was her mother.

And Zero reminds Rovis of that someone.

"Well, then." Her lips twist and stretch into what she thinks should be a smile. "I guess I have always been my mother's daughter."

Rovis growls and looks away, his brows bunching up in frustration. "That's *not* what I meant."

"What else could you have possibly meant? I'm very aware of the fact that I'm a monster. I was raised by a monster. The monster lives on in my blood. It's written in my genetic codes, in my bones, in my eyes."

"No, it's not." Rovis slams the desk, standing. "It's—"

"Actually, come to think of it, you're just like your dad, too."

He deflates, his waves of anger fading to leave the tension trembling in his arms, his hands clawing at the wooden edges.

"Why do you say that?" Rovis hisses, a quiet warning.

And there he is, the Scavenger. The armor Rovis has created to survive the world of the Damned and rule Dyvris. Except he's still too soft. There's one thing in the past that keeps holding him back, that he's forgotten. He refuses to remember, and that's why he still hasn't fully become the Scavenger.

That just won't do, if Zero won't be around much longer to watch his back.

"Your father was weak," Zero taunts. "He was a slave to self-victimization, always allowing everything to happen to him and doing nothing about it. All he did was follow cruel women around like a sad puppy, because he never learned how to be by himself, and you paid the price for it."

"Stop."

"And that's not it. He was so easy to manipulate, I bet he'd never even know that you became a criminal if he were still alive, as long as a pretty woman walks by and tells him that he's thinking too much."

"Zero, *shut up*." Rovis's face flares with red fury, eyes blazing.

But she doesn't care. She knows she's hurting him, and she doesn't care. She knows she's been doing this ever since she joined the Aconites, and she *never gave a damn*, because she was raised by a heartless beast.

Zero has tried all her life to be better, to break out of her laid-out path, but she always messes up and destroys everything she touches, and Rovis needs to see that, on top of the truth about his father. He needs to give up and walk away, because she's not worth it. He needs to turn away, before he can watch her die.

But of course, Lila's obnoxious ghost has to make an appearance at the corner of bookshelves behind Rovis.

"You're really going to throw away everything you've built over the past few years in one mental breakdown?" she demands.

"Go away," Zero growls, her vision blurring.

The knife flies through Lila's nose, and her phantom dissipates.

Rovis looks back and forth between the knife in his shelf and Zero, still radiating with outrage but slightly doused with confusion. He's probably wondering if her knife-throwing has always been this terrible. Or who she was talking to. Zero forgets sometimes that she's the only one who sees Lila, and nowadays Jacek.

"This is my office," Rovis says.

"I wasn't talking to you," Zero waves him off, indifferent.

"Then who—"

"Wake up, will you?" she interrupts. "Do you even remember how your father died?"

That brings back his rage. "Of course I do. What is your fucking point?"

"He was weak," Zero repeats, spitting with disdain. "And he made himself vulnerable, and you're just like him. All you do is make promises you can't keep and tie nooses around your neck. Then when reality hits and you disappoint people, you pull the rope yourself by binding yourself to them with guilt. No one even needs to manipulate you. You do that very well to yourself."

Rovis's chest heaves with barely contained fury.

"N.A.D.E.," he says, sharp and cold like spikes of ice. "Send two closest members of the inner circle to my office. Now."

"Oh, no." Zero laughs, hysteria breaking through her focused malice. "Am I about to get executed?"

"Not another word from you," Rovis seethes. "We're done here."

He's so serious, and he has no idea. He has absolutely no idea that he only has to see her for a maximum of five more years. And Zero's hatching a plan to leave before then anyways, so that he won't ever hear about, know about, or care about her death.

He has no idea.

Zero laughs and laughs, stumbling back, until she feels hands grabbing at her arms and shoulders, pulling her out. Her chest and throat are burning, her tongue drier than the sand around the city. Her eyelids are too heavy, and her head feels as though someone put her brain in a blender.

Faces float in front of her, and Zero realizes they've put her down to sit in the Menders' lounge. *Avery and Daleyza*, she vaguely registers.

"She's really warm," Avery's voice floats through her mind.

A hand brushes against her forehead. Zero shivers, feeling both hot and cold.

"I'm calling Tal," she hears Daleyza say.

"He's in the city still trying to find clues about Levi's murderer."

"This takes precedence. Wait for a Mender with her."

Zero hopes no one tries to test her blood. The WVM-67 virus can probably be detected in her bloodstream. Although, viruses can't be found unless they know to look for it, because the search engine in sample analysis machines only lists the basic information and living bacteria.

So as long as Kagiso keeps his mouth shut, they won't find out that she has the white vein malady.

Tal is suddenly kneeling in front of her, his gloved hands holding her upper arms.

"What happened?" he whispers urgently.

Zero chuckles again, much weaker than before. Her bleary eyes can barely stay open, and her raw throat probably can't pass any words through.

"*Zero*," Tal says, and something's wrong with his tone. Alarms start to go off distantly in her mind, like a nuclear explosion underwater.

"Is Rovis okay?" she manages to ask, her words coming out rough.

Tal frowns. "Why wouldn't he be?"

"Because I'm killing him," she tries to say, but her voice gives up halfway through, the roughness giving away to whispers. If Tal doesn't know anything, then maybe she's just paranoid. Or maybe it's a gut feeling.

"What's going on with you?" Tal's fingers thread through Zero's hair, his concerned gaze tearing her chest into pieces. "Talk to me."

Rovis must have done something, she thinks. *What did he do? What have I done?*

Zero shakes her head, too dizzy to recalculate.

"I'm sorry," she whispers.

"What happened?" Tal asks again.

Her eyes fall shut when she can't keep the darkness at bay any longer. Somehow, her mouth forms a slurred answer.

"My mother."

17
Everyone Has Secrets

Rovis lets the knife clatter into the sink when his head quiets, too focused on the raw pain to torment himself with memories and Zero's words.

He watches the red lines on his arm grow bolder, filling in the space between old scars with color. The sound of air hissing in and out of his nose calms his mind as he slides his eyes shut and welcomes the familiar sting. It feels like fresh air, like toxic gas leaking out of his veins.

The last time he did this was the night before he decided to kill Quade Bianchi, Rovis recalls numbly.

After Bianchi cut off Rovis's finger for keeping his past with Zero a secret, he almost lost his sanity worrying about Zero's fate when she returned from Torch City. He felt as though he was going to explode or boil alive, and the only way he could find peace was to let the blood flow out, along with his anxieties and fears. Just like all those nights after his stepmother beat him up and slashed lines across his back with his father's belts.

His back is crisscrossed with imprints of his suffering.

His forearm is lined with proof of survival, of self-destruction, of revenge against the world by being crueler to himself than anyone else ever could be.

All he can feel right now are his own deep breaths, the blood rushing to his ears, the quiet haze of his mind, the twinkling numbness in his fingers. Nothing gets him back into his body more effectively than this. A soft laugh floats out of his chest when he opens his eyes again to stare himself down in the mirror. His arms rest on the sides of the sink, blood dripping onto the porcelain, fingers trembling just slightly.

"Rovis."

Tal stands in Rovis's bedroom, just outside the open door to the bathroom, eyes stricken.

Rovis knows he's been caught. There's no point hiding the wounds on the inside of his left forearm, contrasting the flawless wolfsbane tattoo on his right one. He washes the blood off the edge of his knife and says, voice blank, "You have your addiction, Tal. I have mine."

"Is that what you call it? An addiction?" Tal steps closer. Rovis lets him.

"Years of a terrible coping mechanism tends to become an addiction." He washes his arm with soap and watches the water run down his fingers with a tinge of sickly red. "You crave oblivion at the end of a bottle; I crave peace at the end of a blade."

"Here." Tal takes Rovis's wrist gingerly. "Let me."

When he takes out a cell-regenerating spider-bot, though, Rovis pulls away and reaches up to grab a roll of bandages.

"I don't understand," Tal says, staring at the bundle in Rovis's hand, a small distance away from the angry carvings that stretch from his wrist to his elbow.

Rovis only shakes his head and begins wrapping his arm himself.

"Truth for truth." Tal shifts closer and stops Rovis with a gentle hand, a challenge. He's pushing Rovis to open up, but he's also giving him the chance to say no.

"I like it when it scars," Rovis answers. "It's proof that my pain is real. Sometimes the scars fade anyways, and I feel like I cheated, like I've been cheated, like everything I felt when I drew these lines was a joke." He shakes his head. "Why were you looking for me? You usually know to leave me alone if I'm not in the office or the studio."

Tal sighs, taking the bandage roll and covering the cuts for Rovis. "Is that really what you're going to use your turn for?"

"Your reluctance to answer is only evidence that I'm asking the right question."

"I don't think now is the time."

"Do not start coddling me now, Talon. This is not the first time I've done this. I won't break."

"That's not very reassuring."

"Now you understand what it's like on the other side," Rovis says, looking back at Tal steadily when his head snaps up. "I'm not trying to make you feel guilty. But now you understand, don't you?"

Tal's fingers twitch on his arm. Resistance flits through his eyes as he clenches his jaw, but the longer he stares at Rovis, the less he seems to able to argue against him. Tal's chest deflates with a deep sigh, his rough edges softening, like a paint brush blurring harsh lines on a canvas.

"Yeah," he finally says, his ungloved knuckles grazing the side of Rovis's face. "I guess I do, Rov. I'm sorry."

Rovis holds Tal's hand with his free one and shakes his head. "You have nothing to be sorry for. We both have our own demons. We can talk about this again later. Answer my question, Tal."

Tal hesitates again. Rovis feels as though he knows the answer.

"Zero," he guesses.

"She asked about you," Tal confirms. "Daleyza said you had another fight. I thought things were getting better between you two."

"So did I," Rovis says bitterly.

"She has a high fever. Ofir stabilized her temperature, and I put her to bed when she passed out. She'll be okay in a few days. I came as soon as I could."

Rovis nods. A fever makes sense, since she sounded like she was losing her voice this morning. He knew something was wrong as soon as she walked in, with that look on her face and the unsteadiness of her steps. It also seemed like she might have been hallucinating, which Rovis finds concerning, paired with her insistence that no one can help her.

Yet none of that warranted Zero's slandering of his father.

She's cold and calloused, but she's not cruel. Rovis doesn't understand why she lashed out so violently.

"Did she say anything else?" he asks.

"I asked her what happened quite a few times," Tal says. "All she said was, 'my mother.'"

Rovis sucks in a breath, pressing his knuckles between his brows. "I shouldn't have brought that up."

"What did you say? What did *she* say to *you*?" Tal demands. "I've known you for years, enough to know that she must have said something really bad for you to react this way."

"That's between me and her."

Tal huffs in frustration, looking away. "This again. Fine. But there's another thing."

"What is it?"

"When I took Zero to the Tower, she got a call from someone named Enyo."

Rovis freezes, his blood chilling. "You don't think..."

"What other Enyo do you know?" Tal retorts. "Zero's only normal friends are from school, all of whom are either dead or Raven, and she's off the grid. I know in my gut that Zero has been in contact with Enyo Zhao. I even heard her speaking Riyssolan the other day, after Levi's funeral."

"Shit," Rovis breathes.

Enyo Zhao, Queen of Loveias and Mistress of the Daggers, is never good news. After a small but deadly Riyssolan organization killed Enyo's parents in a blood feud against the Water Lords, they took her when she barely learned how to walk and raised her as one of them. A killer, a con artist, a devil. When she turned ten, Enyo turned on them and slaughtered every last one of them, from elders to children, and rejoined the Lords.

Except, the Lords condemned Enyo for her bloodlust and absurd deals. She was exiled at fifteen, and to be executed if ever sighted in their territories. After that, she built a drug empire from the ground up in the city of gambling and prostitution, Loveias. The Daggers formed as she collected girls from trafficking rings and made them her personal team of assassins.

Every creature of the Damned knows this.

The only way for Zero and Enyo to be in contact with each other, phone numbers saved and calls without warnings, is if they have a deal.

What has Zero gotten into this time? Her mind can't possibly take any more of this, not after everything her mother has done to her and after Bianchi's tyranny. Rovis has seen how fractured it has become, so why is she doing this?

Rovis really wishes he can be properly angry at Zero instead of constantly worrying about her bizarre choices and implosive tendencies.

Just like how it takes a lot for Rovis to relapse into self-harm, he suspects it takes a lot for Zero to intentionally hurt him, after everything they've been through together.

"What are you thinking?" Tal asks.

"I'm going to see her."

"Rovis," he warns.

"Stars, Tal. What do you think I'm going to do? Torture her? I'm going to check on her and maybe look at her phone."

"I could just hack it," Tal points out.

"Don't. She still deserves privacy." Rovis returns to his bedroom, rolling down his sleeves. "I only need to make sure she isn't doing anything stupid for Enyo."

Tal follows him. "Rivka and Daleyza might be with her. I'm not sure about Avery."

"I'll deal with them," Rovis says and pulls on his gloves.

"What do you want me to do, then?"

"Keep working on finding Levi's killer." He rests a hand on Tal's shoulder. "I'll deal with my issues. I won't take you away from your revenge."

"You're what's in front of me," Tal says, covering Rovis's hand with his own. "If you need me, I'll be there."

"Okay." Rovis squeezes, then he lets go. "I'll be back soon."

Tal nods and watches him leave. Rovis tries to keep his thoughts at bay as he makes his way to the ground floor, where Aconites bustle around. The television plays in one of the lounges, where some members watch Purish authorities demand a hunt for members of the Faceless organization. He ignores the news and heads for the Tower.

When the elevator doors open on Zero's floor, Rovis comes face to face with Rivka and Avery.

"You," Rivka says, eyes widening with fury. She reaches out to push Rovis back, but Avery traps her in their arms before she could get close enough.

"Sorry, Boss," Avery grunts.

"I'm not letting you touch her," Rivka hisses. "If you knife her, you will lose all of the Heartless."

"What's going on?" Daleyza emerges from the bedroom, shutting the door quietly.

"I came to check on Zero," Rovis says coldly. He is not a fan of being questioned by his own people.

"You threw her out," Daleyza states, lingering in front of the door, eyes wary. "We saw the look in your eyes."

Avery keeps their gaze downcast and doesn't refute her.

"I needed to cool down," Rovis says. "Move, before my temper gets the better of me for the second time today."

"No," Rivka growls viciously. "I don't care what she said to you. We are all terrible, fucked up people. We are the Damned, and all we do is commit sins. If you can't come to terms with that, you don't deserve to be the Scavenger. Zero has been loyal from the moment she became an Aconite. You will not exile her because of mistakes she made while delirious from a stars-damned fever."

If Rivka weren't the new head of the Heartless, Rovis would have frozen her legs off with an ice blaster. Unfortunately, she's Zero's friend and hand-picked successor, so he can't touch her. Otherwise, his relationship with Zero might be forever irreparable, and he'd be dealing with another round of internal disputes in the organization.

"There are cameras around this apartment," he says instead. "Trust me when I say that I am only here to check on Zero after hearing about her illness. You have my word. Like you said, she's one of my most loyal Aconites and a member of the inner circle. I do not take that lightly. I understand that she was not in her right mind this morning, so I will only be addressing our disagreement after she recovers, not that that's any of your business. Now, get out of my way."

Avery nods furiously with a sheepish smile and drags Rivka to the side. Rovis steps forward, tilting his head at Daleyza.

"She has a hard time staying asleep," she merely says. "Keep it down when you go in."

With that, Daleyza pulls Avery and Rivka into the elevator, and the trio disappears behind the patterned doors.

Rovis sighs, shaking his head. At least he doesn't have to worry about anyone trying to kill Zero in an explosion anymore. Slowly, he turns the knob and creeps in.

Zero shoots out from her bundle of blankets and a wire flies at him.

Not this again, he internally groans as he twists his body to catch it, the silver tightening around black leather.

"It's me," he snaps.

Bleary eyes blink at him, focusing and unfocusing. Zero struggles through her illness and exhaustion, a knife in a weak grip as she leans heavily on a hand clutching the side of her bed, while Rovis has to patiently wait for his hand to be sliced in half by her stupid ring.

"Rozzie?"

His heart stops.

The wire falls to the floor with a ting.

Rovis's hands tremble as he tries to figure out if his mind is playing tricks on him. Zero hasn't called him that in five years. Anyone can look at her right now and know her mind is barely lucid. With her guard down and filters off, the first thing she says when she sees him is his old nickname.

Perhaps Rovis hasn't been completely stupid for hoping.

The moment shatters when Zero doubles over, coughing her lungs out, saliva dripping onto her carpet. Snapping out of a daze, Rovis rushes to help her back into bed. An unopened bottle of cough medicine sits on her nightstand, so he takes it when he hurries into the kitchen and fills up a glass of warm water. He cuts open the plastic packaging with a knife and looks over the label.

Zero hasn't stopped coughing when Rovis returns, curled up on her side.

"Here," he murmurs in Avyrian and puts a hand on her shoulder. "I'm going to sit you up."

She doesn't protest when he pulls her up and sits behind her so she can lean on his chest. When the coughs let up, Zero wheezes, and Rovis holds up a pill. She takes it and drains the entire glass of water, breathing heavily as her hand drops onto the bed. Rovis moves the cup to the nightstand before shifting to get up, pausing when Zero latches onto his sleeve.

"You seem so real," she mumbles in Avyrian. "If you are, how are you here?"

Rovis isn't sure if Zero is actually speaking to him or if she can hear him, but he says, "I walked."

"Why? Why would you come?"

He frowns. "Why wouldn't I?"

She shakes her head. "This can't be real. The past is dead. But you still don't hate me. Why can't you hate me? What will it take?"

"There's nothing you can do to make me hate you."

"No. No. There has to be a way," she says, almost desperately, though Rovis is sure she's only half-awake. Then Zero stills. Her glossy eyes drop down to his arm, and she frowns. Tentatively, she tugs at the sleeve, almost looking as though she might cry. "You didn't do it, did you? You're not doing it again, are you?"

Rovis snatches his arm out of her fingers and slips off the bed to lie her back down. "Go to sleep."

"You did," she whispers, chest heaving. "Oh, no. I knew it. I felt it. It's my fault. It's my fault. What have I done? Why did I say those words? Fuck, it's my fault. Fuck. *Fuck*."

He puts hand on her forehead, feeling the heat through the leather. Rovis technically did cut because of what she said earlier, so he doesn't deny it and instead answers, hushed, "We'll talk about it later."

"No," Zero mutters over and over again as she clutches his elbow, her breathing becoming erratic and shallow.

A heavy sigh slips out between Rovis's lips, and he reaches into his jacket to dig for a small golden vial. He twists the top off and holds the opening under Zero's nose. Her brows furrow and she tries to move her face away, but Rovis coaxes her back with gentle fingers.

"Just breathe for me. I taught you how, remember? In for five, out for seven," he instructs before he starts counting.

She settles down after several breaths of his chamomile and lavender mixture.

"My head hurts," she croaks, tugging at her hair.

A gloved hand brushes a sweaty strand out of her face. "Sleep."

"Don't hurt yourself, Rozzie." Her words start to slur. "Not because of me. I'm not worth it. I'm not worth it."

Zero keeps repeating the last sentence until she drifts off.

Rovis wipes the water and saliva off of her chin with the edge of his sleeve, then puts the vial back in his jacket. Sighing, he buries his face in his hands.

Things have never been easy between the two of them, but he hoped it might get better someday. While Rovis has scars all over his back and his arm, Zero's mind has been fractured to pieces, and he'd do anything to take that from her. Maybe she has been right all along, and there's no such thing as 'getting better' or 'being okay.'

He also doesn't understand why she's so sick, physically. Zero has only ever been sick once before, bedridden by a migraine and a stuffy nose when she was nine. But all the Aconite members get all their vaccine shots when they take their wolfsbane mark, so the chances of catching anything should be zero. None of it adds up.

Remembering the matter about Enyo, Rovis reaches over to grab her phone off the nightstand. There's indeed a missed call from Enyo, though the screen also displays two new messages.

Harlow: ENCRYPTED FILE (.xg)

Enyo: Pleasure doing business with you again, Ace. (Attached: 1 file)

Again. Zero has made more than one deal with the Queen of Loveias, and she has significantly amplified the irritation simmering beneath Rovis's skin.

Rovis doesn't know who Harlow is, and he doesn't care for the moment, but he's not optimistic at the sight of an encrypted file.

He takes out a mirroring tablet and hooks it up to Zero's phone, projecting her information on his device so that she'll never know Rovis opened her text history with Enyo unless he tells her.

Scrolling up, he sees that Zero sent over the Aconites' file on Didier Whiston. Rovis frowns, nonplussed. Last he checked, everything they have on Whiston comes from his interrogation of Jeremy Wright. And why would Enyo be interested in Whiston?

Rovis decides to just open up the file from Enyo and see what Zero asked for.

It's a profile on a woman named Skylar Wright, Jeremy Wright's wife.

Why the hell would Zero trade for information on an ordinary Dyvrian businessman's wife with someone so dangerous?

His eyes scan over the basics, and Rovis grows more vexed as the endless scrolling gives him useless things like the number of kids and beach houses.

Until he reaches the end.

"Holy stars and bloody cities," Rovis breathes, looking back at Zero's tense sleeping face, the soft blanket rising and falling gently.

She did it. This is it.

He reaches out to set her arms underneath the covers and picks up the dragon ring, putting it next to her phone. Careful not to wake Zero again, he inches toward the door and turns off the light. Almost vibrating with the newfound information, Rovis has to control his legs from bounding over to the Core.

It's almost dinnertime, judging by the smell drifting from the kitchen. He glances in the lounges, looking for a red button-up shirt and black slacks.

Rovis nearly jumps when Tal's face appears a breath away when he turns away from a dimly lit room where Aconites are watching the television.

"I—" Tal starts, then glances down between them, and looks back up at Rovis with a scowl, unimpressed.

A gun presses against Tal's abdomen.

"Sorry." Rovis tucks the weapon back to where it belongs. "Tal, I know who killed Levi."

"I don't care. I need your help."

Rovis stares at him, taken aback. The hallway isn't fully lit, so he has to squint to notice that Tal's face is pale and tense.

"What's wrong?"

Tal opens his mouth, but only a growl of frustration comes out. He looks away, pulling Rovis back into the dark lounge. His chin jerks toward the screen covering the entire wall.

Two lines of Purish law enforcers are escorting a Lasan girl into a caged vehicle. She's wearing a black hooded cloak that intensifies the vibrance of her flame-colored hair, which falls just below her shoulders. She looks about Zero's age, almost an adult but not quite.

As she passes by the camera, her orange contacts flare with fire that matches her hair, and something starts to turn in Rovis's head.

The headline, most of all, roots Rovis to his spot.

ANOTHER MEMBER OF THE FACELESS CAPTURED: SAIGE HARLOW, LASAN, AGE 18.

Harlow.

The encrypted file was sent to Zero hours before Saige's capture.

A feeble part of Rovis wants to believe that the odds are different. What are the chances that Harlow is someone's given name rather than a false family name?

But this is Zero. Nothing can ever be a coincidence when it comes to her. Rovis mentally curses the name of the Ace of Crowns, before he remembers Tal's anxious expression. He half turns, stare flicking between the screen and his second in command.

The facial structure, the careless smirk, the dangerous gleam in her stare.

I miss my sister, Tal told Rovis during the Moon Festival. Rovis remembers how his eyes shone with nostalgia and bittersweet serenity, even while he was watching the sparring show, until the drug experiments destroyed that peace.

The similar features between Tal and Saige, the same blaze of rebellion in their eyes, the approximate age. Even if the physical proof isn't laid out in front of them, Tal has the same edges in his restrained expression that Rovis would have if the Agency ever catches Zero.

Rovis already knows the answer when he pushes Tal out into the hall again and asks in quiet Lasan, "Who is she?"

Emotions flit through Tal's face, and determination flashes in his eyes. He licks his lips and utters the confirmation that Rovis waits to hear.

"My sister."

18

Nothing Lasts Forever

Tal stares at Rovis's grave expression, dreading what the other man might say. The cross-cutting shots of the news flashes different colors onto their faces, but Rovis stays perfectly still, meeting Tal's eyes with an unreadable gaze.

To be fair, Tal himself can't quite wrap his mind around the fact that Saige has been working with the Faceless. Eight years ago, she was still learning geometry. Now, she's part of the revolting force aiming to take down the government?

Even when Lime Gateway High School burnt down, Tal assumed that his parents enrolled Saige into a different school. Otherwise he would've found her when Rovis was bringing in Raven, Jacek, and Ayssa. He thought it was a good thing that Saige wasn't going to be joining him in the crime life. Never in a million years would he suspect that Saige has fallen out of the education system and started breaking laws herself, only in a different organization.

His eyes slide back to the screen in the lounge, where the streets have been taken over by protestors holding up signs to free Saige.

Saige has grown so much since Tal ran away, but the instant he saw her on the news, he knew who she was. She may have dyed her hair and changed the color of her eyes, but she'll always be Tal's little sister. And from the defiant expression on her face, Tal knows she's been involved with the Faceless for a good amount of time.

Either their parents are dead, or Saige ran away as soon as she was able to.

Why didn't you come find me?

She must have had a reason not to, right? Maybe she didn't have enough interaction with the Damned to know about Lithium. He's sure that if she knew about the Aconites, she would have come to Dyvris.

Or maybe she knew, and wanted nothing to do with him. Maybe their relationship was never as deep as he thought it was. Maybe she adopted the ideology that all the other Faceless have, which would explain why she's not part of the Damned.

Revolutionaries and criminals don't exactly run together.

But it doesn't matter, because Saige has been arrested, and she will always be Tal's sister. He intends to break her out of whatever prison they put her in, even if it's Drokklo's Playground.

"Rovis," Tal pleads.

The man lets out a long breath of air. "We'll need to make a plan first."

Finally, Tal can breathe again. His chest still hurts, but the feeling in his gut loosens with Rovis's words. As long as he has the Scavenger by his side, he can do anything.

"Thank you," he breathes, catching hold of Rovis's hand.

Rovis brings up his free one to squeeze their joined grip, his chest heaving a massive sigh. He looks Tal in the eyes and says, "I know."

Once they reach the Tech Hall, Rovis starts barking out orders to every Aconite in sight.

"You have an hour to find out where Saige Harlow is being sent to," he says to the room of Digitals keeping track of all cyber activity in their city.

Even though none of them know who the hell Saige is or what she is to Tal, they don't dare to question their boss. Screens flash as they redirect their energy to programming search engines and national surveillance.

If the Scavenger wants something, he will get it, regardless of the costs and obstacles thrown his way.

"Touch up on all of our best Shapeshifters," Tal says to the Mechs when he takes a detour to the hardware lab. "Make sure the bulletproof platings don't have any weak spots. The engines better function without a hitch. Install the energy shields to the ones that don't have it already."

After Zero taunted him with his prototype, Tal finished the model so that the shields would last for hours and produced hundreds of copies for the Aconites.

"There's not much we can do until we know where she is," Rovis says when Tal meets him at the Poison Core. "I'll do my best to gather the Reapers, but we don't know what we're up against."

"We will." He flexes his metal hand to unsheathe his claws. A bar of whetstone flies out from his sleeve and into the air, landing in his palm. Tal sharpens the tips and says, "We will get Saige out of there. Whoever stands in our way will regret it."

Rovis nods absently and glances away. Something about his posture sets off a faint alarm in Tal's head.

"What?" he demands. "Do you know something?"

"That's not it." Rovis runs a hand through his hair. "I just have a lot on my mind."

"Right," Tal softens his voice, reaching out to brush a hand over the sleeve covering those brutal cuts he saw earlier. It's only been a few hours since Rovis wrapped his arm up like it's nothing, like the mess on his skin is just another one of his paintings. Tal internally berates himself for forgetting and snapping. He can't understand why Rovis cuts, why anyone would cut, but the idea alone makes his heart twist.

"It's fine," Rovis says, voice blank.

"I've been inconsiderate."

"It's *fine*," he insists. "You're going through a lot. Go check to see if the Digitals have made any progress."

"Don't brush me off like that," Tal argues, frowning. "You're not okay, and I'm asking a lot of you."

"Well, what do you want, Tal?" Rovis tilts his head back to glare at the ceiling, exasperated.

"Eat dinner and go to sleep. You need to rest."

"Your sister's in danger," Rovis says flatly. "I'm the most powerful person who can help you right now, and you want me to go to bed?"

"Like you said, there's not much to do until we find out her location. Rov, you are amazing, but you're only human. Thank you for doing what you can, I mean it."

Rovis looks at Tal and pauses. His lips part in surprise. If it were any other day, Tal would take pride in rendering the Scavenger speechless.

"Okay," Rovis answers, still staring. Then he blinks and shoves past Tal toward the kitchen. "I don't take orders from you, though."

Tal rolls his eyes. "Yes, yes, I'm your right hand man. I'm your might and your iron fist — although, technically, my arm isn't made of iron."

"Nerd," Rovis quips without turning around. He takes two plates and passes one to Tal.

Saige used to bicker with him like that, too. She loved literature and had huge stacks of books in her room, especially since their parents got her whatever she wanted. Tal leaned towards the sciences, his walls decorated by an unaesthetic mess of equations and scratch work. They argued often, though it was usually shallow drama and pointless squabbling, unlike whatever Rovis and Zero have going on.

"You wound me," Tal attempts to snark, but it falls flat. He adds, "I may be your servant, but I'm also your advisor. See, I merely *suggested* that you consider your health seriously after a mentally damaging day, and you've clearly taken the suggestion."

He sweeps out an arm to gesture at Rovis's filled plate theatrically.

The corner of Rovis's lips twitches. But he only says, "You're not my servant. Don't ever say that again. Unless I've been treating you like one?"

"It was a joke," Tal refutes, nonplussed.

"Good." He sits down in the dining room. "I just hope the Digitals can track down Saige before the Purish enforcers lock her up. It'll be easier to hijack the transport or brute force attack them while they're moving, compared to breaking through the security of a prison and needing a clear path out."

Tal's face falls. He hasn't been thinking about the details of the plan. Rovis has always been the strategist, while Tal tinkers and runs programs to keep them at a technological advantage.

"What if our team isn't strong enough?" he asks suddenly, starting to panic.

Rovis slants a look at Tal. "That is a concern. Depending on what the Digitals find out, we have to figure out the smartest ways to distribute our resources. It's my job, Tal."

"Why is it taking so long?" he mutters, mostly to himself.

"If they're on the surface roads, we would have heard by now," Rovis answers anyway. "They're either underground or really high in the atmosphere. The latter is more costly, but the Purish have all the money in the world to do whatever they want."

"Don't we have eyes on abandoned subway tracks?"

"We do. That's not the only way to travel under. If the Aconites can have secret tunnels, then the government definitely has ways, too."

Tal rubs his face.

"I'm sorry," Rovis says. "We could really use the Ring's resources, since they basically hold a monopoly over underground activities and cyber networks. Damian Narvaez hasn't responded when I asked if he might know anything, and Jordan Faal..."

He trails off, and Tal tries to come up with a response.

But then his watch starts vibrating. He answers the call and displays the speaker on a holographic projection at the center of his metal palm.

"We found out where they're taking Saige Harlow," Vanneza Otieno, head of the Tech Hall, reports. "It's a prison in Torch City."

"Drokklo's Playground?" Tal's heart pounds.

"No. It's a secure building on the surface near the nuclear plants. They're currently somewhere between Metloxcy and Loveias in some kind of electromagnetic tunnel."

Tal stands. "Tell the Reapers we're leaving."

"Heading where? We don't have a plan yet," Rovis protests.

"We can plan on the way." Tal turns to leave, but Rovis catches him by the elbow.

"We can't go to Loveias unprepared. It's Enyo Zhao territory."

"Rovis," Tal warns. "Let go."

"If we're reckless, we're going to lose people before we can even get to Saige."

"There's no time!" he shouts.

Slamming doors interrupts their argument from the entrance to the dining room. Daleyza pants and takes one uncertain step forward.

"Boss," she says, sounding winded, "Harlow is dead."

The blood runs cold in Tal's veins. He staggers back, his head dizzy and his heart frantically beating his chest. Rovis catches him by the shoulders.

"What?" His question sounds far, far away.

Daleyza taps on her watch and swipes a hand from her wrist to the wall, projecting the news to the side of the long tables. Shots of Saige's body on the floor of a van and masked prison guards flash before Tal's eyes. His legs give out.

"No." The word tumbles out.

First Levi, now Saige. It can't be true. Tal just found his sister again; she can't be dead already. He hasn't seen her in person. He didn't get a chance to talk to her about what happened eight years ago. This can't be the end of Tal and Saige.

He remembers all the times she'd follow him around as an obnoxious seven-year-old reciting all the Lasan passages she read, word for word, thanks to her eidetic memory. He remembers how their parents treated her like a princess and gave her everything they could despite their practically nonexistent income. Even when Tal's mother berated him constantly for being a disappointment and when his father ignored him at home, he never truly hated Saige.

Most of the money he worked for went to making his sister happy. Some days, he resented that his parents never gave him a choice. Other days, Saige's infectious smile makes him forget all the ways that they're different.

"She can't be dead," Tal hears himself say, though he doesn't know how many times he's uttered those words. Through his ragged breathing, he recognizes the walls and messy drawers of his own room. He blinks up at Rovis, who keeps a warm, ungloved hand on the back of Tal's neck. "How did we get here?"

"There were too many eyes in the dining room," Rovis explains. "I led you back here. Didn't think you'd want all the Aconites to watch you break down."

Tal nods, squeezing his eyes shut.

He doesn't want to believe it, but he knows what he saw. The headline is carved into his memories.

ROGUE GUARD KILLS HARLOW BEFORE EXECUTION

She's gone.

"She's gone," he hears himself repeat out loud, as if that would make it easier to get into his head, to figure what to do next, to learn how to live with it.

Saige is gone, before Tal could find her and give her a home again. If it weren't for the Purish guard escorting her to prison, they would have had time to break her out. They needed to be faster. They needed to track her down faster. They needed to get to her faster.

But it's too late. She's already gone.

Tal pants, clutching at his chest. He feels as though he lost a limb. No, he's already lost one before; this is worse. He felt cold when Levi died, and now he feels like someone is tearing the organs out of his body.

He doesn't want to feel like this.

He can't do this again.

The pain keeps building and building, and Tal needs to get it out of his heart. Suddenly the hand on the back of his neck is too warm. It practically scorches his skin. He jerks away from Rovis, wrenching his touch off of his neck.

"This is your fault," he hisses, standing.

Hurt flashes in Rovis's eyes, so briefly that Tal barely notices it.

"We wouldn't have made it in time," Rovis says with false tranquility. "Even if we left when you wanted to."

"We would have found her faster if you actually dealt with all your issues with Jordan Faal," Tal rips out, and he knows his words are unfair, are baseless, but he's only concerned with getting away from his grief right now. He just— He can't. He *can't do this*. Never has he ever cared about the universe treating him like a piñata, but to take Saige's life? And Levi's life? That is way too much cruelty for Tal to handle, too much hopelessness, too much rage.

He barely notices that Rovis flinches back from his accusation. Voice clipped, he says, "You don't know what you're talking about."

"You're right, and I don't care." The words are pouring out now, leaving Tal's mouth before it even reaches his brain. "I don't care what went down between you and Damian Narvaez or Jordan Faal. I don't care about whatever the fuck you have with Zero that gives her the right to know things that you won't tell me about. And I am so sick of the two of you keeping secrets from me, by the way. I am sick of both of you. Your inability to communicate and fix your relationships killed my sister."

"You're grieving," Rovis says, face shutting down.

"What else would I be doing?" Tal growls.

The door swings open. Zero breathes with great difficulty as she leans against the doorframe, face flushed.

"Tal," she says blankly.

Her feigned indifference is nothing new, except Tal caught the flash of concern in her eyes before she schooled her expression.

Realization dawns on him.

"You knew," Tal accuses her.

"Knew what?" Zero blinks at him, and he's had enough of that fake expression for ten lifetimes.

"You knew Saige." He steps forward, feeling as though his entire body has been set on fire. "You knew she was involved with the Faceless. You knew she was my sister. And you kept *all of that* to yourself."

"I promised her I would," Zero says, apathetic.

Tal freezes.

Saige wanted to keep Tal in the dark?

His throat burns, and heat consumes his head, his neck, his arms. He wants to scream, to punch a hole through the ground, to tear this entire mansion apart with his claws. Why would Saige do this? Was none of it real? Did she even love him? Did he really have no one at home who gave a shit about him? What is this sick joke, the way his life has played out since the beginning of his consciousness? He never stood a chance, did he, to turn out to be a decent person, instead of this twisted, loveless monster?

"Your promise didn't keep her alive," he whispers, icy rage and flaming grief rolled into shards as his claws slide out. "I am done with your secrets and lies."

Rovis shoves him in the chest, forcing Tal away from Zero. Tal slowly turns his head, disbelief coloring his face as he stares at his friend.

"Why are you helping her?" Tal demands.

"I'm helping *you*," Rovis shoots back. "I'm not going to let you do something you regret, no matter how much pain you're feeling right now."

"Aren't you sick of her deception?" Tal yells. "The Aconites could have been twenty steps ahead if she bothered to tell us about the Agency. Levi would still be alive. *Saige* would be alive. She kept my own sister away from me!"

"Zero, you should go—"

"*Don't you dare—*"

"No," Zero says, straightening, her voice hoarse. "Tal blames me; he can take it out on me."

"Oh, how noble of you," Tal spits out. "Where was this selfless sentiment all those times you could have told me where my sister was?"

"Tal, for stars' sake, she's sick."

"You really choose her?" he brushes Rovis's arms off. When Tal looks at him again, and processes Rovis's lack of reaction to Zero's admission, his lungs collapse. His eyes widen, incredulous, as he breathes, "You."

Rovis falters.

Time slows, as Tal stares at Rovis. In the span of less than a second, he realizes he doesn't know the other man at all.

"Did you know?" he whispers, terrified of the answer.

"Know what?"

Fire reignited, Tal pushes Rovis's hard chest with both hands. The tips of his claws catch on the violet shirt and tear the fabric.

"Don't bullshit me, Rovis," Tal hisses, voice shaky. "Did you know?"

Everything stills around them. All the members working in the Tech Hall, all the residents strolling on the streets of Dyvris, all the wars threatening to break out in Pureland, all the beings of nature, all the entities among the cosmos. Everything stops. Tal's holding his breath, desperate to hear that he's wrong. Nothing moves, except for Rovis licking his lips.

"Yes."

Tal steps back, releasing the air from his bleeding lungs. His eyes sting from the betrayal. With a will of its own, Tal's lips twist into Lithium's signature warning.

"You always coddled her."

He moves to attack Zero without wondering how far he'd go, only wanting to follow the red in his vision. Rovis is quick to block him and shove Tal away again.

A black stick slides out of Rovis's sleeve and into his hand. He thrusts it outward, and with three snaps, it triples in length, crackling with blue electricity.

"Walk away, Tal," Rovis warns.

"This is *my* room," Tal growls.

"It won't be much longer, if you continue to act this way."

Tal's jaw drops. A cold laugh rips out of his chest. "So this is how it's going to be? What's that Avyrian phrase? 'You flip your face faster than you flip a page'?"

"You leave me no choice. I don't want to do this, but I'll have to if you don't stop. Once you lay a hand on her, you break your vow to always protect your Aconite family."

"This isn't family." Tal jerks his head towards Zero. "And can she even be considered an Aconite? She's practically a quadruple agent."

"Rovis, don't."

"Shut up, Zero," both men snap.

A flash of silver arcs in the air. The stick flies out of Rovis's grip, shrinking and killing the power. Zero hisses as sparks fly in her palm, and her wire turns back into a dragon when it lands back on her finger. She catches the stick with an unsteady hand.

"Both of you, stop it," she says weakly. "You're not going to fight each other. Take three steps back, and go drink some tea."

"Tea?" Tal mocks. "Really? You think some leaves and water are going to fix this?"

"Rovis." Zero ignores Tal's jab. "*Biv'ye nu wanotai.*"

"That's not going to work this time," Tal taunts.

Rovis stares back at Zero silently, jaw clenched. He sucks in a breath and growls, craning his head to crack his neck. He mutters some Toullish words that Tal doesn't understand before turning his attention back to Tal.

"You're grieving," he says again. "I will not punish you for reacting this way, especially after two losses in a row, but you will be stepping down temporarily until you're thinking clearly again."

With that, he stalks out, snatching back his stick as he passes Zero.

Tal feels as though someone doused him with a freezing bucket of water. He has never been on the receiving end of the Scavenger side of Rovis. He's only watched Rovis use his reputation against other people from the side. A deep crack runs through Tal's chest.

How come everyone he's ever cared about can turn their back on him, just like that?

All he's ever done to Rovis and Zero was to protect them, and they'd set aside their issues to close ranks against him, because he's upset about something utterly fucked up that they've done?

It's quite possible that Rovis and Tal will never come back from this.

If that's the case, then Tal would rather not stay here any longer.

"And you?" He challenges Zero. "What are you still doing here, without your bodyguard?"

"You already plan on leaving," she says, correctly guessing his intentions. "Your actions will have no consequences, so why don't you do what you want to do?"

Quick like lightning, he slams Zero against the wall, his claws outlining her jaw. A cough escapes from her mouth, but otherwise she doesn't react.

"I can't tell if you're really that indifferent about death," Tal murmurs, "or if you really think I won't hurt you."

Bleary eyes blink slowly at him, as if Zero can't care less about Tal's words. A suppressed shiver runs through her frame. His eyes flick down to the goosebumps on her arms. Zero's pale face glistens with cold sweat, and snot seeps out from her nose over her pursed lips. He can feel the heat of her fever burning through his metal hand.

Stars, what is he doing?

Tal steps back, releasing her. She stays in place. Their staredown lingers.

He hears her answer, clear as day.

Both.

Zero dances with Drokklo as a hobby, and she has already wormed her way into Tal's heart and taken roots there. She didn't care if things could go either way; she just also knew what was the likely outcome. Once again, Zero was right.

"Go back to bed," Tal says roughly.

She gives him a once over. When Zero seems to find what she's looking for, she leaves without a word, without a glance.

It doesn't take Tal long to pack, since most of his important belongings are digital blueprints and program scripts, all of which is stored safely in his watch, tablet, or phone. A light duffle bag of clothes, and he's set to leave.

The only reason he loiters for another hour at the mansion is to pick through Levi's belongings. His heart seizes when he finds a chunky silver signet ring, an elegant sparrow etched into the hexagonal shape. Levi took it off on the day of the festival because he was afraid to lose it in the crowded streets. The metal fingers holding the ring don't shake because they have no nerves, but the movements are jerky and lack control when he slides it onto his ring finger. Tal belatedly remembers that Rovis was going to tell him who the killer was, before he broke the news about Saige.

Whatever, he thinks. *I'll figure it out another way.*

Tal stuffs a few of Levi's old books into the duffle and takes one last look at the mansion. Four monstrous buildings, filled with monsters. He's the worst of them all, for betraying his vows and leaving them. Too bad he doesn't care anymore.

Unlocking his car in the garage, he swings the bag onto the passenger seat.

"Do you even know where you're going?"

Disbelief chills Tal's anger. He doesn't bother turning around when he says, "I told you to go to bed. You better not try to stop me. You know what I'm capable of. I let you go earlier, but do you really think it's a good idea to approach me right now?" He slams the door shut. "Our entire relationship began with lies. You used me, and I gave you a chance. Then you ground the pathetic, broken, *shattered* pieces of my life to dust when you took Levi and Saige away from me. I'm through with you."

"Saige is alive."

Tal whirls around and gapes at Zero. "Don't play with me."

She walks closer, holding out a disk as large as the size of her hand. At least she's smart enough to wear a jacket this time, black leather gloves matching Tal's.

"Saige sent me a message before she got captured. I didn't see it until after I left your room. Encrypted file, codes within the code. The first few lines were easier to solve, but I think only you can decrypt the rest. I think she tells you where she is."

He closes his fingers over the disk.

"I also added in another file. It's Levi's murderer. Don't ask me how I got the information." Zero steps back, though she hasn't looked at Tal a single time in the garage. "Be careful, Tal."

She turns away before he could get a word out.

Tal watches her disappear upstairs. Silently, he forces himself to let her go with a quiet sigh. She's not important anymore, not after everything she's kept from him.

Then he gets in the car and drives. He's getting out of the city, and he's leaving Dyvris behind. He's leaving Rovis, as much as it hurts him.

Because Tal is going to find his sister, no matter the price.

Epilogue

eneath the high speed roads in Torch City, a man strides down the hall of a facility bathed in neon blue. Two larger men follow after him, covered from head to toe in dull shades of brown and red.

"Who's this woman again?" the man in front asks when they reach a door lit up in red, a Purish teenager guarding it.

"She says her name is Isabella Brown," the teenager answers. "Exiled from the Aconite gang."

The man's eyes darken. "The Scavenger's organization."

"Would you like to speak with her, sir?"

He lifts his hand and flicks his fingers. The teenager nods and hurries to activate the unlocking sequence. The red lights blink and turn into green, as the double doors slide into the walls with a whoosh. A pale woman is sitting on the floor, back against the wall of a small cell. Her dark hair is messy, sticking to her face. A heavy chain that's connected to thick cuffs on her wrists dangles between her knees. The sleeves of her orange prisoner's uniform reach her elbows, exposing the disfigured Aconites mark on her forearm.

The man smiles. "Hello, Isabella Brown."

Brown looks up, green eyes scanning his face. "You're the director of the Agency?"

He opens his arms. "In the flesh."

The woman uses the wall to push herself up to standing. Her limbs are weak, and she trembles on her feet. "I can give you information."

"In exchange for what?"

"Safety. Housing, security, money, food, a job. I will give you information, in exchange for a life at the Agency."

The man raises a brow. "I'm afraid you're living in the wrong universe, if you want all those things."

"But you have all of it," Brown says, unrelenting. "Most of the Purish do, while we Ezclovese are degraded to the same treatment as other immigrants. But we are the same people. If you help me, I'll help you take down the deadliest criminal organization of the east."

The man hums. "Go on."

"I'll give you names."

"We already have all of them."

"I know things about the Scavenger," she hurries to add. "The head Reaper. The second in command, Lithium. And the head Heartless, which you might know as the Ace of Crowns."

The man turns away, bored. "The Ace of Crowns is no longer his head Heartless. She stepped down when her high school friends persuaded her to leave the organization. Oh, that is, until one of my experiments killed one of them, so now she's staying in Dyvris, but no one knows what she does now. Quite a fleeting run as the Ace, to be honest. And Lithium just left the Aconites a few days ago, in the middle of the night. He's off-the-grid. No one knows where he is, not even the Scavenger himself. So, it seems, Isabella Brown, your information is outdated."

"You've already been watching them for a while," Brown realizes.

"Yes." The man crosses his arms and glances at her over his shoulder. "You see, Quade Bianchi and I worked very well together. Then one day, my best source of poison weapons suddenly disappeared."

"I can tell you about the day the Scavenger killed him," Brown offers eagerly, stepping forward. "I can tell you who was involved."

"Oh?" He turns to fully face her again. "You were there?"

"The whole organization was. The Scavenger stole Quade's place very publicly. He walked into the main dining room that evening and challenged Quade to give up his position as the head of the organization. Of course Quade said no, and ordered the Reapers to kill him. Except, the Scavenger was already head Reaper, and none of them moved. Then Quade ordered anyone to kill him, with the promise of more money and freedom. So people went and fought the Scavenger. It was a bloody brawl."

The man's stare gleamed with interest. "And?"

"The Scavenger won. He killed all of the ex-military members who were skilled enough to go against him. When no one dared to challenge him anymore, he shot Quade in the head."

"That's it?"

Brown falters. "The Scavenger killed forty-seven people that night. By himself."

"By himself," the man repeats. "What about Lithium? What about the Ace?"

"Lithium stood watch and made sure no one could leave. He only killed five people that night, for trying. The Scavenger didn't just want to kill Quade; he wanted to thoroughly push the entire organization into a new era." Brown frowns. "As for the Ace, she was in Torch City making deals for Quade, I believe. No one except for Quade could be sure."

"Oh, yes," the man remembers. "She was indeed hiding in my organization, poking her nose into things that don't concern her. Stole quite a lot of information and made one of my experiments utterly useless, too. No matter. I've already ordered the Purity Syndicate to deal with her."

"Zero was..." Brown's eyes widen with shock. "She was spying on the Agency?"

"Crazy, right? No, I don't think Quade knew everything about what she was doing in my city. But that's exactly why I need to control her, don't you think? If she's this dangerous before she's legally allowed to vote— well, *'vote'*— then she might be running this country herself in three years, and that just won't do."

Brown nods. "Of course. I agree with you. I never liked her anyway."

"Enlightening," the man says dryly. "Now, what else do you have for me?"

"The Scavenger has a soft spot for the immigrant groups."

He frowns, disappointed. "Isn't that obvious? That's how they started calling him 'the Scavenger.' In fact, all the major heads of the Damned are children of immigrants. They all have the same weakness."

"The Scavenger and Lithium are in love," Brown tries.

"Literally anyone who's ever been to Dyvris knows that," the man retorts, condescension starting to show on his face, in his voice. "And they're both in my black book already, so what's the difference?"

Brown leans forward. "You can use them against each other. Once you have one, the other will walk right into your arms, without a doubt. Lithium may be off-the-grid, but he'll come out of hiding for his Scavenger. You should capture the Scavenger first."

"That was already the plan." The man lets out a dramatic sigh, smoothing out his suit jacket. "It appears that you're of no use to me."

"But—"

"And since I've told you lots of classified information, I have no choice but to kill you."

"*What*?" Brown tries to lunge at him, but the Agents clad in brown and red catch her by the elbows and force her back. "I never asked for that information. You're the one who chose to tell me. And you said you'd help me."

The man puckers up his lips, considering. "No, I never said that. You just assumed I agreed to your deal and offered up useless facts that I already know about the Aconite gang. And even if I did agree to it, I would be lying. Isn't that what the Damned are like?"

Brown's lips part in disbelief, eyes wide. Then she snarls, "Even Rovis, a lowlife, honored his word. I thought the Agency was such a big deal, but turns out you're just even lower than the Damned."

The man chuckles. He pulls out a semi-auto pistol from inside his jacket, clicking off the safety. He points it at Brown, between the eyes. She struggles, but she's much too weak against his Agents in this state.

"Goodbye, Isabella Brown."

A satisfying bang explodes in the air. The man watches Brown's body slump and crumple into the ground, arms still hung by the Agents' grip.

"Clean up," he orders them, waving a hand and walking out.

"Sir?" the teenager at the door calls after him. "Where would you like to station me next?"

"Your supervisor will let you know." The man waves his arm without looking back. "Whichever one that is."

He strolls down the endless corridor, careless of the monotonic beeping of the underground facility. Most of the cells are empty, since the Agency has long run out of war criminals, and all their recent captures have been sent to the cages of Drokklo's Playground.

Ah, Drokklo's Playground.

One of his family's greatest creations. The man comes from a line of powerful Purish vigilantes who've kept this country under the correct conditions for centuries. Patrikk Feyrer might be the 'chief of state' in name, but he's just a clown who makes a fool of himself on television and keeps the bored Purish citizens at home entertained.

The Marudas family is the true ruler of Pureland.

And it's not going to end because of some naive children running around pretending they're formidable creatures of hell. Or because of cowards who hide behind their screens and disturb everyone else in the country through media channels.

Both the Damned and the Faceless will be purged from this country soon enough.

The man smiles as he steps into the elevator. It shoots up four hundred floors through the Agency's bioweapons building, and he steps out onto the roof.

"Sir," an Agent bows to him.

"Take me to my son's building," the man orders.

"Yes, sir."

He follows the Agent onto the jet, red strands of hair shifting with the harsh wind, and he settles down as the engine whirs to life. An air stewardess, skin as pale as snow, lips red like blood, ambles over to him with a bottle of champagne. She pops off the cap and pours him a glass. The man holds out a hand, and the stewardess hangs the glass between her fingers.

"How's your husband?" he asks, taking a sip.

The stewardess freezes. "My husband's been dead for three years, sir."

"Oh," the man says, unconcerned, "I thought you were the other one. Or the one who was with me on the way here."

"I... I was the one with you on the way here, sir."

The man waves her off, gulping down more champagne. "Whatever. You all look the same anyway. Dead husband, cheating husband, abusive husband. Who cares? You're all working for me, and that's all that matters."

The stewardess chuckles nervously and refills his glass, knuckles turning white on the bottle. She bows her head and says, "Of course, sir. I am grateful for the opportunity to be a part of the greatest organization in the country."

"You should be." The man smiles. "We are doing good work here, bringing the nation back to the glorious days after we destroyed the barbaric Zessroans and before the dumbest chief in history opened up ports for immigration. Soon, Pureland will live up to its name."

"That sounds lovely, sir."

"Yes, and it will be even more so when Riyssola becomes ours. The Ezclovese Empire may have destroyed Toullifuka, but we can take Avyria again with Riyssolan firepower in our hands. And once we have the islands, our technology will be unbeatable. We'd conquer the world within months. It'll just be us, the Purish, on this whole planet."

"I can't wait for such a future, sir."

The man hums. He reaches out and runs his knuckles up the woman's arm. "The real future is off this disgusting planet. When we get rid of all the useless filth, we can open up a million more spaceship development centers on all six continents. We'll be up in the stars, sweetheart."

The jet begins to descend, and the stewardess shoots out a hand to keep herself balanced, but the man's faster. He catches her wrist before her fingers close around the nearest handle, then tugs so that she stumbles into his lap.

"Careful," he says, chuckling.

He snatches the champagne bottle and drinks straight from the bottle. He doesn't notice that the woman is trembling beneath his roaming hand. The alcohol sloshes all over her uniform when he goes for another gulp right as the jet lands.

"Ugh," he groans in disgust and throws the bottle off to the side, uncaring that it shatters against a wall and spills the leftover champagne onto his expensive carpet. Then he shoves the stewardess off, who yelps and catches herself on the floor with her hands and knees.

The man straightens his tie, stretching his neck.

"Now I have to talk to my stupid fucking son," he mutters, words slurring.

He watches the stewardess get up on her feet and fix her clothes while the rumbling of the engine fades. He frowns at her, displeased.

"You know what," he says. "I don't really like you."

The woman's eyes go wide, and she stammers, "Why— Why not, sir?"

He shrugs. "No idea. I just don't. You're too much like... A piece of clay. Anyone could do whatever they want to you, and you'd just let them. That's boring, and I don't like it. But then again, I fired a woman last week because she asked too many questions. Or I might have killed her. I can't remember. No, I definitely killed her."

"Oh." The stewardess inches back.

The man sighs, slapping his forehead. "Damn, I did it again. I've told you all my plans, and I don't even like you."

"Sir," she pleads, holding her hands up. "I can be better. I won't say anything to anyone."

He reaches into his jacket and pulls out the pistol for the second time this evening. "But honey, I just don't like you. I don't need to keep you around. I have more than enough staff for all of my planes."

"Please, sir."

The man wrinkles his nose and shoots her in the heart. He stands and steps over her body right as the Agent opens the door to assess the situation.

"Get rid of..." He waves his hand without the gun. "That."

He nearly falls when he exits the plane, but he rights himself up and walks a perfectly straight line towards the entrance to his son's penthouse. The artificial intelligence program at the door scans his body, then the entire doorway turns red.

"Access denied," the mechanical voice says.

"Don't be ridiculous," the man scoffs.

The lights suddenly turn green. "Access granted."

"That's better."

He stalks in, twirling the pistol in his hand. A younger clone of the man hurries out, silk robes tied poorly around his scrawny body, the mess on his somehow resembling both a red thundercloud and a bird's nest.

"Father," he says, shock evident in his voice.

"Surprised, boy?" The man shoves past his son and saunters to the kitchen, opening the freezer in search of gin.

"What are you doing here in the middle of the night?"

He sneers, "Why? Are you sleeping with more dumb blondes?"

"No," his son answers, affronted. "Actually, I've met someone. A smart girl, who can actually keep up with me."

"As if that's a high bar," the man jibes, finally picking out a bottle and shutting the fridge.

Then he freezes.

He squints his eyes at the purple card hung on the freezer with a magnet, a green crown sparkling in the center. Slowly, he sets the bottle on the counter. He whirls around, eyes blazing, suddenly not so drunk anymore.

"Do you know what this is?" he seethes, jabbing a finger at the card.

And his brainless son has the audacity to grin with excitement and say, "That's from the girl I've fallen in love with."

The man stares at his son, speechless.

Then Emery Marudas switches his grip on the pistol, and strikes the barrel across Didier Whiston's face.

Acknowledgements

I'd like to thank Ian Wang (Instagram @w.3.p.0) for the amazing book cover, and for being one of my greatest friends since high school, who has been incredibly supportive through this whole publishing process. He's one of the most inspired people I know, and I'm honored that we get to walk parallel paths in pursuing our creative passions.

I'd like to thank all of my friends, for keeping me going, during this side quest to publish this book while pursuing a college degree in astrophysics. Self-publishing is a grueling job, and it required a lot of support from people who love me to ensure that I'll see this to the end.

I'd also like to thank my therapist for helping me work through my childhood trauma and find myself over the past couple years. The flashback I chose to start this story with was, in fact, something I wrote of a true event in my life from five years ago, with some changes in details. This is why I picked the quote from *Captain Marvel* as the epigraph, because looking back, I feel that my life truly began that day, when I shied away from an attempt, just as Zero did. This story has been in the works for four years, and it has always been an exploration of mental illnesses and how to learn to live with them. Needless to say, I had a lot to work on for myself, and I'm proud to say that I'm in a much better place than where I was when I started this book.

I wrote the first draft of this story when I was seventeen and bitter against the entire world, the peak of my activist era. I felt helpless, in the face of climate change, poverty, socioeconomic inequity, and my own mental health issues. Obviously, I projected my issues the most onto Zero, with her age, her gender and ethnic identity, as well as her romantic and sexual orientations. She carries my manic and depressive episodes, the swings, the embodiment of "All the best people are crazy." Rovis carries the part of me that keeps everything under a calm mask, silently cutting away on his arm in private to deal with the pain he can't talk about. That was the part of me that walked through the hallways of high school everyday for four years, and the part of me that started to crumble during my first year of college. Tal carries my humor and deflection, the avoidance, the fear of taking advantage of opportunities. He's popular and well-liked, but barely anyone truly knows him. All three of them carry my self-destructive tendencies, the cruelty pointed towards myself so that no one and nothing else could hurt me as much as I do.

Almost everyone I knew in high school, and a lot of my friends at college, they've been through similar journeys of these struggles yet continue to power on and do amazing things out there in this cold world. These are the strongest people I know. I am surrounded by survivors, and I hope this story goes out to others like us.

This book was influenced by early Marvel movies, *Six of Crows*, *These Violent Delights*, *Gearbreakers*, *Iron Widow*, and the *All for the Game* series, so many thanks to the writers/authors of these works for giving me a wonderful place for my mind to escape to when things were difficult, and for inspiring me to write this book.

Lastly, thank you to the readers for listening to what I have to say through this chaotic world of cyberpunk gangsters and shady government operatives. The book world is an incredible place of wonders and possibilities, and I feel honored to have contributed to a small part of it.

Appendix

RULES OF KEEPERS AND THIEVES

There are five ranked suits, not counting the Chosen suit in each round. The suits are, in decreasing order, as such: Crown, Wineglass, Maltese, Anchor, Fish.

Each suit has 10 number cards and 3 face cards. Each deck also has a Drokklo card that overrides every other card in the deck. With 66 cards in one deck, 5 decks and 10 people are needed for this game. Each round has a Chief who calls on 3 Keepers as teammates, and the remaining 6 players form the opposing team of Thieves.

The Chief is chosen in any of the following three scenarios:

- For the very first round of the game, the first person who throws down an Ace, regardless of whichever suit, becomes Chief, unless later overridden. To override the Ace and attempt to claim status as Chief, a player must throw down a greater number of Aces in a different suit or a greater number of Drokklos than the previous player. Once a Drokklo shows up, however, the overriding stops. Overriding is optional; a player can choose not to put down their Aces or Drokklos, even if they have it. The ranking of suits is null in this process, so no Ace trumps another. There is no limit to the number of times players can override, and every player can still override even if their previous attempt failed. This is called the Free Market.

- For the round after a forfeit, the rules to choosing a Chief is similar to above, but each player can only throw down a card that corresponds to their level, rather than an Ace. For example, it's possible that no players are showing the same value on a card, since there are 10 players and 13 levels.

- For future rounds, in the natural flow of the game, the Chief is based on the team that won the previous round. Following the rotation, either clockwise or counter-clockwise, the next person on the winning team becomes Chief.

Each person draws the cards in rotation, and the last 30 cards at the bottom are left for the Chief of the round from which to possibly swap for better cards. Each person thus has 30 cards in total.

Rules of the game:
- Everyone begins at level 1. The levels increase by number, reflecting the 10 possible number cards. After level 10, the levels are Shield, Castle, and Ace, in increasing order. After the first round, the level of each round is the level of the Chief. The cards corresponding to the level, regardless of suit, become the largest cards after Drokklo.

- Each round has a Chosen suit, which follows the same rules as the Free Market.

  - For a round following the natural flow of the game, the Chief has been decided, which means the level of the game is set as well. The Chosen suit is then determined by players throwing down a card of value corresponding to the level, then the overriding system if it occurs. The final declaration of suit, or the player who puts down the most number of cards corresponding to the level within the same suit, becomes the Chosen suit.

- For a round following a forfeit, players put down cards corresponding to their own level. Overrides can occur on another player's level as well. In this scenario, the player that wins the Free Market in becoming a Chief does not necessarily determine the Chosen suit. Other players can decide to allow for someone to be Chief but put down cards of the future Chief's level in a different suit.

- The Chosen suit ranks higher than all other suits for this round of the game and will be redetermined with each rounds. The natural ranking of suits follows after the Chosen suit. For example, if Anchor becomes the Chosen suit, for that round, any Anchor cards would be larger than any Crown cards, except for level-value cards.

- If in the overriding system, Drokklos win, then there is no Chosen suit, and the round would be in Anarchy. Only the natural ranking of suits would be relevant to this round.

- Plays can include: singles, pairs, triples, quadruples, and quintuples of the same suit and value.

- A combination trick is called a train, which is when a player puts down consecutive pairs, consecutive triples, consecutive quadruples, or consecutive quintuples. A train can consist of any number of combined plays. They can be three-pair trains (three consecutive pairs), five-triple trains (five consecutive triples), two-quadruple trains (two consecutive quadruples), etc.

- Advancing to the next level:

  - The Thieves must gather 200 points in order to win this round and earn a chance to become Chief for the next round. Otherwise, the Keepers win and level up for players at a number level, and the next Chief would follow the rotation within the Keepers.

  - The Thieves must gather 250 points in order to win this round, earn a chance to become Chief of the next round, *and* level up for players at a number level. Otherwise, if the Thieves have between 200 and 250 points, they can only have the next turn for Chief.

  - For each additional 50 points the Thieves gain above 250 can add another level of advancement for players at a number level, until they reach level Shield.

  - Players at the levels of Shield and Castle can only advance while playing as Chief. Winning on a team led by another player does not qualify for leveling up.

- A full game of Keepers and Thieves is only complete when a player gets to the Ace level and wins as Chief. However, this game is designed to be entertaining in its individual rounds as well, so time and energy for a full game is not required.

About the Author

Astraea Long is a young adult author from Boston, Massachusetts. She's lived in the states of Oklahoma, Oregon, and Texas, as well as four years spent in school in Sichuan, China. She currently studies astrophysics in college, and she's taking up new language sequences such as Italian and German, rather than focusing on a minor.

She is an avid reader of science fiction and fantasy, and her future works will include a variety of urban fantasy, dark academia, and queer themes. As an aromantic asexual, she intends to focus on sibling and platonic relationships in her writing, and to challenge the popular trends of sex and romance.

Outside of writing and reading, she's a devoted dancer who previously trained as a pre-professional and now spends many late nights choreographing for her college dance groups. Her other hobbies include painting, scrolling through Asian streetwear fashion websites, watching cooking videos of things she probably can't make, and spending too much money on boba.